D0974329

She gave Jamie a strange look. "You believe the South will lose this war, Jamie?"

"Yes. After several long and bloody years. The North has the manpower, the money, and the factories."

"And the South has . . . ?"

Jamie poured another glass of water. He drank it down and set the glass back carefully on the wicker table that was between him and the woman. "Slavery is wrong. No man has the right to own another human being in bondage. But the Federal government does not have the right to tell individual states what they can and cannot do. That is really what this war is all about: central control of our lives. Total control of our lives. If I obey the laws of God, and observe a moral code here on earth, the government has no business interfering in my life. That is why I choose on the side of the Gray."

"And your sons?" she asked gently.

"Falcon is fighting for the Gray in Texas. I suspect Jamie Ian will choose the side of the blue and so will Matthew."

"Father against son."

"And brother against brother," Jamie added. "This war will cut deep across the country. It will leave bitter scars that will last for many, many years, perhaps forever. But a person must always do what they think is right."

"No matter what the consequences?"

"No matter what the consequences."

BEARLY READ BOOKS
by the 1000's
16441 S.E. Powell
Portland, Oregon 97236
(503) 667-9669

BOOK YOUR PLACE ON OUR WEBSITE AND MAKE THE READING CONNECTION!

We've created a customized website just for our very special readers, where you can get the inside scoop on everything that's going on with Zebra, Pinnacle and Kensington books.

When you come online, you'll have the exciting opportunity to:

- View covers of upcoming books
- Read sample chapters
- Learn about our future publishing schedule (listed by publication month *and author*)
- Find out when your favorite authors will be visiting a city near you
- Search for and order backlist books from our online catalog
- Check out author bios and background information
- Send e-mail to your favorite authors
- Meet the Kensington staff online
- Join us in weekly chats with authors, readers and other guests
- Get writing guidelines
- AND MUCH MORE!

Visit our website at
http://www.kensingtonbooks.com

WILLIAM W. JOHNSTONE

TALONS OF EAGLES

PINNACLE BOOKS
Kensington Publishing Corp.
http://www.kensingtonbooks.com

PINNACLE BOOKS are published by

Kensington Publishing Corp.
119 West 40th Street
New York, NY 10018

Copyright © 1995 William W. Johnstone

All rights reserved. No part of this book may be reproduced in any form or by any means without the prior written consent of the publisher, excepting brief quotes used in reviews.

If you purchased this book without a cover, you should be aware that this book is stolen property. It was reported as "unsold and destroyed" to the publisher, and neither the author nor the publisher has received any payment for this "stripped book."

All Kensington titles, imprints, and distributed lines are available at special quantity discounts for bulk purchases for sales promotions, premiums, fund-raising, educational, or institutional use. Special book excerpts or customized printings can also be created to fit specific needs. For details, write or phone the office of the Kensington special sales manager: Kensington Publishing Corp., 119 West 40th Street, New York, NY 10018, attn: Special Sales Department; phone 1-800-221-2647.

PINNACLE BOOKS and the Pinnacle logo are Reg. U.S. Pat & TM Off.
The WWJ steer head logo is a trademark of Kensington Publishing Corp.

ISBN-13: 978-0-7860-2571-8
ISBN-10: 0-7860-2571-9

First Pinnacle Printing: April 1996
Ninth Printing: June 2011

17   16   15   14   13   12   11   10   9

Printed in the United States of America

Book One

I leave this rule for others when I'm dead,
Be always sure you're right—then go ahead.

—Davy Crockett

Prologue

Jamie Ian MacCallister was just a little boy living in the wilderness of Western Ohio when the Shawnee war party killed his parents and baby sister. For reasons known only to the Shawnee, they spared Jamie and made him a slave in their village. Jamie worked hard, did what he was told, and was soon adopted into the tribe, learning the Warrior's Way of the Shawnee. He was named Man Who Is Not Afraid. Before his twelfth birthday, Jamie escaped from the village, taking with him a young woman named Hannah. The pair made their way to a small pocket of civilization in Kentucky, and Jamie was taken into the home of Sam and Sarah Montgomery, while Hannah, who was several years older, was taken in by the preacher and his wife.

But civilization did not take well to Jamie. He was wise far beyond his years, tall and strong for his age, and could hold his own in any fight, fists or blade, with boy or man. There was no back-down in Jamie MacCallister.

Then he met Kate Olmstead, the most beautiful girl Jamie had ever seen, and he fell head over moccasins in love. Kate had hair the color of wheat and eyes of blue. She wasn't very big, but with a smile and a wink she could twist Jamie right around her pretty little finger. Jamie became so smitten the first time he saw Kate, he walked right into a tree and almost knocked himself goofy.

If there ever was a love made in heaven, it was Jamie Ian

MacCallister and Kate Olmstead. There was only one hitch: Kate's father and her brother hated Jamie.

But that didn't stop the two from seeing each other and holding hands whenever they could.

When Jamie was fourteen years old, he looked twenty, was well over six feet tall, and literally did not know his own strength. He wore his thick blond hair shoulder length and shunned store-bought clothes and homespuns in favor of buckskins.

Then he had to kill a man.*

It was self-defense, but suddenly Jamie found himself a wanted man with a price on his head. He took to the deep woods of Western Kentucky, but would not go far because of his love for Kate. After only a few months, Jamie returned and the two of them eloped. They were married in the river town of New Madrid, Missouri, and wandered westward, finally stopping in the Big Thicket country of East Texas. There, they settled in and began to raise a family. Jamie's neighbors were a runaway slave, Moses Washington, and his wife, Liza, and their children. A few years later, several families from back in Kentucky showed up in the Thicket: Sam and Sarah Montgomery, and Hannah and her husband, Swede.

Jamie became involved with those seeking independence for Texas, and the night before the Alamo fell, he was sent out with a packet of letters from the defenders. Jamie was ambushed by one of Santa Anna's patrols and left for dead. A poor Mexican family found him, more dead than alive, and took him into their home, helping to nurse him back to health until Kate could arrive and take him back to their cabin in the Big Thicket.

In the spring of 1837, Jamie and Kate, Moses and Liza, and the families from back east decided to move westward.

They settled in a long and lovely valley in Colorado; in the coming years it would be known as MacCallister's Valley. It was there Kate and Jamie's tenth and last child, Falcon, was

Eyes of Eagles—Zebra Books

born in 1839. All had survived except baby Karen, who had been born in the Big Thicket country and was killed by bounty hunters at five months of age in 1829.

Jamie made friends with those Indians who would accept his friendship, and fought with the others. The name of Jamie MacCallister became legend throughout the West, as scout and gunfighter, and a man who had damn well better be left alone, just as the MacCallister children were making names for themselves as they grew into adulthood. Their oldest boy, Jamie Ian, Jr., who was born in 1827, was a man feared and respected by both whites and Indians. Jamie Ian did not begin to settle down and hang up his guns until he married Caroline Hankins and built a home in the valley.*

The second set of twins, Andrew and Rosanna, showed an early interest in music and were sent back east to school. In the coming years both would become world-renowned musicians, composers, and actors.

Life was good for Jamie and Kate in the valley, and they were content to watch the town they founded grow and their kids mature and marry and have children of their own.

But Jamie MacCallister was too famous a man for the public to forget. When he was fifty years old, he received word that President Abe Lincoln wanted to see him.

*Dreams of Eagles—Zebra Books

1

"You can't go meet the president of the United States looking like you just came off a buffalo hunt, Jamie," Kate told him.

"Why *not?*"

"Hold still!" Kate said, measuring him across the shoulders. "Your good black suit will fit you, but I've got to make you some shirts."

"What's wrong with buckskins?"

"Hush up and hold still."

Time had touched the couple with a very light hand. Their hair was still the color of wheat, with only a very gentle dusting of gray. Kate was still petite and beautiful, and Jamie was massive. The few suits he owned had to be tailor-made because of the size of his shoulders, chest, and arms. His hands were huge and his wrists thicker than the forearms of most men. Even at middle age, Jamie still truly did not know his own strength. He had killed more than one man with just a blow from his fist. But with Kate, the kids, and those he loved, Jamie was gentle.

"What did the letter from Falcon say?" Megan, one of the triplets, asked.

Kate stepped around Jamie and looked up at him, questions in her eyes.

Falcon, the youngest of the MacCallister children, had left home when scarcely in his teens and quickly made a reputation as a gambler and gunfighter. He did not cheat at cards, although he could; he just knew the odds and played expertly. He had his father's size but not his father's easy temperament. Falcon's temper was explosive, and he was almighty quick with a pistol.

Jamie said, "He joined up with some outfit in Texas. He was scout for that bunch who attacked Fort Bliss."

"Then the war is really happening, Pa?" Megan asked.

"Yes."

"I just can't believe that Falcon would fight for any side that believed in slavery," Ellen Kathleen said.

Kate looked at her oldest daughter. Like all MacCallister children and grandchildren, Kathleen's eyes were blue and her hair golden. It was difficult for Kate to believe that Kathleen was in her mid-thirties and had children of her own that were very nearly old enough to marry. "Falcon does not hold with slavery, Ellen Kathleen," the mother said. "I'm told the war is not really about slavery. It's about something called states' rights. Isn't that so, Jamie?"

"Damn foolishness is what it is," Jamie said. "And if Honest Abe thinks I'm going to get mixed up in it, he has another think coming."

"Don't speak of your president like that!" Kate said sharply. "You be respectful, now, you hear? Abe Lincoln is a fine man with a dreadful burden on his shoulders. If he needs your help, you're bound and obliged to help out—and you know it."

"I thought you said I was too old to be traipsin' about the country, Kate?" Jamie said, with a twinkle in his eyes. He let one big hand slip down from Kate's waist to her hip.

She slapped his hand away as those kids present howled with laughter.

"You mind your hands, Jamie MacCallister!" Kate snapped playfully at him. "Time and place for everything."

"I've got the time," Jamie said. "If you've got the place, old woman."

"Old woman!" Kate yelled. "Get on with you!" she said,

amid the laughter of kids and grandkids. She shoved at him, and her shoes started slipping on the smooth board floor. It was like trying to move a boulder. "Get outside, Jamie! I've got to finish these shirts. Megan, you and Ellen Kathleen get your sewing kits and help me. We can't have your father going to Washington looking like something out of the rag barrel."

Joleen MacCallister MacKensie, who had married Pat MacKensie in 1851, came busting up onto the porch. "Pa! Will you come talk to your grandson Philip and tell him to stop bringin' home wolves. He's done it again! Now, damnit, Pa . . ."

Kate pointed a finger at the young woman. "I'll set you down and wash your mouth out with soap, young lady. You mind that vulgar tongue, you hear me?"

Joleen settled down promptly. She knew her mother would do exactly what she threatened. "Yes, Ma. But somebody's got to talk to Philip. Last year he brought home a puma cub and like to have scared us all to death when the mother showed up!"

Jamie rattled the windows with laughter at the recalling of that incident. He clapped his big hands together and said, "I recollect that morning. Pat was on his way to the outhouse with his galluses hangin' down and come nose to snout with that angry cat. I never knew the boy could move that fast." Jamie wiped his eyes and chuckled. "He came out of his britches faster than eggs through a hen. If that puma hadn't a got all tangled up in Pat's britches and galluses, that would have been a tussle for sure. Pat never did find his pants, did he?"

It would be many a year before Pat MacKensie would live that down.

"Pa!" Joleen yelled, red in the face.

"All right, all right. I'll go talk to Philip. Calm down."

"Get your sewing kit, Joleen," Kate said. "We've got work to do. And bring what's left of those buttons I lent you."

"Yes, Ma."

Jamie stepped outside and looked up and down the street of the town. Two nearby towns, separated by only a low ridge of hills, were called Valley. Several hundred people now lived in the twin towns. They had a doctor, several churches, a block each of stores, and a large school house that served both towns.

Jamie thought about his upcoming trip east. He was to ride out in three days, crossing the prairies, then into Missouri, and then catch the train east to Washington. Jamie smiled. Tell the truth, he was sort of looking forward to it.

Jamie stayed to himself as much as possible during the train ride eastward, which was not easy since the coaches were filled with blue-uniformed soldiers of the Union army, all excited about the war. To a person, they were convinced the war would not last very long, and all were anxious to get in it before it was over—promotions came fast in a war.

Jamie was not so sure the war would be a short one. And he was even more baffled as to why the president of the United States wanted him to scout for the Union army. Jamie knew almost nothing about the country east of the Mississippi; everything had changed since he'd left that part of the country, more than thirty years ago.

Jamie looked at the fresh-faced young officers on his coach, and listened to them talk of the war, as the train whistled and clattered and rattled through the afternoon.

"Those damn ignorant hillbillies," one young second lieutenant said. "They really must be stupid if they think they can whip the Union army."

Those damn hillbillies, Jamie thought, can take their rifles and knock the eye out of a squirrel at three hundred yards, sonny-boy.

"The Army of Virginia is a joke," another lieutenant said. "And Lee is nothing more than a damn traitor."

Lee is no traitor, Jamie thought. He is a Virginian and a

damn fine soldier. How could he turn his saber against the state that he loves?

"We'll whip those mush-mouthed Southerners in jig-time," another young officer boasted.

Don't be too sure of that, Jamie thought. He stood up and walked to the rear of the car, stepping out to breathe deeply of the late spring air. The conductor had said several hours before that they would be in Washington sometime during the night.

Jamie felt strangely torn, as a myriad of emotions cut through him. His family, like so many others, had roots in both the North and the South, although his mother's side of the family had settled in South Carolina many years before the MacCallister clan came to America. Jamie had been so young when his parents and baby sister were killed and the cabin burned, he did not know his mother's maiden name.

He sensed more than heard the door open behind him and cut his eyes. The man who was stepping out smiled at him. "Mind if I join you for a smoke?"

"Not at all," Jamie replied.

"Boastful young soldier boys in there," the man said.

"They'll soon learn about war."

"That they will, friend. That they will. Traveling far?"

Jamie smiled. "Not too far." Jamie's smile had been forced, for the man had a sneaky look about him that Jamie did not care for; he took almost an instant dislike for the fellow. Jamie had learned while only a boy to trust his finely honed instincts. They had saved his life many times during the long and sometimes violent years that lay behind him.

"A sorry thing this war," the man said, after lighting a cigar. "After the Union is successful in bringing those damned Southerners to their knees, we should put them all on reservations like we're doing with the Injuns and let the damned worthless trash die out."

"There is right and wrong on both sides in any war, friend," Jamie said.

A dangerous glint leaped into the man's eyes, and he

moved his hand, hooking his right thumb inside his wide belt. "Not in this war, friend. No man has the right to hold another as slave."

"You're right," Jamie agreed, and the man seemed to relax somewhat. But his right hand stayed where it was. Hide-out gun or knife, Jamie thought. Or both. Jamie was carrying a gun and knife of his own. He carried a .36 caliber Colt Baby Dragoon in a shoulder holster, and a knife sheathed on his belt. "Slavery is wrong."

"Southerners are filthy trash," the man said. "You agree with that?"

The man is determined to force an argument, Jamie silently concluded. But why? And why with me? Jamie placed both hands on the iron railing and stared at the countryside as the train rolled on. Only a few minutes until dusk, Jamie noted, and the stranger's stance was aggressive. He's going to jump me! Jamie thought suddenly. But why? "No, mister. I don't agree with that."

"Can't straddle the fence in this conflict," the man said, a wild look in his eyes. "And now I know who you are."

"Oh?"

"You're a damned filthy secessionist! Our intelligence was right."

"What the hell are you talking about?" Jamie asked, irritation plain in his words.

The man's eyes were burning with a fanatical light. He moved his hand under his coat. "Long live the memory of John Brown!" he said, just as the train began moving through a shady glen. That, coupled with the fast-approaching dusk of evening, plunged the train into near darkness. The man whipped out a knife and lunged at Jamie.

But Jamie had anticipated trouble. He clamped one huge hand on the man's wrist and stopped the knife thrust. He hit the man a vicious blow to the jaw with his left fist, and the man's eyes glazed over. Jamie twisted the man's knife arm, and the pop of the bone breaking was loud even over the rumblings of the train. The assassin opened his mouth to scream in pain just as Jamie took a step backward for leverage and hurled the man from the platform of the coach. The man bounced and rolled beside the tracks and then lay still. Whether he was alive or dead, Jamie did not know, and did not care.

"Idiot," Jamie said. The train rolled on, and he quickly lost sight of the fanatical abolitionist.

Jamie, of course, had read of the exploits of John Brown, and considered the man to be a fool.

The car in which Jamie had been riding was the last one of the hookup, so it was doubtful that anyone else had seen the brief confrontation and the man being thrown from the platform—but there was always that chance. Jamie waited for some sort of outcry, but none came.

Jamie stood for several minutes on the platform, wary now of his surroundings, but still deep in thought.

Somebody has learned of my invitation to meet with the president and doesn't want me to attend. But why? I have not committed to either side in this war, and as it stands now, I probably won't. I have no interest in this war.

But if there are any more attempts on my life, I will develop a very personal interest in the conflict.

"And take appropriate action," he concluded aloud, just as the sun sank over the horizon and night covered the land.

2

"I am E.J. Allen," the short, stocky man said, with a definite Scottish burr to his words. "Welcome to Washington, D.C., Mister MacCallister."

The man's real name was Allan Pinkerton, owner and founder of the soon-to-be-famous Pinkerton Detective Agency. And a man who many say founded the United States Secret Service. During the early days of the Civil War, or the War Between the States, as many called it, Pinkerton often worked under the name of Major E.J. Allen.

"The carriage is this way, sir," Allen said.

Jamie picked up his bag and followed the man through the busy train station. Seated in the closed carriage, Allen asked, "Did you have a pleasant trip, sir?"

"Very pleasant," Jamie replied. He had made up his mind to say nothing about the attempt on his life. There were some things he wanted to sort out in his head.

E.J. Allen said not another word from the train station to the White House. Jamie could sense that the man either did not like him, or did not trust him, or a combination of the two. He also, for some reason, did not believe E.J. Allen was the man's real name.

At the rear entrance, Allen finally spoke. "I'll take your pistol and your knife, Mister MacCallister."

"If you get them, you'll take them," Jamie told him, then stepped from the carriage and walked up the steps.

"Sir!" Allen called.

A tall, almost emaciated appearing man stepped into the lamp-lit doorway. "Let him be," the man said in a deep, resonant voice. "And leave us alone, please."

Inside, Jamie was shown to a private room on the ground floor of the huge, three-story mansion and was served a hot meal by a Negro servant. As he was eating, Lincoln appeared and sat down across the table from him. A cup of coffee was placed in front of the president, and the servant left without saying a word, closing the door behind him.

Lincoln took a sip of coffee and smiled. "Your admirers said you were a large man, Mister MacCallister. But they did not do you justice. And you do not look your age, sir."

"Thank you, Mister President." Jamie laid down his knife and fork.

Lincoln waved a hand. "Eat, sir, eat. I know you must be ravenous after such a long and tiresome journey. You eat, I'll talk. Is the meal to your liking?"

"Yes, sir. It's very good."

"You're a very famous man, Mister MacCallister—"

"Jamie, sir. Please."

"Very well. Jamie, it is. Hero of the Alamo. Pioneer. Trailblazer and scout. Indian fighter. I've heard the songs about you, read the books and articles, and I saw the play about your life when it played in Springfield. How do you feel about this war that has started?"

"I don't hold with slavery, sir."

"It isn't about slavery . . . although that does play a very minor part in the conflict. I have friends in Alabama and Georgia, and several other Southern states, who were talking about freeing their slaves long before the war talk started. It's about . . . well, whether this nation survives whole, or tears itself apart and crumbles."

"Looks like to me the tear has already started, sir."

Lincoln shook his head. "The South can't win, Jamie. It is going to be a very long war, and a costly one in terms of human life, but the South cannot win. We have the factories, the man power, and the wherewithal to sustain for years. The South simply does not."

Jamie said nothing. He ate his beef and potatoes and green beans in silence.

"You could help bring this terrible tragedy to a sooner end, Jamie," the president spoke the words softly.

Jamie met the man's eyes, and in those eyes he could see what a burden the man carried. "You're asking me to fight against my own son, Mister President?"

Lincoln stood up, almost painfully, Jamie noted. Bad knees, probably. The president walked around the small meeting room. He sighed and faced Jamie. "I did not know you had a son fighting for the Confederacy."

"Falcon. My youngest. He's twenty-one. And my oldest boy, Jamie Ian, is talking about taking up arms for the Blue. Matt might go with the Blue, too. I don't know. But he's leaning that way. I hope they both stay in Colorado. But all you can give a child is roots and wings. They got to make up their own minds. Andrew is in Europe, and his ma and I wrote him and told him to stay there; stay out of it. My grandfather came from Scotland; my mother's people came from South Carolina, I think. Somewhere in the South. I'm just not sure. I know I feel a great pull toward the Confederacy."

Lincoln smiled very sadly and drained his coffee cup. He said, "Then you must go where your heart dictates, Jamie. I personally despise slavery. But if I could save the Union without freeing a single slave, I would do so."

On August 22, 1862, in a reply to Horace Greeley, Lincoln wrote: "My paramount object in this struggle is to save the Union, and is not either to save or destroy slavery. If I could save the Union without freeing any slave I would do it; and if I could save it by freeing all the slaves I would do it; and if I could save it by freeing some and leaving others alone, I would also do that."

"I want you to think about becoming my chief of scouts, Jamie MacCallister," Lincoln said. "It would be a great boon to the Union if you would accept the position. If you do not, I will understand."

"Yes, sir. I promise you I will think about it."

Lincoln extended a hand, and Jamie took it. "I have made arrangements for you to stay at a nearby hotel. My carriage driver will take you there. Good luck and God bless you, Jamie MacCallister."

"And good luck and God bless you, sir."

Lincoln left the room, and Jamie pushed the plate from him and refused the offer of more coffee from the servant. He walked outside to stand for a moment in the night air. Warm for this time of year, Jamie noted. He felt eyes on him and turned around, glancing up at the second floor. Lincoln was standing, looking out a window at him. Jamie lifted a hand in farewell and Lincoln did the same.

"A great man, there," E.J. Allen spoke from his position beside the carriage. "With a terrible burden on his shoulders."

"Yes," was Jamie's reply. "And it's not going to get any lighter." He stepped into the carriage without another word.

A full decade before the Southern states elected to secede from the Union, another revolution was taking place—in the North. By 1860, the Northern states held four-fifths of the nation's factories, more than two-thirds of the railroads, and nearly all of the shipyards. The term "Yankee ingenuity" had become a commonplace word in all the civilized countries of the world.

The South had slaves and pride and something else: the South knew that should the Federal government win the war and states' rights become a thing of the past, in the years to come, the Federal government would have too much control over the lives of American citizens.

Lincoln was right in maintaining that the South could not win this war. But everybody, the president included, was wrong about the duration. The war would last for four long, bloody years, and during that time, just under three-quarters of a million Americans would die. The war would cut deeply across the fabric of America, leaving wounds that would never heal, and would divide families forever.

Washington was an armed camp, filled to overflowing with soldiers ready to defend the nation's capital. But it was an unnecessary move. At the time, Washington was in no danger from armed invaders.

The morning after meeting with the president, Jamie carefully packed his suit and changed into buckskins. He roamed the city, inspecting several dozen horses before he finally chose one to buy. He bought supplies, a brace of pistols, and a rifle. Then he crossed the Potomac and headed south into Virginia.

Just across the river, he stopped and sat for a time under the shade of a huge old tree and read the newspapers he'd bought in Washington.

About a third of the experienced army officers had resigned to take up arms against the Union; among them were Johnston, Beauregard, and Lee. One-fourth of the experienced naval officers had joined the Confederacy.

Baltimore was about to come under attack, the newspapers stated.

It never happened. General Butler quickly moved troops into place and put down any still-vocal secessionists. Butler further added insult to injury by stating that he had ". . . never seen any Maryland secessionist force that could not be put down by a large yellow dog."

Lincoln had put out the call for volunteers on April 15, 1861. They poured in to join up, hundreds of thousands of them. In contrast, the Confederacy had just less than sixty thousand troops, active and in training. In 1861, the population of America was just over thirty-two million, with more than two-thirds of that number living in the North. The South had barely nine million citizens, with more than a third of them slaves, barred from serving in the Confederate army because of white fear of an armed insurrection.

But it was the North's industrial might that made the South's pale in comparison. New York State had more factories than all of the South.

The South, however, had one crystal clear advantage: they would be defending their homeland. And they were ready and very willing to defend it to the last drop of Southern blood.

Jamie looked up from his reading at the pounding of hooves. A troop of cavalrymen, dashing in appearance in their gray and gold uniforms, with the officers wearing plumed hats, came galloping up and reined in on the road beside which Jamie was sitting.

"You there, woodsman!" the commanding officer said, his eyes taking in Jamie's buckskins. "You've picked a peculiar place to rest."

Jamie smiled at the man. "Oh? Why is that?"

"Well . . . there is a war on, my good fellow! This area could come under attack at any moment."

"Not by me," Jamie said. "I'm a Western man just passing through." He held up the newspapers. "The only thing I know about the war is what I read."

"Rest the men," the captain said, dismounting and handing the reins to a sergeant. He walked over to Jamie and knelt down. "My friend, you are probably what you say you are, but these are tense times. You run the risk of being arrested as a spy."

Jamie laughed. "I'm no spy, Captain. Although President Lincoln would probably settle for that."

"Lincoln?"

"Yes. I met with him last evening."

"I beg your pardon, sir?" the captain was quite taken aback by Jamie's words.

Jamie rose to his full height, and the captain quickly stood up. Jamie towered over him. "I was offered a position in the

Union army. I refused . . . in a manner of speaking. I have a son who is fighting with a Texas cavalry unit."

"Good lad!" the captain said. "And your name, sir?"

"Jamie MacCallister."

The entire troop of confederate cavalry fell silent. Everybody had heard of Jamie MacCallister. *"The* Jamie MacCallister?" the captain asked.

"I guess. Far as I know, there's only one of me. I do have a son named Jamie Ian, but he's back in Colorado."

"Good God!" a young lieutenant breathed. "The man's a living legend."

One quick look from the captain silenced the ranks. He swung his gaze back to Jamie.

"And how was Mister Lincoln, sir?" the captain asked.

"Saddened by the war."

"He has no need to be. He has only to give us independence and there will be no war."

"He won't do that, sir."

"No. No, I'm sure he won't. You have heard the Yankee side, sir. Would you be interested in hearing our side of the issue?"

"I would."

"Excuse me for a moment." The captain walked to the ranks, and a moment later, a rider galloped away, heading south. The captain returned to Jamie's side and extended a hand. "I am Captain Cort Woodville, sir—of the Virginia Scouts. There is someone I would very much like for you to meet."

Kate was sitting on the front porch with Ellen Kathleen, Megan, Joleen, and Jamie Ian's wife, Caroline. The ladies were rocking and talking and sewing.

"Jamie Ian is going off to war, Ma," Caroline said.

Kate did not pause in her rocking or her sewing. "Oh? He tell you that?"

"No, Ma. But I can see it in him."

"Matthew is going to resign his commission as sheriff and join up with the Blue," Ellen Kathleen said. "And yes, he told me. He was scared to confront you himself, Ma."

Kate still did not cease her rocking. But she did lay her sewing in the basket beside the chair. "Then so far we'll have two for the Blue, and two for the Gray."

"Who besides Falcon, Ma?" Joleen asked.

"Your father, dear."

"Pa don't hold with slavery, Ma!"

"No. But he'll almost always take up for the underdog. Did any of you know that Wells and Robert rode out yesterday? We're going to be short on men-folks for a time."

"Wells and Robert?" Caroline said. "But—"

"They've gone to join up with a Negro army somewhere back east. Certainly, no one can blame them. If Titus and Moses weren't so old, they would have gone, too. But the boys talked them out of it."

"Pa ain't no spring chicken," Ellen Kathleen said.

"Isn't," her mother corrected. "Oh, he's still got some spry in him," Kate said with a smile filled with recent nighttime memories.

"I just can't believe that Pa would take up with the Gray," Megan said.

"Your father will do what he thinks is right," Kate said. "It may be wrong, but if he thinks it's right, that's the way he will go." She sighed. "I think he suspected all along that this valley would be split between the Blue and the Gray. There will be others who answer the call. Hannah and Swede's oldest boy might go. Juan has sons that were born in Texas, remember. Sam and Sarah's oldest boy might go. Some will not return."

"I wonder what Pa is doing?" Megan said softly.

Kate smiled. She knew what he better *not* be doing.

3

"General Robert E. Lee, Mister Jamie MacCallister," Captain Woodville announced.

The two men shook hands and Lee motioned Jamie to a chair. It was full dark outside, for Lee had been camped a half day's ride from where Jamie had been found reading the papers. "You stay, Captain," Lee said. "Close the door, Sergeant."

Jamie noticed that Lee's eyes held the same sadness and sorrow that he had seen in President Lincoln's eyes. Nobody in power really wants this war, Jamie thought—oh, a few fanatics on either side, but not thinking, caring men.

"Some supper, Mister MacCallister?" Lee questioned.

"That would be nice, General. It's been a long day, and I missed the nooning."

Captain Woodville hopped up and walked to the door, ordering food to be sent in. He returned to his chair and sat silent.

Lee smiled, and for a moment, his eyes held a sparkle. "I don't suppose Abe Lincoln told you about any up-coming battle plans, did he, Mister MacCallister?"

Jamie laughed. "No. He just wanted me to take over as chief of scouts for the Union army. I promised him I'd think about it. But I believe he knows that I will not accept the position."

Lee smiled.

Cort said, "Then throw your lot in with us, sir. If you don't, you'll be missing a grand fight. Of course, it will be a short one."

Lee's smile faded, and in an emotion-filled voice, he said, "It will be a long and bloody war, Captain Woodville. It will be brother against brother, father against son. Its duration and human cost will make the Revolutionary War and the War of 1812 pale in comparison. But sadly, it is a war that has to be."

"Explain that to me, General Lee," Jamie asked. " 'A war that has to be.' "

Lee picked at his food for a while, then pushed the plate from him. He was silent for a moment. "If the Yankees win this war, MacCallister, it will signal the beginning of the end of many personal rights and liberties that will affect every citizen of the United States. Government is a dangerous thing, Jamie MacCallister. Compare it to fire: a useful servant; a fearsome master. If we allow the North to win, it will be the end to states' rights. The citizens of any state will no longer rule their lives—the Federal government will. Governors will be figureheads only. They will be allowed to make very minor decisions, but the major ones will have to have the blessings of the Federal government. And that is no way for good, decent free men and women to live."

"Slavery?" Jamie questioned.

"Over. It should have ended a long time ago. Should never have started. I am on record as being a disbeliever in slavery and secession. A hundred years from now, historians will still be writing that this bloody conflict was about slavery. They will be wrong in doing that."

Jamie ate in silence for a time, and Lee and Woodville also returned to their food with a bit more enthusiasm. They both stopped eating when Jamie asked, "How could I be of service to you, General Lee?"

Lee smiled. "I feel confident that we could find a place for you, Mister MacCallister."

At the time of the meeting with Jamie, Lee was not commander of the entire Confederate army: he was commander of the Army of Virginia. General Joseph Johnston was the overall commander. Lee asked Jamie to ride with Captain Cort Woodville's scouts for a time, to get acquainted. Jamie, still in buckskins, obliged.

It was early June, 1861. The final day of peace had passed on April 11. On the 12th, Confederate forces had fired on Fort Sumter. At that time, the stars in the Confederate flag formed a circle of seven on a blue background, for only seven states had seceded up to that point. The other four states would quickly follow. The war would really begin on May 24, when Union troops, eleven regiments strong, crossed the Potomac to secure a safe zone for the nation's capital. The next four years would be the bloodiest period in American history.

Matthew and Jamie Ian had left MacCallister's Valley to join with the Union forces. Falcon MacCallister was now a lieutenant leading a band of Texas Raiders in waging a guerrilla war against the Union forces. Two of Juan Nunez' sons had joined the Confederacy in Texas. Wells and Robert had joined the Union's Negro army, now being formed and training in New Jersey. Swede and Hannah's oldest son and Sam and Sarah's son had joined the Union forces of Iowa. The citizens of MacCallister's Valley were quickly choosing sides.

"I don't think the Yankees will ever get as far as Richmond," Cort said to Jamie as they rode south one warm day in middle May. "I think we'll stop them cold long before then. But Lee wants you to see the country. So I'll take this time to show you Ravenswood and introduce you to my wife. We'll have some real home cookin' and sleep in a warm bed this evenin'."

"Sounds good to me," Jamie said. "You have children, Cort?"

"One. A daughter. Page. She might not be at the plantation, though. Her mother is sending her to a finishing school. I know you have children, Jamie."

"Nine living. Karen was killed by bounty hunters in the Big Thicket country of Texas in '29."

The men rode in silence for a mile or so, and then Cort

waved a hand. "Ravenswood begins here, Jamie. For as far as you can see in any direction. I have slaves, but they are not mistreated. I won't allow that and neither would my father. They work hard, if they're able, but they are well fed, housed adequately, and receive some medical care."

Actually, the slaves lived in poorly heated shacks, were fed mostly fatback, cabbage, greens and cornbread, worked from sunup to sundown (can to cain't, as the saying went), and most had never even seen a doctor. But Cort was correct in saying that his slaves fared better than many others. Many Southerners (and Northerners, too, if the truth shall be told) viewed the Negro as just a cut above an animal, strange, savage beings that occasionally had to be whipped into obedience.

"My wife and I had a parting of the ways some time back, Jamie," Cort said. "But both of us chose to not seek a divorce."

"I see," Jamie said. Actually, he didn't see at all, but what the hell was he supposed to say?

The men rode on, and Jamie marveled at the size of the well-tended plantation. He guessed, and guessed accurately, that Ravenswood was completely self-sufficient: everything in the way of food was grown or raised on the sprawling grounds.

"Tell me more about your valley in Colorado, Jamie," Cort said. "Did you have to tame the savages?"

"No," Jamie said with a smile. "I attempted to tame no one. I got along with most and fought the others."

How to explain the vast West to a person who had never seen it? There had been many reporters from Eastern newspapers who had traveled in the West and written about it, but their views were mostly romanticized ones. They wrote about the ignorant red man; but the Indian was far from being ignorant. He did not have schools and colleges, newspapers and books, or a written language, but he certainly was not ignorant. The Indian's way was savage when compared to the white man's, but unlike the white man, the Indian was one with the land he lived on. The Indian did not own land like the white man; but he did claim land, and that would be something that neither side would ever fully understand about the other.

"Ravenswood," Cort broke into Jamie's thoughts, pointing to a huge mansion off to their left.

Jamie had grown used to seeing great mansions in the South. They never ceased to amaze him. He finally had to ask, "What do you do with all the rooms?"

Cort laughed. "I suppose it is a bit much. Tell you the truth, we rattle around in them quite a lot."

Anne Woodville almost died when she looked out the window of her upstairs sitting room and saw Jamie MacCallister riding up with Cort. Although it had been many years since she and her brother had left the valley in Colorado and changed their names, there was no mistaking Jamie. Thank God Page was in Richmond.

She wondered if Jamie would spill the beans when they confronted each other? Not that there were that many beans left to spill to Cort. Cort knew much of the sordid story, having learned some of it from Anne's brother, the rest from Anne herself.*

To make matters worse, during the past year, her brother had fathered a child, during one of his rare couplings with a woman in Richmond. Worse still, the woman was a lady of quality, from an old Virginia family. But her brother had done the right thing and married the woman, although his sexual leanings certainly went the other way. Now there were two more unhappy people added to the list, and a child that was quarter Negro but looked white.

Anne felt there could be no hell after life. This was hell right here on earth.

Being a gracious lady of the South (although if her back-

Dreams of Eagles—Zebra Books

ground were really known, the good ladies of Richmond society would all suddenly develop the vapors and fall over in a dead faint), Anne walked down the curving steps of the mansion and out onto the porch to greet her husband and his guest.

Jamie recognized Anne immediately. But he never so much as blinked an eye in recognition.

"Darling!" Anne greeted her husband, kissing him on the cheek. "What a delightful surprise."

She turned to Jamie, and he bowed slightly. "Mrs. Woodville," he said. "Your husband said you were lovely, but his words did not do you justice."

"Why, sir!" Anne simpered. "You are just too kind."

You always did like intrigue and dangerous games, Jamie thought, wondering where Anne's brother was. Close by, he was certain. He had learned that they had been actors and singers for years, and then dropped out of sight. Right into the lap of luxury, he mentally added.

Cort chatted with Anne for a time, then ordered a man to change his saddle to a fresh horse. To Jamie, "I must go into town for a few hours. You will, of course, stay here. I'll be back in time for drinks and supper." Then he was gone, leaving Anne and Jamie on the porch, looking at each other.

"A drink, Mister MacCallister?" Anne asked, mischief dancing in her eyes. She had fully recovered from her shock and was once more her old self, playing the part to perfection.

"Water would be nice, Mrs. Woodville," Jamie said, thinking, You really must have been a fine actress. Then he put that into words after looking around to be certain they were alone.

"Oh, I was," she said, after sitting down and arranging her skirts.

A servant brought a pitcher of water and glasses.

"Leave us for a time," Anne told the woman. "I'll ring if I need you."

"Yessum."

Anne made certain the servant had gone. "You're a fine actor yourself. That was quite a performance you just put on."

"I'm not here to interfere in your life, Anne. I did not know you were Cort's wife."

"Thank you. But there are no secrets left between us. Cort knows all about me. I made sure of that. Well, he doesn't know that I know you and Kate. Oh, he wouldn't dare divorce me; I could ruin his reputation. Besides, he and my brother are lovers."

Jamie dropped his glass to the porch floor, where it broke with a crash and splash of just pulled, cool well water, and stared at the woman in amazement and disbelief. "I don't believe that." He finally found his voice.

She shrugged her shoulders. "Why would I lie? I don't mean to impugn his bravery, for Cort is a very brave man. One of the first to volunteer for the Gray. It's just . . . well, these things happen."

"Does he know that you . . . ah . . . ?"

"That I know? Certainly. What it means is that neither of us shall ever ask the other for a divorce. He will be discreet and so will I."

"With your, ah . . ."

She laughed at the expression on his face. "Our lovers? Yes."

"Just the one child, Anne?"

"No." Anne knew Jamie MacCallister and knew him to be a man of honor. He would keep his silence; although, she felt he might tell his wife. That was all right, for Anne trusted Kate as much as Jamie. Kate had always treated her well. "No," she repeated with a long sigh. "Page has a twin brother." She laughed sourly. "With good hair," she said bitterly, remembering the words of Selma, her personal maid, that terrible stormy night the twins were born. "He isn't black, but neither is he white. But he is Negro. That is very plain. I never held him. He was given to a woman in the slave quarters who lost a child, and some years later, when he was, oh, I don't know. Time goes by so swiftly. Anyway, he was sent north on the

Underground Railroad. I don't know where he is or what he looks like or even if he made it across the line to freedom."

"You ever think about him?" Jamie asked softly.

Anne smiled sadly. "Yes. Not as often now as I used to, but yes, I do think about him." She sighed and straightened up in her chair, squaring her shoulders. "I should write my memoirs and have them published. I could make a fortune, but then, I'm already worth several fortunes."

"You'd better invest in something outside of the South, Anne," Jamie warned.

She smiled. "Oh, but I have. I have this clever little man in Richmond who has been secretly investing sums of my money in factories up north. I own a factory that makes uniforms, another that makes guns, and yet another that manufactures boots and shoes. And I own bits and pieces of several other factories . . . all located far above the Mason-Dixon line." She gave Jamie a strange look. "You believe the South will lose this war, Jamie?"

"Yes. After several long and bloody years. The North has the manpower, the money, and the factories."

"And the South has . . . ?"

Jamie poured another glass of water. He drank it down and set the glass carefully back on the wicker table that was between him and the woman. "Slavery is wrong, Anne. No man has the right to own another human being in bondage. But the Federal government does not have the right to tell individual states what they can or cannot do. That is really what this war is all about: central control of our lives. Total control of our lives. If I obey the laws of God, and observe a moral code here on earth, the government has no business interfering in my life. That is why I chose the side of the Gray."

"And your sons?" Anne asked gently.

"Falcon is fighting for the Gray in Texas. I suspect Jamie Ian will choose the side of the Blue and so will Matthew."

"Father against son," Anne murmured.

"And brother against brother," Jamie added. "This war will

cut deep across the country, Anne. It will leave bitter scars that will last for many, many years, perhaps forever. But a person must always do what they think is right."

"No matter what the consequences?"

"No matter what the consequences."

4

Oddly enough, there was no tension at supper that evening. Cort and Anne were more than cordial toward each other, and Jamie could sense a real feeling of affection between them. Anne was a beautiful woman and Cort a handsome man. After supper, Jamie left them to chat while he took a walk around the grounds. He strolled down into the slave quarters and, whenever possible, listened to the slaves talk, some of the older ones in their native tongues. Usually though, the slaves fell silent at his approach. A lot of the homes were no more than shacks, but Jamie suspected that for many, had they wanted a better place to live, they could have fixed up the shacks, for there was lumber stacked all over the place.

But that still did not excuse slavery.

On the walk back to the mansion, Jamie muttered to the night, "What am I doing here? I live in the West. This isn't my fight."

He walked and thought for over an hour. Back at the mansion, he found that Cort had already gone to bed, and Anne to her room. Jamie was shown to his room and elected to read from the stack of newspapers he'd found in the downstairs. Many were several months old, but much of what they contained was still news to Jamie.

Jamie read that just after the fall of Fort Sumter, a mob of angry New Yorkers had stormed the offices of the pro-Southern *New York Herald* and threatened to smash and destroy everything in sight if the publisher did not display the stars and stripes.

Jamie learned that Jefferson Davis, the president of the Confederacy, had stated that war was not necessary if the North would just leave the South alone.

Lincoln had then issued a call for seventy-five thousand men to suppress the South . . . he believed then that he could do that in three months.

Jefferson Davis called for a hundred thousand volunteers. And they answered the call in droves. The upcoming war took on an almost mystical aura.

Kentucky, Maryland, and Missouri refused to send men to aid Lincoln, but neither would the governors of those states openly support the South.

Confederate troops had seized the Gosport Naval Yard at Norfolk and managed to salvage the burned-out hulk of the USS *Merrimack* and refit it, naming it the CSS *Virginia.* The Confederates also seized eleven hundred heavy naval guns.

Slowly, the battle lines were being drawn. In Florida, Fort Pickens held and beat back Rebel attacks.

On May 20, 1861, when North Carolina finally seceded from the Union, the eleven state confederacy was complete and both sides were ready for war . . . just about.

The Union forces at that time numbered just slightly more than thirteen thousand regular army troops. Thousands and thousands more were undergoing training at a fever pitch, but they were not yet ready for combat. Federal militias were being activated, and were on the march, such as the elite Seventh New York Militia, the Sixth Massachusetts, the Vermont Volunteers, the Guthrie Grays from Ohio, the Michigan Volunteers, the Twelfth New York Militia, and dozens of other local militia units, large and small.

But the South had their local units as well, such as the Louisiana Zouaves, a mostly French-speaking unit, who patterned their uniforms after the famous French Zouave regiments who fought in North Africa. A few of the many others included Virginia's Old Dominion Rifles, Sussex Light Dragoons, the red-shirted Wheat's Tigers—another Louisiana based unit led by six-foot, four-inch, three-hundred-pound Major Roberdeau Wheat—and the South Carolina Volunteers.

Jamie laid aside his papers and magazines and went to bed. So far there had been a lot of hot air coming from both sides, and damn little action.

All that was about to change.

As he was drifting off to sleep, Jamie wondered why Cort had worn such a secret smile all during and after dinner. He woke up around midnight at the sounds of a galloping horse, followed by muted conversation on the front porch. The rider soon rode off, and the great house grew dark. Sensing no danger, Jamie turned over in the feather tick and went back to sleep.

During breakfast, Captain Woodville explained the secret smile.

"I've been *what?*" Jamie blurted.

"You've been commissioned a major in the Army of the Confederacy, sir," Cort said.

"By whose orders?"

"General Lee, Major. You are to assume command immediately of two companies of Confederate guerrillas and commence harassing the enemy, sir."

"The rider I heard last night."

"Yes, sir. General Lee telegraphed all his commanding officers that could be handily reached by wire, seeking their opinion on your commission, and I am proud to say the returning word was unanimously in favor."

"Well, I'll just be damned!" Jamie blurted, then cut his eyes to Anne. "I beg your pardon, Mrs. Woodville."

She laughed and poured them all fresh coffee. "No need to apologize, Major MacCallister. I'm very happy for you."

"General Lee predicted that three days from now, when I am to ride with you to a staging area about thirty miles from here, volunteers would be lined up fifty deep and an acre across to join you, Major," Cort said.

"I never commanded men before."

Cort smiled. "You just *thought* you weren't commanding them, Major. But they were following you."

Anne almost blurted out that she could certainly testify to the accuracy of that. She bit back the words just in the nick of time.

That would have really shocked her husband right down to the soles of his polished cavalryman's boots.

Since they were to be guerrillas, Jamie was adamant about uniforms: there were to be no military uniforms worn in his unit.

"Then you run the risk of being shot as spies," Lee pointed out.

"Not as long as we stay in our own territory," Jamie countered. "Although the Yankees might not see it quite that way," he added with a smile.

Lee and his other generals agreed—Johnston had been unable to attend. He was meeting with President Davis.

Jamie was stunned at the size of the contingent that had volunteered to ride with his command. Hundreds of men had arrived at the staging area in hopes of being chosen to ride with MacCallister's Marauders—that name not of Jamie's choosing, but of Cort's.

Jamie stepped in front of the group and shouted, "I want men who can ride like the wind, shoot like Davy Crockett— and remember this: I fought beside Davy for days at the Alamo—and who possess the courage to charge the gates of hell at my command!"*

The entire group of men stepped forward.

Lee shook his head, smiled sadly and murmured, "Brave lads all."

Eyes of Eagles—Zebra Books

Jamie had read over the records of the officers who had volunteered and chose Captain Jim Sparks from Texas as commanding officer of First Company, and Captain Pierre Dupree of Louisiana as commanding officer of Second Company. As his command sergeant major, he chose an Alabama man, a career soldier who had left the Federal forces after years of brave and loyal service, and many commendations, to fight for his homeland: Louie Huske.

"Make out a list of the men you want," Jamie told his two captains and his sergeant major. "They've got to be men who can get along with each other, and men who will stand. When you've done all that, we'll go over the lists together, interview the men, and choose together."

Each company would be comprised of one hundred and three men and officers. They would carry only light rations, depending for the most part on the good will and generosity of the people of the South for food. Each man would carry four pistols, two on their person and two on special-made saddle holsters, one left and right, butt facing to the rear. Each man would carry one Sharps .54 caliber carbine. Cort tried to persuade Jamie to add sabers to the list of weapons, but Jamie stood his ground against them. He would equip each Marauder with a long-bladed Bowie knife. The officers could carry sabers if they chose to do so—and they all did—but the rest of Jamie's men would carry Bowie knives.

Before any further men were chosen, Jamie personally selected the horses. He would have preferred the tough mountain horses that he knew and loved, but mustangs were impossible to find in Virginia. The horses he chose were not the prettiest of the lot, but they were tough and strong. He chose no animal that he knew had been raised on grain, for grain was something that was going to be hard to come by. The color of the horses was also very important, for he wanted no horse that would stand out, day or night.

Lee and J. E. B. Stuart watched Jamie closely that first day and part of the second. By then, they knew they could not have picked a better man to command the guerrillas. Jamie Mac-

Callister had proven himself in battle dozens of times over the years, and he had the unwavering loyalty and respect of the men.

Lee and Stuart summoned Jamie to a meeting at the close of his second day at the staging area.

"Jamie," Lee opened the meeting, held in a tent set off in a meadow, away from any unfriendly ears and eyes—and Lee knew they were about. "The Army of the Shenandoah is ready. General Johnston has just over ten thousand men, trained and ready to fight." He moved his finger along a map spread out on a table. "They're here." His finger left that position and moved along another line. "Up here and over here, under the command of General Robert Patterson, are the Union forces, some twenty thousand of them. Patterson is a fine man, but he is too old and much too timid for a field command. General Winfield Scott made a blunder by appointing him to command the Union forces now preparing to advance on Harper's Ferry. Scott will soon discover his mistake, but it will be too late.

"Begin training your Marauders hard, Major, for I am going to thrust you all into the lion's mouth very soon. You and your Marauders are going to cross the river and begin harassing actions against Patterson's green and unproven troops. I want you to convince Patterson that he has many more men attacking him than he does in truth. Buy us some time, Major. For God's sake and the sake of the Confederacy, buy us some time."

"I'll do my best, sir."

"I know you will. Here is the reason for your daring actions: General Irvin McDowell is training thousands of troops to add to Patterson's force. General Beauregard's troops will be shifted over here to add to our forces. It is going to be a great battle, Major. One that we can win if we play our cards close to the vest. Johnston is going to let Patterson think he has him on the run. As Patterson advances, Johnston is going to retreat from Harper's Ferry, pulling the Yankees deeper into the trap. The Yankees may or may not fall for the trap—I suspect they will sense something is wrong and quickly turn around and head back across the Potomac. If that is the case, we put another plan into action."

Jamie studied the map for several long moments, his frontiersman's mind working hard.

"If you have anything on your mind, Major," Stuart said, "for God's sake, share it."

"What does intelligence say about McDowell's force over here on this flank?" Jamie asked.

"Many of them green troops or old, inactive veterans, poorly trained and poorly equipped. They are short on supplies and short on weapons and ammunition."

"And the major offensive is scheduled to begin . . . when?"

"As near as our spies can pinpoint it, the date will be July 8th. We'll be ready by that time. McDowell's troops will not be ready."

J.E.B. Stuart said, "We will, in all probability, be facing the largest army ever assembled in North America. Probably more than thirty-five thousand men."

Jamie's finger drew a circle around another area. "This place here, what's this called?"

Stuart looked at the map. "Bull Run."

5

Jamie began pushing his men hard. What he had to do was knock all sense of fair play out of them and then start from the ground up retraining them in guerrilla warfare. To a man they knew that Jamie MacCallister had been raised by Shawnee Indians, and was a master at what was called dirty fighting. To Jamie's mind, that was nonsense; there was no such thing as a fair fight. There was a winner and there was a loser, and that was all. In war, you killed the enemy, and that was that. You did it as humanely as possible, but a soldier kills. Period.

His two companies were chosen, and he had personally handpicked fifty men to stand in reserve, for only a fool did not expect casualties.

Jamie adopted little of the established cavalry tactics. Other people could fight gentleman's wars. Despite all the talk of how he was to disrupt supply lines and create confusion among the enemy, Jamie knew he and his men had really but one function: to kill as many of the enemy as possible.

Jamie had no way of knowing how many men had left the twin valleys back home to join up with either the Blue or the Gray, but he suspected many of the young men had made up their minds and were now in training with their chosen side.

Jamie had written Kate, telling her that he was now a major in the Confederate army, but not telling her exactly what he was doing. His guerrillas were to remain a secret for as long as possible. He knew that would not be for very long, for once his men began raiding in full operation, the cat would soon be out of the bag.

Jamie had put aside his buckskins and now dressed like his men, in civilian clothing that he had to have made for him. But he still wore his moccasins and high leggin's. The horse he had chosen for himself was a monster. A mean-eyed, dark, sand-colored brute whose owner had been threatening to shoot when Jamie arrived at the farm.

"Sell him?" the man almost shouted the words. "Hell, yes, I'll sell him. I can't ride him. Nobody can ride the bastard. You can't keep him in a stall; he kicks it all to pieces. He'll sneak up on you and bite the crap out of you. I got him in a trade and it was a sorry day that I did. My mares are scared to death of him. He ain't good for nothin'."

The man looked at Jamie. "Say, you'd be Jamie MacCallister! Major MacCallister! Take him, Major. He's yours. God bless you, sir."

"What's his name?" Jamie asked.

"That's a horse straight out of hell, Major. Man I got him from named him Satan!"

Captain Jim Sparks took one look at Satan and asked, "You got a death wish, Major?"

Within a week, Satan was eating out of Jamie's hand and following him around like a trained dog.

In the first real test of armies, the Rebels soundly defeated the Federals at a place called Big Bethel in early June. President Lincoln became exasperated and ordered General Scott to launch a campaign against the Confederate forces in Northern Virginia. Scott and McDowell worked out a plan, and the date of the assault was to be July 8. Confederate spies learned of this and got the information to Johnston and Lee. Lee sent an aide to Jamie with this terse message: Ride. Attack. God speed.

Within the hour, Jamie and his Marauders were riding toward the north. Jamie broke his command up into small groups so as not to arouse suspicion among the Federal spies who seemed to be everywhere, just as Confederate spies were all over Washington and near any Federal troop encampment.

Jamie's aide was a young Virginia lad not yet out of his teen years. Private Benjamin Pardee. He had picked Ben for several reasons: Ben was small and light in weight, and could ride like the wind. And the young man's parents were dead, his only close relative a sister living down near the Virginia/Tennessee border. Jamie had a suspicion that before this war was over, there would be damn few original members of the Marauders left. He had thought at first to select only single men, but as it turned out, about half of his men were married.

Jamie's Marauders began gathering in four places just south of the Potomac River. Across the river, clearly visible to the naked eye, were the camp fires of the Federals. Although President Davis and General Lee had forbid General P. G. T. Beauregard from taking any type of offensive action against the Yankees, that order did not apply to MacCallister's Marauders; they were militarily designated as guerrillas and therefore could attack any Federal position they chose.

On this night, the Marauders would not attack in force. Jamie had other plans. Captain Sparks was an experienced Indian fighter with years of fighting Comanches and Apaches behind him, and so was Lieutenant Casten. Jamie chose nine other men with experience fighting Indians, and at full dark, they left their horses on the south side of the river and rowed across the river, using boats that had been hidden in the brush the day before. Jamie and his men were armed only with pistols and knifes and packets of explosives.

The green troops of General McDowell were about to experience the terror of sneak attack by men who had learned it firsthand from the greatest guerrilla fighters the world has ever known: the Indians.

Sparks and Casten marveled at the ability of Jamie to blend in with his surroundings and move as silently as a ghost, in spite of the man's large size. Many times during night training Jamie had slipped up to experienced men and tapped them on the shoulder. Startled one man so badly he soiled his underwear—it would be a long time before he lived that down.

Jamie took Casten and three enlisted men and circled the camp to his left, while Sparks took the remainder and went to his right. Sparks knew what to do, for this had been researched several times, using information supplied to Jamie from Confederate spies.

Jamie placed his black powder charges gently, choosing his spots with care. One smaller charge went between two senior officers' tents. Another huge charge was planted behind the rough-built powder house. The men with Jamie and Sparks planted small charges around artillery pieces; when that was done, they backed off just inside good pistol range and waited for Jamie's signal.

Jamie could have killed several of the sentries, but elected to spare them . . . for this night. Once the war began in earnest, he would not be so generous.

Neither Jamie, Sparks, nor any of the other men could cut the fuses for the charges until they were actually on the site. So all breathed a silent prayer to the gods of war that they were allowing themselves plenty of time to get clear before the charges blew.

Mostly it was the skill of the men with Jamie, but some of their success had to be placed on the shoulders of the green troops guarding the encampment. The Marauders did their work, lit the fuses, and slipped away to lie belly down in good pistol range of the camp without being detected.

When the several hundred pounds of explosives blew, it must have sounded like the end of the world to those green troops in the camp. Four senior officers were killed instantly by the charge that Jamie had planted between the tents, and several more were badly wounded. When the block house went up it leveled everything within a five-hundred-foot radius. The charges under the artillery pieces went off, and for some inexplicable reason known only to God and the inexperienced artillery crews, the cannons were fully charged and ready to fire. Sparks from the exploding charges ignited the powder in the fire holes, and the cannons began going off. Since many had the wheels blown off them, the balls went ripping off at ground level, doing terrible damage to tents, wagons, and people.

The men of MacCallister's Marauders all let out fearsome screams in the violence-shattered night and let their pistols bang into the running, milling, confused mass of Federal troops.

When their pistols were empty, they headed for the river and the boats. They did not attempt to row, just lay flat on the bottom and let the current move them along downriver until the gloom of the cloudy night had swallowed them.

They left behind them several hundred dead and wounded, a camp in shambles and confusion, and morale considerably lowered. Jamie and his Marauders made it back to their horses on the south side of the river and were quickly gone into the night.

Many Northern newspapers put out special editions with huge headlines, denouncing the assault as a COWARDLY ACT, a VICIOUS SNEAK ATTACK, and THUGS ATTACK SLEEPING UNION CAMP.

"Somebody forgot to tell those editors that war is hell," Jamie said, although the credit for that remark would be attributed to someone else.

Then strategists in the Confederate camp decided it would be a good thing to let just a bit of news leak out about MacCallister's Marauders and the actual number of men who had attacked the Union encampment.

It was said that General Winfield Scott went into a rage upon hearing that only ten or so men were responsible for the terrible damage that was wreaked upon McDowell's camp along the Potomac. Most Northern newspapers called the number false. Several Union generals loudly proclaimed that no ten 'hound dog Southerners' could inflict that much damage on a Northern church choir, much less upon an armed camp. One of those generals was Thomas Thornbury, a pompous, lard-butt loudmouth who commanded a Pennsylvania home guard. Thornbury, who came from a very wealthy Philadelphia family, had commanded his small militia for years, and his rank was self-imposed. He had never experienced actual combat, but he did make good copy for the newspapers because he always had something outrageous to say. This time, Thornbury was quoted as saying, "If those yellow-bellied Southern riffraff ever come to Pennsylvania, I'll personally kick their ignorant butts back across the Mason-Dixon line."

Jamie read with interest the remarks of General Thornbury. Then he sat in his tent for a time, deep in thought, a smile occasionally playing around his mouth. Without telling anyone what he had planned, Jamie met with Captains Sparks and Dupree, and in twos and threes, Marauders began quietly saddling up and riding out. Jamie took scissors and cut his long hair short, dyed what remained black, and laid out his good dark suit.

When Lee was asked by one of his aides what MacCallister was up to, Lee was reported to have replied, "I don't know and I don't want to know."

Jamie left Satan and rode out of camp on a horse that had been deemed unfit as a cavalry mount—he would turn it loose once he got past enemy lines and to a train depot—and headed north. His handpicked men were already well on their way, posing as drummers, wandering itinerant laborers, and so forth. Jamie figured if he could successfully pull this off, he and his men would really tweak the noses of the Yankees.

Safely past Yankee lines, Jamie turned his horse loose and bought a train ticket for Philadelphia. There were several of his own men on the same train, but they did not speak to one another and managed to find seats in different cars.

Having initially ridden the steam cars much of the way to Washington to meet with Abe Lincoln, Jamie had gotten used to the railroads, but it still bothered him somewhat to be speeding along this fast. When the locomotive hit the flats, the driver really sped along. Jamie didn't have any idea how fast they were going, but to his way of thinking, it was just too damn fast. It was unnatural. Progress was, of course, a good thing, but this was ridiculous. Next thing a fellow knew, a man would invent some sort of machine to fly through the air like a bird.

Jamie smiled at that silly thought. He made himself as comfortable as possible in the seat and took a nap.

Jamie got himself a room in a rundown boardinghouse on the seedy side of the city; the rest of his men found equally dismal lodgings. Jamie bought a horse and arranged for other horses at various stables and liveries around the city. But for now, he used a rented horse to get around.

Thomas Thornbury lived a few miles outside the city, in a large home on several hundred acres of land. He had never married, and rumor had it that he enjoyed the company of whores several nights a month. Usually three or more of the soiled doves . . . at a time.

"Fellow must really be a ladies' man," Sparks remarked.

"Either that or he is a little bit on the strange side," Jamie replied.

Sparks gave him an odd look but said no more about it.

Jamie wasn't really sure what he was going to do to Thornbury, but for certain he was going to teach the blowhard a lesson about shooting off his mouth.

But before he did anything, Jamie had to sit down and figure out an escape route. If they hit Thornbury's house at ten or so in the evening, and did whatever they intended to do, they might have six hours at the most before Thornbury and the whores worked themselves loose and sounded the alarm. So the escape route had to be as foolproof as possible. And Jamie did not want to hurt Thornbury and certainly not the women. He just wanted to show the Yankees that they were not as safe in their homes far north of the war as they might think.

Far in the back of his mind, Jamie was thinking long range,

thinking of another operation that was perfect for the Marauders. But that one was months or even years down the road. For now, it was best to dwell in the present and let the future play itself out.

In the few days that he had been in the city, Jamie had made friends with several working prostitutes, and being very careful how he approached the subject, only after buying the ladies several bottles and getting them drunk, had learned a great deal about Thornbury and his home guard.

Thornbury was a man who liked his food and especially his strong drink. And as more than one of the ladies had told Jamie with a wink, Thomas Thornbury was a bit peculiar when he entertained the ladies. Each morning, when it wasn't raining, Thornbury hoisted the American flag on a pole outside his mansion. On the evening of the attack, there certainly was going to be a flag raised, but it damn sure wasn't going to be the Stars and Stripes that would be fluttering proudly in the morning's breeze come sunup—for Jamie and his men had brought with them a dozen Confederate battle flags, and come the dawning, the Stars and Bars would be flying in certain spots all over the city.

Sparks had carefully reconnoitered the home guards' armory and was busy working out a plan to blow that up in order to create a diversion just as the Marauders slipped out of the city.

When the deed was done, the Marauders were going to scatter in all directions.

"If we can possibly do it, I don't want anybody hurt or killed," Jamie told his men. "What I do want is to kick some of the high and mighty arrogance out of these people and show them they are vulnerable."

"When do we do the deed, Major?"

"Tomorrow night."

6

Jamie had paid for a week's lodging in advance; on the night of the attack, he dropped his bedroll and saddlebags out of the window to one of his men waiting below, then walked down the steps and strolled out the front as if he were simply going out for a bite to eat and some drinks at a local tavern. Jamie walked around the block to where his man was waiting with their horses.

"The rest of the men, Sergeant McGuire?" Jamie asked in a low voice.

"On their way, Major."

"Let's do it."

The two walked their horses until they were at the edge of the city, attracting no undue attention from anyone. A mile out of town, they met up with several more Marauders. Fifteen of Jamie's men remained in town, each with a different assignment.

Jamie linked up with his group in a stand of timber about half a mile from the Thornbury mansion, and they waited for a time. Conversation was in low whispers. Jamie opened his pocket watch—a present from Kate with her picture inside the cover—and checked the time. They had one hour to do the deed, for at midnight, all hell was about to break loose in various parts of the city.

"Stay with the horses and keep them quiet," Jamie told young Pardee.

He nodded his head in understanding as Jamie and his band made their way silently toward General Thornbury's great house. Just as they reached the rear of the house, a shrill cry came from inside.

"Oh, love!" a woman's voice cried out, a definite Irish lilt to the words. "You do make a darlin' lassie!"

Dupree and Jamie exchanged quick glances. Jamie smiled and motioned McGuire on ahead to check out the house.

A dog started barking; but Jamie had anticipated that and softly called the dog to him, opening a packet of food he'd prepared. The dog ceased its barking and immediately began eating the huge portion of meat and bread Jamie laid on the ground.

McGuire returned and said, "You boys have got to see this to believe it. The general's all dolled up in a *dress!*"

Corporal Bates had to put a hand over his mouth to stifle his giggling.

"And the ladies?" Jamie asked.

"Two of them is nekked as jaybirds, and the third one ain't far behind." He shook his head. "The general sure likes his ladies on the hefty side."

"Perfect," Jamie said. "Let's go."

After several nights of observation, it was determined that no guards patrolled the mansion. And since this was a party night for Thornbury, Jamie felt sure the general would not risk having his antics observed by anyone.

The lock on the back door was jimmied, and the men silently entered the house and made their way to the huge room located in the center of the mansion. Jamie stood in the shadows, just inside the archway, and watched the goings-on for a moment. General Thomas Thornbury was all dressed up in an evening gown, complete with gloves and a hat. He was dancing with one of the naked prostitutes while the other two sang a rather bawdy little ditty.

The two singing spotted Jamie and his Marauders and abruptly stopped their singing, their mouths dropping open in surprise.

"Oh, don't stop, Maggie!" Thornbury said. "You're just getting to the good part."

"The good part is over," Jamie said, stepping into the room, a pistol in his hand.

Thornbury whirled around, his face paling at the sight of armed men. "Get out of my house, goddamn you!" he shouted.

"Isn't he cute?" Dupree remarked, stepping forward with several lengths of rope.

"Who are you men?" Thornbury shouted.

"Some of those yellow-bellied Southern riffraff you talked about, General Thornbury," Captain Dupree said. "We came to pay you a little visit. My, but don't you look military?"

"Get out of my house!" Thornbury squalled.

"Secure them," Jamie ordered. "Just as they are. And throw some logs on the fire. We wouldn't want any of these ladies to catch cold now, would we?"

Jamie had already told his men that nothing was to be taken from the house . . . except for any papers that might have some bearing on the war. But he suspected that nothing of any military value would be found, and after a careful search he was found to be correct in that.

Thornbury and the Soiled Doves were trussed up securely. Sergeant McGuire noticed that Thornbury was in bare feet, and he looked around for the man's shoes. He found some ladies' slippers that appeared to have been made for a big foot and knelt down on the floor.

"Let's cover up those little tootsies, now, missy," he said with a grin, slipping the shoes on Thornbury's feet.

"You vile oaf!" Thornbury said.

At that moment, one of Jamie's men in town was giving a sealed envelope and a five dollar gold piece to a local man he'd found to be reasonably trustworthy. "At seven o'clock in the morning, you take this to the editor of the *Inquirer*. Don't forget now. It's important. He'll have another five dollars for you." The Marauder had no idea whether the editor would give the man any money or not, but it insured the delivery of the letter. His job done, the Rebel walked to his horse and rode out of the city.

At the Thornbury mansion, Jamie unfurled the Confederate battle flag and ran it up the flagpole in front of the house. Jamie stood for a moment, looking up and grinning. So far, so good. Not a drop of blood had been shed—thus far. But all that could change, quite abruptly.

At the home guard's armory, the explosives had been planted, and the men waited, one occasionally checking his pocket watch.

At the Philadelphia shipyards, Marauders had swum out to naval ships in the harbor and planted explosives, while others of the band of guerrillas had placed explosives on ships under construction in the yard.

"Who are you, sir?" Thornbury demanded, from his trussed-up position on the floor. Blankets had been tossed over the naked ladies. Thornbury's pretty party bonnet had been securely tied to his head, with a very tight square knot under his chin.

Jamie smiled at the man. "Major Jamie Ian MacCallister. The Army of the Confederate States of America. We are the Marauders, General. And you Yankees have not heard the last from us. Now I'll give you a word of advice, sir: There are good men on both sides of this struggle. The next time you want to question the courage of those who chose to wear the Gray—*don't*. Good night, General Thornbury. Pleasant dreams now, you hear?"

Chuckling over the screaming curses and wild threats of Thomas Thornbury and the high, shrill laughter of the ladies, Jamie and his men faded into the night and ran to their horses, Jamie stopping long enough to pat the general's dog on the head and slip him a biscuit from his saddlebags. Jamie and his bunch scattered to the winds.

When the home guard's armory blew, it shook that entire end of the city, sending flames shooting high into the night skies and scaring the daylights out of the citizens of the city who lived near there—Thomas Thornbury had been stockpiling arms and powder for months, and there was enough ordnance in the warehouses to outfit an entire division for a long campaign. The shipyard, too, erupted into a series of rocking explosions. One ship was totally destroyed, two others partially sunk and several others badly damaged.

The actual damage inflicted upon the Union cause by Mac-Callister's Marauders was really not all that great once the dawning came and things began settling down. But it was a terrible blow to Yankee pride . . . which was exactly what Jamie had wanted.

The editor of the newspaper did send a reporter out to the Thornbury mansion. Unfortunately for General Thornbury, the reporter took his wife out there with him. No story was ever written about the general's strange attire—or if it was, it was never printed. But following the Marauders' attack upon the city of Philadelphia, Thomas Thornbury did retire his commission and step down as commanding general of the home guard. In a public statement, he said it was time for a younger man to take over. Thomas Thornbury dropped out of the public's eye and never made another comment about the bravery and courage of the Southern fighting man. Two of the ladies who were found with General Thornbury immediately retired from prostitution (to the absolute amazement of all their friends) and opened successful businesses of their own in the city. Where they got the money to do all this remained forever a mystery. The third Soiled Dove, who was approximately the same girth as the general, married Thomas Thornbury in a private ceremony, and the two dropped out of sight. A dress shop was kept busy for years making dresses . . . in duplicate. The general's dog ran away from home and took up residence at a nearby farm, where he lived to be fifteen years old.

The citizens of Philadelphia screamed for revenge over this dastardly act, but not one Marauder was ever caught. When it was learned that Jamie MacCallister was the commanding officer of the Rebel Marauders, a bookstore that had sold many, many copies of *The Life and Times of Jamie*

Ian MacCallister, Hero of the Alamo and Frontier Scout, and still had copies in stock, was looted and burned.

To Jamie's mind, it had been a very successful raid, for no one had been killed and only a few people injured, none of them seriously.

What really irritated the people of Philadelphia was the Confederate battle flags flying high and proud at various locations all around the city.

One senior Federal officer summed it up this way: "Jamie MacCallister is going to be a royal pain in the Union butt until this war is over."

7

Training in Massachusetts, Wells and Robert looked at each other in amazement when they learned that Jamie was commanding a guerrilla unit for the South.

"I never thought Jamie would fight for slavery," Robert remarked.

"He ain't fightin' for slavery," Wells said, soaking his aching feet in a pan of warm water—the black army did not as yet have shoes and boots and were training in what they had arrived wearing, often bare feet. "He's fightin' for the right of a state not to be totally run by the Federal government."

"Don't that still amount to slavery?" a friend asked.

"It might in the minds of some, but not to me. Jamie never believed in slavery, and neither did any of his children, or anyone who ever got close to Jamie. He just don't hold with it."

"I ain't got no use for the white man," another Negro said. "Never have, never will."

"Then your thinkin' is all screwed up," Robert said. "You ain't never met no man like Jamie MacCallister."

The former slave looked at him. "Why should I want to? He fightin' for the South, ain't he?"

"Yeah," his friend said. "I want my mule and forty acres like I hear we gonna git when the war is over. And I know where I'm gonna git it. And I hope that white trash that whupped me tries to stop me from gettin' what's due me. 'Cause if he do, I'm shore gonna kill him."

"You got a lot of hate in your heart," Wells said.

"Yeah?" The man looked at him. "Well, nigger, I got the scars on my back to prove I earned that hate—do you?"

Jamie and his men returned to a hero's welcome at the encampment. Even Lee and Johnston were smiles when they greeted Jamie. Johnston had a commendation for him from President Davis.

"You struck a mighty blow for the South, Major," Johnston said, unfolding a map. "But as soon as you and your men get some rest, I want you to ride north and join up with Beauregard here." He pointed a finger at the map. "Between Centerville and Manassas, on the south bank of Bull Run. General Beauregard will have orders for you when you get there. Good luck and good hunting."

When Jamie reached the area, he did not immediately report to General Beauregard; instead he spent several hours riding back and forth over as much of the area as he could, talking with Rebel troops. Jamie did not know much about commanding huge armies, but he did know guerrilla tactics. In his mind, he wondered if the Yankees had any outfit such as his own—they did, but were not as yet ready for action. If the Union army had men such as those Jamie commanded, he saw a flaw in Beauregard's positioning of troops, for the general was so sure the Union forces would attack across Mitchell's Ford, that he had spread too few troops on the left side of his lines. Jamie understood why the general had done that, for the left side of the line consisted of either thick, almost impenetrable woods, or narrow, twisting roads that no advancing army of any size could use with any speed.

But if the Federals had guerrillas . . . ? Jamie shook his head at that thought.

Jamie had to hide his smile when he reported to Beauregard, for the next words out of the general's mouth, after he greeted and congratulated him, were, "I want you and your Marauders on this side of my line, Major." He tapped a map position. "Right here at Sudley Ford. But you are not confined to that area alone. Go where you are needed." He smiled. "And a man of your many talents will surely be needed, I assure you of that."

"I'll get settled in then, General, and get my men in position."

Jamie turned to go, and Beauregard's voice stopped him. "Major, we'll probably be falling back some few thousand yards." He smiled again. "Be prepared to move out hurriedly."

"Yes, sir. I was briefed down south."

"I assumed as much, but I wanted to be sure."

Jamie saluted and left the tent.

It was July 16.

Beauregard's army stretched for more than six miles along Bull Run. The Confederate government in Richmond had expressly forbidden Beauregard from taking any type of offensive action, and after seeing that the Rebels were not going to bring the fight to them, the Yankees began a slow advance toward Rebel positions. They had no way of knowing that it was a trap, for when the Federal troops had advanced far enough, Beauregard's plan was to flank them and cut them off from the nation's capital.

The Yankees' advance was slowed to a snail's pace in the sparsely populated area, filled with thick brush, dense forests, and creek bottoms that seemed to swallow the wagons up to their axles. Many of the Federal troops became separated from their units and got lost.

Jamie's men captured more than two dozen of them, and they were disarmed and brought to Jamie.

Boys, Jamie thought, looking at the scared young men standing in front of him. They should be playing games and sparking young girls.

Jamie walked the short line, eyeballing each prisoner for a

few seconds. The imposing figure of Jamie MacCallister stalking up and down in front of them caused many of the soldiers to tremble in their hot and ill-fitting uniforms. Jamie wore his customary black shirt and gray britches, a yellow kerchief tied around his neck. With his moccasins and high leggins, deeply tanned face, and muscular build, he looked sort of like a pirate to the young men. They didn't know who the hell had captured them.

Jamie cleared that up promptly.

"I am Major Jamie MacCallister, MacCallister's Marauders."

"Oh, shit!" a young private muttered. "They're gonna shoot us for sure."

Jamie hid his smile. "You boys are the lucky ones. You're out of this war."

Jamie ordered the young soldiers to be taken to Beauregard's HQ for questioning and then settled down to wait for some action. But none came that night, and the Marauders all got a good night's sleep. Mid-morning of the 17th, a runner found the major and told him to fall back; Union troops were only about a mile from Fairfax Court House.

Dupree grinned. "The Yankees are takin' the bait, Major. It won't be long now."

Jamie looked toward a black spiral of smoke. "Beauregard's set the Orange and Alexandria Railroad Bridge on fire. Fall back, boys."

Beauregard had given orders to his troops at Fairfax Court House to leave food still cooking on the fires, giving the Yankees the impression they were so frightened they had fled without eating. The Union soldiers were jubilant. They ate the hot food and sang victorious songs with their coffee. Their jubilation was to be short-lived.

The Union general, McDowell, was giving conflicting orders to his commanders and being forced to rethink his strategy every hour or so. Nothing was working out as he had planned. He had reached Fairfax Court House expecting to find another of his generals, Heintzelman, waiting for him. But now he had no idea where General Heinzelman might be (Heinzelman and his men had been slowed down to a crawl by the dense brush and poor roads). McDowell was also beginning to suspect a trap. He had just learned that Centerville had been abandoned by the Rebels and also that all along the Rebel line the Confederates were pulling back. That seemed very odd to him.

McDowell ordered another of his generals, Dan Tyler, to ride through Centerville at first light to check out the situation. And McDowell also gave him firm orders not to engage the enemy—just check it out and report back with his findings.

Jamie and his two companies of Marauders had pulled back as ordered and were cooling their heels in the dense timber, hoping to see a blue coat to shoot at. So far, they had seen nothing, nor had they heard the first shot.

A runner found Jamie and handed him orders. Jamie was to take his Marauders over to a stand of timber not far from Mitchell's Ford and throw up a line. Beauregard suspected something was up.

Something sure was.

Just moments after Jamie and his Marauders got into place, after having circled wide and come up from the south, Tyler exceeded his orders and decided to take the town of Manassas. His thinking was that since the Rebels seemed to be in full retreat, why not take advantage of it and forge on ahead. It would be quite a feather in his cap.

That decision not only got the plume in Tyler's hat shot off, it almost cost him his life.

Since his men were going to be engaged in regular army field tactics for a time, Jamie had taken the rifles from the dozen captured Yankees and passed them out to his best shots. The rifles were British Enfield rifles, which could use the American .58 caliber bullet and could fire farther and with more accuracy than the shorter barreled carbines.

"When they come into range are they fair game, Major?" one of Jamie's men asked.

"As far as I'm concerned they are."

The snipers looked at one another and grinned.

Tyler was at that time giving orders to send several companies of the First Massachusetts forward and at the same time ordering several twenty pounders to open fire where he suspected Rebel artillery to be hidden in the thickets. He also ordered two other companies of infantry to seize and hold a wooded area that lay off some distance from the suspected Rebel artillery battery. He had no way of knowing that Jamie and his men were in those woods waiting. The batteries commenced firing as the two companies began advancing on the hidden positions of the Marauders.

Jamie told his men to open up.

Twelve Rebel riflemen fired, and ten Union soldiers went down, four of them dead and the others badly wounded.

Tyler ordered the companies back and into cover. He looked toward the timber, confusion in the glance. Then his gaze was averted as the First Massachusetts came under heavy fire from Rebel snipers far to the right side of Jamie's position.

Tyler not only ignored his orders, but threw all caution to the wind and ordered his men to take the Rebel positions. But they could not. They were caught in a heavy cross fire and pinned down. Tyler called for his entire command, just over a brigade strong, to come up.

Tyler had no way of knowing that General Beauregard had more than half his army facing his one brigade.

"Pull back, you damn fool," Jamie muttered. "You're throwing good men out to be slaughtered."

"That's what it's all about, Major," Sparks said, standing a few feet away. "One side slaughters the other."

Jamie could not argue that.

Dupree called, "Them facin' us is showin' a white flag, Major. I reckon they want to get their wounded."

"Let them. I've done the same with Indians and with Santa Anna's men at the Alamo."

The colonel commanding the Massachusetts waved his men out to collect the wounded. The dead would lie where they fell. After a few minutes, both sides started once more banging away at each other.

Tyler ordered another line set up facing Jamie and his men, but Tyler's only option was to place them on the crest of a hill. After a few minutes of deadly fire from the Marauder snipers, they were withdrawn.

"If this is the best showin' their officers can do," Corporal Bates remarked, "we just might win this war." But it was said without a lot of conviction. Bates had traveled the North and East with his father, a railroad engineer. He knew full well the might of the Yankees.

In a desperate move, General Tyler placed men from the Twelfth New York, the First Massachusetts, and the Second and Third Michigan stretched out along a line facing the Rebels. But they could not advance. After less than a half hour of fierce fighting, Tyler ordered his men to withdraw.

The weakest point of the miles-long line was at Blackburn's Ford, but that was due to the terrain and not the resolve of the Southerners under the command of Longstreet.

Now General Tyler was faced with some tough decisions. He had no way of knowing that Jamie's Marauders were only two companies strong without a single cannon to back them. Had he taken a chance, he might have broken through and begun a flanking movement. But he did not. He elected to pull back the Twelfth New York and send them directly at Longstreet's men. But Beauregard had sent Early's brigade to beef up Longstreet and went there himself with his men. He and Longstreet stood up behind their troops, sabers in hand, the sight of them braving the bullets only adding to the courage of their men.

After only twenty minutes, the Twelfth New York began to retreat, and it was not an orderly withdrawal . . . it was a rout. That retreat left other Union troops under Tyler's command wide open, and Longstreet sent men from his Virginia command charging across the stream. The Union line broke, and the troops began running toward the rear. Longstreet did not pursue—a decision that was questioned for some time by other Confederate officers; instead he ordered his Rebels back and to resume their positions south of the creek.

The battle for Blackburn's Ford was over, with the Rebels clearly victorious.

McDowell arrived on the scene, clearly irritated, and took Tyler into a hastily erected tent and posted a guard and closed the flap. It was not known exactly what McDowell said to Tyler, but congratulations certainly were not in order.

For the next several days, all was mostly quiet along the long lines. Jamie and his men held their positions in the woods and rested, wrote letters home, and talked among themselves.

The men of the Marauders were gradually adopting a battle dress, and Jamie did not object. While Jamie wore a black shirt and gray trousers, the men were now nearly all wearing gray shirts and black trousers. All now wore the yellow bandanna around their throats and the standard Confederate cavalryman's hat. Dupree's wife had gathered together several Louisiana ladies and sewed a battle flag for the Marauders. Jamie smiled when he saw it, but offered no objections to its use . . . as a matter of fact, he was rather amused by it.

It was a black flag with a pirate's skull and crossbones in the center.

Leaving his two companies resting in the woods, Jamie rode over to Beauregard's headquarters—his aide, Little Ben Pardee, rode with him. General Joseph E. Johnston was there. Johnston, being the senior officer, was in command of the entire Rebel army. But for the Battle of Manassas (the Yankees called it Bull Run), he left Beauregard in complete command.

It was the 20th of July, 1861.

Reinforcements were arriving almost hourly. General T.J. Jackson and his Virginia Brigade had arrived, as had General B.E. Bee from South Carolina and General E.K. Smith and his men. General Theophilus Holmes had arrived with his troops, as had Colonel Hampton and his South Carolina Hampton Legion and Colonel Bartow's Georgia Brigade. Many had their own flags, and it was getting confusing, for the flags were all different, some of them not even using the Confederate colors. The flag of the Florida Independent Blues, for example, was a blue background with seven white stars on top, a flower in the middle, and the words ANY FATE BUT SUBMISSION, in a half circle on the bottom. One flag from South Carolina had blue and red squares with a fox, a cannon, a quarter moon, and a palm tree embroidered on the flag. Soon most of the flags would be replaced by the Rebel battle flag, which had thirteen white stars against a blue X, the stars representing the eleven Confederate states plus the two that the Rebels claimed, Missouri and Kentucky.

General Beauregard's HQ during the Battle of Manassas was a private home near Manassas Junction. President Jefferson Davis would meet with Beauregard there, and some fifteen months later, President Abe Lincoln would meet with some of his generals in the very same house.

In addition to the thousands of Confederate troops already gathered, by July 21, more than nine thousand other Rebels had made the trip by railroad to beef up the Confederate army. At the same time, the Union forces were also being increased—by reporters and civilian well-wishers who came bringing picnic lunches and kegs of beer and stronger spirits. They pitched tents and laid down blankets and cots. They came by the hundreds, getting in the way and in general making a nuisance of themselves. They were in high spirits, some having traveled long distances to witness firsthand the Union army give the Confederate army a good sound licking and to teach these upstart Southerners a lesson. They settled in under whatever shade they could find and uncorked their spy glasses and field glasses and got ready to have a party after the battle that would soon and forever after be called the Battle of Bull Run.

8

One of Jamie's men who had lived for a time in Ohio, and did not have a pronounced Southern drawl, slipped into Yankee held territory and mingled with the crowds for a day, before slipping back across the lines that night.

"Must be near 'bouts a thousand civilians over there, Major. Man name of Matt Brady is over there with his cameras, and there are congressmen and senators from Washington, D.C., there. And they got troops comin' in just like we have."

One of General Johnston's aides was in camp, and he asked, "Civilians? Why?"

"To watch the Yankees whip us, sir."

The aide smiled. "They just might be in for a slight disappointment."

"We're counting on that," Captain Dupree said.

"Major MacCallister, General Johnston has orders for you and your Marauders. When the battle starts in earnest, he wants you and your men to cross the stream and launch a flanking action here." He pointed to a map. "Create a lot of confusion."

"We do that right well," Sparks drawled.

"Yes," the aide said with a smile. "We know."

Long after the aide had left, Jamie studied the crude maps and the overall battle plan carefully and again immediately picked up the flaws in it. The northwest, or left, side of the line was grossly undermanned. Beauregard had placed the bulk of his troops far to the right, down around Mitchell's Ford, Blackburn's Ford, and McLean's Ford, leaving the left side of the line very nearly wide open.

But Jamie wasn't about to openly question the commanding general on his battle tactics. However, he could see to it that the Union forces he was to face in a few hours would think they were up against a much larger force. He didn't know quite how he was going to do that, yet, but he'd work it out.

He was awakened at three o'clock on the morning of July 21 by a runner. "The Yankees are on the move, sir," the young man told him. "They were rousted out about an hour ago. Them that could sleep that is. Our people in the observation posts say the Yankees hardly slept at all."

Pulling on his moccasins and tying his leggins, Jamie looked at the young man. "And you, son?"

The runner grinned. "I ain't slept none, Major. War's in the air, I reckon."

"Indeed," Jamie replied, standing up.

Jamie and his men drank coffee and ate cold biscuits, then doused their small fires and saddled up. With Jamie in the lead, they moved silently through the brush and timber over to Colonel Evans' position between Young's Branch and the stream called Bull Run.

Jamie and Evans shook hands, and Evans asked, "Your orders, Major?"

"To raise some hell with the Yankees, sir. I figure they'll hit us at dawn."

"If they can ever get into position. My forward people report a lot of confusion and cussing over there."

He was right about that. The terrain was totally unfamiliar to the Union troops, and many were stumbling around and tripping over things and falling down. The rattle of Yankee equipment clattering against rocks and such was enough to raise the dead.

The Rebels waited behind their guns, silent in the gloom of night.

From Ewell's command far to the right, all the way over to Evans' command, some six or seven miles away, the Rebels shared the same fear as the Yankees. It was hard to get enough moisture in their mouths to even spit. In a few spots along the snakelike line, Union and Confederate troops were only a few yards away from each other, with many of them taunting the other.

"You come acrost this crick, boy, you gonna die."

"You go straight to hell, Rebel!"

"Hell's waitin' for both of us, I reckon."

"Not for me, I don't own human beings as slaves."

"I don't neither. Never owned a slave in my life. Ain't nary a slave on either side of my family. Never has been."

A long silence followed that. Finally, the unknown Union soldier asked the equally unknown Rebel, "Then what the hell are you doing fighting?"

"So's you Yankees will stay out of my business, I reckon."

"I'm not in your business!"

"The hell you say. You here, ain't you?"

The Yankee could not argue that.

"If you blue-bellies had tended to your own affairs, I'd be home asleep 'side my wife instead of on this damn cold ground."

"Where are you from?"

"South Carolina. You?"

"New York. We're both a long way from hearth and home."

"You damn shore got that right."

"Silence up and down the line!" Rebel and Union sergeants ordered.

Both Yankee and Rebel told the unseen voices where they could shove their orders.

Both men would be dead in a few hours. Neither man quite sure what he was fighting for, but each firmly convinced he was on the right side.

At dawn, Jamie had moved his people several hundred yards away from Evans' position and was keeping them hidden in a stand of brush and timber. Nothing was happening down the line, and Jamie felt a sinking feeling in the pit of his stomach. He had a strong suspicion that the whole of the Union army was going to come pouring right over and through his and Evans' men.

He wasn't that far from being right.

Just a few minutes after seven that morning, Colonel Evans sent a runner to tell Jamie, "The colonel thinks the Yankees are bluffing. They aren't going to attack in strength along our positions. He thinks they're going to strike at Sudley Ford. That's Burnside's Yankees. The colonel wants you and your people over there. He'll join you as quickly as possible."

Jamie quickly shifted his Marauders over to the left, and they waited. Just a few minutes later, he saw the glint of Union bayonets flashing in the morning sun as the first troops moved into position in the trees around Sudley Ford.

Jamie sent Ben Pardee on the fly to tell Evans of the news. After Pardee blurted out the message, Evans quickly shifted his command around, putting Major Wheat and his redshirted, five-hundred-man Louisiana Tigers just to Jamie's right.

Wheat's Tigers were a unit known for its bravery under fire. Later on during the Battle of Bull Run, one Union colonel, after witnessing his men being soundly thrashed by the Louisiana Tigers, called them, "The most belligerent bunch of bastards I have ever faced."

Jamie rode over to meet with Wheat. He could look Wheat straight in the eye, for both men were over six feet, four inches tall, although Wheat outweighed Jamie's two hundred twenty-five pounds by a good seventy-five pounds. Major Roberdeau Wheat was a very imposing figure of a man.

"We're slightly outnumbered down there, MacCallister," Wheat remarked, after lowering field glasses.

Jamie smiled. "About twenty-five to one, I'd say. But I have a plan."

"Oh?"

"We'll charge!"

Wheat roared with laughter. "You're damn right, we will. I'll get my boys ready and wait for your signal."

Jamie rode back to his Marauders and told them what he planned to do. His men grinned at him. Jamie, at the far point of the left side, watched for a time longer and then sent Ben Pardee racing back to Evans.

"We're being flanked, sir," Pardee panted out the warning. "Just north of the Stone Bridge."

"What's Major MacCallister going to do?"

"Us and Major Wheat is fixin' to charge, sir."

"What?" Evans blurted, but Pardee was already back in the saddle and galloping away, not wanting to miss the charge against the Yankees. His haste was uncalled for. The first charge would not come for a couple more hours.

Colonel Evans was thoughtful for a moment; then he smiled. "That just might be a pretty good idea," he said aloud.

Evans then began moving very fast. He ordered out skirmishers but kept the bulk of his troops well hidden. He did not want the Yankees to know just how few men he really had and just how vulnerable he was.

Then the Union troops came in a rush. Evans committed more of his Rebels, and they caught the Union troops in a blistering fire, pinning them down. The Yankee commanders started shifting troops around, somehow realizing how thin the Rebels' lines were. Just as the Union commanders were shouting the orders to charge, a thundering pound of hooves and spine-tingling Rebel battle cries filled the air.

The Federal troops must have thought somebody opened the gates to hell. On one side there were some two-hundred-odd gray-shirted and black-trousered men on horseback, screaming as they charged them, a horrible-looking black flag with a ghastly white skull and crossbones against the black flapping in the wind. The mounted charge being led by a black-shirted man who held the reins in his teeth, both hands filled with pistols.

On the other side, there came what appeared to be a sea of red-shirted soldiers led by a huge man with a pistol in one hand and a Bowie knife in the other. Wheat and his men were screaming Rebel yells as they charged down the hill, straight into the startled Union troops. Jamie's Marauders hit the Union forces from one side, and Wheat's Louisiana Tigers slammed into them from the other.

Jamie emptied both pistols, holstered them, and grabbed for the two on the left and right of his saddle and began firing. He charged Satan into the sea of blue, and the big horse knocked men spinning in all directions.

The charge was costly for both the Marauders and Wheat's Tigers. In Jamie's unit ten men were killed and a dozen wounded. Wheat lost almost fifty men, dead and wounded, and was hard hit himself.

Jamie's and Wheat's men retreated, having created chaos and confusion, giving Beauregard time to send in reinforcements. Wheat was badly wounded, so gravely the doctors told him he didn't have a chance and to make his peace with God.

Wheat, showing all the belligerence he and his Louisiana Tigers were famous for, was reported to have told all the doctors (among other things) to go right straight to hell; he had no intention of dying just yet. He turned over his command to his executive officer and was back on his feet in a month, once more leading the Tigers into battle.

But it was the Union forces who took the greatest casualties: several hundred blue-shirted troops lay dead or wounded as Jamie and his Marauders and Wheat's Louisianans retreated back over the ridge to safety, carrying their dead and their wounded.

Their combined actions had bought a little time for Evans. But after assessing the situation, Evans decided it was time for a major pull-back; he had received word that another Yankee column was crossing the bridge at Sudley Ford. Evans ordered a withdrawal just as two Confederate brigades came running and riding up, bringing with them much needed artillery.

"We're out of here!" Jamie shouted to his men, swinging into the saddle. "Follow me!"

Units from Alabama and Mississippi, under the command of General Bee, and units from Georgia, under the command of Colonel Bartow, formed a line facing the Yankees, some of the Rebels as close as fifty yards from the Union forces. The Rebels began alternately taunting and shooting at the Yankees. They would jump up, fire, fall down in the ditches or behind whatever cover they had, and reload and yell at the Yankees. Where they were, on the extreme left side of Beauregard's line, looking at the Union troops over on Matthews Hill, there were approximately five thousand Rebels facing some fifteen thousand Federal troops. Even though, or probably because, they were outnumbered at least three to one, the Rebels charged the Yankee lines, the bold move surprising the Union commanders. General Bee's troops quickly pulled out in front of the rest of the Rebels, leaving both flanks badly exposed. Bee ordered Evans and Bartow back and withdrew to Young's Branch.

Jamie sat on a ridge not far away and watched the action through field glasses while his men rested behind him. He could see no reasonable course of action for his men to take. Just as he was rising to his feet, a runner from headquarters reached his side.

"Orders from General Beauregard, sir. You are asked to take your men up to the Warrenton Turnpike and try to prevent Burnside's troops from flanking Evans."

Jamie smiled. "Less than two hundred lightly armed men against five thousand? Of course! We're riding now."

It was eleven o'clock in the morning, the fight had been raging for several hours, and both sides had taken terrible losses, the dead and badly wounded littering the ground.

General McDowell ordered General Tyler to mount an attack—to take his troops across Bull Run. Jamie and his Marauders and about three hundred other Rebels, men who had gotten cut off from their units, were gathering in a thickly wooded area along the Warrenton Turnpike. Jamie looked around for an officer among the regular soldiers; there was none.

"What do we do, sir?" a badly frightened young Rebel asked. He was gripping his rifle so tightly his knuckles were white from the strain.

Jamie looked at the lad; no more than sixteen or seventeen years old. He put a big hand on the boy's shoulder as twenty or thirty others gathered around him. "First of all, men, we calm down and get our wits about us." The group around him had swelled and now fell silent, listening, those men cut off from their units glad to finally have some leadership.

Jamie had no way of knowing that more than five thousand men were bearing down on him, only minutes away. Had no way of knowing that two Union brigades, commanded by Sherman and Keyes, were heading directly toward his position.

Command Sergeant Major Huske galloped up and leaped off his horse, pushing through the crowd to Jamie's side. He whispered in Jamie's ear.

Jamie did not change expression at the news. Huske stepped away, and Jamie said, "Fall in and start moving back. And we will do this in an orderly fashion. You're soldiers, so act like it. Sergeant Major Huske will take command of you men. Now move out."

The Union army had broken through the Rebel lines and very nearly put the Confederates in a rout. Jamie and his men were trapped.

9

When the news of the Confederate retreat reached the spectators behind the Union lines, they cheered and shouted and waved flags. Two divisions of Federal troops had now crossed Bull Run, and a third division was not far behind. General McDowell's goal for this day was to cross the turnpike and head straight for the railroad and seize it. Once there, he believed, he would have a clear route to Richmond.

For more than an hour, General McDowell rode up and down the ranks of his advancing Federal troops, a smile on his lips. He would occasionally shout triumphant words to his men, who grinned and waved their caps at him.

McDowell was certain the battle was very nearly won. Victory was his.

However, the Rebels had other plans.

Astonishingly enough, General Beauregard did not really know what was going on for some time. He was at his headquarters and could only occasionally hear some gunfire. But to his way of thinking, it was coming from the wrong direction. The bulk of his army was far to the right of the scene of the actual fighting.

He finally sent an aide to find out what was going on, and the aide returned, pale and shaken. "Our boys are in a rout!" he shouted. "The Yankees are hard upon us, sir!"

Beauregard was stunned into momentary silence. It was then that General Joe Johnston took over as commander of all Confederate forces in Northern Virginia. He grabbed the situation in a strong hand and began issuing orders.

It was just after noon, on the 21st of July, 1861.

Jamie and his men, and the three-hundred-odd regular Rebel infantrymen with him were trapped in a pocket on the north side of the Warrenton Turnpike, with the stream called Young's Branch behind them. Jamie quickly counted heads. He had just over five hundred men, all armed with plenty of ammunition. He thought fast, knowing he had to get out of this pickle.

"Dupree," Jamie said. "Take your company and act as vanguard. The infantry will be in the center of the column and Sparks' company behind that. I'll take ten men and try to plug up the hole that we make getting out of here. We'll cross the turnpike and throw up a line. If anything happens to me, you're in command. Now move out."

Jamie turned to Little Ben Pardee. "Ben, ride like the wind and find whoever the hell is in command and tell them what I'm doing. Go, boy!"

Sparks' company just barely made it out before Union forces came charging into the thicket after them. Bad mistake. Jamie and the ten men with him opened up with rifles and pistols, and those Yankees who survived that fusillade decided it would be a very wise move to get gone from that area of the woods.

Jamie and his group found themselves alone and unchallenged as they crossed the turnpike and threw up a line on the south side. The heaviest fighting was about two miles away, to their right. Jamie and command found themselves with nothing to do. But that was not going to last long, for Little Ben came galloping back with orders from General Joe Johnston himself.

"Our boys have abandoned the line, Major," Ben said, leaping off his horse. "Some South Carolina boys under the command of Colonel Hampton is on the way up to the front, and they damn near got stampeded over by those retreatin.'

They're all alone, sir. General Johnston says if at all possible, get over there and lend a hand."

Jamie turned to the infantrymen. "Shuck out of those heavy coats and tie them over a shoulder." He looked at Sergeant Major Huske. "Top Soldier, double time them over to the fight. We'll see if we can't pull some Yankee stingers before you get there."

"We'll be right behind you, sir."

But the Federal forces hesitated in attacking. They had suffered terrible losses that morning, due to the stupidity of their leaders. When the battle first began, Evans' men were grossly outnumbered, and the Union leaders could have sent a division, or at least a brigade in to overwhelm the Gray by sheer numbers. They did not. They wasted human lives by sending small units in what amounted to suicide charges, instead of committing fully. Now they were simply unable to attack in anywhere close to full strength because their commands had been so badly mauled and chewed up.

But McDowell could muster about ten thousand troops . . . some six brigades, holding one in reserve. Still, McDowell did not attack immediately.

As Jamie and his Marauders were galloping toward the battle, General Jackson was moving there also, with five regiments of Rebel infantry. However, at the time, Jackson's 33rd Virginia wore blue uniforms, and some Union troops wore gray. Jackson later said, "It was a hell of way to fight a war." Jackson instructed his men to tie white pieces of cloth around their arms so they would not be shooting each other.

One sage in the ranks got a withering look from Jackson when he called out, "You gonna tell them Yankees all dressed up in gray to do the same, sir?"

History does not record Jackson's reply, but it was probably rather salty.

Jackson formed up his men just behind the crest of a hill and waited. By now, parts of five batteries of Confederate artillery were in place, commanded by an Episcopal minister turned colonel.

He looked at the retreating line of Gray. "Give those gallant boys some support!" he thundered. "Fire!"

"Where the hell is Jackson?" a captain shouted out.

General Bee pointed to the crest of a hill. "Standing over there like a stone wall."

Jackson's nickname was born.

Bee rallied his men and urged them on to one more charge, riding among them, waving his saber. It was to be his last effort of the Battle of Manassas. He was shot off his horse and died a short time later.

It was one o'clock in the afternoon.

Johnston and Beauregard arrived on the hill just after General Bee was killed and just in time to see Jamie's Marauders hit the Union troops on the left side of the line, firing their pistols point-blank and slashing with Bowie knives at the clearly startled Federal forces, who had not expected anything like this wild bunch of screaming men flying a pirate's flag. About three quarters of a mile behind the Marauders, the two generals could see several hundred Confederate soldiers double-timing their way toward the fight.

There was damn little for the commanding general to smile about that day, but he smiled at the battle flag of the Marauders and shook his head in disbelief at the bravery of the guerrillas and at the efforts of the battered men of Colonel Nathan Evans, who, with the action of the Marauders, was now able to regroup and fall back out of the Union trap.

Johnston watched as Jamie hand-signaled Sergeant Major Huske to position his men between the Union forces and the hill. Then Jamie and his Marauders galloped away to safety. The Marauders had lost two men dead and five wounded in this latest action.

Seeing what was happening right before their eyes, witnessing five hundred or so men abruptly stop the Yankee advance cold for a few moments, what was left of the Fourth Alabama once more surged forward, as Bartow managed to piece together what was left of his Georgia men and joined him. And the line held.

Moments after Jamie and his men staged their daring charge, Colonel Jubal Early and General Bonham's brigade rushed into battle, further strengthening the line. Within moments, Colonel Jeb Stuart's First Virginia Cavalry put some more steel into the Rebel defenses.

Jamie rode up the hill to Johnston. Johnston looked at him and said, "Fine work, Colonel MacCallister."

"I'm a major, sir," Jamie replied.

"Not any more, sir," General Johnston said. "Pull your men back here to me and act as my guards while I set up a new HQ."

He looked more closely at Jamie. "You've been wounded, Colonel."

"In several places, General. But they're minor." He waved toward the battle below them, a battle which was softening in sound and fury now as the Union forces were beginning to understand that their earlier jubilation at victory was a bit premature. "Nearly every man down there has a cut or a tear."

"Indeed," Johnston agreed. "Take over here, Pierre," he said to Beauregard. "Come, Colonel."

Jamie turned to his color bearer. "Case that flag, Jones."

"Oh, no, Colonel," Johnston said. "Let it fly. It helped to save the day. I'd feel proud to ride under its banner for a time."

"Very well, sir."

Johnston found new quarters for his HQ about three quarters of a mile behind the front while Beauregard began repositioning his men as reinforcements arrived. The Forty-ninth Virginia marched onto the scene, plus about a dozen other companies from various units. Beauregard stiffened left and right flanks and rode up and down the line, quietly talking to his men, urging them to stand and hold.

By mid-afternoon, Beauregard now had about seven thousand men on the line and several batteries of cannon placed on the crests of hills, and the Union troops were ready for a charge.

"That's fine with me," Stonewall Jackson said, and ordered his men to fix bayonets.

Meanwhile, Jamie had pulled in his reserve to bring his two companies of Marauders up to strength. But Johnston ordered him to hold his people around his HQ, saying he had other plans for the Marauders.

At the front, the Yankees began their charge against Stonewall's position.

"Let them come," Jackson told his men. "Let them come."

Just as the Union troops were close enough to be almost eyeball to eyeball with the Rebels on the hills and ridges, Jackson ordered his men to stand and fire.

It was slaughter for the Federal troops. Jackson's men cut them down with volley after volley, and the Union troops broke and ran.

The first reported civilian to die in the battle was killed by enemy artillery. Yankee gunners believed the house to be a stronghold of Rebels and poured round after round into the home, blowing a leg off of an elderly, bed-ridden woman. She died a few hours later. The man responsible for ordering the shelling of the civilian home was later made a general in the Union army.

A Virginia regiment, one of the few whose uniforms were blue, began an advance on a Federal artillery and infantry position. The commander of the Union forces mistakenly thought they were Federal reinforcements. The advancing troops were less than fifty yards away when the Union commander realized they were Confederate troops. But it was too late. The Rebels swarmed over the position and slaughtered the Union troops, seizing valuable cannons, powder, shot, shells, and horses. What remained of the Union troops fled.

Many of the Federal troops at the front began retreating, some in wild panic as the battle now turned. The Southerners, although badly outnumbered, had begun fighting with a ferocity that was frightening to the Northern troops. The fear spread as those retreating mingled with inexperienced fresh troops coming up from the rear.

The Federal commanders finally stopped the retreat before

it got completely out of hand and pushed their men back to the front with threats and curses and taunts.

The cheering of the hundreds of civilians behind the front had ceased when the retreating began, now it resumed as the Yankees rallied.

For the next three hours, the battle lines changed and shifted, and positions were lost, retaken, lost again, and retaken many times. In many areas along the front, the fighting was cut and slash with bayonet, saber, and Bowie knife, eyeball to eyeball and nose to nose; so close the men of the Blue and Gray could smell the sweat and the fear of the other. The Rebels would use the captured cannon against the Yankees; the Yankees would retake the pieces and use them against the Rebels without having to move the cannon except to turn them around.

Johnston kept MacCallister's Marauders close to his HQ until one event caused the general to call Jamie in and ask him to lead his men briefly into battle. It appeared Beauregard himself was so caught up in the heat of battle he personally led the Fifth Virginia in a wild charge up a hill, waving his saber and cursing the Yankees. He and his men took the hill and captured more Union artillery pieces. They turned the cannon around and began shelling the retreating Federal forces.

"Colonel, take some of your men and get my field commander off that damn hill, please!"

Jamie personally escorted a reluctant-to-leave Beauregard off the hill just as Colonel Frances Bartow, commander of the Seventh Georgia, was shot through the chest. He died urging his men to never give up.

Men on both sides were dropping not only from grievous wounds, but from the terrible heat of the day, choked with dust and arid gunsmoke. Drinkable water was scarce, and besides, the battle was so intense, no one had the time to waste drinking what water could be found. The creeks were running red with blood from the bodies of the Blue and the Gray.

Johnston came up to view the battle from atop a high hill

and told Beauregard to stay with him. "I need you," was his explanation.

"They could overwhelm us at any time," Jamie muttered. "But they don't. Why?"

Why indeed? Why, because McDowell would never commit his Union troops to a charge in anything other than brigade strength. He needlessly lost several hundred lives because of his timidity. But even had he committed all his troops, he might not have won the battle, for the Rebels were fighting for loved ones and homeland, and there is no stronger incentive to stand or die.

As one Union brigade was driven back, another took its place, and they, too, were driven back by the men of the Gray. The New York Highlanders charged up a hill and were slaughtered by Rebel rifle fire and the lowered barrels of point-blank cannon using grapeshot.

It was four o'clock in the afternoon when McDowell finally called up his unbloodied reserves, men from Vermont and Maine, nearly four regiments strong. But by now the Union lines were so disorganized and confused, with commanders from the company level up and the essential sergeants wounded, dead or missing, McDowell was about to hurl his last fresh troops into and through the gates of death, the gate masters the men of the Gray.

In the dust and smoke and confusion of battle, it is doubtful that General McDowell even knew where the fresh troops were committed to the line; but committed they were and died by the score.

The first attack from the four regiments was thrown back, the Union troops thoroughly demoralized by the fierceness of their adversaries. The fresh Union troops were further disheartened by the sight of bloodied and mauled Federals limping back from a previous assault.

The Federals charged again—some of them, at least. The others did not know what to do. Orders could not be heard over the crash of combat. Some men went forward while others, confused, turned toward the rear. Others became disoriented.

Fresh Rebel troops had been added to the line of defenders, and they bolstered the resolve of their tired comrades. One fresh-to-the-scene Rebel commander of Maryland troops vowed to ". . . walk away from this day victorious or be buried here." He led his men against the far right of McDowell's troops, and the Union line began to crumble.

Jamie, watching through field glasses, saw Union soldiers throw away their weapons and packs and run toward the rear.

It was late afternoon—about five o'clock.

Beauregard left the hill over Jamie's protestations and galloped to the battle, personally leading his men forward, chasing the fleeing Union soldiers. The retreat soon turned into something else: a panic seemed to grip the Union soldiers, many of them running blindly in any direction that would take them away from the terrible carnage.

Soon, Beauregard and his cavalry had to stop chasing the Federals, for they had taken so many prisoners the captured Union soldiers were badly outnumbering the guards.

President Jefferson Davis had reached the battlefield, and Johnston and a contingent of Marauders personally escorted the Confederate president to the hill overlooking what had been the main battle area.

"They were good men all," Jeff Davis said, speaking of both the Blue and the Gray. "And they believed they were right."

Jamie sat his horse and said nothing as Johnston and Jeff Davis turned their mounts and rode back to Johnston's headquarters.

"Good men all, indeed," Jamie muttered. "And every man on either side was right." And the winds from the gathering storm clouds blew the words away.

A furious storm developed early in the evening of July 21, and it only added to the misery of the retreating Federal soldiers slogging wearily and dejectedly back to Washington, D.C.

General Johnston decided that the Confederate troops, just as tired, plus being hungry and short on ammunition, would make no pursuit of the enemy. Many believed that was a mistake, for as tired as his men were, they could have seized the nation's capital and possibly ended the war right then. Others heatedly disagreed. It was an argument that would never be settled one way or the other.

General McDowell managed to put together a force and throw up a defensive line around Centerville, but he knew they could not stop an all-out Rebel offensive. More than half of his army was still retreating toward Washington, D.C.

On the morning of the 22nd of July, McDowell ordered the rest of his army back to the Potomac. There were no bands playing, no cheering crowds. The retreating men had fought all the past day and then marched more than twenty miles through the stormy night, and they were exhausted. The rain continued to fall and that added to the misery of the beaten soldiers.

Many of the ladies of Washington turned out to help in the feeding of the hundreds and hundreds of bedraggled-looking soldiers. They used wash kettles to cook soup and coffee. Others stayed up all night baking bread. After wolfing down the first food many had consumed in thirty-six hours, the weary soldiers dropped down to sleep wherever they could, oblivious to the rain.

The battle had cost the Union army more than six hundred dead, nearly fifteen hundred wounded, and more than two thousand missing. Whether captured, dead or deserters, the exact figure would never be known.

Lincoln's comments upon hearing the figures was terse. "It's bad."

The Confederate army lost four hundred dead, over sixteen hundred wounded, and twenty-three missing.

On July 25, President Lincoln summoned General George McClellan and named him commander of the Union army around Washington, replacing McDowell. But the old soldier was not put out to pasture, for he would go on to command other divisions in the Union army and blunder through the war.

One firm conclusion did come out of Bull Run: it forever wrote in blood the unwavering promise—on both sides—to wage this war to a bitter conclusion.

It did that. But a hundred and thirty years after the Civil War officially ended, a lot of bitterness would remain, and even after hundreds of thousands of classroom hours, the real reasons for fighting the war would still be murky in the minds of many.

10

War news was slow to reach the small and all but isolated communities in the West. By the time Kate received the letter Jamie had posted to her, telling her of his appointment to major in the CSA, the Battle of Manassas was days old, and he had already been field promoted to lieutenant colonel. And he and his Marauders had been given a new assignment.

Two more young men had left MacCallister's Valley to join in the fight, one for the Blue, one for the Gray.

In his letter, Jamie had asked her not to write him for he had no idea where he and his command would be sent. Instead, he would write her and keep her abreast of happenings.

Kate began keeping a daily diary, listing everything that took place in the twin valleys; she felt Jamie would enjoy reading it when he came home.

But Kate knew more about her husband than he thought, for the newspapers had written extensively of the exploits of MacCallister's Marauders. The nation's press now knew that he and his men had been responsible for the events in Philadelphia prior to the Battle of Manassas, and of his daring charges during what they referred to as the Battle of Bull Run.

The Marauders were making quite a name for themselves, and much of it was unfavorable. Jamie was aware of that, and it bothered him not a whit.

The Eastern press could not understand how a man who had

fought so bravely for freedom at the Alamo could now fight for slavery with the South.

"Idiots!" Jamie said, wadding up the newspaper and tossing it into the fire.

The press, Jamie felt, just simply did not understand the real reason behind the War Between the States. And probably never would, he concluded.

Jamie had brought his companies up to full strength and then some by pulling up the men he had held in reserve. While the Battle of Manassas was going on, other men had been training to join the Marauders. Jamie now had four full companies. Little by little, all his men had adopted a standard uniform, and Jamie offered no objection to it. The Marauders wore gray shirts, black pants, yellow bandannas, and gray Confederate cavalrymen's hats with gold-colored braid. As the weather worsened, they would wear black waist-length jackets. The Marauders were officially listed as a Special Operations unit.

Jamie preferred to think of them as guerrillas.

A few days after the Battle of Manassas, Jamie was called to a meeting with General Johnston.

"Colonel, I have been asked if I would lend you to the fight in the West, namely Missouri and Arkansas. I said I would ask you."

"I'll go wherever I'm needed, sir."

"Good! Good! I felt you would." He held out a hand and Jamie shook it. "Good luck and God bless you, sir."

Jamie and his four companies of men rode out one hot morning in the last week of July, 1861, with Captain Malone commanding the Third Company, and Captain Jennrette commanding the Fourth. They rode out without fanfare, the more than five hundred man column and wagons heading first south, then cutting to the west.

As they rode through the small towns of Virginia, people lined the streets and cheered the guerrilla fighters, for by now, everyone knew who they were. The standard bearers rode with the Confederate battle flag and the Marauders' own flag unfurled and flying. The citizens of the South pressed food upon the guerrilla fighters: Virginia hams and sides of bacon and fresh-baked bread and containers of stew and soup. So much food was given them that Jamie had to stop along the way and buy two more wagons and mules to pull them.

Toward the end of the long and bitterly divisive war, many citizens of the South, in order to survive, would be forced to eat all manner of things that would have been totally repugnant to them prior to the war.

But for now, food was plentiful, the South had just won a major victory against the Yankees, and the citizens were in a jubilant mood.

West Virginia was divided in loyalty, but stayed with the Union. There were a lot of hostilities toward the Confederacy in the state, so rather than have to fight his way through, Jamie chose to take the long way west.

The Marauders were a proud unit, for just getting picked to be interviewed was hard, and the few weeks of training they received was brutal. Each man knew exactly what was expected of him, knew that the life of a guerrilla could be very short, and knew that if captured, they could well face a firing squad or a hangman's noose.

The Marauders put the miles behind them as they rode farther and farther into territory many had never seen before—including Jamie. The cheering crowds, the blaring bands, and the adoration from the people soon became an embarrassment to the men, and Jamie began searching for ways to avoid towns whenever possible, taking back roads and sometimes blazing new trails around the populated areas.

The men of the two new companies were all seasoned combat veterans, having fought against the Federals in Florida and Texas and South Carolina and in pitched battles in other areas.

Whenever they camped for the night, Jamie would study the reports given him by General Johnston. Missouri had already seen dozens of battles of varying intensities between Union forces and Southern troops. Missouri was split in its loyalties almost along geographical lines: the northern part of the state was pro-Union, while the southern part was pro-Rebel. There had been riots in St. Louis where Union troops had fired into civilian crowds, killing many men and women and several babies; hatreds were running deep and bloody in Missouri. The state capital, Jefferson City, had changed hands several times, but by the end of July was firmly under the control of Union forces, under the command of General Harney and the home guard commander, Nat Lyon, a man who hated the South and all Southerners.

By the time Jamie and his Marauders reached Memphis, conditions were totally out of hand in Missouri. Missouri and Kansas were waging a bloody border war, with the Kansas Jayhawkers, the Red Legs, and Lane's Raiders fighting several bands of guerrillas, including Bloody Bill Anderson, Quantrill's Raiders, and the Missouri Bushwhackers. Lane, too, despised the South and Southerners, but his hatred was almost fanatical. The rift between Kansas and Missouri would not heal until decades after the war.

"We're riding into a hornet's nest," Jamie told his company commanders. "In Missouri, it's going to be damn difficult to tell friend from foe."

The leaders of the South had already and with much conviction disavowed any connection with William Quantrill, for the man was nothing but a cold-blooded murderer, and several of the men who rode with him were certifiably insane, including the man who would soon split and form his own gang, Bloody Bill Anderson, who often rode into battle foaming at the mouth like a rabid beast. Just before the war officially started, Quantrill had been given a commission in the Confederate army, but that commission had been quickly pulled, though Quantrill proclaimed himself a colonel.

By the time Jamie and his men reached a Confederate post just outside Memphis, General Lyon had been killed in a Missouri battle called Bloody Hill. Although it only lasted for half a day, the fight was one of the bloodiest battles in Missouri, with several thousand Rebel and Union soldiers wounded and over five hundred men killed.

"Missouri is a bloody killing field," the commanding general at Memphis told Jamie. "And it is going to get worse . . . much worse. I've sent word to General Johnston that I am not going to order you in there—yet—and he has agreed. But the Mississippi River, as much as we can hold, must remain in our hands. For as long as possible," he added grimly. "I want you to start raiding Yankee encampments on the east side of the river. Range just as far north as you dare, Colonel."

"Kentucky?" Jamie asked.

"It will soon be lost to us," the general said. "I don't know how long I can hold Memphis."

Longer than most expected. Memphis would remain in Confederate hands until May of '62, when Union gunboats, after a blistering naval battle, won them the city.

In a way, Jamie was relieved about not having to go into Missouri and get all tangled up in a divided state's internal war. However, Jamie was now a soldier until the war's end, and he would obey orders, even those orders he personally considered to be stupid ones—he would receive several of those.

After the Battle of Manassas—or Bull Run, as it is better known—even the most optimistic on either side realized in their hearts that this war was going to be a long and bloody one. And the war would age both combatants and leaders alike with a speed that seemed virtually impossible. Lee, at the war's outbreak, was fifty-four years old, tall and with dark hair showing almost no gray. At war's end, he was totally gray and worn far past his years. The Southern spirit was so strong that before the terrible conflict ended, boys as young as ten and eleven would be fighting in the front lines for the South . . . and no one made them go. Confederate soldiers, near the war's end, so weak from hunger they could barely stand, would be facing Federal rifles, pistols, cannons and sabers, armed with only rocks and clubs and knives. Old men armed with shotguns loaded with birdshot would die fighting the

Union forces. Old women and young girls would stand near the road and throw rocks at Union cavalrymen as they passed, hoping to spook their horses into throwing the despised blue-coated riders. Young boys would point wooden guns at blue uniforms as they passed. So hated was the Federal occupation after the war that young children would grow into adults before realizing that Damn Yankee was not one word.

Many people still believe that the Civil War was fought over slavery, yet ninety-five percent of the enlisted men who fought for the Gray, and many of its officers, never owned a slave.

For the rich plantation owners, the Southern gentry, to survive (and most of them became officers—many self appointed), the war had to be, for they could not continue their grand and lavish and selfish lifestyle without slaves. For if they had to pay people to work the fields, they'd be out there in the fields, pickin' cotton and pullin' bolls and choppin' weeds right along with the working class. Many of the Southern gentry owned hundreds of slaves; some owned as many as three *thousand* slaves. For them, the war was about slavery. But for the average Southerner, it was not. Men do not leave hearth and home and businesses and farms to pick up a gun and fight for something they have no part of and don't earn a dime from.

In truth, the Civil War, or the War Between the States, was fought over many issues; slavery, which was morally, ethically, and spiritually wrong, certainly close to the top of the list. Insidiously encroaching Federal Government Imperialism was the second and glaring reason that many historians have strangely remained mute about. For the latter alone, in the years after the war, many people wondered if they had fought and supported the wrong side.

11

Jamie and his Marauders struck at a Federal gun emplacement deep in Western Kentucky, overlooking the Mississippi River, and held the gun crews captive until they had packed the barrels of the huge thirty-two pound cannons with explosives.

"You boys better get gone," Jamie told the men with a grin on his face. "There's about to be one hell of a bang here."

The gun crews took off at a flat run, wanting to get just as far away as possible from the site before those massive charges went off and sent pieces of cannon flying in all directions.

"MacCallister's Marauders," one Union officer said, a disgusted note in his voice. He looked at the young artillery officer standing in front of him. "You were treated well after the surrender?"

"Yes, sir. They had a doctor with them and he saw to the wounded while the guerrillas packed the barrels with explosives."

The young officer was clearly embarrassed, and the Union colonel noted his discomfort. "You were outnumbered, Lieutenant. There is no disgrace in an honorable surrender. You saved lives by doing so."

"It isn't that at all, sir. It's just that, well, I don't really know how to say this. But . . ." Then he blurted out the words. "The Rebs were so darn nice to us after the fight. I mean, they weren't nice at all *during* the fight, but after it was all over, while they were tending to the wounded and holding the rest of us at gunpoint, why, they were just as friendly as could be, sir. It was as if there hadn't even been a fight at all. They asked about our families and what we did for a living before the war . . ." He hesitated, shuffling his feet on the floor and slowly shaking his head.

"Go on, Lieutenant," the colonel urged, although he had a pretty good idea what the young officer was having so much trouble putting into words.

"Well, sir . . . it's just . . . It's hard to explain. They didn't seem like . . . they didn't act like the enemy, sir. One of my gunners, Henderson, why, he was talking with this man, and it turned out they were related by marriage . . . sort of. This guerrilla's brother, why, he'd married one of Henderson's cousins a few years back. And Henderson's father had even bought a horse from this guerrilla's father. I don't understand this war, sir. I really don't."

The colonel waited, sensing there was more.

The young lieutenant frowned, then said, "Just before we were told to take off running, this one man—I think he was an officer, but it's hard to tell, since the Marauders don't wear any type of insignia—he looked at us and smiled and said, 'Y'all take care now, you hear?' " He met the colonel's eyes. "What the hell kind of war is this, Colonel?"

The colonel thought about that for a moment. "A very confusing one, Lieutenant." He was not a career officer and added, "And if both sides hadn't of had such stiff necks, a war that could have been avoided. Should have been avoided." He smiled. "However, if you repeat that last bit, I'll swear you were lying."

Jamie and his men beat it back into Tennessee with dozens of Yankee patrols nipping at their heels.

For weeks, Jamie and his Marauders raided installations deep in Federal territory, always working in small groups of ten to fifteen men. Sometimes they dressed as river men, using commandeered boats, sometimes as drummers, peddling everything from pots and pans to the latest in corsets, and sometimes as laborers looking for work. They became experts in the sneak attack, the hit-hard-and-run tactics that Jamie had learned as a boy in the Shawnee villages.

But one thing slowly became apparent to the Yankees: Jamie and his men did not kill needlessly; they would not kill at all if they could avoid it. So the Federal commanders in the West, as this front was called, met and decided that was the Marauders' weak point and they could use it to their advantage.

They were very wrong.

Summer waned and turned into autumn and autumn brought cold winds that introduced winter, and a very hard and early winter all but closed down the war in Northern Virginia. The Rebels, nearly fifty thousand strong, huddled in tents and huts and hastily built log cabins around Centerville. About twenty miles away, just across the Potomac, thousands of Federals were massing. The fancy uniforms of militia were gone; the Union army wore blue, the Confederate army gray. McClellan commanded the Blue, Johnston the Gray. The armies stared at each other and did little else. The South had stated that it only wanted to be left alone; they would not take the offensive. The North would have to move against them.

But it would be some months yet before those two armies met. For now, most of the action was to the west. The greatest battle of American history, to that date, was shaping up in Tennessee. It would be known as Bloody Shiloh.

The cold winter brought the war in Northern Virginia to a halt, but out in the West, in Cairo, Illinois, an-up-and coming general named Ulysses S. Grant was massing some eighteen thousand troops for an assault against Tennessee. His

attack and the offensive against the Rebel troops in Northern
Virginia was originally planned to start on Washington's
birthday, February 22, 1862. But Grant was ready to go and
didn't plan on waiting. He pressed his superiors for permission to attack and received them despite their reluctance. He
planned on heading down the Tennessee River on February
2, 1862.

Jamie and his men were under orders to begin harassing the
outposts of the Union garrison at Paducah, Kentucky. It was
there the boats of Grant were to take the river to Fort Henry,
the first objective of his offensive. Grant crowded steamers
with some sixteen thousand troops and, with heavily armed
Union gunboats escorting, shoved off.

Confederate sympathizers got word to Jamie of the flotilla,
and the Marauders cut across country to try to intercept
Grant's army, knowing there was very little they could do
even should they get there in time.

At Fort Henry, the commanding general, Tilghman, realized he was about to be overwhelmed and ordered most of the
infantrymen out and over to Fort Donelson.*

Tilghman kept a small unit of men with him and planned
to hold long enough for the main garrison to get safely away.

Grant landed his troops on both sides of the river, and the
commander of the flotilla ordered his gunboats to open fire
on the poorly defended fort. Less than two hours later, General Tilghman was forced to surrender to Foote, the commander of the naval gunboats. On his flagship, Foote accepted
Tilghman's surrender and invited the Confederate general to
his cabin for dinner.

Jamie and his men bypassed the fallen fort and headed
straight to Fort Donelson, where its defenders had been put
to work digging trenches. The Rebels at Donelson, number-
ing less than five thousand, were up against a Union army of

---

*Fort Campbell, Kentucky, lies not far from this site.

now more than seventeen thousand and steadily growing in number.

General Beauregard had just arrived at Donelson to act as second in command. Beauregard, not an easy man to get along with at his best, had quarreled with President Davis several times about how to fight the war, and the Confederate president was only too happy to oblige Beauregard's request that he be sent west to serve under Albert Sidney Johnston, which he did, promptly.

Jamie was liked by both Albert Sidney Johnston and Beauregard, and at Bowling Green, Johnston's headquarters, Mac-Callister was privy to the men's argument about how to defend Fort Donelson.

"We dig in and defend the fort," Beauregard insisted for the umpteenth time that cold and dismally cloudy day.

Jamie, although he didn't put his opinion into words, thought that was nonsense at best and suicidal at worst, as it turned out, so did Johnston, the commanding general not at all hesitant about speaking his views.

"Then I'll just go back to Virginia," the Louisiana Frenchman said.

For an instant, Jamie thought Johnston was going to tell Beauregard to carry his butt back to Virginia, for Johnston had a temper, even though he usually kept it in check. Instead, Johnston controlled his temper and became tactful, moving to a map.

"I have approximately forty-five thousand troops, Pierre," he said patiently. "Many of them poorly armed. Our spies tell us that the combined total of Yankees, which includes Grant's army, Halleck's men, and Buell's army here"—he pointed to the map—"is in excess of a hundred and ten thousand men. We've lost the river down to Fort Henry and can only be supplied by land. Now how in God's name are we to defend this fort?"

For once, Beauregard kept his mouth shut, which, Johnston said later, was a momentous event that should be chiseled in stone.

"And finally, Pierre," Johnston concluded, "it is my belief that the Union navy alone could destroy Fort Donelson. As witnessed at Fort Henry, the Union gunboats can fire their cannon accurately from two thousand yards away."

Johnston turned his back to the men, and the meeting was over. The very next day he issued orders that directly contradicted his own words. He ordered Fort Donelson defended and sent in just over ten thousand more men to beef up the five thousand already there in place. Johnston then ordered Beauregard to take over the evacuation of Confederate soldiers from Columbus, up in Kentucky, and Johnston personally saw to the retreat from Bowling Green. Furthermore, he left an inexperienced general in charge of Donelson, a man who was totally incompetent and whom General Grant knew and publicly held in total contempt: General Pillow.

Grant launched his assault on the 2nd of February. The day was warm and sunny; Grant did not see and his commanders did not report to him or stop many of their men as they discarded their heavy winter coats and threw their blankets in ditches along the road as they marched.

Grant began slowly surrounding the fort on three sides, the north protected by impassable swamps. One of Grant's generals was Lew Wallace, who later became a very popular novelist, penning, among other books, *Ben Hur*.

That night, as Grant was getting his troops into position to attack, the temperature suddenly began dropping, finally leveling off at about twenty degrees with sleet and freezing rain. The Union troops who had thrown away their coats and blankets were miserable. There were not nearly enough tents, and no one dared to light a fire, on either side, for both Rebel and Yankee snipers had killed a half dozen men who tried that. Without fire, there was no coffee which might have helped ward away the cold. For food, the soldiers had only field rations, which at that time was hardtack.

On the morning of the 14th, Grant asked the navy to attack the fort using their gunboats. Four ironclads and two wooden gunboats steamed and sailed into position and began the attack early that afternoon. The ground was covered with a blanket of fresh-fallen snow, glistening white in the wan sunlight. In twenty-four hours it would be stained red with blood.

The gunboats opened fire on the fort, but the Rebel gunners did not return the fire. The Yankee gunboats drew closer and opened fire again. Still the cannons behind the earth-and-log walls of the fort remained mute. The gunboats drew to within about five hundred yards, and the Rebel gunners opened up with everything they had, which was twelve cannons, all lowered and positioned to do the maximum damage.

The damage they inflicted was terrible.

Four of the six Federal gunboats were so badly damaged they were forced to retreat, one of them in real danger of sinking. The captains of the two wooden gunboats had wisely stayed out of range of the cannons in the fort.

About a dozen Union sailors were killed and another dozen wounded. The Rebels in the fort suffered not a single casualty.

Jamie and his Marauders had escorted Johnston and his aides to Nashville before the battle had even begun. The general seemed to enjoy Jamie's company and certainly felt secure with these hard men guarding him.

The Rebels, even though they had won a victory that day, still made plans to evacuate the fort that night, as Johnston had ordered through a note sent to the senior general at the fort.

Moments before dawn, the Rebels started their pull-back, which meant they had to attack the Union lines in order to open a hole. The Yankees held the first time, but broke during the second charge, and the Rebels poured through. The Union forces had to be quickly repositioned, but Grant could not be found to give the orders. General Wallace finally took the initiative and swung troops around to plug the gaping hole.

But the Federals did not realize the attack was to allow the Rebels to break out; they thought the Rebels had taken the offensive and were seeking a victory. The Union troops were ordered to attack the fort, where only a small garrison had volunteered to stay.

Then General Pillow lived up to his reputation of being incompetent. With a hole in the Union lines large enough to sail the entire Confederate navy through, he ordered the troops under his command *back* to the fort.

One of the other generals refused the idiotic command and started making plans to take his men out and to the road that would lead to Nashville. Then, for reasons that would forever remain unknown, he relented and took his men *back* to the besieged fort.

An up-and-coming cavalry officer, Nathan Bedford Forrest, barely managed to hold his temper after he learned that two of the commanding generals were talking about surrender.

It is said the colonel's ensuing conversation with the generals was liberally sprinkled with invectives. Forrest said he would surrender when "Hell freezes over!"

The generals then began passing the buck and finally handed the entire command over to General Buckner. Buckner immediately called for a messenger with a white flag. Colonel Forrest told him to go to hell (among other things and places) and left. He gathered his men and began pulling out toward Nashville.

Generals Pillow and Floyd finally found some backbone and quickly followed suit.

Buckner's command was captured, but thousands of other Rebels managed to escape and make it to Nashville, where they quickly regrouped and continued on to finally stop and turn in Northern Alabama.

Jamie and his men, all of them disgusted to the core at this sour turn of events, met on the outskirts of town while in Nashville itself, rumors were flying about that the South had lost and surrender was in the wind.

"General Johnston has cut us loose," Jamie told his four companies of Marauders. "We really have no orders other than a request from Colonel Nathan Forrest. We can go, or we can stay."

"What's all this damn talk of surrender?" Captain Jennrette asked.

"Just that," Jamie replied. "Talk. Colonel Forrest is taking over from General Floyd and calming matters in Nashville."

"What's Colonel Forrest want with us?" Captain Sparks asked.

Jamie told them and Captain Dupree smiled. "Now I like that. I surely do."

12

What Colonel Nathan Bedford Forrest was doing was stripping Nashville of anything of military use and controlling the frightened mobs of civilians now that the Federal army was drawing closer to the city.

He asked if Jamie would take his men outside of the city and discourage any advancing units of Yankees, giving him time to complete his task.

Jamie and his four companies of guerrilla fighters rode north and took up positions and waited.

"Finally get to do some damn fightin,' " Captain Sparks said. "Maybe."

Just as Forrest was finishing up his work in Nashville, and preparing to head south to the Alabama/Tennessee border, the first forward units of Union cavalry reached Jamie's position.

Union spies in Nashville had sent word to the Federals that Jamie and his Marauders were acting as rear guard.

"They won't fight," one Union commander scoffed. "We all know that. Over the past few months we've all seen that. Jamie MacCallister is a big blowhard. I'll personally lead the first troops into that damn nest of Rebels and clean their plows."

The Yankee cavalry came riding up, singing a popular war song as they rode along. Jamie and his Marauders came galloping out of the woods, screaming like Comanches, and slammed into the Yankee colonel's command. The colonel, a lawyer from Massachusetts, had about as much business commanding a cavalry unit as tits had on an alligator, and he was promptly knocked off his horse and landed on his butt in the dirt. Just as he was getting to his feet, a Rebel galloped past him and conked him on the head with the barrel of his pistol, knocking the colonel unconscious.

The four companies of Marauders and the four companies of Union cavalry mixed it up briefly . . . very briefly. The Union troops (a volunteer unit of militia) had never been bloodied before that brief encounter. It was a morning those who survived would never forget. The Marauders killed and wounded over a hundred before the second in command, thinking his colonel was dead, ordered his bugler to sound retreat and galloped away with the remnants of his shattered companies in full rout.

Jamie, seeing the big-mouthed colonel was not dead, got water from a nearby creek and poured it on the man's head, rousing him. The colonel opened his eyes and began coming to his senses. Seeing himself surrounded by hundreds of hard-eyed guerrilla fighters, a terrible-looking pirates' flag stiff in the breeze, the man promptly fainted.

Jamie stripped him down to his underwear, tied him backward in the saddle, and sent the spooked horse galloping back to the north.

The colonel, after his men found him and restored some of his dignity (and his pants), resigned his commission, went back to Boston, and never went past the northern boundaries of the Mason-Dixon line again.

Never again would the Union commanders entertain the thought that the Marauders would hesitate to kill. Jamie Ian MacCallister's reputation grew another notch, and he and his Marauders became one of the most hated and feared units in the Confederate army.

The winter dragged on, and the fighting slowed to a standstill in the East. Out west in Texas, Falcon MacCallister had joined up with Henry Sibley, a former U.S. army officer, who now was commanding officer of a brigade of Confederate militia. In January of '62, Sibley and his men marched out of El Paso and straight into battle with four thousand Union troops at what is now called the Battle of Valverde. The Rebels whipped the enemy soundly and then, full of confidence, proceeded on to Albuquerque and took that city. Sibley then sent several companies on to Santa Fe. His plan was to take Fort Union and then march straight into Denver and the gold and silver mines of Colorado. But that was not to be.

Colorado, solidly on the side of the Union, sent a volunteer force who called themselves the Pike's Peakers to help the Federal Regulars. The Blue and the Gray clashed at a place called Glorieta Pass in the Sangre de Cristo mountains late in March. The Rebels won the day but lost the battle when a group of Union forces captured their supply wagons. That was the end of Sibley's brigade. It took Sibley and his men more than seven weeks to retreat back to El Paso.

Falcon had left Sibley shortly after the battle and, after visiting briefly with his mother, headed east to try to find his dad.

In Arkansas, General Van Dorn came up with a plan to invade Missouri and secure it firmly under the flag of the Stars and Bars. He had about seventeen thousand men in his command, and the only force that stood in his way was about ten thousand Union troops. They met in what is called the Battle of Pea Ridge, and it was there that the Rebels learned that the Yankees could fight, and fight damn well.

Near New Madrid, Missouri, a major battle was shaping up for Island Number Ten, a small Rebel-held island blocking the Mississippi. But the major battle for the spring of '62 would be fought near Pittsburg Landing in Tennessee. Nearly forty thousand men in the Gray, against almost seventy thousand wearing the Blue.

Bloody Shiloh.

All during March, General Grant moved his army into place by boats on the Tennessee River, landing the thousands of troops at Pittsburg Landing. General Buell's army, some fifty thousand strong, marched from Nashville to join Grant. Neither man, nor their chiefs of staff or aides, ever even entertained the thought that the Rebels, under the command of General Johnston, just might attack them first.

Jamie's Marauders, acting as the eyes and ears for Johnston, constantly were bringing back reports of new troops arriving and where they were being positioned. Jamie wanted to slip into Grant's headquarters, in the small town of Savannah, Tennessee, and kidnap the man. Johnston nixed that firmly, thinking it could not be done.

Jamie thought it could, but obeyed orders, and the plan was dropped.

Grant was over-confident about the outcome of the upcoming battle, feeling he could easily whip the Rebels. He was flat wrong about that.

Jamie, known for speaking his mind and not adhering very much at all to military protocol, told Johnston, "We need to strike before Buell's army gets in place. Once he joins the troops already in place, we'll be facing about eighty thousand men."

Beauregard beamed, for he, too, felt the same way.

General Bragg offered his support to the plan, even though General Van Dorn's army had not yet arrived. General Johnston finally agreed and ordered battle plans to be drawn up.

Beauregard was put in charge of drawing up the plans and shaping the army. There would be four armies, each with at least two divisions. First Army would be commanded by Major General Breckinridge, who had been vice-president of the United States during Buchanan's administration. Second Army was commanded by General Polk, an Episcopal bishop. Third Army was under the command of General Hardee, and Fourth Army would be commanded by General Bragg.

Beauregard, frankly, did not know what to do with Jamie and his Marauders. "Wait until the battle starts," he told Jamie. "We'll find a place for you and your men."

The Confederate troops blundered about getting into place.

"They make enough noise to raise the dead," Jamie remarked. "There is no way this attack will come as any surprise."

Buglers tooted away in practice and drummers hammered. Rifles were accidently discharged, and Jamie shook his head in disbelief at all the racket.

"Personally," Captain Malone said, "I wish Beauregard would send us to Jackson, Mississippi. With all this commotion, the Yankees will be in place and ready for us."

Incredibly, the Union forces were not ready for the Rebels, having paid absolutely no attention to all the noise of thousands of men milling about and stumbling over things in the dark and cussing.

On April 4, Rebels captured some Yankee stragglers and took them to Johnston for interrogation. Acting on a hunch, Jamie and his single company rode over to near the spot where they had been taken and, rounding a bend in the narrow road, ran right into a company of Federal cavalrymen.

Jamie and his Marauders put the green Union troops on the run, after killing several and wounding several more. The Union officer raced back to his commanding general's HQ—William Tecumseh Sherman—and slid breathlessly off his mount.

"The Rebels!" he shouted. "They're on the move."

But Sherman just waved it off and returned to his maps, leaving the young cavalry officer standing there feeling very much like a fool. "But . . . ," he stammered.

"Leave the general alone," one of Sherman's aides told him. "Don't bother him with twaddle."

The next day, plenty of Rebels were spotted by the Union troops, and those sightings were consequently reported to various Union commanders. No actions were taken. Patrols reported seeing light reflecting off of brass cannons. The sightings were dismissed. Union troops got into a small skirmish with a group of Jamie's Marauders. The report went no farther than the regiment commander's field desk. The hours ticked by, the day waned, and the Rebels drew closer to Union lines.

Jamie watched, astonishment on his face, as Rebel troops exchanged shots with Yankee troops for a few minutes, until the Union troops ran away to report the incident. Jamie and his men braced for an attack. None came. The Yankee commanders had dismissed the report as only a minor action.

"Great God!" Jamie breathed. "If this is the best they can do, we might actually win this war."

Night fell around the thousands of Blue and Gray, and the Union troops still took no offensive action.

In the early morning hours of Sunday, April 6, a probing force was sent out from the Union lines. The front was about five miles wide, with Sherman's command on the extreme western side and Stuart's men on the far eastern side, only about a thousand yards from the Tennessee River. On the north side of a creek, near the center of the miles-long front, Union troops saw movement across the water and opened fire. The Rebels returned the fire, and the battle was on.

General Sherman would later call that Sunday "The devil's own day."

Without any orders, Jamie was acting on his own. He rallied his men and rode off to the east, to throw up a line facing Stuart's troops along the Savannah Road, just north and west of Lick Creek, an area that was wide open and undefended by Rebel troops.

"We're not here to commit suicide," Jamie told his men. "We'll hold as long as possible. If we aren't reinforced, we'll gradually fall back." He looked at Little Ben Pardee. "Ride, boy. Tell Johnston we need help. We're facing some ten thousand troops."

Beauregard had drawn up the battle plans, and in a word, he goofed.

But Stuart did not cross the road. He had no orders to do so and stubbornly held to the east side, not knowing that for more than an hour, he was facing only five hundred men.

Johnston was furious when Little Ben found him and made his report. His entire right side was exposed, and Breckinridge and Jackson were more than a mile away, to the southwest. He immediately ordered reinforcements up to Jamie's position, with several artillery pieces.

But Stuart had still not crossed the road when the additional Rebel troops arrived.

"What the hell's he waiting on?" the commander of the newly arrived Rebels questioned.

"I don't know," Jamie replied. "I'm just glad he did."

Then Stuart attacked. Jamie quickly observed that he had not been facing a full division as he had first thought, but a small brigade. His men, all battle-tested and expert rifle shots, on the vanguard of the line, opened fire and stopped the Yankee charge cold before the first Union soldier could set his boots on the Savannah Road.

The commanding officer of the reinforcements was young, green, inexperienced, and scared. Jamie quickly took command and ordered the field pieces up and the muzzles lowered, for the range was no more than a hundred yards.

"Load 'em with grapeshot and stand ready," he ordered the gunners. He glanced at Little Ben. "Get back to Johnston and tell him we can hold. We're facing only a short brigade."

Little Ben jumped into the saddle and was off. A half mile away, his horse was shot out from under him, pinning the young man under its weight and badly spraining Pardee's ankle. It would take him precious minutes to dig his way free and more lost minutes finding a branch to use as a crutch to limp around on.

Unable to find Beauregard in the heat and smoke and confusion of battle, Johnston worried about his right flank and finally ordered Breckinridge's reserve up to assist Jamie. The troops were not needed there; they were badly needed elsewhere. But Johnston had no way of knowing that.

Stuart again ordered his men across the road. They didn't make it. Jamie opened fire with his six cannons, and the grapeshot shredded human flesh and drove the Union troops back and into whatever cover they could find, mostly a few ditches and a low ridge. And there they would stay for some time.

It was nine o'clock on the morning of Bloody Sunday. And the blood was just beginning to pour.

13

Sherman was forced to admit he had made a terrible mistake, and at ten o'clock that Sunday morning, he ordered his men to fall back, but make the Rebels pay in blood for every inch of ground.

Both sides would pay in blood.

All along the line, from eight positions, the Rebels charged the Union line with fixed bayonets, waving the Stars and Bars and screaming the Rebel Yell. Years after the war had ended, Union veterans said they could still hear that awful battle cry in their dreams.

General Prentiss' line was the first to break, sending hundreds and then thousands of men running toward the river. They clogged the trails and roads and prevented reinforcements from reaching the front.

Sherman's line began to buckle, but not break. He gave ground, his men fighting fiercely as they slowly withdrew.

With so many of the Federals pulling back in huge clumps of blue uniforms, Beauregard and Johnston now massed their troops into three attack lines . . . and then the whole shebang halted for breakfast.

When the battle resumed (both the Blue and the Gray on the front lines had paused for a bite to eat), there was no longer a clearly defined front and damn little organization. All up and down the chain of command, leaders lost touch with each other, and shattered platoons joined other equally shattered and leaderless platoons to form units of company size, often being led by officers from other divisions. For a time it was chaos.

Back at the Savannah Road, Stuart had received reinforcements and was massing for a charge across the road.

"We'd better get some help over here damn quick," Jamie muttered.

Help came rushing up just seconds before Stuart was to begin his charge, and the Union officer held his men back, for he was now facing the massed troops of Generals Chalmers and Bowen.

"Colonel," a general's aide said to Jamie. "You and your boys have fought gallantly this day. Now you rest and let us put these Federals to rout."

Jamie could read between the lines of that statement but curbed his tongue and pulled his people back.

Stuart's brigade and several brigades from Ohio and Illinois were now facing the bulk of two divisions of Confederates, and they made ready to be slaughtered; for their orders were to hold at all costs, and the costs would be high.

But in terms of slaughter, it was give and take that day. At just about the same time Stuart was preparing a defense, Rebel General Cheatham urged his men forward, and they went screaming and charging toward a Union stronghold that was called the Hornet's Nest. Closer they came, then closer, and the Yankees held their fire. When the charging Rebels were less than a hundred yards away, the Union troops opened fire with rifle and cannon and it was carnage. The bodies dressed now in bloody Gray lay in heaps and piles. Some had been blown apart by grapeshot at nearly point-blank range.

Moments after that attack failed, Bragg ordered Colonel Gibson to lead a bayonet charge against the Hornet's Nest. Gibson led men from Louisiana and Arkansas into the battle. They were thrown back at a terrible cost of human life.

Again the Rebels charged, and managed to breech the lines, only to be thrown back once more. The battleground was now covered in Blue mixed with Gray.

Exhausted, Gibson was replaced by Colonel Allen. Allen's charge was beaten back, with Allen losing almost half of his men. Gibson rallied his troops and charged the Hornet's Nest for a third time, and for a third time, his battered brigade was thrown back. Gibson had no more men to give to the Cause on this Bloody Sunday.

While Gibson's brigade was being destroyed trying to take the Hornet's Nest, Johnston was preparing to personally lead a charge against Union troops just to the Rebel right of the Hornet's Nest. Jamie and his men had joined up with Jackson's men on the other side of the Savannah Road and were locked in combat. The Marauders had dismounted and were fighting as infantry.

Johnston led the charge into the peach orchard, now in full bloom. It was to be a successful charge, for the Union troops fled under the onslaught of Confederates; but it was to be Albert Sidney Johnston's last charge. A minié ball tore through his right leg and he bled to death, lying on the ground, amid pink peach petals that had been torn loose by cannon fire.

The command of the Rebel army in the West now was passed to Beauregard. But Beauregard was a mile and a half to the rear, at his own Command Post, so far back from the front lines he did not have the foggiest notion what was actually going on.

It was about three o'clock in the afternoon when General Johnston was killed. It took almost an hour for a runner to find Beauregard and lead him back to the fallen general. Standing over the body, Beauregard was momentarily distraught; then with a mighty sigh, clearly heard over the booming of battle, he personally covered the body with a gray cape, straightened up, and called for field reports to bring him up to date.

"If we don't start using artillery up the middle and start flanking the Yankees left and right," said Jamie, who had ridden up shortly before Beauregard arrived, "we're going to be chewed up and had for supper."

Beauregard's aides fidgeted as the general gave the guerrilla fighter a sharp look, for the general wasn't accustomed to anyone giving *him* orders. Then his soldier's mind realized that MacCallister was right. "Your commander on the right, Colonel?"

"They're all dead, General."

"You are the ranking officer over there?"

"Yes, sir, I am."

"Then you are in command." He turned to an aide. "Make a note of that." He turned to Jamie. "Return to your position and wait until the last echoes of cannon fire have ceased, Colonel," Beauregard said to Jamie. "Then take your right flank and swing your men in."

"Yes, sir." Jamie mounted up and was gone.

"That is a very impudent and disrespectful man," one of Beauregard's young aides sniffed.

"My God, I wish I had ten thousand more just like him." Beauregard put a very abrupt end to any further criticism of Colonel MacCallister.

Jamie waited with the remnants of half a dozen different shattered and battered commands that he had gathered around him. Soon more than seventy cannons began to roar from the Confederate side, lashing out shell and shot. The cannonade lasted for about forty-five minutes, and it demoralized those Union troops it was directed upon, mainly those defending the Hornet's Nest. The Rebel gunners were pouring on the fire, sending more than one hundred and ninety shot and shell per minute into the Yankee lines.

The center of the Union line began buckling and finally gave way. On the Rebel left, Jamie and his men charged and put the Union forces into a wild retreat. On the Rebel right, Sherman and the other Union generals began a withdrawal.

Some say the Rebels were fighting so fiercely because of the death of their beloved general, Johnston, but that was not so. Beauregard had ordered that his death be kept secret, and only a handful of officers and men actually knew he was dead.

Jamie and his men smashed into the Union lines and secured their objective on the Rebel right. Jamie, following orders received during the devastating cannonade, stopped his advance and held, allowing his men some much needed rest.

The Union troops defending the Hornet's Nest began to scatter as the word came down the line that it was every man for himself, for they were very nearly surrounded by screaming, blood-thirsty Rebels. Most of the Union troops headed for the river—or where they hoped in all the smoke and confusion the river would be.

Several battered units of Confederate cavalry had linked up with Jamie, and Jamie sent Little Ben Pardee, limping badly but very much still in action, galloping on a fresh horse to find Beauregard and get permission to attack straight on toward Pittsburg Landing. But Little Ben could not find the commanding general, for the general, by this time, had moved all the way over to the Rebel left to join Morgan's cavalry, smashing against Sherman's forces.

Jamie obeyed orders and held his position.

In the center of the Union line, General Prentiss was forced to surrender more than twenty-five hundred of his men, all that he had left after more than a dozen bloody charges against his position. Troops from Iowa began to show the white flag. They were cut off, surrounded, out of ammunition, and their situation was hopeless.

General Grant kept looking toward the rear, where more than six thousand fresh troops, under the command of General Wallace, were expected to come marching in. It was five o'clock in the afternoon of this Bloody Sunday. Wallace would not show up until almost three hours later. He had received the wrong orders and then, when he got that straightened out, had taken the wrong road.

At the river, hundreds of Union soldiers, confused and leaderless, were swimming across to the other side, having thrown away or lost their rifles. Fresh Union troops, almost forty thousand strong, who had just arrived on the scene, could not understand what was happening.

Union cavalrymen tried to beat the frightened men back with the flat sides of their swords, but were soon overwhelmed by the hundreds of retreating soldiers.

Union chaplains prayed for the men to turn around and fight. That ended when one nearly exhausted Union veteran told a chaplain, "Get out of my way, you damned fool. I've been to hell and it's right across the river."

The chaplain and the infantryman got into a fist fight on the east bank of the Tennessee River.

There is no written record as to who won the bare-knuckle altercation.

As for the soldiers, both Union and Confederate, they were completely exhausted as night fell. Most had not eaten in twenty-four hours, and they just simply could not go on. The fighting for that day was over.

It was a horrible night. Neither side had adequate medical teams or a way to transport the wounded, and both sides were fearful of snipers. The wounded, hundreds of them, lay on the cooling ground along a five-mile stretch. They cried, begged, moaned, screamed, and many mercifully died as a cold rain began falling. Yankee and Rebel wounded found each other and huddled together for warmth and some degree of solace during the night.

"Where you from, boy?"

"Iowa. You hard hit?"

"I reckon. My left leg's shot off at the knee. I done stopped the bleedin' by bindin' it up tight, but it hurts somethin' fierce."

"I'm belly shot," the Union soldier spoke around the awful pain in his stomach. "And it's bad. I don't think I'm gonna make it."

"I know I ain't. I'm from Alabama."

"Pleased, I'm sure."

"Hell of fight, weren't it?"

"For a fact, Alabama. Say, what's that awful chomping sound coming from over there near the woods."

"Them's hogs, Iowa. They're rootin' around, eatin' on the dead. Hog'll eat damn near anything."

"You believe in God, Alabama?"

"Hell, yes! Don't you?"

"I guess. You believe in the Hell-Fires?"

"I seen that today."

"Yeah. Me, too. Everything is fading, Alabama. I think I'm about to pass."

"I'm right behind you, Iowa."

They were found the next morning, arms wrapped around each other, the Bloody Blue and the Bloody Gray, brothers, finally, in death. They were too stiff to separate, so they were buried together. They had found something in common after all.

14

The next morning brought a sight that none of the combatants had ever before witnessed. Even Jamie, who had seen scores of Mexican soldiers piled up in death outside the Alamo, was shocked.

Surgeons had worked all night sawing off limbs, and outside of makeshift hospitals, severed arms and legs were piled head high. Both sides had to post guards to keep the hogs from nearby hurriedly abandoned farms away from the amputated limbs. The badly wounded were laid out in neat lines among the stiffening dead, the doctors knowing they could do nothing for them.

Bloody Sunday was about to move into Bloody Monday as the two sides rose as one and stared across the battle lines at each other.

Both sides were disorganized and scattered. But even in disorganization they were soldiers, and soldiers fought. They fixed bayonets and took ammunition from the dead and made ready to resume the fighting.

During the night, Nathan Bedford Forrest and Jamie had dressed in captured Union uniforms and, with a group of their men, slipped into the Federal camp. Both were stunned at what they saw. Both raced back to inform their generals of the news.

"Thousands of Yankees are massing over yonder," Forrest told several Rebel generals.

"If we don't mount an attack right now," Jamie said, "we're done."

"Go tell Beauregard," was the reply.

But Beauregard could not be found. The searchers went to Beauregard's tent, but General Bragg was sleeping there. No one thought to look in Sherman's abandoned headquarters. Had they done so, they would have found Beauregard, sound asleep in Sherman's bed.

On the other side of the battle lines, Grant spent the rainy night under a tree, wrapped in a greatcoat against the elements, a cigar clamped between his teeth. "We'll be victorious in the morning," he told his aides, then went to sleep.

Forrest began cussing the missing Beauregard, loud and long, calling him some very uncomplimentary names, not giving a damn who heard him do it.

"I'll be on the right, near the river," Jamie said.

"I'll be on the left," Forrest said, shaking hands with the guerrilla colonel.

The first skirmish of the day came just at dawn, while the mist was still clinging close to the ground. The Federals beat them back.

Grant had over fifty thousand men, twenty-five thousand of them fresh troops. Beauregard could muster up no more than eighteen thousand troops. By mid-morning, the Union forces had retaken much of the ground lost on Bloody Sunday. By mid-afternoon, the Rebels had sustained huge losses and were falling back to the south, many of them to protect the road leading to Corinth, Mississippi.

"Tell Forrest and MacCallister to act as rear guard," Beauregard ordered. "Tell them to round up as many stragglers as they can to assist them." Beauregard slumped in the saddle. "Retreat," he said softly, the words bitter on his tongue.

The Union troops, flush with victory, charged down the road leading to Corinth. They were met by some three thousand men with two dozen cannons, two thousand of the Rebels under the command of a Colonel Jordan, and the Rebels held at the road long enough to let their comrades retreat in a soldierly and orderly fashion. It was about four o'clock in the afternoon when the retreat started.

Jordan ordered Forrest and Jamie to pull out, and he held while they made their retreat.

The retreat did not lay as heavy on Jamie as it did with the others, for Jamie had been trained well in the guerrilla fighter's credo: he who fights and runs away lives to fight another day.

But he did understand and sympathize with the Rebels' feelings. The Federals were about to push, or attempt to push, deep into homeland. Jamie also had a hunch that the Union army had not seen the determination and fierce fighting that they would meet deeper in the South.

Grant ordered his troops not to pursue the retreating Confederates . . . for several reasons: It would soon be dark and the sky threatened rain. His own troops were exhausted. And Grant knew once he entered the domain of the deep South, the fighting was going to be brutal—his men were simply not up to that. Yet.

The entire town of Corinth was turned into a hospital once the retreating troops arrived. At least six thousand wounded were sprawled all over the town, in every building and on the boardwalks and even in the streets and alleys. The piles of amputated limbs seemed to be everywhere waiting to be gathered up and burned. Two out of every three amputees died of infection. At the height of a dysentery and typhoid epidemic the number of men officially listed as sick was more than sixteen thousand.

At Shiloh battlefield, stiffening and bloated bodies lay so close together that a man could walk for long distances without his boots ever touching the ground. The stench of hundreds of human bodies and nearly a thousand dead horses and mules was more than many in the burial detail could stomach.

The exact number of dead on either side could never be accurately tallied. But it was close to being equal. Each side lost approximately two thousand dead and approximately nine thousand wounded. Four thousand dead and eighteen thousand wounded, total.

On April 8, Island Number Ten, near New Madrid, Missouri, finally fell to Union hands after more than a month of fighting. That action opened the Mississippi River toward Memphis.

Grant, whom many held responsible for the near defeat at Shiloh, was relieved from duty as a field commander, and General Halleck took over—and more than lived up to his nickname of Ol' Cautious.

Halleck did not attempt to take the town of Corinth until his troops had been heavily reinforced, and that took almost a month. When he had just under a hundred and twenty thousand men and several hundred cannons, Halleck proceeded to overtake the Rebels . . . very, very slowly. It took him twenty-five days to march the approximately twenty-two miles to Corinth. When he arrived, the town was almost deserted. Jamie and his Marauders had been sent up into East Tennessee. Nathan Bedford Forrest had been sent away on special assignment.

Beauregard pulled his troops away from the town, and Halleck's two-day shelling and then the taking of Corinth was nothing to write home about.

But a very vital objective on the Memphis and Charleston railroad had been taken. Now the Union forces could turn their attentions to East Tennessee.

Bloody Shiloh had been a terrible blow to the South. Many Federal officers felt sure the South would surrender after Shiloh. Those who thought that vastly underestimated the fighting spirit of the Confederates.

It was said that the South never smiled again after Shiloh.

When Colonel Jamie MacCallister heard that, he said, "Who the hell says you have to smile when you fight?"

15

Central Tennessee was now under firm control of the Union army. The Mississippi River was in Union hands all the way down to just north of Memphis. Vital rail lines had been taken by the Yankees. But if the Federals thought that the war was nearly over (and many did) they were badly mistaken.

East Tennessee was a hotbed of pro-Union feelings, with civilians and soldiers alike prone to taking potshots at each other. Neighbor feuded with neighbor over the war, and as in other parts of the divided country, families would be forever split.

Jamie and his Marauders had made it through East Tennessee on the way west without incident. It was much different this time. The four companies of Marauders had been ambushed by civilians half a dozen times on their way to Chattanooga, and to a man, they were getting damn sick and tired of it. Just across the Tennessee border, Jamie received orders by wire to turn his Marauders around and ride back to northeast Alabama. The Yankees were burning civilian homes in retaliation for attacks on Union held railroad lines.

"Now that is evil," Captain Jennrette said.

Jamie agreed. "We'll see if we can't do something about that."

For a very brief period of time, the North had come up with its own version of the Marauders, a group of Union soldiers led by a spy named Andrews. They called themselves the

Raiders. But they weren't too successful at the guerrilla business. Early in April, they did manage to steal a Confederate train in Georgia and drive it to within about twenty-five miles of Chattanooga. There, their luck ran out. They were stopped and captured, and the leader of the Raiders and half a dozen of his men were hanged as spies.

The Union just didn't quite have this business of guerrilla warfare down pat as yet.

But Jamie MacCallister did.

"This Yankee bastard come up to our house," an elderly man told Jamie, pointing to the burned-out hulk of what had once been a modest house. "Said there had been an attack on a train. Said we was gonna have to suffer the consequences. The son of a bitch then kilt our cows and hogs and chickens, stole our horses, and then burnt down our home. He and his men been doing that all over this part of the country."

"Does he have a name?" Jamie asked, feeling rage building deep within him. If the Yankees wanted to fight this war in such a despicable manner, Jamie would show them that both sides could play at this game.

"General Ormsby Mitchell and some foreign-talkin' bastard named Turchin. We call him the Turd."

Colonel John Turchin had been born in Russia and spoke heavily accented English.

"So they're making war on civilians?" Jamie asked.

"You bet," the old man replied. "And that ain't all. Turd Turchin turned his men loose over in Athens, and the Damn Yankees looted the town and raped women. Now they've started hangin' men."

Jamie gave the old couple some food from the Marauders' supply and led his men up the road for about a mile, then halted them.

"Sparks, take some men and find out if what that old man said is true. If it is, we've got a little score to settle."

With a grin, Captain Sparks and a dozen men rode off.

"The Yankees had no call to do harm to that old man and

woman," Captain Dupree said, anger evident in his tone. "Just no call at all."

"No," Jamie replied. "But for every home they burn, we'll kill ten Yankees. For every town they loot, we'll kill fifty, for every man they hang, we'll kill a hundred, and for every woman they rape, we'll kill two hundred. And that is a promise."

The next few weeks were going to be bloody ones in North Alabama.

Jamie sent a messenger to Beauregard, telling him of the atrocities committed against civilians. Beauregard was furious. He sent the messenger back with orders for Jamie to "Act as you see fit against the Yankees who are waging war against civilians in North Alabama."

Captain Sparks had returned and verified that Union troops were indeed looting and burning and terrorizing and sometimes raping Southern women in retaliation for Rebel raids against the railroad.

Other men Jamie had sent out reported back that the commanding general of the Army of the Ohio, Major General Carlos Buell, knew nothing of the rapine and rape taking place by some of his troops.

"He will before long," Jamie vowed. "When he starts finding shot, hanged, or horse-whipped Yankee soldiers."

The words were spoken with such a cold hardness that the men close to Jamie had to suppress a shudder.

Jamie walked off, his back stiff with anger.

"He's takin' this right personal, ain't he?" Sergeant Major Huske said.

"Rape has touched his family, I believe," Captain Dupree said. "And his home has been raided more than once by renegades. Yes. He takes such things very personally."

Beauregard's message to Jamie concerning the unsoldierly like behavior of some Union troops, and Jamie's disposition of the same, was one of the last orders he would give as commander of the Army of the Mississippi. Davis replaced him early that summer with General Bragg.

Jamie sent scouts out to locate the camps and the strength of those troops who seemed to take satisfaction in the looting of towns and the raping of women and the hanging of civilians. Two days later, he had the locations of ten camps, and the information checked and verified.

One camp was less than eight miles away from Jamie's present location. His companies had been broken up into small units so they could better hide in the brush and timber. With his scouts back, he had gathered all his men together.

"What is the strength of this unit here?" Jamie asked, pointing at the map.

"Two companies, Colonel."

Jamie was thoughtful for a moment. Then he smiled a very hard curving of the lips. "We'll hit them late this afternoon. Just when they're settling in for supper. We take everything we can, and what we can't, we burn. Those left alive we strip naked and tie them in a line and put them on the road."

Captain Jennrette chuckled. "I wouldn't miss this for the world."

Just as the sun was beginning to set over the horizon, Jamie and his Marauders had walked their horses to within easy striking distance of the Union camp. This particular bunch of Yankee renegades were so confident their guards were careless and not very alert. They were standing at their posts, rifles on the ground, eating supper.

The Marauders hit the unfortunate camp from four sides, screaming like banshees and striking hard. The Federals must have thought the devil had unleashed his demons from hell; for many of them, that was their last thought as the Marauders shot and cut and slashed their way through the camp.

These troops were accustomed to ordering unarmed civilians about; they were used to taking what they wanted by brute force. Up to now, they had seen no real combat. The survivors would know the horror of it and remember it for the rest of their lives—as well as the humiliation that was about to follow.

The attack had been so sudden and so completely unexpected, Jamie's companies suffered only four wounds, and they were minor. The two companies of Federals sustained more than fifty dead and at least that many wounded, some of whom would not last out the night.

When the Federals saw the battle flag of the Marauders, a few of them became so frightened they dropped to their knees and began praying.

The battle—if it could be called that—lasted for less than two minutes.

Jamie's men worked swiftly. They loaded up the supplies on pack horses, tore down the tents, and threw the blankets and spare clothing onto the growing pile.

Jamie faced the line of prisoners. "Strip," he told them. "Right down to the buff."

"I'll do no such thing!" an officer blurted, his face red from anger and embarrassment.

Jamie hit him in the mouth with the butt of a Sharps rifle with such force several teeth were knocked out and the officer hit the ground, unconscious.

"Strip!" Jamie roared, and the troops quickly began peeling out of their uniforms.

The Marauders had brought hundreds of feet of rope with them, and it was quite a sight: a hundred men buck naked right down to the soles of their feet, all in a line, hands tied behind their backs, their ankles hobbled so they could only take very short steps. Another rope was lashed tightly around each waist, then running to the next man, until they were all tied together, from the front of the line to the rear.

Using the Yankee's own meager medical supplies, the doctor and his assistant assigned to the Marauders did what they could for the wounded.

Then Jamie repeated what he had told his own men several days before. "Tell your commanding officer this," he told the line of naked men. "For every home you burn, I'll kill ten Yankee soldiers. For every town you loot, there will be fifty dead Yankees. For every Southern man you hang, we'll kill a hundred of you bastards, and for every woman raped, there will be two hundred dead Union soldiers. Now get the hell moving!"

The long line of troops silently began shuffling off up the road.

"I wish we could give these tents to the people whose homes were destroyed," Captain Malone said.

"No," Jamie told him. "If they're found with Yankee property, that would be grounds for imprisonment. Burn everything."

The out-of-uniform Yankee soldiers were found by a Union patrol just after dark and quickly taken to the nearest encampment.

Colonel John Turchin was livid with rage when he was awakened later on that evening and informed of the events.

"I'll not have my loyal troops humiliated in such a manner," he said. "I want this goddamned Jamie MacCallister. Dead or alive." He moved to a map and pointed to a tiny settlement located in the northeast corner of the state. "Burn this town to the ground," he ordered.

The settlement was wiped from the face of the map the next morning.

The next day, Jamie and his Marauders struck a Union camp, and the few soldiers who were left alive staggered wild-eyed into Turchin's camp in a near hysterical state.

Turchin was taken to the battle site and stood stunned for a moment: dead troops lay all about, at least a hundred of them. But the wounded had been taken care of as best they could be in the field.

"What manner of man is this Colonel MacCallister?" he murmured.

"He's a devil!" one of the surviving officers of the attack said. "And so is every man who rides with him."

Turchin said nothing in reply to the frightened officer.

Back at his headquarters—a nice home that he had commandeered, throwing the owner and his wife out into the road—
Turchin ordered the looting and burning to continue and an
all-out search for the capture of Jamie and his Marauders.

Before those orders could be carried out, Major General
Don Carlos Buell came in and took command. He ordered the
looting and burning to stop and vowed to hang any Union soldier who engaged in rape or pillage of civilians. He very
quickly had Colonel Turchin arrested and court-martialed
and drummed out of the service. But not for long, however.
President Lincoln earned the everlasting hatred of many
Southerners when he personally intervened and ordered not
only that Turchin be returned to active duty, but promoted to
general. It was one of Lincoln's major blunders.

The looting and sacking and raping and burning in North
Alabama ceased—for a time, anyway. But for several weeks
during the summer of 1862, Jamie and his Marauders left their
mark forever in the minds of those Union soldiers who served
in North Alabama.

Their orders completed, Jamie and his men took a different route to the border of Tennessee, crossing without incident, and rode on toward Chattanooga.

Except for a few minor skirmishes, Union and Confederate forces had spent the first few weeks of summer rebuilding their armies, for Bull Run and Shiloh had taken a terrible
toll on both sides.

Now they were ready to bloody each other again.

16

Jamie and his Marauders had just made camp and set up picket lines when they heard the sounds of approaching horses. Two heartbeats later, the Marauders were in a defensive position, behind cover, with rifles and pistols at the ready.

But the approaching men were Rebels, dressed in plumed hats and gray coats with a red sash around the middle. One was a lieutenant, and he let out a rousing yell at the sight of the Marauder's battle flag.

"By God, it's MacCallister's Marauders!" he yelled, and jumped from his horse. He strode up to Jamie and saluted smartly. "I'm Lieutenant Will Smith, from Morgan's Raiders. And I have some news for you, sir."

After introductions all around, the lieutenant and his men settled down for bacon, pan bread and coffee.

"The news, Lieutenant?" Jamie pressed the young officer.

"By all means, sir. We are attached to General Edmund Kirby Smith. We, being Colonel John Hunt Morgan and his Raiders. Colonel Morgan got a wire from President Davis telling him that you and your fine band of men were on the way and instructing you to join us, if you will."

"Fine with me," Jamie said.

Will Smith beamed, fairly busting with more news. Jamie, amused, waited, sipping his coffee and eating bread and bacon.

"Your son, Falcon, is a scout with us, sir."

Jamie smiled, and then slowly nodded his head. "I want to see him as soon as possible, Mister Smith."

"How about tomorrow morning, sir?"

Father and son first shook hands, and then embraced for a moment, to the cheering of Morgan's Raiders and MacCallister's Marauders. Then they walked off to stand alone for a few moments of private conversation.

"I got some letters for you, from Ma," Falcon said, handing his father a packet of letters, tied with two ribbons, one Blue, one Gray.

Jamie smiled. "Your mother always did have a touch of the dramatic in her, Boy." Jamie put the letters in his pocket. "How'd you come by these?"

"I went home for a visit. Stayed a few days. Ma is well. Ian is fighting for the Yankee side; so is Matt. Two of Juan's boys, Jorge and Tomas, have joined up with the Gray. Joleen's husband is with the Blue. Sam, Jr., joined up with the Blue. Wells and Robert are with some Negro regiment up north. Swede and Hannah's oldest boy left to join up with some unit in Iowa. Of course, Morgan is still scouting for the army out west. I hope he stays out there."

"There are plenty of men still in the valley to protect the people?"

"Ample, Pa. Ample." He smiled. "I heard about you and your men teachin' the Yankees a hard lesson about ridin' roughshod over civilians."

"I think they got the message, all right." Jamie gave his youngest son a good once-over. Falcon had leaned down some, but was still almighty big, with bulging muscles in his arms and shoulders. He was a handsome young man, lean-hipped and cold-eyed; but his eyes could fill with good humor in an instant. "But those men weren't representative of most Union soldiers, Falcon. We have an equal amount wearing the Gray who are just as bad, or worse."

Falcon studied his father for a moment. "How come, Pa?"

"How come what, boy?"

"How come you joined up with the Gray?"

"I don't know that I can put the why of it into words. It just seemed like the right thing to do."

"Me, too, Pa. Thing that worries me is, when this war is over, no matter who wins, is this goin' to tear our family apart?"

"I don't believe it will, boy. We'll probably argue about it for years to come. There might even be a few blows exchanged. But we're too close a family to let it destroy the way we feel about each other."

"I hope you're right, Pa. But it's not been that way among a lot of other men. Right here in Morgan's command there's a man named Ferguson who has a brother fightin' for the Blue. They've sworn to kill each other. They hate one another. Really hate. They go into battle lookin' for each other. Here in East Tennessee and Eastern Kentucky times are cruel. Meaner than any place I've seen fightin' in this war. Some units—on both sides—kill prisoners."

Jamie gave him a sharp look. "Colonel Morgan?"

Falcon shook his head. "Oh, no, sir. He wouldn't stand for that. His men hit hard and fast and they don't mess around. But a prisoner is treated well. But I never seen such hate as I've found in these mountains."

"I would imagine, son, some of these families have been feuding for years. The war is just an excuse for many. I hold no rancor toward any man who follows his conscience in this conflict. And when it's over, it will be over, and then we've all got to get in double harness and pull together to rebuild this nation . . . or nations, as the case may well be."

Falcon smiled sadly. "You know as well as me, Pa, that we ain't gonna win this war. But I'm gonna fight 'til it's over. The Federal government just don't have the right to tell me what I can or can't do as long as I'm doin' my best to live right."

Jamie put a big hand on his son's shoulder. "I think, boy, you just summed up why the both of us are here."

Morgan's Raiders and MacCallister's Marauders had a combined force of over sixteen hundred men, and they were an awesome sight as they rode west the following morning. General Smith had ordered the guerrilla fighters to harass and disrupt Federal forces along the supply line between Nashville and Louisville.

Along the way, Morgan acted as recruiter for the Southern Cause, and enlisted several hundred volunteers. As they rode toward a town just across the border in Kentucky, where a unit of Union troops were garrisoned, pro-Union bushwhackers harassed the long column.

After one of his own men was shot and wounded from ambush, Jamie personally charged Satan into the brush and came back half-dragging a young boy of about twelve or thirteen. His musket was taller than he was.

"You better throw that one back, Colonel," one of Morgan's men good-naturedly called. "He's not big enough to be a keeper."

"I'll have the cook make him up a sugar tit," Morgan said with a laugh. "Then we can send him on back to his mama."

Jamie dismounted and put the boy over his knee and proceeded to tan his butt proper until the boy's rear end, under his homespun britches, was hot enough to heat bathwater just by sitting in it.

Then Jamie set the lad on his bare feet and glared down at him. "Boy, you use this rifle to help keep your family fed. You use this rifle to defend hearth and home in case of attack. But we're not attacking your home or bothering your ma." He handed the lad his musket. "Now you git, boy. Move!"

The boy took off like the devil himself was nipping at his heels. He did not look back.

Years later, he would still be boasting that Jamie MacCallister was the one who put him squarely on the path of righteousness.

Jamie walked over to the man the boy had wounded. The ball had just grazed the man's arm; it was a burn, but not a serious one.

"You all right, Jennings?"

"Oh, I'm fine." He chuckled. "But that boy will long remember that hidin', I'm thinkin'."

With a twinkle in his eyes, Morgan had personally mixed up a bit of sugar and butter, tied it in a knot at the end of a clean handkerchief, and solemnly handed it to Jennings. "Here, son," he said. "With a terrible wound like that you'd best be pacified with your own sugar tit!"

Red-faced amid the laughter, Jennings climbed back into the saddle, and the column rode on . . . but with a grin, Jennings sucked the sugar tit dry.

"I'd like to have one of them myself," Falcon muttered.

The Raiders and the Marauders attacked the garrison just across the border in Kentucky without losing a man. The battle lasted about fifteen minutes before the Union commander, seeing that he was badly outnumbered, surrendered. Jamie noted with satisfaction that the prisoners were all well-treated. One of Morgan's men, Ferguson, a man who hated Yankees, wanted to kill them all.

"Restrain yourself, Champ," Morgan told the man. "Or leave my command."

The man gave up his habit of killing Yankee prisoners— for the time being.

In less than a month, Morgan and MacCallister seized tons of supplies, hundreds of horses, tore up miles of railroad track, took more than fifteen hundred prisoners, captured twenty towns, and demoralized the Union forces between Nashville and Louisville. By the time the Union forces were strong enough to launch any type of effective assault against the guerrillas, the Raiders and the Marauders were heading back to Chattanooga, to receive accolades for a job well done.

Matthew and Ian MacCallister, now both officers in the Union cavalry, were on the march toward Tennessee. Jorge and Tomas Nunez were part of Hood's cavalry, and they were on their way from Texas to Tennessee, as part of an advance unit. Sam Montgomery, Jr., and Jamie's son-in-law, Pat MacKensie, were part of a cavalry unit from Ohio. And Swede and Hannah's boy, Igemar, was part of an infantry unit coming in from Iowa.

Tennessee was about to come under full siege, with members of the MacCallister family caught up right in the middle of it . . . some in the Blue, some in the Gray.

General Bragg finally came up with a plan of action. But it was a plan that no one, on either side of the conflict, expected. Bragg was to march north through Kentucky, securing that state for the South, and then take Louisville and Cincinnati. The news of that quickly spread, and the citizens of both cities went into a panic. Which was exactly what General Bragg wanted.

Meanwhile, Jamie and his Marauders, Morgan and his Raiders, and Nathan Bedford Forrest were still busy raising hell with the Union's supply lines and railroads. But this time they concentrated on Yankee forces in Tennessee. Their objective was twofold: by constantly harassing the Yankees, the commanding general of the Union army in Tennessee could not advance his troops to Chattanooga . . . he was too busy dealing with the Confederate guerrillas.

Jamie came up with a plan, and it was met with approval and smiles.

Launch a sneak attack against the Federal garrison at Louisville.

The commanding general of the Union forces around Louisville put out a call for civilian volunteers to aid his forces, in the form of a militia; his regular troops were mostly green recruits, as yet not battle tested. They were about to be, in a limited way.

In small groups, Jamie and his Marauders had left Tennessee, riding north through Kentucky, heading for Louisville. Thanks to the hundreds of Southern sympathizers along their preplanned route through the state, the Marauders were able to get supplies and be warned of any Yankee patrols that might be in the area. They also had places to stable and rest their horses, sleep, and have a hot meal they didn't have to cook.

Far in the back of Jamie's mind, another raid was still just a tiny seed; but it was growing, and just the idea of it amused Jamie. But he spoke to no one about it. He would let the idea nurture for a time—for the more he thought about it, the better he liked it.

While Jamie was moving his men toward Louisville, and Forrest and Morgan were raiding south as a diversion for Jamie, Lee handed the Federals a smashing defeat in Virginia when McClellan tried to take Richmond in a campaign that would be known as the Seven Days' Battle.

Up to now the war had been going decidedly in the Union's favor; now it had become more like a seesaw. The Federals would attack and be victorious; then the Rebels would attack and take back the ground. In the nation's capital there was much grumbling and finger pointing and placing of blame. Generals on both sides (but mainly in the Union army) were losing their jobs and being demoted and promoted, and transferred and shifted around from post to post. In many instances, after only a few weeks, or at best, a few months, many of them would be returned to their original commands. It was difficult to keep up with just who was commanding what army and where.

To make matters worse, as they always had and always would, the Congress of the United States stayed busy running their mouths, constantly attempting to direct the war while sitting on their penguin asses in Washington . . . that much would never change.

In mid-August, 1862, Jamie and his Marauders began massing just a few miles outside of Louisville and only a mile from a garrison of very green Union troops. They would not be green after this night, for the ground was about to be stained red with their blood.

My darling Jamie,

As I take pen in hand this lovely afternoon in our valley, my thoughts are of you and the boys—all the boys from this valley who have chosen to follow their hearts in this terrible conflict.

I pray this letter and all the others I have written will find you well. It is lonely here without you, but I am staying busy. Sarah, Hannah, Maria, and our girls and other women of the village all get together at someone's home for a couple of hours each day, to have coffee, and to sew and talk and give each other comfort. So many of our young men have left. I pray that all will return.

By reading the newspapers I know that you are now a colonel and the leader of a guerrilla band called the Marauders. Was that name of your choosing? The newspapers we receive all make you out to be some sort of monster. I have to laugh at some of the reports concerning your daring-do. Perhaps I should write some of these newspapers and tell them of the time you forgot to tighten your cinch strap and fell off your horse right into a watering trough. Remember that incident? The children were so delighted they pestered me for a month to allow them to deliberately distract you so they

*could loosen the cinch strap and see you do it again.
Naturally, I refused . . .*

Jamie chuckled at the memory. For exactly one month after he landed in the horse trough, his saddle went under his horse's belly again, and he got dumped out on the ground. It would be just like Kate to do that.

*The crops look good and the livestock are all fat and
healthy. I go out to the pasture every day to feed Horse
his daily apple or bit of sugar and to stroke his muzzle.
He misses you, too. I can tell . . .*

If anyone else had tried to pet Horse or hand feed him, the aging mean-eyed monster would have taken their hand off at the elbow. But with Kate, he was as gentle as a kitten.

*I keep a daily diary of events taking place in our twin
valleys so you will have lots of reading to do when you
return home. And I know you will come back to me.
While you are in the midst of life-taking, here, new life
is being born. We have a number of new babies, for before the boys left, they wanted to be sure they would
leave something behind for their wives to remember
them by. They certainly did. You are a grandfather—
again.*

*Caroline had twin boys, Joleen had a girl, and Megan
delivered twin girls. One thing about it, my darling, the
world will never run out of MacCallisters or their kin.*

*I miss you so very much. Take great care and come
back to me.*

Love, Kate

17

Jamie sat under a tree and read all the letters twice before wrapping them carefully in oilskin and tucking them away in his saddlebags. He had already read them a dozen times over. Not all the letters had been from Kate; his kids had written him, and several of his grandchildren had written short notes.

Jamie closed his eyes and rested for a time. He tried to recall just how old he was. He thought he was fifty-one, but he wasn't sure. He might be forty-nine; he just wasn't sure.

Sergeant Major Huske approached Jamie and squatted down. "The boys is rested and ready to go, Colonel."

Jamie opened his eyes and nodded his understanding. "You made it clear to everyone what they're to do once the raid is over?"

"Yes, sir. They know to git and where to scatter to."

Jamie consulted his watch. Huske noticed the tiny picture of Kate.

"Your wife, sir?"

"Yes. We've been married . . . ah, thirty-seven years, I think."

Huske shook his head and again looked at the picture of Kate. "That don't hardly seem possible, Colonel. She don't look a day over thirty in that pitcher."

"Well, to tell you the truth, the picture is a few years old. But she still doesn't look her age by a long shot."

Huske knew that Jamie had fought at the Alamo. But he

still found that hard to believe. Jamie just did not look his age. "How old are you, sir? If you'll pardon my askin'."

"I think I'm fifty-one, Top Soldier. But I'm not real sure about that."

"You don't look nowheres near that, neither, sir."

"Thank you. But some mornings I sure feel it."

Huske chuckled. "I know what you mean, sir. I ain't no spring chicken, myself. When this damn war is over, I'm takin' my wife and them rug rats of ourn that's still to home and headin' west. Git me a section of farmland and live out my years in peace. Sit on the front porch in the evenin's with my good woman and my dogs and smoke my pipe and be at peace with the world."

"You'll certainly be welcome in our valley, Sergeant Major."

"I'll sure take you up on that, sir."

"You ever own slaves, Top Soldier?"

"Oh, no, sir. No one in my family ever did, neither. Hell, sir, we wasn't gentry."

Jamie smiled sadly. "What is your feeling toward Negroes?"

Huske thought about that for a moment. "I don't rightly know, Colonel. I never had much truck with them. I guess they're all right. Their ways is a sight different from mine, but that ain't no crime. Back home, our land butted up on plantation land, and I been around blacks all my life. But I only got to know a few close-like." He grimaced. "That was a mighty mean man that was overseer of that plantation. White trash, my daddy used to call him. He'd whip a slave for little or nothin'. I mean, take the hide off with that black-snake he carried, then slip off down to the quarters at night and bed down with some young high-yeller wench. That ain't right atall."

Huske paused to light the stub of a cigar. "Colonel, you got a few men right here in this command that'd as soon shoot a black as look at him. They consider them to be less than animals. And you got men in this command who flat don't believe in slavery. And then you got men like me who, I guess, is all caught up in the middle. Blacks, I think, is sorta like the red savage Indians I fought out on the frontier 'fore this caper started. They ain't like us and they ain't never gonna be like us. But they're here. And some of them been here for nigh on two hundred years. When I was stationed up east I seen blacks that was free and had some education. But they still wasn't like us. Not to my way of thinkin'. I think the blackman is gonna be the white man's burden plumb up to the end of time. But that don't give the white man no call to make them slaves or abuse them. I don't want to live with blacks, Colonel. Not with no whole passel of them, anyways. I would have to say that I like blacks as individuals but dislike them as a group. But for me, this war ain't about slavery. I don't care if they're freed or remain slaves. That don't make a whit to me one way or the other. But I would like for the whuppin' on them to stop. For me, the main thing is this: the damn government just ain't got no right to tell me what to do and who to live with and how to conduct my business. That's my affair and none of theirs. If a man annoys me whilst I'm tryin' to live right, I'm gonna tell him about it, and he damn well better straighten up. If he don't, I'm gonna take action, and that action just might involve gunplay.

"Colonel, I been jerked around from pillar to post servin' the United States in the army cavalry. It's been a hardship on my family; but me and my wife has raised seven good kids, and we done it the best we could on damn little money. I hear tell that the government is promisin' that when the Yankees is victorious, every black man is gonna get some money, forty acres and a mule. For free. Don't no man deserve nothin' for free. And the land, the money, or the mule had damn well better not belong to me or there's gonna be a killin'. Whichever way this war goes, the South ain't never gonna be the same again. That's why if I live through it, I'm pullin' stakes and headin' west. Colonel, the United States is sending troops to invade my homeland. That ain't right. Jeff Davis has said over and over that this war need not be if the North would just let the South alone.

"I read where some of these Yankee abolitionists is sayin' this nation was built by the slaves. Well, to my way of thinkin', those people don't know hog jowls from horse shit. There ain't never been a slave in my family for as far back as we go in America, and that's more'un two hundred years. And that's written in the family Bible that's been handed down for long generations. Whatever the Huske family has got, the Huske family worked for—without slaves. And I don't like some goddamn Yankee son of a bitch sayin' we used slaves to git what we got. 'Cause we didn't. Talk about slaves, I believe that if we don't stop the Yankees now, right now, our grandkids and their kids and forever on until another war comes along to tear this nation apart—and it will—is gonna be virtual slaves to the Federal government. To me, that's just as plain to see as the snout on a pig. All Abe Lincoln has got to do is leave the South alone and this war is over right now. But he ain't gonna do that. Now, to be honest, I can't lay all the blame on his doorstep, for there's other folks who's proddin' him to interfere in other folks' lives. Their the ones who need to be shot. That's what I believe. I'm done now, and I reckon that's the longest speech I ever made in my en-tar life. But you asked me, and that's what I think, Colonel."

"You're an honest man, Top Soldier."

"If you say so, Colonel."

Before Jamie could reply, Captain Dupree walked up, an angry expression on his face and a civilian by his side.

"What's the matter, Pierre?" Jamie asked, getting to his feet.

"The operation's been called off, Colonel. This is Edward Oldsman. Our spy network sent him a coded wire and everything is off."

Jamie stared at the man for a moment. The fellow seemed at ease enough, but there was something that struck a discordant note with Jamie. "You have new orders for us, Mister Oldsman?"

"Yes, Colonel, I do. You are to proceed westward and join the Confederate forces in their attempts to retake Memphis."

Now Jamie knew the man was lying. There were no plans to retake Memphis. It was solidly in Union hands. "I see. You have a route of travel for us?"

Now the man's face fairly beamed. "Yes, sir, I surely do." He quickly produced a map and spread it out on an old stump of a tree. "You're to go straight down here, following this route, and cut due west at this little town."

Only an idiot would have dreamed up such a route, Jamie thought. Or someone who felt that *he* would be idiot enough to take it. "I see," Jamie said softly. "And we are to pull out when?"

"Immediately, sir."

"Are you going to guide us, Mister Oldsman?"

"Why . . . ah . . . no, Colonel. My orders are to return at once to Louisville."

Jamie snaked his right-hand Colt out of his non-regulation holster so fast Oldsman's eyes bugged out. Jamie placed the muzzle against the man's forehead, and the sound of his earing the hammer back was loud. It brought a sudden bead of sweat to Oldsman's face.

"No, Mister Oldsman, or whatever your name is. You are not going back to Louisville. You are going with us. But we are not going to Memphis."

"What . . . what is the meaning of this, sir?" Oldsman managed to stutter.

Jamie smiled at the frightened man. "That should be real clear, Mister Oldsman. You got caught!"

Jamie quickly pulled his men back and, after an hour's careful ride, made a cold camp in a deeply wooded area along a sluggish creek. He jerked Oldsman off his horse and faced the man.

"My scouts say the nearest home is about two miles from here, Oldsman. So your screaming won't be heard."

"What screaming?" Oldsman stammered.

"I was raised by the Shawnee, Oldsman. I know ways to get information out of people that you haven't faced in your most terrible nightmares."

"You're making a horrible mistake, Colonel! I swear to you before God I am a true-to-the-cause Southerner."

"What you are, sir, is a liar. One of my men, who was a telegrapher before the war, tapped into the telegraph wires this morning to send a coded message down the line. Our orders still stood. There are no plans to retake Memphis. Furthermore, only an idiot would have chosen the route you pointed out to me. I hold no rancor toward you, Mister Oldsman. You are a Union man just doing your job. But I am a colonel in the Army of the Confederate States of America, and I also have a job to do. I want the truth now, Mister Oldsman."

"I have spoken the truth to you, Colonel. I stand by my words."

"Then you, sir, are a fool," Jamie told him. "Sergeant Major, build a small fire under that limb over there." He pointed. "Corporal, tie Mister Oldsman's hands behind his back and then string him up by the feet, head down, over the fire. This is a little trick I watched the Shawnee do several times. It makes quite a sight when a man's hair catches on fire and his head cooks. The pressure builds up inside the skull until finally it explodes."

"Great God!" Oldsman yelled. "I'm a white man, Colonel. You can't treat me like a damn ignorant nigger!"

Every Marauder head within hearing range turned at that remark. The encampment fell very silent.

Captain Judd broke the silence by asking, "I thought you Yankees loved colored folks, Oldsman. Are you saying that it would be all right to burn a black but not a white man?"

Oldsman looked at the lieutenant for a few seconds, and then cussed him.

"I have a new name for Mister Oldsman," Jamie said. "Talks Out of Both Sides of Mouth."

"Go to hell, Colonel!" Oldsman said.

"Still want the fire, Colonel?" Huske asked, standing with an arm load of dry wood.

"Yes. We'll see how well Oldsman stands up to pain."

"You're bluffing!" Oldsman blurted.

Jamie's smile could not, by any stretch of the imagination, be called pleasant. "You want to bet your life on that, Oldsman?" When the man did not reply, Jamie said, "Get the fire started, Top Soldier. String him up by his feet, Corporal."

Oldsman's bravery lasted until he felt the heat from the nearly smokeless fire on the top of his head. Then he broke and started begging.

"For the love of God, MacCallister!" he shouted. "Don't do this to me. I'll tell you all I know. Please don't set me afire. I implore you!"

"Cut him down," Jamie ordered.

The badly shaken and trembling man was freed and set on the ground. He was given a cup of whiskey. He gulped it down and started talking.

"I didn't think you would actually do it," he said.

"Get to the point," Jamie told him.

"We have a spy high up in your command, Colonel. Not this command, but in General Smith's headquarters. And no, I don't know who it is. I honestly do not know that."

"I believe you," Jamie said. "Go on."

"Had you fallen for my story, this unit was to be ambushed about thirty miles down the route I showed you. The Union cavalry is there now, in place. On both sides of the covered bridge. You're a very hated man, Colonel MacCallister. And this unit of yours is much feared. That's all I know, Colonel. If you don't believe that, then I am prepared to meet my Maker, for as God is my witness, I have told you the truth."

Jamie believed him.

Oldsman said, "I suppose that I will be charged with being a spy and hanged, Colonel?"

Jamie shook his head. "Not by me, you won't. Kentucky is not officially part of the Confederacy. You cooperated, so I am going to send along a note asking that you be paroled."

"Thank you, Colonel."

He ordered four men to escort Oldsman—or whatever his name was—back to General Smith's HQ for further interrogation. They left immediately.

It was almost dusk, so Jamie decided to remain in the cold camp where they were for that night. He had some thinking to do. A lot of thinking.

Jamie lay long and sleepless in his blankets that summer's night. Hated and much feared, Oldsman had said. Very well, Jamie thought, making up his mind. He would give the Union army more grist for their fear mill.

Right in their own damn backyard!

18

Jamie had the telegraph wires tapped into by his man and a coded message sent to Smith's HQ advising him of the spy in his camp. And just in case the spy intercepted the message and could break the code, he added that he was calling off his attack on the garrison of Union troops outside Louisville and instead heading down into Central Tennessee to launch guerrilla strikes against the Yankees. Then Jamie ordered his men to get ready to hit the Union garrison outside of Louisville.

At the beginning of the third week in August, 1862, MacCallister's Marauders struck the green troops garrisoned outside of Louisville and raised bloody hell with them. The Marauders rode their horses right down the center of the camp, over tents filled with sleeping men, shooting and slashing and burning their way through.

The Marauders stampeded horses, destroyed supplies, and blew up the armory. Then they skedaddled into the hills and thickly timbered area south and east of the city, toward the Kentucky River, and melted into the landscape, with the help of Southern sympathizers.

At the same time Jamie and his men were terrorizing and demoralizing the Union troops around Louisville, Confederate troops, under the command of General Smith, were moving deep into Kentucky—their objective was to take Lexington.

It was a daring move on the part of the Confederacy, and

one that struck fear in the hearts of those citizens who supported the Union forces in the struggle.

Meanwhile, Jamie and his Marauders were busy blowing up railroad bridges and attacking small garrisons and roaming patrols of Federal troops. For the first time in the war, a price was put on Colonel Jamie Ian MacCallister's head, for "Scurrilous, traitorous, treacherous, and cowardly assaults against the Union forces."

Matthew MacCallister, who was now leading a unit of Union cavalry, found one of the wanted posters tacked to a tree and ripped it down and took it to his commanding officer.

"Sir," Matthew said, holding out the flyer. "If the Federal intention was to make my father angry, and have him go on a rampage that will cause more damage than a hundred tornadoes, they will soon find out how successful they are with this piece of garbage."

The commanding officer took the wanted poster and quickly read it, shaking his head in disbelief as he did so. "Somebody has lost their mind!" he said. "This is going to backfire right in the Federal face."

"You bet it will, sir," Matthew agreed, unaware that General Buell was standing just behind him and to the right of the opened tent flap. "This is a direct challenge to my father. And believe you me, sir, it is a challenge that he will be more than happy to take."

Buell stepped into the tent, and both Matthew and his commanding officer snapped to attention. "Stand easy, men," General Don Carlos Buell said with a smile. "Let me see that paper, Major." He read the flyer, and his frown deepened as his face, under his beard, darkened with anger. "All this will do is further strengthen Colonel MacCallister's resolve. Colonel MacCallister is certainly no coward. As for these other accusations, they're nonsense. This is war, not a church social. You cannot condemn a man for fighting for what he believes in his heart is right."

"Oh, my father doesn't necessarily believe the Southern cause is right, sir," Matthew said.

"I beg your pardon?" Buell gave him a sharp look.

"My father is adamantly opposed to slavery, General. I grew up working right beside Negroes, going to school—such as it was—with them, and playing with and spending the nights with colored boys my age. My father was captured by the Shawnees when he was about five or six years old and made a slave in their village, General—he hates slavery."

The general sat down in a camp chair and waved Matthew to a seat. "I don't understand, Lieutenant. Colonel MacCallister hates slavery yet he fights for the South."

"He's fighting for the right of a people to govern themselves, General. For states' rights. Not for slavery."

Like many men on both sides of the issue, Buell shook his head in confusion. "Do you have any idea where your father is at this time, Lieutenant?"

Matthew smiled, then chuckled, and Buell could not keep his own smile from showing. "General, my pa was raised by Indians and taught the Way of the Warrior. The Indians called him Man Who Is Not Afraid. Man Who Plays With Wolves. He could be standing right behind this tent at this very moment, listening to every word that is being said. My father is about fifty years old and still does not know his own strength. He's the most powerful man I have ever known. He can move like a ghost and fight like fifty men. And I am not exaggerating, sir."

"And when your father sees this . . . document?" He held up the wanted flyer.

"I think he and his men will go into action immediately. They'll begin striking at any Union garrison or patrol they encounter. And it's not going to be pleasant."

"For us, you mean?"

"Yes, sir. For us."

The bridge blew up just before the Union patrol reached it, sending timbers and deadly splinters flying in all directions.

Before the blue-coated troops could get their frightened and rearing and bucking mounts under control, the Marauders struck them from ambush. Only a very few got away.

The next day, the Marauders attacked a Federal supply train and plundered it, taking rations and ammunitions and explosives. Then they destroyed the locomotive's boiler and set the cars on fire before vanishing into the woods.

During a three-week period, MacCallister's Marauders destroyed miles of railroad track, attacked and destroyed three Union trains, blew up three supply depots and one armory, captured hundreds of Union soldiers, and sent a dozen or more terrified prisoners back to their commanding officers with this message from Jamie: "I am no coward nor am I a traitor. You can keep the price on my head, but you'd damn well better reword that flyer!"

By the 15th of September, 1862, the price had been taken off of Jamie's head, and no more wanted posters were printed.

Even the usually dour Buell was secretly amused at how fast the government could act . . . when they were being poked in the ass with a Bowie knife.

Jamie and his men and horses had very nearly reached the stage of exhaustion as they rode into a small Kentucky town that was solidly in the Confederate camp. A scout had been sent ahead to check out the town and alert the citizens that they were coming.

The town's band tuned up, and the citizens gathered along the street. The band played "Dixie" while the folks cheered and shouted as the weary Marauders rode slowly up the street.

The townspeople took care of the tired horses and put the Marauders up in private homes, where they could bathe and shave and have a few hot meals. The mayor personally took Jamie home with him. After the colonel had taken a long hot bath, shaved, and changed into clean clothing, the mayor took Jamie into the sitting room of his home.

Over whiskey, the man said, "You don't remember me, do you, Jamie?"

Jamie stared at his host, then slowly shook his head. "I'm sorry, sir, but I do not."

The man smiled. "I'm Jim Jefferson, Robert Jefferson's brother. His younger brother. We went to school together after you and Hannah escaped from that Shawnee camp."

"Well . . . I'll be darned. Sure, I remember you now. How is Robert?"

Jim shook his head. "Killed years ago, Jamie. By some kin of the Jacksons' or the Olmsteads'. We never did know for sure who did that awful deed." He sighed. "I don't reckon that feud will ever die."

"I'm sorry. I truly am. Robert was the first friend I made in that village."

Jim smiled. "But you put a pretty good dent in that feud, so I hear."

Jamie laughed. "I sure tried."

The two men talked until the long shadows of afternoon lay dark upon the ground; then his wife called that dinner was ready—and it was excellent, the table fairly groaning under the weight of food. Jim tactfully kept the talk away from the war, something that Jamie was very grateful for.

Jamie slept well and deep that night on a soft feather tick and ate a hearty breakfast, then, after seeing to Satan, napped the remainder of the day away, as did most of his men. On the morning of the third day in the village, Jamie received orders by coded wire.

The Marauders were to proceed at once, by the shortest route, to an area just north of the town of Perryville, located on the Chaplin River, and wait for orders.

"What the hell is goin' on there?" Captain Jennrette asked.

"I don't know," Jamie replied. "I never heard of the place. I don't even know where it is."

"I do," a young Marauder spoke up, opening a map and spreading it out. "It's right here, Colonel."

Jamie looked. "So it is," he muttered. "But what's there?"
No one knew.

"Saddle up," Jamie ordered. "Let's go find out what's so important about Perryville."

19

While Jamie and his Marauders were carefully making their way toward Perryville, events were unfolding very quickly all around them, but without their knowledge, since the Marauders were traveling cautiously, avoiding villages and towns. Rebels, under the command of General Smith, had taken Lexington. The Federal forces, under the command of Buell, had pushed north to Bowling Green. General Bragg, meanwhile, had circled around and was now close at hand, ready for a fight. But he hesitated, and Buell pressed on to Louisville, leaving the Rebels far behind and without adequate supplies.

It had taken Jamie and his Marauders days to reach the Chaplin River, and when they got there, they found absolutely nothing. They still had no way of knowing they were about to be caught smack in the middle of a raging fight.

"I got a bad feelin' about this whole thing, Colonel," Sergeant Major Huske confided in Jamie.

"So do I," Jamie replied. "Send out scouts, Top. Let's find out what is going on."

Plenty, as Jamie was about to find out. But for now, he was cut off with no way of communicating with any of his commanders; having no orders countermanding his original orders, Jamie and his men made camp and waited, unaware that a Federal force of more than seventy-five thousand men were camped to his east, and getting ready to move . . . in his direction.

The days dragged on and Jamie and his men rested, reread letters from home, and fished in the shallow river to supplement their supplies. To make matters worse, the river was growing dangerously low because of a terrible drought.

A scout came boiling back into camp, all smiles. He leaped off his horse and reported. "Confederates in Perryville, Colonel. 'Bout ten thousand of 'em. We're fixin' to mix it up with the Yankees right soon."

"Who's in command?"

"Generals Wood and Johnson, sir."

Jamie quickly saddled up and rode into the town.

"Where in God's name have you been, Colonel?" Bushrod Johnson asked, when Jamie reported in.

Jamie told him.

Johnson's mouth dropped open. "By whose orders, Colonel?"

"They came out of Chattanooga. That's all I know. General, I don't even know what month it is."

"It's October, Colonel. The fifth of October. Get your men in here to draw supplies. We're about to have one hell of a fight on our hands. When you're supplied, waste no time, sir. Get over to link up with Wheeler's Cavalry." He pointed to a map. "Right here."

Wheeler's face brightened noticeably when he saw the Marauders ride up, battle flag uncased. "MacCallister's Marauders reporting as ordered, General," Jamie said.

"Glad to have you, Colonel. Most glad. Let's dismount and give our butts a break and go over a very bad situation."

When Jamie looked at the map, his heart sank. He could see at a glance that General Bragg had his men positioned all wrong. Wheeler read the big man's face.

"Yes, Colonel. I know. But I'm a soldier, just like you."

"My God, sir," Jamie blurted. "We're going to be cut off

way down here to the south, with a short regiment of cavalry, facing a full division of Federals."

"That is correct, Colonel. And we are expected to hold this road and keep that division from advancing and flanking Powell, up here."

"But Powell is facing more men than we are!" Jamie lost his temper. "What the hell are all these brigades doing being held in reserve?"

Wheeler shrugged his shoulders and said nothing.

"Well . . . I'll do the best I can, General."

"I'll not throw away good men, Colonel. You may be assured of that. We'll fight, and fall back, regroup, fight, and fall back. But do it slowly. And while we're doing that, we've also got to watch this Federal force south and west of us. We don't want to get flanked."

Jamie met the man's eyes, and both realized that the other knew Bragg's plan was badly flawed. "Yes, sir," Jamie said softly, as in the distance, shots were heard.

Wheeler held out his hand, and Jamie took it as he towered over the much smaller man. "God be with you, Colonel Mac-Callister."

"And you, sir."

For the next several days, God chose not to smile on either side. About seventeen thousand Rebels were poised to strike at over sixty thousand Yankee troops. Bragg thought the number of Union soldiers was much less than that. When he discovered the true figures, it was too late to turn back. He was committed. On the morning of October 8, Bragg gave the orders to attack.

The Confederates charged under a covering fire of artillery, and Wheeler's Cavalry and Jamie's Marauders held firm, much to the surprise of both of them, for they were vastly outnumbered.

During a lull in the fighting, Jamie rode over to Wheeler.

"What's happening over there?" he asked. "The Federals have enough troops to shove us all the way across the river."

"I can't imagine," the hard-charging Wheeler replied. "Something is certainly all haywire over there."

It certainly was. The commanding general of the troops on the road defended by Wheeler and Jamie, Crittenden, stayed well back, at least several miles back, and refused to commit his troops. He had sent out several advance parties, company strong, and they had been so thoroughly bloodied by Wheeler's Cavalry and Jamie's Marauders, Crittenden was convinced he was facing a much larger force than he actually was.

That first day was to be a series of Federal foul-ups, one right after the other.

The Federal troops did advance at widely scattered points, mainly the hard-fighting Sheridan, but those few units under his command that did advance found themselves in danger of outdistancing their allies and were forced to pull back for safety's sake.

Back on the road some two miles from the town and about the same distance south from the heaviest fighting of the day, Jamie and Wheeler could but look at each other in astonishment.

"I don't believe it," Wheeler said.

A scout rode and whispered in Jamie's ear, then quickly withdrew. Jamie shook his head in disbelief, and then turned to Wheeler.

"General, my men just finished questioning several Union officers. Are you aware that we've been fighting the whole damn Army of the Ohio this day?"

Stunned, Wheeler stared at Jamie for a moment. "Let's ride for Bragg's HQ!" he said. "We've got the Yankees on the run, and if we press hard right now, we can strike a major blow for the South."

"No," Bragg said. "No. We could not possibly hope to win by doing that. We retreat back to Harrodsburg. Now."

It was yet another case where the South won the battle, but eventually lost the war.

Surprisingly, General Buell did not pursue the retreating Confederates as they reached their objective and began setting up a strong defensive line. Their objective, which surprised everyone, was to march over two hundred miles, clear out of Kentucky, and all the way down to Knoxville, Tennessee. With a victory at hand had he pressed it, Bragg instead chose to retreat, and his officers and men had no choice but to obey. Jefferson Davis was furious. The comments about Bragg from general officers ranged from his being an idiot to an incompetent—and those were the nice things said, the others being unprintable.

But Davis and Bragg were close friends, and Bragg was not replaced.

To make matters worse, many of Bragg's troops were sick and all were hungry, even though warehouses around the area were bulging with tons of food and warm clothing. That food, they were told, was to be sent to the Army of Virginia. They had to remain healthy in order to repulse any attack.

Jamie's reply to that was, "Hogwash!" He immediately started sending teams of his men out on night forays to break into the Confederacy's own warehouses to steal and cache enough food to keep body and soul alive.

Winter lay white and heavy on the ground when Bragg received orders for his command to head for Stones River. Davis also appointed a new overall commander of the Army of the West: General Joseph Johnston. But the South had the same problems with command as did the North: the damned politicians insisted upon running the war, especially Jefferson Davis. Johnston and Davis came nose to nose and eyeball to eyeball in Richmond at a private meeting.

"Get your goddamn aides out of here!" Johnston thundered at Davis. "Let's settle this command issue once and for all."

The room cleared, Davis took off his coat and rolled up his

sleeves, preparing to fist-fight the general. It would not have been their first fight, for the two had gone out behind the barracks several times while at West Point and duked it out. They just simply did not like one another.

Reason quickly overrode anger, and the respect the men had for one another prevailed. They didn't like each other, but they did respect each other.

"Mister President," Johnston said, after the men had passed a few amenities and passions cooled. "You have thirty-five thousand men sitting over in Arkansas doing nothing. Use them to reinforce Vicksburg. Don't strip men away from other vital areas."

"I'll think about it," Davis replied, and the meeting was over.

He didn't think on the suggestion nor did he act on it.

Back in Chattanooga, Jamie was chafing at the bit to get into action. But Davis was coming for an inspection soon, and Bragg wanted Jamie and his Marauders to be there to act as personal guards for the Confederate president.

"I suppose that's better than a lick up 'side the head," Sergeant Major Huske lamented.

For more than six weeks, the war had been reduced to skirmishes, and the South was clearly the victor in most of those brief battles.

It was the middle of December, 1862, when Davis came to Tennessee for a visit and dealt Bragg a terrible blow. He ordered Bragg to send more than ten thousand of his troops to Vicksburg. That cut Bragg's forces by one third and left him with about thirty-five thousand men to face a Federal force estimated at more than one hundred and ten thousand. General Joe Johnston hit the ceiling and immediately traveled to meet with Davis. The home where they were meeting cleared like a whirlwind when the angry general stormed in.

One aide later said that when the door slammed closed, he heard Johnston yell at Davis, "Strip your blouse, goddamn you!" Then there were several loud crashes.

When the two men emerged a few minutes later, Davis had a black eye and Johnston had a bloody nose.

But ten thousand troops from the Army of Tennessee were sent to Vicksburg anyway.

Around Christmastime, the war virtually came to a halt— on both sides—and Colonel Morgan got married in Tennessee. While that was going on, Jamie, with no orders to remain now that Davis had returned to Richmond, provisioned his Marauders and hit the trail for Kentucky. During the next three weeks, Jamie and his men stopped and seized three Federal trains, burned the cars and blew up the locomotives, tore up miles of track, raided armories and supply depots, and captured over nine hundred Union prisoners.

"What the hell are we goin' to do with them?" Sergeant Major Huske asked.

"Watch," Jamie told his Top Soldier.

"Go home," Jamie told the startled prisoners. "Spend some time with your families if you can. I wish to God I could."

Jamie and his men left the stunned Union prisoners standing alongside a ruined stretch of railroad and rode off into the cold afternoon.

"My captain is just not gonna believe this," a sergeant from Indiana said.

"Hell with your captain," another sergeant said, picking up his rucksack.

"I've said that a time or two myself."

As Christmas day came and ebbed into night, the Rebel and Yankee armies in Tennessee prepared to fight. Peace on earth and good will toward men was about to be shattered by gunfire.

"Strike wherever you feel is necessary." That's what Jamie's orders said.

"Idiotic orders," Jamie muttered, as he wiped the cold rain from his saddle and mounted up.

"Which end do we support?" Captain Sparks asked, riding up alongside Jamie.

The Rebel lines were south of Nashville, stretched west to east, a line almost forty miles long.

"We have been ordered to strike wherever I feel is necessary."

Sparks blinked. "Beggin' your pardon, Colonel, but we're gonna be needed damn near everywhere."

Jamie smiled. "Yes. I know."

They sure would be needed, for the Rebels were badly outnumbered.

After studying the battle map for a moment, sitting in the saddle, Jamie chose to once more link up with General Wheeler, knowing that the hard-charging young cavalryman—Wheeler was not yet thirty years old and one of the youngest generals in the Confederate army—would be right in the thick of things.

When Jamie reached Wheeler's position, he had to smile, for Joe Wheeler had chosen a position far north of the established Rebel lines. General Wheeler was determined to be the first to draw blood.

"People might say you were spoiling for a fight, Joe," Jamie remarked, riding up to the young general's side.

But Joe did not smile. He tried, but the smile just couldn't form on his lips. He looked at Jamie through sad and serious eyes. "My men just took a few prisoners, Jamie. From a Yankee cavalry unit. That one facing us not five hundred yards away." He pointed. "They're in those woods right over there. And they're not green troops; they're a crack outfit. Colonel MacCallister, you might ought to take your men over to the west some; get out of this area. Join up with General Hardee. As a matter of fact, I strongly suggest that you do that."

Jamie studied the younger and smaller man for a moment. "Now why would I want to do that, Joe?"

Wheeler sighed. "Because the newly promoted and appointed commanding officer of one of those companies of Yankee cavalry is your son, Captain Matthew MacCallister."

20

Jamie sat silent for a moment. The day he had been dreading had arrived, as he had been certain it would. In one of the letters, Kate had asked him what he would do when the moment came. At the time, he did not know; but now he did. "I am needed at this location, General," Jamie said. "And here I will stay unless you order me away."

"I won't do that, Jamie. I do need you here. All right, here it is. I have Maney's Tennesseans to my right. You and your men take the left. It's going to get very hot over there very quickly, Colonel."

Jamie smiled. "Considering the weather, Joe, we could all stand a little heat." Jamie gave the young general a very sloppy salute, lifted the reins and rode back to his Marauders. He said nothing to any of his men about Matthew commanding a company of Federals.

When one of Crittenden's senior officers saw the battle flag of the Marauders through his field glasses, he immediately rode over to Matthew's company. "Shift your company over to that ridge, Captain." He pointed. "You support those green troops from Illinois. They're going to need help."

"Yes, sir." Matthew had no idea that he had been facing his father.

All the remainder of that day, the Union troops threw themselves against the Confederate lines and were repulsed each time, sustaining heavy losses. The Rebels were beginning to stiffen their lines and dig in, and the fighting was fierce.

The Federals would charge, and each time, the men under the command of Joe Wheeler would drive them back. When night fell, the ground was littered with the dead and the wounded. Joe called for a ceasefire to gather the wounded, and the Union commander readily agreed. Jamie volunteered to be one of the men to enter the bloody grounds.

"You didn't even have to ask, Colonel," Wheeler said, sadness in his voice.

Jamie walked among the dead in his section, looking for Matthew. He knelt by a wounded Union soldier and found the boy could not walk; one leg was badly mangled by grapeshot. Jamie picked him up and carried him through the Union lines and to a field hospital.

Nearly everyone knew who the big man with the black shirt and black waist-length leather jacket was, and the lines parted as he walked through, softly talking to the boy, whom Jamie guessed to be no more than seventeen at the most. The field hospital fell silent for a moment as Jamie was shown in.

"Colonel," one of the doctors said, even though Jamie wore no insignia. He was that well-known. "Put him here, please, sir. If you would."

Jamie laid the boy on a table, actually a kitchen table scrounged from somewhere, and stepped back.

"Thank you, sir," the wounded private said. "I do thank you deeply."

"It's all right, boy."

"All you goddamn Southerners have to do is surrender and it would really be all right," a man with a slight wound said.

"Shut your mouth!" a voice barked from the front of the tent, and Crittenden stepped inside the tent. He walked up to Jamie and nodded. "Thank you for bringing that lad in, sir. It was most kind of you."

"Wars are savage, sir. But men don't have to be."

"Well put, Colonel."

Both men looked at the boy Jamie had carried in. He was

already out from laudanum, and the surgeon was lifting a saw to cut off his leg, just above the knee.

"General Wheeler asked to tell you that this cease fire will hold until the ground is cleared of all wounded. I can't speak for the other commands; just this one."

"Thank you, sir. Litter bearers!" Crittenden snapped. "Move it!"

"Dad!" the voice came from behind the men.

Jamie turned to look at Matthew, a bloody bandage around his forehead and one sleeve of his jacket damp with blood, the arm hanging limp.

"Your . . . son?" General Crittenden questioned. "Of course. I should have guessed."

Matthew limped to his father's side, and Jamie caught him just as Matthew collapsed. A doctor rushed to the men and quickly cut away Matthew's jacket sleeve.

"He'll keep the arm," the doctor said. "But he's out of this battle. Will you put him on that table over there, Colonel?"

Jamie carried his son to the table and then walked back to where Crittenden stood. "The sad thing is," Jamie said, "before this war is over, I may have grandsons fighting each other."

"Sadder still, Colonel," the general replied, "I know men who do!"

Jamie did not get to speak with his son that night, but left the hospital tent with the certain knowledge that at least one of his sons was out of the war for now. He had no idea that Ian, his oldest, was there also, but the unit he commanded was being held in reserve. As the year of 1862 drew to a bloody close, Ian would be called to the front at a place named Hell's Half Acre.

Yankees and Rebels fought to a virtual standstill for several days. A little ground would be taken, a little ground would be lost, and a little ground would be retaken. The dead and wounded continued to mount.

On the next to last day of the year, Jamie and his Marauders rode with General Wheeler's cavalry to attack at the rear of the Union forces. As dawn broke they spied almost four hundred Federal supply wagons moving with only a light guard.

"Take them," Wheeler shouted to Jamie. "I'm moving on northward."

Jamie and his over five hundred men swept down and took the wagons after only a light skirmish.

"Go home, go back to your units, or head west and get out of this damnable war," Jamie told the almost eight hundred prisoners, which included about a hundred Negroes who were serving as drivers and laborers.

"Do that include us?" a Negro asked.

"Of course, it does," Jamie told the startled Negroes. "Just don't head South," he added with a grin. "That would be the wrong direction to take."

Those in Jamie's command who believed strongly in slavery, and who would not hesitate to shoot a Negro—and there were still a few—had learned to curb their passions if they wished to remain a Marauder. Jamie had rid himself of most of those men until only a few remained. The unit was such a proud one, with such a distinguished and colorful history—albeit a short one—that Jamie never lacked for volunteers. Once in, only death or a grievous wound would cause a man to leave.

"You're Colonel MacCallister, aren't you?" a captured major asked.

"I am, sir."

"Well, sir," the Union major said, "if you don't believe in slavery, which you obviously do not, what the hell are you doing fighting for the South?"

Jamie looked at Sergeant Major Huske, sitting his saddle beside him. Huske rolled his chaw of tobacco to the other side of his mouth and spat. "Well, sir. Most of us here don't hold with enslavin' another human bein'. You Yankees got this here war all wrong. I'm in this tussle for my homeland, not for slavery. Y'all run along, and be careful now, you hear?"

Jamie personally escorted the wagons, filled with much needed medicines, including a large supply of laudanum, along with warm clothing (even if it was the wrong color), food, and ammunition, back to the Confederate lines and turned it over to Wheeler's second in command.

An hour later, Wheeler rolled and rumbled in with an additional two hundred wagons, filled with the same kind of supplies. It was a rich haul for the Rebels and a demoralizing strike against the Union forces, and those two actions very nearly ended the fighting that day, except for light skirmishing.

But the next day, the last day of 1862, and for the following three days of the new year, the ground around Stones River would live up to its name of Hell's Half Acre.

In some places along the line, the Blue and the Gray were less than fifty yards from each other. They called back and forth. Some of the calling was filled with rancor; most was friendly during the periods of quiet.

"You Yankees love 'em so much, we gonna bury you bastards with your goddamn niggers!" one Rebel called out.

"Aw, shut up, Jones," another Rebel said. "Me and this Yank was talkin' about farmin'. What all do you raise up yonder in Michigan, Yank?"

"Niggers," Jones butted in, hate in his words.

"Jones," his comrade in arms said, about to lose patience. "You fixin' to let your ass overload your mouth most directly. I'm gonna take the butt of this rifle and loosen some teeth in your mouth if you don't close it right promptly. You got any coffee and sugar with you, Yank?"

"Lots of it. What you got to trade?"

"We got plenty of tobacco. That fair with you?"

"Sure is."

"Hold your fire up and down the line!" Rebel and Yankee sergeants hollered. "We're fixin' to make a swap here and don't nobody get itchy trigger fingers."

Trading back and forth among the Blue and Gray went on until war's close. These little unofficial truces were very common when both sides faced each other across creeks. Both sides would use tiny makeshift sailboats to swap articles back and forth.

Then, at their officers' commands, the savage fighting would once more resume.

On the last day of 1862, the armies began massing for attack several hours before dawn. As the night gave way to a foggy dawn, Union pickets along the west side of the now backward L-shaped lines blinked their eyes and stared hard into the gray mist. All of them thought they'd seen gray shapes moving toward them. But the shapes quickly melted into the haziness of the morning, and the pickets did not report what they felt was only an illusion.

It was not an illusion. It was twelve thousand gray-clad Rebels moving to attack on the west side of Stones River, between Franklin Road and Wilkinson Pike.

At the curve of the backward-shaped L, one full division of Confederates were supposed to attack at the same time, theoretically severing the Union lines. Had that happened, the terrible battle yet to come would have been avoided and the Rebels would have secured a clear victory. But the commanding general of that crucial division of Rebels was drunk that morning, having consumed about half a gallon of Tennessee-brewed Who-Hit-John the night before. He couldn't even get on his horse, much less command troops.

Since the lines had shifted dramatically during the night,

ith the Federals pulling back and regrouping, Jamie and his
Iarauders were now at the extreme north end, at the top of
e backward L, facing a regiment of Crittenden's men, on
e east side of the river.

"Now how in the hell did we manage this?" Captain Dupree
iestioned, staring across the river at the Blue, who were star-
g back at him.

"I don't know," Jamie said, lowering his field glasses. "But
:re they come!"

The Marauders had dismounted and formed up in a line.
hey laid down a withering fire that stopped the Federal ad-
ince cold on the west bank of the river, for one of the re-
iirements to get in the Marauders was being a crack shot
ith rifle and pistol. The first volley killed or wounded sev-
al hundred Union soldiers. The Blue line pulled back and
ayed back.

On the south side of the Union lines, the right side of the
ldly shaped lines, the Rebels had advanced and pushed the
nion forces back until they were in full retreat.

For several hours the Blue and Gray smashed at each other.
adly outnumbered to begin with, Confederate losses were
ow so great that every troop being held in reserve was called
) and committed to the fight. Shortly after noon of that
oody day, the Federal lines had been hammered into a V-
iape, the V surrounded on three sides by hard-fighting
ebels.

Jamie had gathered together, in addition to his own men,
»out four companies of Rebels who had been cut off from
eir units or were leaderless due to the many wounded and
:ad. He sent Little Ben Pardee galloping to General Breck-
ridge asking for permission to cross the river and close the
p of the V, thereby completely boxing in the Union forces.

But Breckinridge could not be found. He was right in the
iddle of his own men, on the ground by the river, fighting
ith a pistol in each hand, his color bearer right beside him,
)lding the Confederate battle flag.

Ben did find a colonel who told him to race back to Mac-Callister with orders to "hold, by God, hold!"

"Hold what, goddamnit!" Jamie thundered. "We've got them on a rout. You ride back to that colonel and tell him that, Ben."

But the colonel was dead, shot through the head.

Jamie could do nothing except hold, for he had no one to support him if he crossed the river.

By two o'clock that afternoon, the Federal V had begun to straighten out somewhat. Jamie was still on the east side of the river, but he was now facing a full division of Union troops.

"Have we been forgotten up here?" he roared.

Yes, for all intents and purposes. But so, too, had the Yankee general, Price, who had a full division all ready to cross the river at the only fording place for a mile in either direction. But Price thought he was facing a division of the butternut boys, for Jamie had sent men back down the line to beg, borrow, or steal as many cannon as they could.

Jamie started a cannonade that sent Price's men ducking for cover. Price sent out a message that read, "Am facing a full division of Rebels with artillery. Need help desperately in order to cross the river. Orders?"

The orders came back: Hold on the west side.

The troops of the Blue and Gray, a mile north of the heavy fighting, sat and stared at each other across the river.

Bragg had been reinforced by some three brigades who had just arrived, and as dusk began to settle, he ordered a charge against Yankee positions at the center of the line. The fresh troops charged point-blank against the guns of the Federals. The charge was a terrible blunder, and the Confederates were forced to withdraw; they had lost almost half of the men from the three fresh brigades.

That ended the battle for that day. Both sides could not have fought another minute had their commanders given the orders to do so. Confederate and Union soldiers simply collapsed where they were, too exhausted to go on. After an hour of rest, both sides began evacuating the wounded.

General Bragg, commander of the Confederate forces engaged in battle at Stones River, sent a message to Jefferson Davis in Richmond wishing him a happy new year.

Then he retired to his tent and went to bed.

21

The battlefield was littered with thousands of wounded, and since the killing field was so long, stretching for several miles, many of the wounded did not receive aid until the next day. Still others froze to death, their blood sealing them to the cold ground. A cease-fire had been ordered from both sides. Rebels aided wounded Yanks, and Yanks aided wounded Rebels. Nearby towns were filled with the injured, no one paying any attention to the color of the uniforms. Makeshift hospitals were set up, and the doctors were so busy sawing off mangled arms and legs, a lot of the severed limbs were just tossed out the nearest window.

No one on either side slept much that bitterly cold night, for both sides were busy regrouping their exhausted and widely scattered troops. Many of the troops were short on food and ammunition, but it was desperate on the Union side, due to those hundreds of wagons that had been seized by Jamie and Wheeler containing badly needed supplies.

No commander on either side slept that night, for they were too busy rallying their men, preparing them for the fight that both sides felt sure would resume at dawn.

Dawn broke gloomy and sunless, and the men were simply too cold, too hungry, and too tired to pick up the fight. Both sides finally rose stiffly to their boots and roamed the miles of battlefield, picking through the equipment and taking what could be used, and that included taking weapons and ammunition off of the stiffened and frozen dead.

Few shots were fired at Stones River on that first day of the year 1863. During the night came the rain, then sleet, and then the whole mess turned to snow, making life even more miserable for the Blue and the Gray.

But on the second day of the new year, the commanders roused their men and the battle resumed, reluctantly at first, for the overall commanding general of the Confederate troops at Stones River, Bragg, very nearly had a mutiny on his hands: one of his own generals was threatening to kill him over some point or slight that was never really brought to light . . . although many rumors persisted for months. Whatever the reason, passions cooled and the threat never materialized.

Fighting commenced at about twelve o'clock, in the midst of a raging sleet storm.

Jamie and his men had been ordered back to plug up a gap in the Confederate lines. Jamie now commanded over a thousand men, with some thirty pieces of horse-drawn artillery. He forded the river and positioned his men on a ridge near the center of the now U-shaped Union lines and, without orders (nobody really had orders other than to attack), opened fire with his cannons until he was forced to halt the barrage for fear of hitting Rebel troops who were charging across an open field and up a slight hill. Leaving a captain in charge (the captain's company had been virtually wiped out several days back), Jamie and his Marauders mounted up and joined the charge.

They broke through the Federal lines, putting the Union troops into a retreat. Cresting the hill, Jamie stared at what seemed to be thousands of blue-coated men running to help plug the hole the Rebels had torn in their lines.

The Rebels thought they had the Yankees on the run. From where he sat his horse, Jamie knew better. "Fall back and take up positions on the hill!" he shouted.

"No!" a full colonel countermanded his orders. "By God,

sir, we have them on the run." Waving his saber, he ordered the charge to continue.

They charged straight to their deaths. The foolhardy colonel took a bullet in the head and was dead seconds after he ordered the charge, as were the color-bearer and all the other men in gray who had followed his orders.

That seemed to turn the tide for the Blue. They mustered up their courage and began pushing the Gray back on all fronts. As night fell, the Confederate officers managed to halt the retreat and turn their weary and bloodied men around. They were out of food, out of ammunition, and very nearly out of hope.

The Union forces on the other hand, as Jamie reported verbally to Bragg, "Have received several brigades of reinforcements and hundreds of wagons of supplies."

Bragg brushed the report aside. Filled with anger, Jamie left the command post and returned to his men. "It's over," he told his company commanders. "Bragg doesn't realize it, but it's all over for us here."

With the breaking of dawn, Bragg could see with his own eyes that the situation was hopeless. Jamie's scouts had brought back prisoners who confirmed Bragg's feelings.

"They've been reinforced all during the night," General Wheeler told the man. "They've got almost eighty thousand men, and we'll be lucky to field twenty thousand. It's over, Braxton. It's over."

Bragg would later say, "I had the coppery, bitter taste of defeat in my mouth." But that day he was forced to utter the hated words, "Retreat. Fall back. Chattanooga must be saved."

Jamie's Marauders and Wheeler's Cavalry stayed to act as rear guard as the weary Rebels picked up their gear and began moving out toward the east. They left behind them over twelve thousand dead and wounded comrades. The battleground was still littered with the dead and the dying.

The Union forces did not immediately pursue the retreating Confederate army. Jamie and his Marauders were the last to leave Hell's Half Acre.

Sparks twisted in his saddle for one last look at the still smoky killing fields. "What the hell did all that death and suffering accomplish?" he questioned.

"Nothing," Jamie replied. "Absolutely nothing at all."

Jamie had lost twenty men killed and fifteen wounded during the battle. But as usual, he was back up to strength within a week as volunteers flooded in to join the Marauders. Bragg ordered him to take his Marauders and roam from, "Border to border of this state, wreaking havoc on any Union soldiers who might dare to pursue us."

"And in addition," Captain Dupree added acidly, well out of earshot of the general, "we get to blow up bridges and tear up railroad track."

"And raid Yankee supply wagons," Captain Jennrette finished with a boyish grin.

Jamie had learned that Matthew had recovered fully from his wounds and was once more commanding a company of Union cavalry. Ian had been promoted and had his own command of cavalrymen. Jorge and Tomas Nunez were with Hood and were heading toward Chattanooga. Pat MacKensie and Sam Montgomery, Jr., had arrived as part of an advance unit and were in Central Tennessee. Swede and Hannah's boy, Igemar, was with the Iowa Fifth.

But Jamie had other troubles that he was unaware of, in the form of one Colonel Aaron Layfield, a blue-nosed Yankee who hated all Southerners with something that far surpassed mere fanaticism. He hated anything and everybody south of the Mason-Dixon line. His idol was John Brown, whom he considered to be the second finest man to ever walk the face of the earth. The first was Jesus Christ. The third was himself.

Aaron Layfield was the organizer and commanding officer of something called the Pennsylvania Revengers, a unit of brigade strength made up of rabid anti-slavers and anti-everything Southern, and they were fast approaching Tennessee. Aaron Layfield considered himself to be a very religious man, a person who insisted upon his men praying before every meal and Bible reading before retiring for the night. Every man in his command considered himself to be an extension of the arm of the Lord, and of course they interpreted the Bible to suit their own bloody aims.

Aaron Layfield was not originally from Pennsylvania; no one knew exactly where he was born, but he had lived there for a number of years, where he had run a variety store six days a week and filled the pulpit on Sundays, where his church was well-attended. It was thought he was from New Hampshire, and it was rumored he had been run out of there for his radical views. Many in Pennsylvania felt the same way, but the town where he lived and worked and preached just loved the Hellfire- and Brimstone-spouting radical, and they filled his church every Sunday and Sunday night to listen to him spew hate toward the South in general and Southerners in particular. They came from miles around to shop at Layfield's General Store, and there, they got the same message: hate. He was so loved that the citizens changed the name of the town to Layfield.

It was going to have a very short history.

As Layfield and his heavily armed brigade, complete with horse-drawn artillery, rode south they had information as to what towns were sympathetic toward the Southern Cause. So far the Revengers had burned and looted and sacked half a dozen towns, killed several hundred men, either shooting or hanging or dragging them to death, and terribly abused several dozen women—all in God's name, of course.

During the long ride south, Layfield picked up several hundred more volunteers along the way, swelling his ranks with fanatics, all of whom waved Bibles in one hand and pistols in the other, shouting out hate to anyone who would listen; fortunately, not many did.

But enough did, and his ranks continued to grow as he pressed on through the mountains of West Virginia and Kentucky . . . gathering not only men and supplies, but pocketfuls of money from people who fell under his snake-oil charm.

Layfield especially hated one man in particular, a man who had lived with Godless savages (Layfield also hated Indians), and who had adopted many of their heathenish ways, and then had turned his back on the Union to fight for the Confederacy—Jamie Ian MacCallister.

Exactly why he hated Jamie so was never really established, but men like Layfield, and those who listened to him and followed his wild teachings, never really need a valid reason. They're just real good haters. They live to hate; they love to hate. It fills them with meaning and gives them a purpose.

Layfield didn't really have a great deal of use for Negroes, either; but he loved the Union, or so he said, and anyone who fought for the South, or supported the South, deserved to be punished. And Layfield was God's appointed punisher. God told him so, personally and up close. And he really believed that he could talk to God and God would answer. And to prove it to any who might doubt that, during his services Layfield sometimes got the spirit and talked in tongues.

Most Pennsylvanians thought Layfield to be about as full of shit as a fattening Christmas turkey . . . but there were always a few who would follow.

In this case, a few too many.

The long, cold winter drifted by with only the occasional raid by one side or the other; the war on all fronts seemed to lag for a time. General Rosecrans' Army of the Cumberland still had Chattanooga to wrest from General Bragg's Army of Tennessee, but he seemed to be in no hurry to do so. Meanwhile, Bragg was slowly rebuilding his army while Grant was sending wire after wire to Washington, demanding more men be sent to him down at Vicksburg.

The only troops in Tennessee active during the winter months were the Confederate cavalry. Bragg had just over sixteen thousand men mounted, and he used them with great effectiveness. He sent Joe Wheeler, Nathan Bedford Forrest, Morgan's Raiders, and Jamie's Marauders on rampage after rampage all over Central Tennessee, especially against the railroad, which was busy night and day supplying General Rosecrans' army.

As the warm breezes began to blow, signaling an end to the bitter winter, the commanders of the two great armies in Tennessee started making plans for attack.

Rosecrans knew that Chattanooga must be taken, for it was a vital railroad link; Bragg was not going to give it up without one whale of a fight.

Rosecrans knew nothing of Colonel Layfield's reputation and his hatred of anything pertaining to the South; he was just glad to have the reinforcements of such a capable-looking group of cavalry, for more reasons than one. Rosecrans himself was a deeply religious man, a convert to Catholicism, and he was glad to have another man so firmly committed to the Lord in his command—even if the man was a Protestant.

"I want you to concentrate on finding and destroying Jamie MacCallister and his band of Marauders," the general told Layfield.

"You can count on me, sir!" Layfield said. "The Union must be preserved and kept from the bloody and lawless hands of the brigands from the South. Tell me, sir, is it true that MacCallister actually worships the pagan gods of the red savages he once lived with?"

"I have heard that."

"The goddamn heathen!" Layfield roared, causing Rosecrans' aides in the next room to stop what they were doing and look up.

Rosecrans blinked at that but said nothing about it, figuring that every man has his own idiosyncrasies. "Good luck, Colonel Layfield."

"I don't believe in luck, sir. For I have God with me at all times."

"I'm sure you do," Rosecrans said drily. "I try to keep Him with me at all times, too."

Layfield saluted smartly, wheeled about, and marched stiff-backed out of the room.

"The man's a bit odd, don't you think, sir?" a Union colonel asked.

"Oh, I suppose so," the general admitted. "But he is committed to the Cause."

Committed was a good choice of words, if only the connotation had been changed.

22

Vicksburg was a surrounded and besieged city, with only a few more days to exist as a Confederate stronghold—it would fall on July the 4th, after weeks of fighting, with the Confederate forces trapped there scarcely able to function, soldier and citizen alike staggering from sickness, exhaustion and hunger. Gettysburg would also be a major Union victory in July.*

But in Tennessee, the fighting had just begun.

"Do you know a man named Aaron Layfield?" Jamie was asked.

Jamie thought for a moment. "I don't think so. I'm not familiar with that name. Why?"

"He has sworn to kill you," Captain Malone said. "Says that if he only accomplishes one thing during this war, he will consider it a great event and a day for celebration if he kills you."

"That's odd. I never heard of the man. Who is he?"

"He's from a town up in Pennsylvania named after him. He came South with a full brigade of cavalry. They're called the Revengers."

Jamie shook his head as he tightened the cinch on Satan.

---

*So bitter were the memories, many regions of the South would not celebrate Independence Day for many years after the War Between the States. Some sections of the South only began celebrating it again in the 1950's.

"Well, I have never met anyone named Layfield. This war is certainly producing some strange characters."

"Including our beloved general," Dupree said with a sour look.

Jamie couldn't argue with that, for General Bragg was one of, if not the, most disliked man in all the Confederate army. He was a harsh disciplinarian, and constantly peevish. No tactician, to a man, his officers considered him incompetent, and more than one of them plotted, at one time or another, to kill him.

But still Davis would not replace him.

Jamie swung into the saddle. "I'm going to take a look around. I can't believe that General Rosecrans has waited this long to attack." It was June 23, and the sky was threatening rain.

The two great armies were lined up about thirty-five miles apart—the front was miles long, stretching north to south—and each side was constantly patrolling. Chattanooga was about ninety miles east of Bragg's westernmost position, and Bragg was determined to hold the Yankees at bay. The Union forces under Rosecrans' command now numbered around eighty thousand. Bragg's troops had dwindled down to about thirty-eight thousand due to the shifting of much needed troops to various other hot spots, including Vicksburg.

Several miles out into no-man's-land, Jamie spotted a small Union patrol and reined up in the timber, uncasing his field glasses and studying the patrol. He smiled, and then chuckled. Tying a white bandanna onto his rifle, he rode out of the timber and into the clearing. He was spotted immediately, and Jamie Ian recognized the rider as his father.

"Hold your fire," he told his men. "I know who that is and we're going to talk. Come on. I'll introduce you to a living legend."

"Who is it, Captain?" a sergeant asked.

"My father."

"Howdy, boy," Jamie said to his son.

"Pa." The two men rode close, leaned out of the saddle, and

hugged one another. "Matt told me he saw you some months back," Ian said, wiping his eyes. "But his memory was sort of fuzzy about that night."

"Is he all right?"

"Fiddle-fine, Pa. I got a batch of letters from Ma. Meet me here tomorrow and I'll give them to you to read."

"Best not, son. Your general might call that fraternizing with the enemy. You save them for me."

"All right, Pa. Pa? You're on the wrong side, damnit. You know what you're doing isn't right."

"It is to my mind, boy. As well as Falcon and Jorge and Tomas."

"All right, Pa. You seen my little brother lately?"

"Last week. He's fine."

"Who's he ridin' with?" the burly sergeant asked.

Jamie smiled at him, although he had taken an immediate dislike to the man. He returned his gaze to Ian and started to say something when the sergeant suddenly rammed his horse close to Jamie and said, "I asked you a question, Reb. And you'll goddamn well answer it."

Before Ian could order the man back, his father hit the sergeant, knocking him clean out of the saddle. The blow sounded like an overripe watermelon hit with the flat side of a shovel.

"Miller!" Ian shouted. "I'll have you court-martialed for this. Colonel MacCallister rode up here under a flag of truce."

The big sergeant got slowly to his boots, blood leaking from his smashed lips. He clawed for his pistol, and a corporal jumped his horse into the man, knocking him down. "Come on, Carl. You're in the wrong and you know it."

"Git off that hoss and I'll kick your ass, Colonel Reb," Miller snarled.

Jamie laughed at him. "You're not worth the effort it would take, Sergeant. Now cool down before you get into real trouble."

"I don't take orders from no goddamn stinkin' Reb!"

"You're a fool," Jamie told him.

"Place that man under arrest!" Ian shouted.

"Hell with you all!" Miller said, and jumped on his horse and galloped off.

"Chase him, Captain?" the corporal asked.

"No," Ian said. "Let him go. We've seen the last of Carl Miller and good riddance. I never did like the man."

"You're not alone in that, sir," another Union rider said. "No one liked him."

"Sorry about that, Pa."

"Forget it. I had a few men like him in my outfit at first. They didn't last long."

Ian could damn well believe that.

Father and son sat their saddles for a moment, looking at each other. Both of them had a lot they would have liked to say, but neither man could put their feelings into words.

"Going to start raining soon, boy," Jamie finally broke the silence.

"Sure looks like it, Pa."

There was another uncomfortable silence. Jamie sighed and said, "Well, boy, you take care of yourself and you be sure to write your mother whenever you have time."

"I'll sure do that, Pa."

"I'll tell Falcon I spoke to you."

"Give him my best, Pa."

Jamie turned his horse and rode slowly back toward his own sector. At timber's edge, he turned in the saddle; Ian was leading his patrol back toward his own lines.

Father and son had passed no hard words, but the meeting had been a tad on the strained side. If they all came out of this war alive, Jamie felt it would take some time before the family was whole again. It would take a lot of healing.

For many families both north and south of the Mason-Dixon line, the invisible wounds would never heal.

The battle for Chattanooga began in a driving rain on the afternoon of June 24, 1863, when General Rosecrans threw his entire army at the Confederates. Rosecrans had armed many of his men with the relatively new seven-shot Spencer rifle, while most of the Rebels still used the older model single-shot rifles, and many of them had converted muskets and shotguns. The Confederate line broke at several points, and the Union forces swept through, cutting vital Rebel supply and communication links.

The rain did not stop. It rained almost constantly for three days, and for three days the heavily outnumbered Rebels took a beating from the Yankees.

The rain finally stopped, but the mud was knee-deep on many of the roads. Even that didn't stop the determined Union forces; they marched on, taking only a few casualties, while inflicting some terrible damage on the Confederates. On the first of July, General Bragg ordered his men to start retreating into the mountains of East Tennessee, putting the Tennessee River between them and the slowly but steadily approaching Yankees.

Jamie and his men were on the north, or the right, side of the Rebel lines, and his scouts reported that a huge force of Union troops were fast advancing toward them, coming down from Kentucky.

"If we stay where we are," Jamie mused, "we're going to be caught in a trap."

Two weeks later, Knoxville fell, and the troops there were ordered out and told to fall back to Chattanooga. Caught between two huge advancing armies, unable to reach Chattanooga, and without orders, Jamie and his Marauders slipped through enemy lines and rode into North Georgia. There, Jamie and his men linked up with a Rebel force advancing north to aid Bragg in his defense of East Tennessee—General James Longstreet and his army.

"The tracks have been destroyed from this point on," Jamie told the general, after identifying himself. "It's march from here on in."

Longstreet nodded his head and pointed to a spot on the

map. "You and your men spearhead, Colonel," he told Jamie. "This place right here looks like a good spot to make a stand. It appears ideal. What's it called?"

"It's an Indian name, sir," Jamie told the famous cavalry officer. "Chickamauga. It means the River of Blood."

Book Two

Keep it; it tells all our history over,
From the birth of the dream to its last;
Modest and born of the Angel of Hope,
Like our hope of success it has passed.

—Major Samuel Alroy Jones

23

Jamie and Longstreet arrived just in time to take part in the bloodiest fighting along the Chickamauga, and during the late afternoon, the stream did run red with the blood of the Blue and the Gray.

Even though it was not yet true fall, somebody forgot to tell Mother Nature, and the weather took a turn for the worse. Neither side was dressed for the cold, and both sides suffered during the near freezing night.

With the addition of Longstreet, the Rebels now outnumbered the Yankees, but just by the barest of margins. Longstreet wanted to attack at first light, for his men were spoiling for a fight, and Bragg agreed and gave the order for the division on the Rebel right to charge at dawn, the rest would follow in waves.

But dawn came and went and nothing happened. Jamie sent Little Ben Pardee racing back to find out what was wrong.

"How the hell should I know?" General Bragg yelled, waving his arms in anger and frustration. "Go find that goddamn Polk. His division is supposed to open this dance."

When Ben Pardee reported back to Jamie, there was a very puzzled look on his young face. "What's the matter?" Jamie asked. "What's the delay?"

"General Polk is waiting for his breakfast."

"Somebody get me a bowl of mush and I'll ride over and hand feed the son of a bitch!" Longstreet said.

No one dared to bring the fiery general any mush, for Longstreet would have done just what he threatened to do.

Both armies waited for the other to make a move. Any element of surprise the Confederates might have had was now long gone. At about eight-thirty, Jamie sent Little Ben riding over to once more check on Polk.

Little Ben reported back. "His aide said he was in the woods, takin' his mornin' constitutional."

"The whole damn war waits for him to take a crap," Sergeant Major Huske said, then spat.

The battle finally got under way just after ten that morning. History did not record whether General Polk's constitutional was to his liking.

When a Union general made a terrible mistake in tactics and shifted his full division, leaving a gap in Yankee lines, Longstreet shifted Jamie and his Marauders around to beef up Forrest's men, fighting at the extreme north end of the Rebel lines, about four miles away from the heaviest fighting. Then Longstreet plunged his entire command straight into the gaping hole and broke the Union lines.

Miles to the north, Huske listened to the faint sounds of battle and remarked, "What's that sayin' about always a bridesmaid but never a bride?"

"Yeah, that's us, all right," Captain Jennrette said.

"Hey!" Captain Sparks yelled across the road to where the Union troops were dug in. "You Yankees gonna fight or not?"

"Try this on for size!" came the shout from the Union lines, and that was followed by a hail of rifle fire that hit nothing but air.

"Well, at least we know they're over there," Jamie said. He turned to Little Ben. "Find Forrest and ask him what we're supposed to be doing."

Little Ben returned and said, "His orders are to harass the enemy and hold."

"A man could interpret those orders in a lot of ways, Colonel," Captain Malone said.

Then the faint sounds of a bugler blowing "Charge" came to the men.

"Somebody is gettin' right into the thick of things," Captain Dupree remarked. He listened for a moment. "Hell, Colonel. That's comin' from the north of us. Whose command is way up there?"

"There isn't supposed to be anyone up there," Jamie said. "We're the northernmost unit."

Suddenly there was wild cheering from the Union troops across the road.

"Now what the hell is all that about?" Lieutenant Lenoir tossed the question out.

"Ben!" Jamie called. "Where did you find Forrest?"

" 'Bout three-quarters of mile south of us, sir. Down yonder on the road."

The firing from across the road grew very intense just as the woods to the north of Jamie's position suddenly filled with blue-coated cavalrymen as they burst out into the clearing, waving sabers and pistols in the classic mounted charge.

"Companies three and four wheel to face the infantry dug in!" Jamie shouted. "Companies one and two, follow me!"

Colonel Layfield had been briefed that Jamie and the Marauders did not like to face the taste of cold steel in a cavalry charge; he had been told they would cut and run. The south-hater had been badly misinformed.

Two companies of Marauders, led by Jamie, smashed into Layfield's as yet to be battle-tested Revengers. Jamie's bugler was blowing "Dixie" with everything he had as the Blue and the Gray clashed in the time-honored tradition of the cavalry charge.

The Marauders were badly outnumbered; but they were, to a man, experienced fighters, having been tested in the heat of battle in almost two years of bloody fighting. Jamie's bugler, a young man named Gibson, tore the fancy new bugle out of the hands of Layfield's bugler and conked him over the head with it, his hat the only thing saving the man from a fractured skull.

Jamie's horse, Satan, was trained to respond to knee commands, and Jamie rode right into the midst of things, both hands filled with Colts. Union saddles were being emptied at an alarming rate under the fury of the Marauders.

Layfield looked around for his bugler; he could not be found. It wouldn't have made any difference, for the young man didn't have anything to toot on.

Layfield was wild with hatred as the sounds of "Dixie" filled his head. Layfield rose up in the stirrups and shouted for his men to fall back and regroup just as Little Ben Pardee triggered off a round from his pistol. The bullet ricochetted off the back of Layfield's saddle and took a small piece of his pompous ass with it before sailing off.

Roaring in rage and pain, waving his saber and cussing, Layfield managed to get his message across, and the Revengers got the hell gone from the clearing.

"Sound recall!" Jamie yelled. "No pursuit. Recall, Gibson."

Forrest had heard the heavy firing and came galloping up, his command right behind him. But while Layfield's attack had failed miserably, the Union troops across the road had been beefed up. For Forrest to charge across the road would have been suicide. All he could do was hold. He jumped off his horse and walked up to Jamie, who was bleeding from a slight head wound.

"Who the hell was that attacked us?" Jamie looked up, as one of the doctor's aides was cleaning up the wound.

"I just received word that a brigade called the Revengers was moving into place north of here. Had to have been them."

"Layfield's bunch."

"You and your boys put them on the rout, Jamie."

"I shot a colonel in the ass," Little Ben Pardee said proudly, a wide grin on his gunsmoke-grimed face.

That tickled the funny bone of both commanders, and they burst out laughing.

"And I got me a brand-new bugle!" Gibson added, holding up the shiny horn.

That set Forrest and Jamie off again. "Well, play, boy!" Forrest said, wiping his eyes.

Gibson lifted the bugle to his lips, and the strains of "Bonnie Blue Flag" drifted out over the dead and the wounded.

The next day the Rebels put the Yankees into full retreat, but while it could be called a Confederate victory, the cost in human life was terribly high. Bragg had lost more than nineteen thousand men, killed, wounded, or taken prisoner. The Union army had lost more than seventeen thousand men, killed, wounded, or taken prisoner. Chickamauga proved to be the bloodiest battle of the war.

Jamie's men had seized a train of supply wagons on the third day, during the Union's retreat. And it was a boon. The wagons were filled with the new Colt revolving rifles and the new Spencer repeating rifles.

Jamie's Marauders became the most heavily armed cavalry unit in the Confederate army, now being able to wheel, dismount, and lay down an awesome field of fire. Jamie didn't know it, but he was revolutionizing cavalry tactics by having his men dismount and fight as infantry. That tactic would soon be adopted by both sides.

Layfield, meanwhile, was unable to ride due to the wound suffered in the right cheek of his buttocks. He found that the greatest balm for the pain in his ass was his ever-growing hatred of and for Jamie Ian MacCallister.

But the siege of Chattanooga was under way, and it was to be a miserable time for civilian and soldier alike. The soldiers had little to eat and the civilians had less. The Union supply lines were being constantly harassed by the Rebels, and before it was all over, some civilians and soldiers would starve to death.

During the first couple of months after the battle of Chickamauga, many drastic changes took place within both the

Union and the Confederate armies. Grant became the commanding general of all three armies operating in Tennessee, and he pulled them all under a single military force. He replaced Rosecrans and sent him home to Ohio. On the Rebel side, Davis still refused to replace Bragg; instead, he shifted several ranking generals around and left Bragg in command, much to the disgust of all.

Grant now turned all his attentions toward clearing East Tennessee of all Rebels, and during the last week of October, he put that plan into action. Jamie and his Marauders had been ordered up close to Knoxville, where the Union general, Burnside, was headquartered. Jamie did not know it, but Bragg had learned that Jamie had some fairly strong opinions of Bragg's ability to command and this was Bragg's way of getting rid of Jamie. Two days later, he would order Longstreet and his force to hit the trail for Knoxville. Finally, Bragg would be rid of Longstreet and Joe Wheeler and his cavalry—Wheeler was attached to Longstreet—the two generals who were the most outspoken against him.

Burnside was ordered to hold Knoxville at all costs.

"Stupid," Jamie fumed on the ride north. "Knoxville is pro-Union. We'll get no support from the citizens there."

Indeed, when Burnside had arrived in Knoxville, he had been wildly greeted by throngs of cheering people.

Pausing for the night, Jamie's wire-tapper hooked into the lines and scurried back down with the news.

"Longstreet and Wheeler have been ordered up to Knoxville, Colonel. They're comin' up by train. 'Bout a week behind us."

"Now I know Bragg is a damned fool," Jamie said. "We'll never be able to hold Knoxville, even if we take it, with such a small force, and Bragg will never beat back the Federals at Chattanooga after cutting his force. What the hell is the man trying to do, lose the war single-handedly?"

That was an opinion shared by many.

Jamie and his men waited for Longstreet and joined the man's forces in the middle of November. He was assigned to

Wheeler's cavalry and immediately began harassing the Union forces stationed along the river and stealing their food and equipment, for the supplies that Bragg promised to send never came and winter was covering the land.

Longstreet never admitted openly that he felt all was lost in Tennessee, but Jamie could read sign better than most and could often see it in the man's stance and in the timbre of his voice. Longstreet's men lacked proper winter clothing, and the shoes and boots of many were falling apart, the men having to tie rags around their feet.

Still, no one suggested they give up the fight.

Inside the city, many Union troops were faring no better than the Confederates, for Jamie and his Marauders were raising hell with the supply boats on the Holston River, managing to seize about one out of every three. But even those supplies barely kept body and soul alive. Longstreet's men were forced to fish the dead carcasses of horses and mules from the river and eat them.

Longstreet called for a meeting of his commanders during the last week of November, 1863. It had turned bitterly cold and the rain had changed to sleet. Longstreet's face was grim under his heavy beard. "I have just received word that Chattanooga is about to fall—it may have fallen by this time. I don't know where Bragg is and I have no orders. Telegraph lines have been cut, and as far as I know, we are alone."

Jamie sat quietly as some of Longstreet's officers urged him to give up the fight and retreat over to Virginia. But Longstreet would not even consider that.

"The last order I received was to fight," Longstreet said. "And fight we shall. We strike at the city tomorrow morning."

That was one of the worst decisions Longstreet ever made.

In less than thirty minutes' time, Longstreet lost a thousand men. He called off the attack and, after a brief pause, ordered his soldiers to begin an orderly retreat. The terrain was unsuitable for cavalry tactics, so Jamie squatted on a ridge and watched the massacre through field glasses, his Marauders packed up and ready to go, waiting some yards behind him.

When Longstreet had been informed that Jamie and his men were packed and ready to pull out, he said, "He probably has the right idea, but I have no choice in the matter."

Jamie had seen similar sights outside the walls of the Alamo and viewed the carnage without change of expression. Telegraph wires had been repaired, and he had heard only moments before the brief battle began that Chattanooga had indeed fallen and Bragg's men were now retreating into Georgia.

"Is it over," Captain Jennrette asked, walking up behind Jamie.

"In more ways than one," Jamie replied, standing up. "Let's go."

"Where to, Colonel?"

"Georgia."

24

During the grim year of 1863, the war had taken a heavy toll. Among the dead was Stonewall Jackson, killed at Chancellorville; a death that was mourned throughout the entire Confederacy.

For the first few months of the new year, the Confederate army was in disarray, with retreats on nearly all fronts. The Army of Virginia was holding, but cracks were appearing even there as the Union army grew stronger. Longstreet had been shifted up to Virginia to reinforce the Rebels there; Robert E. Lee was now recognized as the overall commander of the Confederate army. President Lincoln had called for volunteers to aid in the fight against the Rebels, and more than half a million men had lined up to enlist.

Jamie found himself without orders, and attached to no particular division. In the haste to reorganize, the Marauders had been left out of the planning.

The spring of 1864 brought with it several of the most unusual and least written about events of the bloody struggle. Colonel Aaron Layfield loudly and publicly stated—to anyone who would listen—that once the war in the East was over and the Union was victorious, he was going to take his men out west and stamp out any lingering pockets of Rebels and then turn his attentions to the Indians and wipe them out.

Jamie found the latter highly amusing, for Layfield would

last about a day against the Ute or the Cheyenne or the Dakota or any of a dozen other tribes.

Then Layfield specifically mentioned Valley, Colorado, and the MacCallister clan, calling the area a "Hotbed of insurrection, filled with Southern whores, white trash and traitors fit only to be wiped from the face of the earth and the land they squat upon burned bare and the earth salted down so nothing will ever live there again."

"What the hell is the matter with this lunatic?" Jamie questioned, after reading the article in a Eastern newspaper which thrived on such news.

Jamie and his men were camped in North Georgia, with no orders from the Confederate high command. They had seemingly fallen through the cracks of the military bureaucracy.

Jamie had lost his temper when he rode the train down to Atlanta to try to find out what they were supposed to do—he kept getting the runaround, and when he did get to see a senior officer, the man didn't have the foggiest idea of what to do. So Jamie decided to send the smooth-talking Pierre Dupree to see if he could find out something. Dupree found out a lot of things, including the reason for Layfield's wild hatred of Jamie Ian MacCallister.

"He's being bankrolled by a rich turncoat Louisiana man name of Jubal Olmstead, who's in cahoots with the Yankees, and they have promised him the governorship of Louisiana once the war is over. This Olmstead fellow is originally from Kentucky, I think, and for whatever reason, he has an almighty deep hatred for you, Colonel."

"Dear God," Jamie whispered, shaking his head in disbelief. "Is it ever going to end?"

Over coffee, Jamie told his men the long and twisted story of Kate's father and brother and all their kin, and about the Jacksons and the Saxons and Newbys and all the rest of the men who carried a blood feud against him.*

"What about orders?" Jamie asked.

Eyes Of Eagles—Zebra Books

"I finally got in to see a General Carson, and he said he didn't have the authority to order us to do nothin', Colonel. We don't even show up on any official war documents that he has, and he's got a whole damn room filled with them."

"So . . . officially, we can do whatever we damn well please?" Jamie said with a smile.

"I reckon so, Colonel."

"Including," Lieutenant Dawson said, with a glint in his eyes, "maybe goin' after this damn Layfield, if we was to decide to do such a thing, that is?"

A low murmur of approval came from the throats of the over five hundred men all gathered around, minus ten who were on picket duty and Sergeant Major Huske, who had asked for and received a few days' leave to go visit some kinfolks who lived in a small town about forty miles away from the encampment.

"But if we don't exist, Colonel," Captain Sparks pointed out, "we can't draw supplies. I'm not worried about gettin' paid; Confederate money isn't worth a damn, anyway. But how would we get supplies?"

"Steal them," Lieutenant Broussard said.

"From our own boys?" Sergeant McGuire asked.

"Here comes the Top Soldier," a picket called out.

"He's comin' back early," a Marauder remarked.

Sergeant Major Huske's face was set in anger as he marched up to Jamie and said, "Colonel, I don't want you to think me a quitter, but I would like to be discharged from this outfit. I got me some manhuntin' to do."

"Have some coffee and food, Louie," Jamie said. "Let's talk about it."

Louie calmed down enough to eat a plate of bacon and beans and swallow two cups of coffee. "That town I went to, Colonel? It ain't there no more. Burned to the ground. What men they didn't shoot, they hanged. Then they had their way with a lot of women who didn't run off into the woods. Then they branded them on the forehead with a *W*—for whore. They hanged my brother. Only reason he didn't join up with the Confederacy was because he was born with a clubfoot; he didn't get around too good."

"Who did all this, Louis?" Dupree asked.

"I can answer that," Jamie said. "Colonel Aaron Layfield and his Revengers."

"That's right, Colonel. I'm gonna kill that man. If it's the last thing I do on God's earth, I'm gonna kill him."

"One of us will," Jamie said softly. "Sparks, I want you to pick five other men who don't have a pronounced Southern accent to change into civilian clothing and get ready to take a trip."

"Sure, Colonel. Where to?"

"New York City. Somebody get me pen and ink and paper."

"What's up, Colonel?" Louie asked.

"We're going to have us a very private and personal little war, Top. That's what Layfield wants. A private and personal war with me. None of you have to go on this. It's strictly volunteer all the way."

"Shit, Colonel!" Lieutenant Lenoir said. "You think any of us would miss this?"

"Sparks, you and the men you choose will be bringing back a hundred thousand dollars in gold and Federal paper money. From my personal account. One of many, I assure you."

That shook his men right down to the rowels of their spurs.

Jamie started writing to his banker and attorney in New York City. If Layfield wanted a war, he was damn sure going to get one.

Jamie took a few men with him and rode over to where the town used to be. It was exactly as Top Soldier had said: burned to the ground. There were several dozen fresh graves in the cemetery, and the ropes used to hang the men were still dangling from the limbs of trees. Huske had marked his brother's grave and now set about carving him a wooden marker until he could get a stone mason to chisel a permanent stone.

Jamie walked the paths of what had once been a permanent settlement, filled with people of all ages, working, playing, worshipping, living, loving. Now there was nothing except the smell of ashes and death. Jamie looked up at the sounds of shuffling footsteps. An elderly Negro was making his way toward Jamie.

"What army is you?" the old man called, staying a safe distance from the big man.

Jamie smiled. What army, indeed? "The Army of the Confederacy," he finally said.

"I didn't have nothin' to do with this," the old man called, waving his hand at the burned-out remnants of buildings.

"I know it. I know who did it."

The old man came closer. "Turrible thing, this. I knowed most of these people here. They was some bad amongst 'em, but mos' of 'em was good folks. Them Yankee soldiers didn't have no call to do this. I never seen so many white men so filled plumb up with hate agin they own kind."

"A tall, loud-mouthed man with side whiskers leading the bunch?"

"Yessuh. He personal tooken the hot iron and branded the furst lady on the forehead. That was after his men had they way with the white ladies that didn't run off. Them men of his, they lined up to take they turns with the ladies; some of 'em they raped no more than chillen."

"The men who did this were not really Union soldiers," Jamie said.

"They wasn't?"

"No. Most soldiers of the Blue are like the soldiers of the Gray. They would have no part of rape and torture." Jamie left out the burning of homes and businesses, for the Yankees had begun to do that; something that Jamie found disgraceful.

"The men who done this, they rampaged through all the stores and homes 'fore they put 'em to the torch. They give the money and the finery to any colored folks they could find. Mos' of the colored I know threw the clothes away; they feared of bein' punished if they was caught with it later. The money ain't no good. It's Confederate money."

"Where do you live?"

The old man shrugged his shoulders. "Nowheres, now. Them bluecoats burned down the massa's house and stole the horses and mules. They gathered up all the livestock and took 'em when they lef'. Massa Nations, he dead and so is his wife. The bluecoats kilt 'em both. There wasn't no call to do that, 'cause they was both old and didn't treat us bad like a lot of white folks do. Tell me, sir, is it true that President Lincoln done freed all the slaves?"

"Yes. It's called the Emancipation Proclamation. You're free."

"Lord have mercy. You mean I could just walk down that road as far as I want to go?"

"Technically, yes."

"Well . . . what do I do when I gets to where it is I might be goin'? That is, if I had anywheres I wanted to go."

Jamie then realized the enormity of what Lincoln had done. What he had done was a wonderful thing; only a hate-filled fool would deny that. But on the other side of the coin, with one stroke of the pen, Lincoln had turned loose millions of Negroes who had no training, no jobs, most of whom could not read or write, and had no place to go in a part of the country torn and ripped by war and hatred.

"Who is gonna feed me?" the old man asked. "I'm hungry, mister."

"We have some food with us. We'll share with you."

"But that's today," the old man pressed. "What about tomorrow and the next day and the day after that?"

Jamie shook his head. "You're on your own. You're free. Making do is part of being free."

The old man thought about that for a moment. "What are we 'pposed to do from here on out, mister?"

"Plant a garden. Hire yourself out for wages."

"I be somewheres around eighty years old, big man. Hands all stiff and no good to work no more. All I know is workin' in the fields. Liftin' and totin'. Something ain't quite right about this here freedom. Seems like Mister Lincoln done a good thing with one hand and put a turrible burden on us with the other hand."

Jamie didn't quite know how to answer that. "Come on. I'll get you some food."

"Nosuh. I bes' not. I got to be lookin' after myself from now on, so I bes' get to doin' it. I know where they's some greens and I'll get that and some poke. I'll get by."

Jamie stood and watched the old man shuffle off into the woods. "The slaves should have been freed from bondage immediately, but total freedom should have been a gradual thing," Jamie muttered. "Over a period of years. With education and training. This is going to be a great big mess."

"Did you say something, Colonel?" Louie asked, walking up behind Jamie.

"Just talking to myself, Top." He turned around to face the sergeant major. "What are all these ex-slaves going to do now that they are free, Louie?"

"I don't know, sir. Damn sure won't be much work for a long time to come . . . not any work they can be paid to do, 'cause there isn't any money. It's goin' to be bad, isn't it, Colonel?"

"I'm afraid so, Louie. For many, many years to come."

"Now what, Colonel?"

"We go after Layfield."

25

Jamie took his Marauders into the mountainous section of East Georgia and there holed up until Sparks and the others could return from New York City. Jamie began sending out men dressed in civilian clothing and riding the poorest of stock to act as spies, to learn the whereabouts of Layfield and his Revengers. For when the time came, Jamie was going to hit Layfield so hard the man would think a mountain fell on him.

Layfield, meanwhile, was busy looking for Jamie, but he was over in Central Tennessee and North Alabama, several hundred miles away from Jamie's position.

For a time, the war seemed far away to Jamie and his men. They hunted and fished and picked berries and mended clothing and did all the other things that soldiers do when not fighting—including waiting.

It was late spring before Sparks and the men returned, laden with gold and Federal paper money.

"That New York City is some place, Colonel," Sparks said. "I sure hadn't ever seen anything like it. And I'm not sure I ever want to see it again. Too damn many people to suit this country boy."

The men were also very relieved to be rid of all that money.

Jamie had heard no real news of the war, and Sparks brought him up to date. "Forrest really got the Yankees all riled up against us after that raid on Fort Pillow."

"What raid?"

"Happened a few weeks ago just north of Memphis. Forrest and his boys stormed the place and took it, but the Yankees is sayin' it was a slaughter. The newspapers back east is sayin' that Forrest's boys bayonetted and clubbed to death most of the colored soldiers 'cause they was fightin' for the Blue. The Yankees lost more than three hundred men, most of them blacks . . . accordin' to the newspapers, that is."

"It might have happened that way, too," Jamie said. "Nathan's got some ol' boys fighting with him that hate colored people. Some of them were with us originally, if you'll recall."

"That's not to say they weren't good men in their own way, Colonel."

"Oh, no. I've fought shoulder to shoulder with men who felt the only good Indian was a dead one. I disagree, but I still called them friend and comrade."

At this time, Jamie was well aware that his friend, General Joe Johnston, was over in Dalton, Georgia, with his army, preparing to face off with Grant. Jamie didn't care. Suddenly, that war was far away. He was ready to face his own war, as, he felt sure, was Layfield. Up close and personal. Very personal.

"Sherman is sending troops out to forage, Colonel," Sparks added. "And sometimes they're right cruel with the civilians in doing it."

"Are they paying for what they take?"

"Sometimes, but not often. In something called script." He looked around. "Where is the Top Soldier?"

"Out headhunting," Jamie replied.

With Joe Johnston was John Bell Hood, in his early thirties, one of the youngest generals in the Confederate army. John had lost a leg at Chickamauga and had an arm shattered at Gettysburg, but he was still able to sit a horse (he had to be strapped in the saddle) and was a respected leader of men. The men liked Hood, but they idolized Joe Johnston.

Sherman was asked what he intended to do with Colonel Aaron Layfield's brigade.

"Keep him just as far away from me as is humanly possible," Sherman replied.

Layfield had made the mistake of attempting to preach to Sherman one day. Very poor judgment on Layfield's part.

Jamie very carefully laid out his plans to the men driving the supply wagons, and they rumbled out. Each Marauder carried five days' meager rations in his saddle box, to be used only in an emergency. Jamie had given each man money enough to buy food along the way if they had to. Mainly they would depend on hunting and fishing to sustain themselves.

During the first week in May, 1864, Sherman launched his Georgia campaign, and Grant crossed the Rapidan, signaling the beginning of the campaign against Lee in Virginia. Jamie and the Marauders rode off to tangle with Layfield and his Revengers.

When Sherman learned that Layfield was going to wage a personal war against Jamie MacCallister, he smiled. "Maybe that pompous bag of wind can keep MacCallister occupied enough so he'll not have time to harass us." Then he chuckled and called for an aide. "Take this down as a direct order, Captain. It's to Colonel Aaron Layfield and his Revengers."

He then made it official: Layfield was to keep Jamie Mac-Callister and his Marauders away from Sherman's army. Try to contain the Marauders up in Northeast Georgia if at all possible.

"And make sure that blowhard has sufficient supplies," Sherman added, then leaned back in his chair and lit up a cigar, smiling around the thick swirl of smoke.

War certainly made for strange allies, he thought.

Jamie certainly had ample supplies. He had his men cache supplies and ammunition all over Northeast Georgia: from

Blue Ridge up near the Tennessee line, down to Gainesville, then over to the South Carolina line and up to the North Carolina line, following the river. The white citizens of Georgia knew what he was doing and helped Jamie whenever possible. To a person they despised Layfield and his men . . . and their opinion of Sherman and his army wasn't much better, for the man had started his campaign of burning everything that stood in his way.

"In some small way, the Yankees will pay for this," Jamie promised a group of citizens one summer's afternoon. "I promise you that."

They certainly would. There was one small town in Pennsylvania where the citizens would never forget or forgive Jamie and his Marauders.

The mountains of East Georgia were pimples compared to the Rockies, but they were mountains, and Jamie was at home in the mountains.

"We won't be doing many mounted charges," he told his men. "But we're going to teach Layfield and his men some very hard lessons."

On the same day that Sherman and his Union troops attacked the Confederate stronghold of Rocky Face, Jamie and his men were getting into position in a tiny town in East Georgia. Layfield had been trailed by some of Jamie's scouts, and they had learned that the Southern-hater was planning to loot and burn the village.

Jamie ordered the civilians—mostly older men and women and children—out of town and into ravines about a mile from the settlement. He had some of his own men—the smaller men—dress up in dresses and bonnets and sashshay up and down the streets so Layfield's vanguard would see them and not suspect anything.

"You shore look precious, there, Luke," Sergeant Major Huske told a Marauder, all dolled up in dress and bonnet and parasol.

Luke told the Top Soldier where he could stick his comments . . . sideways.

Layfield had halted his men about a mile from town, where Aaron was busy praying to the Lord to give his men the strength to wipe this wretched town from the face of the earth, and to teach these Southern whores a lesson in humility. Layfield did not think of rape as wrong—as long as the rape was being committed against Southern women. Layfield considered them to all be whores and trollops anyway. Why shouldn't his men relieve their tensions? Weren't they doing God's work here on earth?

Not this day. On this day, Layfield was about to step up and shake hands with the man he considered to be the spawn of the devil: Jamie Ian MacCallister.

Layfield rode up to within a few hundred yards of the sleepy little town. One of the "ladies" parading up and down the boardwalks flipped "her" dress up and made a hunching motion toward Layfield.

"Whoor!" Layfield yelled. "Filthy Southern whoor!"

Yet another "lady" made a very obscene hand gesture toward Layfield.

Layfield waved his saber and shouted, "Charge, men! Remember, we are doing God's work!"

God must have surely winked at that, for He certainly wasn't looking with favor on Layfield that day. Layfield's men came galloping into town, screaming and yelling. Jamie's Marauders cleared a hundred saddles during the first volley. The roaring of gunfire was enormous. Horses reared and screamed in fright and dumped their riders to the dirt. The dust and gunsmoke limited vision to only a few yards, and that helped to save Layfield's life. When the man finally realized he had been suckered into an ambush, he shouted for his bugler to sound recall and then wheeled his horse and got the hell gone from the dusty, bloody streets of the small town. Layfield retained vivid memories of the last time he'd tangled with the Marauders and tried to keep his butt planted firmly in the saddle.

There was just something very unseemly about getting shot in the ass.

Jamie had forewarned his men that there would be no pursuit after the ambush, for Layfield's force was much larger than Jamie's four companies of Marauders, and out in the open the Marauders stood a good chance of getting badly mauled.

On this warm early summer's day in East Georgia, Jamie's men had killed just over fifty Union Revengers and wounded another fifty or so. Jamie ordered all the guns, ammunition, supplies, and horses to be taken. Any money found on the men was to be given to the townspeople. The badly wounded and the dead were loaded into wagons and taken several miles out of town, while the lesser wounded were told to get the hell gone and tell Layfield to come get his wounded and see to them.

Jamie added this: "You tell that hypocritical psalm-singing son of a bitch who ramrods your outfit that his war is with me, not against civilian men and women and kids. If he retaliates against this town for what happened today, you have my personal word that I will hunt down every man jack of you and stake you out over an anthill and pour honey over your eyes and let the ants have you. And don't you doubt for one second that I won't do it. You be damn sure he gets the message."

The slightly wounded and badly frightened Revenger believed every word Jamie said as the man towered over him, his pale blue eyes burning with the heat of emotion.

Jamie threw the man onto a horse and slapped the crowbait on the rump, sending him galloping out of town.

Moments later, Jamie and his Marauders were gone, vanishing into the mountains like ghosts.

Layfield and men returned to pick up their dead and wounded and then retired some miles away, to lick their wounds and let their hate fester.

Jamie had not lost a single man, to death or wound.

All through the months of May and June, 1864, the Marauders and the Revengers fought each other in small battles all over the northeastern corner of Georgia. To the west and south, the Union army was slowly clawing their bloody way toward Atlanta. On June the first, the Yankees were on the north side of the Chattahoochee River, only a few miles north of the city. But it would take the Union forces almost seven more brutal and bloody weeks to reach the city. They would measure their daily advance in yards and sometimes feet. Atlanta was being evacuated.

Jamie and his Marauders and Layfield and his Revengers had been all but forgotten by Richmond and Washington. For them, the war was each other. But it was about to turn decidedly in Jamie's favor.

The Henry rifle had just been introduced, and a train load of them, along with other supplies, was on its way to Sherman's troops, now almost within spitting distance of Atlanta.

The train never made it. Jamie and his men blocked the rails and seized tons of supplies and all the Henry rifles and .44 ammunition for them. The Henry lever action rifle was a marvel, holding fifteen rounds in a tube under the barrel. Each Marauder carried two in saddle boots and a third in hand, across the horn. It gave them awesome fighting power, for counting the rounds in the pistols they carried, each man could now fire over eighty rounds before having to reload—unheard of in those days. And Aaron Layfield and his Revengers would soon experience the killing effectiveness of those new Henry Rifles.

Jamie and the Marauders set fire to the freight cars, and then blew up the locomotive, blocking the Western and Atlantic tracks for several days. Then they rode off with their wagons of booty, Gibson tooting on his bugle.

The loss of a small train and locomotive did not disturb Sherman nearly as much as the loss of those rifles; he had been counting heavily on them. For a brief time he considered sending a brigade of men after Jamie and his Marauders. A dozen commanders immediately volunteered.

But Sherman had been studying maps of East Georgia, and the terrain was not to his liking. Moreover, he knew that Mac-

Callister was right at home in the mountains and was a master at setting up ambushes.

"No," Sherman finally decided. "We'd lose too many men in rooting him out, and besides, we might not succeed."

"But if he should come in behind our lines . . . ?"

Sherman waved that off. "MacCallister has four companies of cavalry, with no artillery to back him up. He could pester us, but not to any large extent. His war is with this Layfield person and I want it to remain so. Send someone to tell Layfield to force the issue with MacCallister or I will replace him with someone who can do the job."

The message stung Layfield, and he immediately went to his tent after telling his officers he must be left alone in order to seek Heavenly guidance on how best to deal with Jamie MacCallister and his band of Southern trash.

Actually, what he was doing was drafting a letter to Jubal Olmstead in Washington, outlining the problem and asking if he could do something to aid the Vermont Revengers.

While he was composing the letter, a plan came to mind, and Layfield thought hard for a moment. He smiled, a cruel curving of the lips, and wadded up the paper, discarding it. Layfield knew that Southern men held their women in high regard, placing them on almost a spiritual plane. Layfield found that amusing, if not downright sacrilegious, for to his way of thinking, Southern women were nothing but trash and whores.

Layfield chuckled. Oh, yes, indeed. He knew a way to lure MacCallister and his band of thugs into a trap. And he was sure it would work. He called for a meeting of his officers, and they immediately began making plans to rid the world of Jamie MacCallister, once and for all.

Layfield did not take into consideration that Jamie just might have a thing or two to say about that.

On September the first, Rebel commanders finally realized the futility of any further holding on, and Atlanta fell. During the night, Confederate troops began slowly retreating. The next day, the mayor of Atlanta officially surrendered the city to the Union forces.

From the very outset, from the moment Sherman had marched out of Tennessee, it had taken a hundred and thirty days of combat, much of it with knife and bayonet, to finally reach and conquer Atlanta. No one could ever offer any disparaging remarks about the bravery of the men of the Blue and the Gray. The casualties were staggeringly, unbelievably high. Both sides combined suffered over seventy-five thousand men dead, wounded, captured, or missing. It was an incredibly bloody price to pay.

But on both sides, the survivors could boast that their fallen comrades had, "Died for the Cause."

26

In Virginia, Federal troops were gradually putting the squeeze on Richmond; but the Confederate lines hardened, and they held back charge after charge of Yankees. At the Battle of the Crater, the Federal commanders made the mistake of pitting Negro troops against the Rebels. That so outraged the Southerners they threw caution to the wind and charged the Union line and turned what might have been a Federal victory into a slaughter. Finally, the Union troops were forced to build breastworks out of mud and clay and the bodies of their own dead comrades in an effort to hold back the enraged Southern troops. From behind the bodies of their own troops, the Yankees finally stopped the wild Confederate charge and held. For a time. Then the Rebels regrouped and came over the top after them in what would be some of the fiercest fighting of that battle. When it was over, the dead Union troops, white and black, would be stacked twelve feet high.

All during the summer of '64, Union troops fought against Lee's troops around Richmond, sometimes as close as four miles from the Confederate capital, but they could not break through the Rebel lines.

There were several dozen black regiments fighting against Lee's Army of Virginia, and they distinguished themselves well against the Confederates. Although led by white officers, the black troops often had to act on their own initiative and proved their mettle time and time again.

Even diehard Rebels were forced to admit, albeit grudgingly, that, "The damn niggers can fight, by God!"

That they could, and did. Twenty-three of them won the new Congressional Medal of Honor for gallantry during the Virginia campaign alone.

In mid-September, Falcon MacCallister and his company of cavalry joined the Virginia fight, as did Wells and Robert, assigned to a colored regiment from Massachusetts. Sam Montgomery, Jr., and Pat MacKensie were there, and so were Jorge and Tomas Nunez. They would soon be facing each other across the battle lines of the Blue and the Gray.

The troops of Lee's Army of Virginia would hold on for about six more bloody months.

"It's a trap," Jamie said, after a few minutes of thought. He looked at the scout who'd just returned from a nearby town. "Who told you this, Will?"

"It's all over town, and the people are scared, Colonel. Really scared. Most of the younger men are in uniform. Only men in town are real old or those who was bad wounded in the war and sent home."

"Layfield must think I'm stupid to fall for something like this. But for the time being, we'll let him think I'm going to blunder into his trap."

Jamie knew exactly where Layfield was camped, but since Jamie and his Marauders kept on the move, the South-hater had no firm idea where Jamie was. Jamie kept his men split up into units small enough to hide, but large enough to easily repel any unit of comparable size.

Despite Jamie's threats, Layfield had kept up his attacks on small towns, and so far, at least, the Union commanders had done nothing to stop the man.

"They just might not know about it," Sparks told Jamie.

"The villages Layfield's been hitting are tucked 'way off the beaten path."

Jamie had to admit that was a possibility. "But some of them know. They have to know. There have been too many complaints for them not to know that something is going on."

"Some of our boys have been raiding in Maryland and Ohio, Colonel," Dupree reminded Jamie. "Maybe the Yankees think what Layfield is doing is tit for tat?"

Several raids had been carried out up north by Confederate raiders; Morgan had hit installations in Ohio and Indiana. "They haven't raped and plundered," Jamie reminded the man, although Jamie knew there were rogues and rakes on both sides in this conflict. But so far he had heard of no officially sanctioned excursions into the north that involved the manhandling and molestation of women, or the hanging of civilians at Confederate hands.

There was only one narrow and curving road leading to the small village that Layfield had threatened to destroy, and anywhere along the road was ideal for ambush. No military man, Layfield fully expected the Marauders to come riding headstrong along the road, open for ambush. Layfield was only a couple of days away from learning a very hard lesson about Jamie MacCallister.

"We handpick the very best woodsmen. A hundred and fifty men and go in here. We leave our horses here," Jamie said, pointing to a map. "And go in on foot. Rifles and pistols. Pick your men."

Even though all the Marauders wanted to go, they were so well disciplined that none questioned their commanders' choice of men who would participate in the raid.

Jamie knew there was no way a hundred and fifty men had any chance at all of putting Layfield out of business, but he could not bring his entire command through the timber without running a real risk of being spotted.

The day had dawned cool, almost cold, and mist hung in

pockets all over the mountains; the leaves of trees dripped with moisture. Jamie and his men slipped silently thought the dense timber, moving on moccasined feet. They had tightly wound pieces of cloth around the barrels of their rifles to prevent any stray bit of sunlight from reflecting off of metal. Layfield and his men were good in the woods and good in the mountains; but they were too confident—too sure of themselves. And they had made the mistake of attempting to second-guess Jamie. Many Indians and white bounty hunters had tried that same thing, and died for it.

Jamie had started a hundred mounted men down the road so Layfield and his men would be all eyes on the road, not suspecting trouble coming up behind them—Jamie hoped.

About a mile from the ambush site—townspeople friendly to Jamie had confirmed the spot—the mounted Marauders would swing off, and Jamie and his men in the woods would strike.

Jamie crept to within a couple of hundred feet of the ambushers, and silently his men moved up in a line beside him, spread out left and right.

"Here they come, men!" Layfield's voice carried through the timber. "Get ready."

Layfield's voice could be heard, but the man himself could not be seen. Jamie knew the only way he was going to end this personal battle was to get lead into Colonel Aaron Layfield.

"They stopped!" a man called. "What's going on? They just stopped."

"Relax," another said. "They just stopped to finalize their plans, that's all."

"Silence," Layfield commanded. "Something is wrong. I feel it."

He stood up.

Jamie quickly pulled his rifle to his shoulder and shot him. But just as he squeezed the trigger, Layfield turned, and Jamie knew it was not a righteous hit. Layfield screamed and pitched forward, rolling down the embankment to the rutted narrow road below. The woods erupted in gunfire from the Marauders, Jamie's men firing as fast as they could work the levers on their Henry rifles.

A hundred and fifty men poured hundreds of rounds of rifle fire into the ranks of Layfield's Revengers, working closer in a line as they fired. When their rifles were empty, as they had planned, seventy-five started using pistols while seventy-five reloaded; then the sequence was done over and over again until the Marauders were close enough to touch those Revengers who had not fled in panic across the road to their horses.

Jamie had been wrong in thinking that a hundred and fifty of his men could not break the backs of Layfield's Revengers, for they did that bloody, foggy, misty day in the mountains of East Georgia. When the shooting stopped and the Marauders began counting the damages, over five hundred of Layfield's men lay dead or wounded.

"You played hell, Johnny Reb," one wounded man said, looking up at Jamie. "The colonel's hard hit. Busted his shoulder and collarbone."

"He started this personal war, not me," Jamie told the man.

"And he'll end it, too," the man replied, just then realizing who he was talking to. "Might not be during this fracas; maybe out west in your valley of whores and trash. But he'll do it. You mind what I say, MacCallister."

Jamie squatted down and opened the man's shirt. He had taken two in the belly and there was no hope for him. "You've not got long, Yankee. Tell me, why does Layfield hate me so?"

When the man hesitated, Jamie said, "The way I hear tell it, you're all supposed to be fine, up-standing Christian men if you ride with Layfield. That being the case, you wouldn't want to die with a lie on your lips, would you?"

"I'll not tell a falsehood to any man, MacCallister. You

killed Layfield's brother some years back, and you killed other kin of his, too."

"I have no knowledge of ever killing a man called Layfield."

"Well, you done it, whether you remember it or not. They was bounty hunters."

Jamie grunted. He had killed his share of bounty hunters, for a fact. But they had all been riding after him, for crimes he had not committed.

He started to ask the man another question, then bit back the words. The Revenger was dead.

"Colonel," Louie Huske called. "Come take a look at this contraption, will you? It's the damndest thing I ever did see. Whatever it is."

Jamie stepped over the dead and the wounded and made his way over to Huske, who was standing beside a strange-looking piece of equipment on metal and wooden legs. The thing had a huge round metal tube with a crank on one end and a thin metal rod sticking out of the top.

"What is that thing?" Jamie asked.

"Damned if I know, Colonel," Top Soldier said. "But these metal tubes is filled with cartridges. There's three cases of the things over yonder."

"What caliber?"

".45-70."

Jamie went around to the front of the contraption and looked. There were a series of muzzles all in a circle."

"For God's sake, Johnny Reb!" a wounded Revenger called. "Don't turn the crank. That's a Gatling gun."

"A what?" Jamie asked, turning around to face the man.

"It's a rapid-fire gun. You turn that crank and the barrel revolves and feeds the ammunition down from that tube. It's a fearsome weapon, Johnny Reb. Spits out lead faster than anything ever before invented." He smiled. "That machine thing is going to kill a lot of slavers like you."

Jamie had grown so tired of telling people that he didn't

believe in slavery that he ignored the man's last comment. "Gatling gun, huh? Well, whatever the thing is, boys, we've got us one. Some of you find the wagon they used to bring this thing here and load it up. Take all the ammunition for it. Take all the guns and ammunition from the dead and the wounded, and leave their horses so they can get out of here. He looked at the sprawl of wounded men, all looking at him.

"You're not going to hang us, MacCallister?" a man asked.

"I don't hang prisoners or civilians," Jamie told him. "Or molest women and kids and old people. I'll leave that to trash like you."

The man flushed under his beard and wisely chose to keep any further comments to himself. But another Revenger elected to keep it going.

"The Union must be preserved, MacCallister. You damn Southerners want to tear this nation apart. So as far as I'm concerned, you're all traitors and deserve nothing better than the torch and the rope. Now I've made peace with the Almighty, so if you want to hang me, you go right ahead. For if you let me live, I will return to fight you. And that's a promise."

Jamie stared at the man for a moment. "Back when the war was just getting started, President Abe Lincoln told me that a man must go where his heart dictates. I made my choice with no rancor toward a person who chose the Blue. Obviously, you are not a big enough man to do the same."

Several of the wounded Revengers smiled at that and nodded their heads in agreement with Jamie's words. Jamie could sense that for them, their minds were made up. The war was over; they would be heading for home as soon as possible. But for most of the Revengers who were sprawled on the damp ground, staring at him, open hate in their eyes, as soon as their wounds permitted, they would be right back in the saddle, riding for Aaron Layfield and his Revengers.

"Let's go," Jamie told his men. "The hate around here is getting more than I can bear."

"We'll meet again, MacCallister," a Revenger called out. "Count on that."

"Damn right," a Revenger officer said.

Now that the men realized they were not going to be executed, their courage had returned and traveled up to their mouths. "Yeah," another one said. "And if by some miracle you make it through the war, if I ever seen you again, I'll kill you, you Godless bastard!"

Jamie chuckled at that. His humor could surface at the strangest of times. "If I make it through the war, and I fully intend to do just that, I'll head back home. Don't come west with hate in your heart for me or mine, for if you do, I'll kill you."

Jamie and his Marauders took the horses of the dead and rode off, the Gatling gun on a small wagon.

Aaron Layfield and his Revengers were, for the most part, through with this war, as far as being able to mount any type of effective fighting force. But Aaron Layfield would see Jamie again. After his broken shoulder and collarbone had been seen to, Aaron had sworn with his hand on the Bible that someday he would kill Jamie Ian MacCallister. God had told him that was his sole mission in life.

Through his pain, not fully dulled with laudanum, he turned to his new sergeant major—one Carl Miller, who had deserted from the Union army, grown a beard, and joined the Revengers—and said, "I will never rest until I can spit on the grave of Jamie MacCallister."

"I'll be right beside you, Colonel," Carl said. "I ain't got no love for the MacCallisters, neither."

"You're a good man, Sergeant Miller," Layfield said. "I'll pray for you."

What was left of Layfield's ambush force began trickling into camp, and Layfield was sickened at the damage done to his brigade, which had been effectively reduced to about a battalion. And many of them were badly wounded and would not live long.

"God *damn* Jamie MacCallister!" Layfield said. "Damn his black soul to the eternally burning pits of hell."

"They got the Gatling gun, too," a Revenger told him, one arm in a bloody sling.

"Shit!" Reverend Layfield said.

27

With Layfield out of the picture for some time to come—and he was out of it, with a badly broken shoulder and collarbone—Jamie assessed his situation and felt he should link up with some unit and try to explain what had happened. Jamie contacted General Hood and told him all that had transpired since last they had seen one another.

Hood was stunned. He wired back: THOUGHT YOU WERE DEAD. WERE TOLD YOU WERE DEAD. CONGRATULATIONS ON RISING FROM THE GRAVE. START TEARING UP RAILROAD TRACKS NORTH OF ATLANTA ASAP. HOOD.

"We're back," Jamie told his men. "Let's go to work on the railroad."

Now Jamie had something else to worry about: did Kate think him dead? He didn't believe so, for if Kate had been notified of his death, she would be moving heaven and earth to come east to see his grave site, and she would also check with Falcon, Morgan, Matt, Pat, Robert and Wells, and Sam, Jr., and Igemar. Jamie would have to get word to her, somehow. The pony express had not lasted long, but there was always a way.

"Buck Masters' home is in Missouri," Huske reminded Jamie. "His wound ain't healin' right, and he needs to go home anyways. His pa was killed in a skirmish with Kansas Jayhawkers, and he's needed to run the farm. He could take the note to Missouri and get someone there to carry it on."

"I'll do that. Thanks, Louie."

By the time Jamie got his men ready to go, it was the third week in October, and North Georgia was crawling with Union troops. Jamie and his men were lucky to be able to advance fifteen miles a day. It was one battle after another with much larger forces. Georgia was filling up with Union troops; Jamie's own command was taking a beating, and they had yet to tear up even one foot of railroad track.

On October 27, he learned that Jorge Nunez had been killed while fighting with Young's Texas Brigade, and Swede and Hannah's boy, Igemar, had been badly wounded while fighting with the Seventeenth Iowa, under the command of Colonel Weaver.

Jamie also learned that months before, both Wells and Robert had been shifted over to the Fifty-fourth Massachusetts Infantry and were somewhere in South Carolina. He would not learn until war's end that both had been killed during the assault on Fort Wagner.

Jamie's men, now less than four hundred strong, were halted in their tracks by several full brigades of Union troops. Jamie had his wiretapper send a coded message to Hood: CAN GO NO FARTHER. HAVE LOST ONE FIFTH OF MY MEN. ORDERS?

It was the middle of November, 1864. Hood wired back: GO WHERE YOU THINK YOU CAN DO THE MOST DAMAGE. GOD SPEED.

The War Between the States would struggle on for another six bloody months.

Jamie cut northeast, planning to ride up through North Carolina. Just across the border, he first came upon a cemetery with dozens of fresh graves, and about half a mile farther, the ruins of a small town. Every building had been burned to the ground. He could see dozens of ropes still dangling from tree limbs.

"Somethin' tells me Layfield's been through here," Lieutenant Casten drawled.

"I thought he was all shot up bad?" Huske said.

"That was a month ago," Jamie said. "Wasn't it?"

All the men had lost track of time.

"I guess it was at that, Colonel," Huske replied. "What month is this?"

"October, ain't it?" a Marauder said.

"I think it's November," Captain Sparks said. "If it isn't, it damn sure feels like it."

It was the first day of December, 1864.

"I wonder who's winnin' the war," Bugler Gibson asked, his words soft and steamy in the cold air.

"You can bet your bugle we ain't," Corporal Bates told him.

Several elderly people came hesitantly out of the timber behind what had once been a town; one man, three women. The old man was on makeshift crutches that looked extremely uncomfortable to Jamie.

"Pickets out," Jamie ordered, then dismounted and walked over to the old people.

"You'd be Colonel MacCallister of the Confederate Marauders," the old man said.

"Yes. What happened here, sir?"

"We don't hold it agin you, sir," one of the elderly women told him.

"I beg your pardon, ma'am?"

"This." She waved her hand at the ruins of destruction. "It ain't your fault."

"I . . . don't understand, ma'am. What happened here? Who did this?"

"Colonel Layfield and his Revengers," another elderly woman spoke up. "Two weeks ago. They shot or hanged every man they could find. They . . . had their way with the young women, and then looted and burned the town. All the businesses and all the homes. Then Colonel Layfield lined up all that was left and preached us a sermon. Said all this was done because of you, Colonel MacCallister. Course we all had heard by then 'bout you and your brave lads defeatin' him in battle some weeks before. Doesn't take a real smart person to see that Layfield is a coward. I guess the only thing he didn't do here is brand the poor women on the forehead like he's done before."

"No," the old man said, bitterness in the words. "This time Layfield ordered his men to shoot the women after his men had their way with them."

"Did they?" Jamie asked, anger growing within him.

"Yes, sir. Ten young ladies. But the ladies stood proud and did not beg. They were forced to stand naked after Layfield's men had raped them repeatedly. Then they were shot down. We buried them yonder in the cemetery."

"Dear God in Heaven," Lieutenant Broussard whispered, his words breaking the silence that had followed the old man's damning statement.

"Do you know much about what is happening in Georgia, Colonel," the old man asked.

"I know practically nothing, sir. We've been cut off for weeks. What is happening?"

"Sherman and his men are burning plantations and towns. Destroying mills and cotton gins and everything that stands in their way. They're looting and pillaging. War is one thing, but they're destroying the lives and livelihood of civilians. That damn Sherman is a devil."

There were many acts of brutishness and barbarism against the civilian population of Georgia by the Union forces, but there were also many acts of individual kindness. Still, civilian lives and livelihood were needlessly destroyed. And no one could legitimately or reasonably excuse the wanton looting of homes before they were set afire. It was war at its worst. The Union troops took ladies' dresses and undergarments and made mockery with them. They killed family pets for no reason and laughed as the children cried. On more than one occasion, weapons taken from private homes were given to newly freed slaves. Many historians have been careful not to record much of what took place after the Union troops left, although some newly freed slaves risked their lives to stand between howling mobs of ex-slaves and their prior masters, preventing, in some cases, wholesale rape and murder. The looting and burning and pillaging grew so bad that flyers were circulated urging Southern civilians to kill any Yankee they could. Of course, that only made matters worse.

Sherman's march through Georgia helped to break the back of the Confederacy, but it also caused a deep-seated hatred of the North that would last for generations . . . and to one degree or the other, among many families, still exists to this day.

To Sherman's credit, he repeatedly stated that he wanted his men to only take what they had to seize to survive, not to loot. But his orders were routinely ignored. He could not keep an eye on eighty thousand men, not including deserters from both sides who followed the Union forces, committing even worse acts upon the civilians.

One old woman handed Jamie a handkerchief that had been tied in a knot. Jamie looked at the handkerchief; he could feel something in the knot.

"That's all we have left," the old woman told him. "Those are our wedding rings. You sell them and buy supplies and bullets and kill those damn Yankees, Colonel. You kill them for us, you hear?"

Some of Jamie's men had to turn their heads so the old people would not see the sudden tears. Jamie himself knew that he could not refuse the worn rings; to do so would be a great insult to the ladies.

He nodded his head and pocketed the rings. "I will see that they are used to fight for the South, ladies. You have my word on that."

Jamie and his men mounted up and rode out. Several miles outside of the scorched remains of the town, and its fresh graves, Jamie halted the column and gathered his officers around him.

"I want you to select the toughest and bravest men in your commands, gentlemen. I want one hundred and fifty men who will ride with me on what could very well be the last ride of their lives. If we're captured, we will be shot or hanged as spies. Impress that upon the men who volunteer. Any man who has been wounded, any man with a family who is depending upon him to return, stand to one side."

While that was being done, Jamie ordered his wiretapper to locate and hook on to the nearest telegraph line and find out what was going on, and find out in detail.

It was late afternoon before the wiretapper returned. "I think the South is finished, Colonel. Sherman has almost reached the sea, and things are going badly for us everywhere else. Hood just lost about seven thousand men at the battle of Franklin. Lee is holding on, but won't be able to for long. More and more Southerners are urging Davis for an honorable surrender."

Two weeks later, the Army of Tennessee would be finished. Hood would ask to be relieved of command, and Davis honored his request. Hood was through, and his army would never fight again.

"What do you have on your mind, Colonel?" Sergeant Major Huske asked.

"You're relieved of your duties, Louie," Jamie told the suddenly very startled sergeant major. "I want you to strip that uniform, get into civilian clothing, and go home. Get your wife and family and head west, for my valley." He handed him a small leather sack. "There is money enough for mules, wagon, and supplies."

"But, sir! I . . ."

"No arguments, Louie. Do as you're ordered. And take Little Ben with you."

"I'll be goddamned if I will!" Little Ben Pardee said, quickly adding, "Sir!"

Jamie smiled tolerantly at the much younger, much smaller man. "Ben, you're a top-notch soldier. I couldn't ask for any better. But this mission . . ."

"I'm goin' with the unit, sir," Ben said. "Sir, I got nobody. I ain't seen my sister in years. I'm not really sure she's still alive. Gibson over yonder, he's the same way. The Marauders are my family."

Jamie nodded his head. "All right, Ben. You can stay."

Many of the men had tears in their eyes as the unit began breaking up. They had been together for three years, and were as close as brothers.

Jamie gave each of the men enough money to get home and to buy some seed to plant and food for their families. He saluted each one as they rode out, then turned to face the one hundred and fifty men who had crossed the line and volunteered to stay.

"When we get up into Northern Virginia, we are going to do some midnight raiding, boys. We are going to steal some Yankee uniforms and become part of the Federal army."

The men started looking at one another and smiling.

"We are going to be soldiers just freed from a Confederate prison—men from all over the North and East—who have been given leave to spend some time with our families."

"We goin' to Pennsylvania, Colonel?" Sergeant McGuire asked.

"That's right, Mac."

"Layfield, Pennsylvania, Colonel?" Doctor Prentiss asked.

"That's right, Tom."

The men's grins changed to laughter.

"There will be no looting of buildings or homes, absolutely no raping or manhandling of women, and no harming of citizens unless they shoot at us. But we are going to burn that goddamn town to the ground until nothing is standing except the flagpole. And just before we leave we are going to hoist up the Stars and Bars, and beneath that, the battle flag of the Marauders. We're going to give the North a little taste of what the South has had to endure for years."

"Do we have anyone's permission to do this, Colonel?" Captain Dupree asked, quickly adding, "Not that I give a damn one way or the other."

"Who cares whether we do or not?" Captain Sparks blurted out.

"No," Jamie leveled with his men. "We do not have permission to do this. And to tell you the truth, if we are successful I really don't know whether it will help or hurt the South."

"Colonel," a man spoke from the ranks. "We get letters from home. We know how the war is goin'. And it ain't goin' no good at all for the South. If our boys can hang on 'til the flowers bloom, it'll be a damn miracle. So, hell, let's us give the Yankees a taste of war."

"I agree," Lieutenant Broussard said. Lieutenants Casten, Dawson, Smith, and Russell had left with the men Jamie had dismissed.

Jamie nodded and gathered up the reins. He swung into the saddle. "All right, boys. Let's go give the people who supported Colonel Layfield a taste of their own medicine."

28

As the Marauders traveled north through Virginia, they kept to the back trails, avoiding towns and remaining out of sight. Winter had begun early, and Mother Nature was just beginning her cold onslaught. For Lee's troops, that winter would literally be a killer. They were desperately short of everything except fighting spirit. They had little food, their clothing was in tatters, their blankets were rags, and many had no shoes. But still the South kept fighting as best they could on all fronts.

Jamie and his men rode on as a unit until they were forced to split up into small groups for safety's sake. Jamie grew a full beard that was mostly gray, and cut his hair short. Each man had now taken an assumed name: Jamie was Colonel Callahan.

Jamie bought a dozen wagons and pairs of fine mules. For a week they worked fitting false bottoms into the beds of the wagons. In the hidden compartments they put the Yankee uniforms they were picking up a piece at a time, and also their weapons. Then Jamie turned the wagons into ambulances, in which his "sick" men could ride in comfort during the long ride back home. They also hid the Gatling gun and the cases of ammunition in the wagons. Jamie had a hunch that when the deed was done in Layfield, they'd have some real fights on their hands getting back across the lines.

After being stopped a dozen times by Union patrols—all

within a twenty-mile stretch—Jamie finally told a rather fat and pompous major that he and his men were all suffering from TB and then coughed in the man's face. The major wired ahead with orders to let Colonel Callahan and his sick men pass, and they were not bothered again.

"You should have told him we all had leprosy," Dupree said. "That would have really given us a wide path."

"I didn't think of that," Jamie replied.

When they crossed into Pennsylvania, Jamie went over the plan one more time. After the raid, they were to ride like hell for the Allegheny Mountains and then try to make their way east to join up with Lee's command. If any were unable to do that, they were to throw their uniforms away and head for home; the war would be over for them.

Layfield was just over seventy-five miles deep into Pennsylvania and had never been touched by the war. All that was about to change.

Gettysburg lay far to the south and east of Layfield, the bloody ground and hundreds of graves silent under a fresh blanket of snow as Jamie and his men approached the town on a Saturday morning. The wagons had been abandoned the night before, the Gatling gun now drawn on a specially built caisson, made out of one of the wagons.

The Marauders had all shaved the night before and, on the morning of the raid, had dressed in their battle uniforms. About a mile from town, just before the crest of a ridge, Jamie said, "Uncase the colors."

The Stars and Bars and the battle flag of the Marauders now stood stiff in the cold breeze.

"Your mouthpiece warm, Gibson?" Jamie smiled at the young bugler.

"Yes, sir!"

Jamie twisted in the saddle and looked at Little Ben Pardee. "You ready, Ben?"

"Yes, sir!"

"Forward at a walk," Jamie ordered, and the line of men

and horses moved out, topping the ridge. "Forward at a trot!" Jamie ordered.

A man who lived on the edge of the town stepped out onto his front porch and dropped his cup of coffee at the sight before him on the road. The Confederate Stars and Bars and the Marauders' battle flag fluttered in the cold breeze. "Holy Jumpin' Jesus Christ!" he hollered.

"Sound the charge!" Jamie yelled. "Forward at a gallop."

The notes of "Charge" split the cold air, and Gibson changed to "Dixie" as the cavalrymen thundered around the wooden bridge and galloped right up the main street of Layfield, the Marauders screaming the Rebel yell.

Women fainted and grown men shit their pants as the Marauders struck the town, which was filled with people from the outlying areas for Saturday shopping.

The first shot was fired by a citizen. He missed, but the Marauder who returned the fire did not. The citizen took a bullet through the chest and died in front of Stottlemire's General Store. That ended the resistance from the citizens of Layfield.

The townspeople were quickly herded into the streets. The elderly and mothers with babies in arms were escorted to a church (after Jamie made sure the church was not where Colonel Layfield spewed his hate). All others were forced to watch as the Marauders began burning their town.

"Where is Aaron Layfield?" Jamie asked a group of badly frightened citizens.

"Out of town. Why are you doing this to us? We've done nothing to you."

Jamie stared at the man. "You've done nothing? You're either a liar or a fool, sir." He rode on.

Jamie threw a leather dispatch case on the ground in front of a man who had been pointed out as the mayor. "There, sir, are the official reports of the rape, looting, arson, torture, executions, pillaging, and plundering done by your goddamn Aaron Layfield and his Revengers. We thought you *good* citizens of the town would like just a small taste of what you supported and sent, with your blessings, to the South."

The flames were roaring like banshees as fire quickly ate the town.

Dupree rode up to a group of citizens all huddled together and smiled down at them. "Y'all have a nice day, now, you hear?"

Jamie led his men out of town, leaving behind them the Stars and Bars and the battle flag of the Marauders fluttering from atop the flagpole.

Now the chase was on.

The news of the raid spread all over the eastern half of the nation. Telegraph wires sang with reports of the daring act. But the White House remained strangely silent about the attack on Layfield. Eastern newspapers hypocritically wrote damning stories about the assault on innocent civilians, glaringly forgetting that innocent civilians in the South had been enduring much worse for several years.

Along the cold and hungry and tired battle lines of Lee's army in Virginia, men were joyous at the news, while the Union side stoically endured the taunts and cheering.

It is said that when Lee heard the news about the raid, he smiled. He would have little else to smile about the next few months.

That was the last raid for the unit known as MacCallister's Marauders. Just outside of the ruins of Layfield, Pennsylvania, Jamie split his unit up and told the men to go home. The war for them was over.

Ten of the Marauders were killed in the days following the raid. They refused to surrender and fought to the death just inside the West Virginia state line. The patrol that trapped the Marauders was led by a newly commissioned captain in Layfield's Revengers, a man named Carl Miller. Carl Miller personally slipped the noose around the neck of young Gibson, the Marauders' bugler, and hanged the badly wounded young man. Gibson went to his death whistling "Dixie."

Deep in the mountains of West Virginia, Jamie smashed the Gatling gun, rendering it useless rather than see it fall into Yankee hands.

Jamie and the ten men with him spent the month of January and part of the month of February hiding in a cave in the mountains of West Virginia, fishing, trapping, and hunting for their food.

When Kate heard about the raid against the town in Pennsylvania, she smiled. Her man would never change, and she didn't want him to—she just wanted him to come home.

Jamie was unaware that peace talks had begun between Davis and Lincoln, with Davis asking for two countries. Lincoln refused, and the war dragged on through the bitter winter months. But many on both sides had lost their zest and zeal for the battle. Desertions ran high among the ranks of the Blue and the Gray. The majority of men just wanted to get this thing over with and go home. Jamie Ian MacCallister included.

"The war is lost," he said one night in early March, sitting with a few of his men around a camp fire in Kentucky. "There is no point in any further deaths."

"Many of the men still fightin' don't have no homes to go back to, Colonel," Little Ben Pardee said. "For them, the Cause is their whole life. They've lost everything else."

The next day, on March 4, 1865, Lincoln would deliver his second inaugural address at the United States Capitol. Among the lines he spoke that day were, ". . . with malice toward none; with charity for all; with firmness in the right, as God gives us to see the right."

Pretty words, but for many citizens of the South, white and Negro alike, there would be damn little charity shown them over the next ten years.

Exactly one month and one week after his address, Richmond was abandoned by the Confederacy, and the capital moved to Danville. Lincoln entered Richmond on April 14, 1865. He had just ten days left to live.

Jamie, Ben Pardee, and Doctor Tom Prentiss were in Western Tennessee when the South officially surrendered on Palm Sunday. The war that had divided a nation was over. The toll was staggeringly high: three quarters of a million men dead, and three times that number were wounded.

For the Cause.

Jamie, Ben Pardee, and Doctor Prentiss were in Central Missouri when Lincoln was assassinated at Ford's Theater in Washington, D.C. The president had been sitting with his wife and another couple, watching a comedy on the stage below.

Jamie, Ben Pardee, and Doctor Prentiss were on the Great Plains when Lincoln was entombed in Springfield, Illinois, with his son, Willie, who had died in 1862.

On May 14, 1865, Major Falcon MacCallister and his forces fought against the troops of Major Matthew MacCallister in Texas, the last battle of the Confederacy. Both Mac-Callisters were wounded, by each other.

On May the 28, 1865, Rebel troops west of the Mississippi River officially surrendered. The war was over.

General Robert E. Lee died five years after his surrender in the home of Wilber McLean at Appomattox Court House.

General Sherman died in 1891. His old enemy, General Joe Johnston, attended the funeral and stood at attention by his casket. Fightin' Joe Johnston died a month later.

John Bell Hood died in 1879.

Nathan Bedford Forrest, who coined the phrase "Git there fustest with the mostest men," died in 1872.

General Ulysses Simpson Grant became the eighteenth president of the United States. He died in 1885.

Dozens of Confederate soldiers went back to their ravaged homes and gathered up their friends and families and began a long journey to South America, where they set up a community known as Little Dixie; it flourishes to this day, flying both the American and Confederate flags.

General "Little Phil" Sheridan became general in chief of

the United States Army. He died shortly after his retirement in 1888.

President Jefferson Davis was accused of having a part in Lincoln's assassination and was arrested in Georgia and imprisoned for several years. Four years after the assassination he was cleared of all charges and formally released. But he remained bitter over his imprisonment until the day he died, in 1889. He passed on still a proud, unrepentant, unbowed, and unreconstructed Rebel to the end.

On a warm summer's day in 1865, Jamie and his companions topped the ridge that looked down on the peaceful valleys called MacCallister's Valley.

"It's beautiful," Doctor Tom Prentiss said.

"I'm gonna rest here awhile and then move on," Little Ben Pardee said.

"You'll probably be married in six months and live here for the rest of your life," Jamie said. "Lots of girls down yonder, Ben."

"There ain't no petticoat ever been born who will ever tie me down permanent, Colonel," Little Ben said. "I got places to go and things to see and lots to do. I like to wander. I just ain't the settlin' down type."

Jamie smiled at that.

Five months later, Ben Pardee would marry one of Jamie's granddaughters.

Kate stepped out onto the porch of her house and looked up on the ridge. Indians had told her days before that Man Who Is Not Afraid was on the way home. "It's about time," she muttered, then went back into the house to put on a fresh pot of coffee and fix lunch.

"Do you want me to uncase the colors, Colonel?" Ben asked.

Jamie thought about that for a moment. "No," he finally said. "Let them forever be cased. It's time to unite the country. Let's go home."

Kate stood on the porch as her husband rode up. "Well, you look familiar," she told him. "I guess it's you. I'm surprised you remembered the way home."

"You still have a mighty sharp tongue on you, woman."

Kate ignored that. "Well, get down, old man. I have hot coffee and hot food inside."

"Is that all?" Jamie questioned, stepping out of the saddle.

"Hell, no!" Kate told him with a smile, then walked into the house.

Jamie stepped inside and closed the door behind them.

Book Three

Always do right. This will gratify some people, and astonish the rest.

—Mark Twain

29

Those who had left the valley to fight in the war were beginning to return—all those who were coming back. Igemar returned minus his left hand. It had been blown off in Tennessee. Tomas returned and told his parents where Jorge was buried. Wells and Robert were buried with several hundred others in a mass grave in South Carolina, along with their white officers.

Falcon and Matthew came riding in from Texas together, arguing and fussing about the war.

"The both of you shut up!" their brother Ian told them. "Before I whup the pair of you."

Louie Huske and his family pulled in and were made welcome by all. The old soldier promptly bought some land from Jamie and settled down to farm during the summer and opened up a small saloon to run during the fall and winter.

Little Ben Pardee immediately started sparking one of Ellen Kathleen's daughters and began changing his mind about wandering.

Doctor Tom Prentiss opened his office in Valley, Colorado, and for a time, everybody put the war behind them. All around them the Indians were going on the warpath, but never against any of those who settled in MacCallister's Valley.

Union troops visited the twin valleys several years after the war's end, and they were received warmly—much to their surprise, for they knew all about Colonel Jamie MacCallister and his Marauders—and stayed for several days. They were stationed at Fort Lyon—located on the Arkansas River, just below the mouth of the Purgatoire—and were on a scouting expedition.

"Any Indian trouble?" the major in charge asked Jamie.

"We don't have trouble with the Indians," Jamie told him. "We live with the land and those who inhabit it. There are some tribes the white man will never get along with, but with most, they're peaceful if you give them a fair chance to be."

"You sound as though you really like the Indians," the major said.

"I do," Jamie said simply.

"I have never seen so many blond-haired and blue-eyed children in one place," a young lieutenant remarked. "And adults, too, for that matter."

Kate smiled at the young man. "Most of them are our kids, grandkids, and great-grandkids."

The young officer blinked at that, for Kate, like Jamie, did not look her age. *"You* have *great-grandchildren?"* he blurted.

Jamie laughed at the expression on his face. "Son, me and Kate got married when we were both fourteen. Our oldest twins are forty years old and they married young. You figure it out."

Truth was, if pressed on the issue, Jamie could not begin to name all his grandkids and great-grandkids . . . but Kate could, of course.

The major leaned forward. "Sir, our trip here was twofold. One, we wanted to see this peaceful place in the middle of hostile territory, and two, I wanted to warn you that you have powerful and influential enemies back east."

Jamie smiled. "Major, I've had powerful enemies since I was about six years old and taken by the Shawnees. As far as my enemies back east, I can just about tell you their names: Olmstead and Layfield, to name two of them."

The major studied Jamie for a moment. "That is correct,

sir, as far as you took it. But there are others just as power-ful, or more so. Do you know a man named Newby?"

Both Kate and Jamie chuckled. "The Newbys again? Good Lord. Talk about a name from the past. Uneducated trash, the whole lot of them."

"One side of the family, yes. The other side, no. But the educated and wealthy side is much more devious and dan-gerous. Then we have the Saxons—"

Kate groaned. "Is it never going to end, Jamie?"

"Doesn't look like it, does it, Kate."

"You killed a man named Bradford down in the Big Thicket country years ago, Jamie," the major said.

"I might have. The name doesn't ring a bell."

"Some of his relatives have struck gold and silver in the Colorado mountains, and have become quite wealthy. They are also your sworn enemies. Be careful, Colonel," the major used Jamie's old military rank. "These mountains abound with men who have sworn to kill you."

"That's going to take some doing, Major."

"Yes," the major said drily. "I just imagine it will."

Matthew had taken over his old job of sheriff. Back before the war, there had been precious little to do, but since the dis-covery of gold and silver, all sorts of trash and human ver-min were flooding into the state, and Matthew found himself staying busy. Sometimes those types even made the mistake of entering MacCallister's Valley. They usually did not linger long, but as more and more people pushed west, there were those who tried to settle in the lushness of the twin valleys. Jamie sold land to a few people, but most he turned away.

Most went quietly, but a few kicked up a fuss about it. One of those who got all up in Jamie's face was a man who called himself Grover Ellis.

"You can't own the whole goddamn area, MacCallister!" Grover blustered.

"Oh, but I do," Jamie said. "Check it out. You'll find it all legal and proper."

"You can't keep me from prospectin' up yonder in the mountains, MacCallister!"

"I don't own the mountains, Ellis," Jamie told him. "Prospect all you like." Jamie pointed to one of the small peaks in the distance. "I would suggest you look there. At the base on the southwest side."

"Huh! Fat chance I'll do that. You'd have me diggin' there for the rest of my life and findin' nothin'. Hell with you, MacCallister. I'll move on, but I got kin. I got kin. And you ain't heard the last of Grover Ellis."

If Ellis had gone where Jamie had told him to go, and worked hard at it, he would have found a small vein of the yellow metal, enough for the man to live out the rest of his life in some degree of security. But instead he chose to dig on the other side of the peak, and got himself killed because of it.

Cort Woodville never returned to Ravenswood Plantation, and it was two years after the war before Anne found out what had happened to her husband. Cort had been wounded during the battle of Spotsylvania, taken prisoner, escaped, and was wounded during the escape. It was presumed he died in the timber around the Union encampment; but his body was never found, and no one really knew what happened to Cort Woodville. Bodies of hundreds of men, on both sides, were never found.

Since Anne Woodville owned bits and pieces of many factories up north, a fact that was quietly passed on to Union commanders around Richmond before it fell, Ravenswood came through the war unscathed. And while Anne was a ruthless and cunning woman, she was also a very smart woman. She doled out parcels of land to the most trusted of her slaves, and they began farming the land on shares. The South was hungry, and Ravenswood stopped growing cotton and began producing tons of vegetables to feed the hungry. Ravenswood's ex-slaves were content to own and farm land on shares, the Federal government was content with what Anne was doing, and Anne was making money hand over fist. She was probably, at the time, the richest woman in the state of Virginia.

Page Woodville had grown into a beautiful young woman, even more beautiful than her mother. She was just as intelligent as Anne, but twice as cunning and devious and dangerous . . . when she wanted to be. Page had dark hair, and dark eyes, and a figure that turned men's heads wherever she walked. But when angered, her eyes could be as cold as frozen black water.

Anne's brother, Ross, had done well enough on his own. He had married the woman he'd gotten pregnant (the daughter of a wealthy Southern family), and was the father of fine young boy the couple had named Garrison; Gar, for short. Just before the South had exploded in war, Ross fathered another child, this time a girl. On the afternoon of the birthing, Ross sat in the parlor with a loaded pistol by his side, ready to blow his brains out if the child was born with Negro features. The girl was born white, with dark hair and dark eyes; but definitely white. Ross breathed a sigh of relief and put the pistol away. The girl was named Chastity.

When the South began to fall, Ross' wife simply could not endure the thought of those horrible Yankees taking control, and she took to her bed, forbidding Ross to ever touch her again, which suited Ross just fine, since his sexual appetites certainly leaned the other way. Ross' wife succumbed to the vapors and drifted peacefully off to that great cotillion in the sky just before Lee's surrender, and Ross was left with a huge plantation and two kids to raise. Being no fool, Ross followed his sister's actions and parceled out the plantation, which met with the smiling satisfaction of the reconstructionists (Ross eventually bought back all the property from the ex-slaves, as did his sister), and began producing vegetables to feed the South.

"What a joke," Ross said to his sister one afternoon as the two of them were having lemonade on the porch of Ravenswood. "Two half-breeds running the two largest and most profitable plantations in the whole damn state. God certainly must have a sense of humor."

Anne glared at him, but said nothing. She sighed as Ross said, "What about that field hand you whelped, sister? Do you have any idea what became of him?"

"Yes," she replied, startling her brother. "It took some doing, but I did it, with a lot of very discreet help. His name is Ben Franklin Washington and he lives in Boston. He graduated from a fine college and is now a writer for a newspaper. He's doing quite well, but has learned, somehow, that the family that raised him was not his own. He's beginning to make inquiries."

"What can come of it? Georgia Washington is dead. Selma and Tyrone are both gone; outside of us, they're the only ones who know the truth. Cort was killed in the war. What can come of his inquiries?"

"I don't think Cort is dead. I never felt that he was dead. He's out there." She waved a hand. "Somewhere."

Ross was silent for a moment. After a huge sigh, he said, "I never thought he was dead, either, sis. Cort was more of a man than either one of us thought. I think he survived the war and headed west, to start all over. To put all this behind him. And I sure as hell don't blame him."

"His holdings were quietly liquidated," Anne said. "I went to his attorney just a few months ago and tried to find out something, anything. He told me it was a closed book; Cort was dead. I didn't believe him. I didn't like the way he smiled. He was smug. He was lying." She looked at her brother. "You haven't been out here in a long time, Ross. Why did you choose this day to come visiting?"

"You are aware that Page has been seeing a young man from the university?"

"I heard. So?"

"He's a fine young man."

"I've made inquiries and discovered that. You think I would let my daughter see anyone who wasn't a proper gentleman?"

Ross smiled and Anne braced herself. Her brother had a wicked sense of humor. "Do you know his name, Anne?"

"His name is James William Haywood. I'm going to meet him this weekend. There will be a gala here at Ravenswood. You're not invited."

Ross chuckled. "I'm told the young couple appear to be very serious about each other. And they do make a lovely couple. So I'm told." Ross laughed out loud.

Anne glared at her brother. "Page kept it a secret from me for months. I don't know why. She's . . . devious about things like that."

"Sneaky is a better word for it, and she certainly comes by it naturally."

"You're a fine one to talk about being sneaky." She sighed. "Will you, for God's sake, get to the point of all this, Ross? You're beginning to bore me."

"A Western young man, I'm told, Anne."

"Yes. From Colorado." Anne froze in the lifting of the glass to her lips. "Oh, *shit!*" The word exploded from her mouth.

Ross smiled. "He's quite the handsome man, I'm told. Tall and muscular, with blond hair and blue eyes. Not my type at all. Much too virile for my tastes. He'd be rough, I'm afraid."

"You miserable son of a bitch!" Anne cussed him.

"You sure have that right," Ross said with a laugh.

"Say it all, Ross. You know much more than you're telling."

"Of course, I do, sister dear. And you'd better put a stop to this romance right now. The young man courting your daughter, my quarter-breed niece, is the grandson of Jamie Ian Mac-Callister."

30

"Falcon is bringing that Indian girl to supper Saturday night," Kate told Jamie.

"Do I detect a note of disapproval?" Jamie asked, looking up from the newspaper.

"Oh, no! Jamie! You know better than that. I ought to slap you for even thinking that of me." Kate removed her reading glasses and gave her husband a very dirty look.

Jamie smiled and tickled her ribs with a blunt finger. She slapped his hand away. "Son marry Cheyenne princess," Jamie said. "Have heap many papooses."

"You are disgusting!" Kate said, moving her chair away from his. They were sitting on the front porch enjoying the warmth of early spring in the valley.

"Besides, she's only half-Indian," Jamie said. "Her father was French. Marie Big Wind."

"Gentle Breeze!" Kate said with a giggle.

"Well, that's not quite it either, but close. She's a beautiful girl."

"Yes, she is. And I'm happy for Falcon."

Spring, 1869. Kate and Jamie were in their late fifties, and their ages were beginning to show, although neither of them looked as old as they were.

"Has anyone heard from James William?" Jamie asked. "That boy sure doesn't like to take pen in hand and write home."

"Ellen got some letters posted to her this morning. I'm sure one of them was from James. There she is now, coming up the way."

Down the street, Ellen waved an envelope at her parents.

"She heard from him," Jamie said. "Kate? How old is Ellen Kathleen?"

"She and Jamie Ian were born in 1827. She'll be forty-three this summer."

"Forty-three," Jamie spoke the words softly. "It doesn't seem possible. Kate, we're *old!*"

She moved her chair closer to him and patted him on the arm. "We certainly didn't behave as old folks last night, dear," she reminded him.

Jamie grunted.

"You can still work younger men into the ground, Jamie. I think we have a few good years left us."

Ellen Kathleen climbed the steps to the house and sat down in a chair beside her mother.

"Heard from James William, did you, dear?" Kate asked.

"He's got himself a girl, Ma. Sounds serious to me." She handed her mother the letter.

Kate began silently reading the letter.

"Am I supposed to read your mind?" Jamie asked. "Read it aloud."

"Hush," Kate told him, thoroughly engrossed in the letter from Virginia.

"I'll get you a cup of coffee, Pa," Ellen said.

"That would be nice. Your ma and I are gettin' on in years. Especially your ma." That got no response from Kate. "It's nice to have someone wait on us from time to time." He jerked a thumb at Kate. "The old woman here is gettin' down in the back. I'm goin' to have to get her a cane, I reckon."

Ellen gave her father a very queer look and, with a shake of her head, walked into the house for coffee.

"Old woman, you mind telling me what that damn letter says?" Jamie asked.

"Don't curse in front of the children," Kate said, not lifting her eyes from the letter.

Jamie looked around for children. "What children?"

"Ellen Kathleen."

"Ellen! Hell, woman, she's a *grandmother!"*

Kate reread the letter while Jamie sipped his cup of coffee, Ellen reading over her mother's shoulder.

"It sure is nice to be so well-informed," Jamie groused. "I'll be practically a well of information after this morning."

"Then go do it," Kate said, without looking up. "But don't overdo it."

Jamie blinked. "Do what?"

Kate looked up. "You just said you had to dig a well, didn't you?"

Jamie's tongue started to get sharp until he noticed the twinkle in Kate's eyes and realized she'd been funning him all along. "Very funny," Jamie said. "Very funny."

"James has him a girl and he's in love," Kate told him.

"In heat, more than likely," Jamie said.

Kate frowned and Ellen Kathleen giggled.

"They want to get married," Kate added.

"He's too damn young. Besides, he's got his education to finish."

"He's nineteen years old, Jamie," Kate said. "And he's been out there in Virginia two years. We were fourteen, remember?"

"That's different. It was a different time, different circumstances. Tell him he can't get married, Ellen. You and Bill forbid it."

"Pa, telling a MacCallister they can't do something is like tossing grease on a fire. You know that."

Jamie handed her his empty cup. "Get me some more coffee, girl. Your ma and I have to talk."

"Yes, Pa. I guess when you get feeble it's nice to have a lot of kids around to wait on you."

"What?" Kate asked.

"He said the both of you were getting on in years. You especially, Ma. He said you were broke down in the back. Said you wanted him to get you a cane."

"Oh, did he now?"

"Well, now, that's not exactly what I said," Jamie vocally backed up.

"I think it's time for you and I to have a little chat, Jamie Ian MacCallister," Kate said, her eyes flashing.

"I think it's time for me to go home!" Ellen said, handing her mother the coffee cup and exiting the scene.

Jamie chuckled. "What else did the letter say, Kate?"

"Yes, I'd best read it to you, since you've reached such an advanced age your eyesight is failing you."

Jamie had the eyes of an eagle.

Kate laughed at the retreating figure of Ellen. "Our kids still move along smartly when they think you and I are going to fuss, don't they?"

"That they do. Tell me about this girl that James William is in love with."

"Well, she's from an old Virginia family and is beautiful."

"What part of Virginia?"

"Around Richmond."

"Kate, does she have a name?"

"Yes." Kate opened the letter. "Ah, Page."

Jamie sat very still for a moment. "Last name, Kate?" he asked softly.

She cut her eyes to him. "What's wrong, Jamie."

"Last name, Kate?"

"Woodville."

"Kate, I think we'd better go inside and have us a little talk."

"Listen to me, you little fool!" Anne shouted at her daughter. "This boy is not right for you."

"Why, Mother?" Page returned the shout.

"Because I know, that's why. I'm your mother. I know what is best for you, and James is not the right boy."

"Name one thing that is wrong with him. I challenge you to name just one thing, Mother."

"I forbid you to see this boy!" Anne screamed at her daughter.

"Go to hell!" Page said, and started to walk out of the room.

Anne grabbed her by the arm and spun her around. Page broke free and shoved her mother. "Don't manhandle me, Mother! I won't stand for it."

"Page, for God's sake, listen to me. I—" Anne cut her eyes as her brother entered the room to lean insolently against the arch, that sarcastic smile on his lips. "What the hell do you want, Ross?"

"Why, I just came for a visit, sister. Did I arrive at a bad time?"

Page looked at her mother, then at her uncle. She could never understand why her mother did not get along with her brother. True, Uncle Ross was a fop, but everybody knew that. "You tell her, Uncle Ross," Page said. "Tell her that James is a nice young man. You've met him. You know."

"He's a nice young man, Page," Ross agreed. "But he's not the young man for you."

"Oohhh!" Page threw her hands into the air.

"Tell her, Anne," Ross urged. "Tell her. She's got a right to know. She has to know. Tell her."

"Shut your goddamn mouth!" Anne screamed at her brother.

"Tell me what?" Page asked, looking first at her mother, then at her uncle.

"Nothing, dear. Nothing at all." Anne faced her brother. "Get out of this house, Ross. Get out, and don't ever come back. Do you understand that?"

"Perfectly. Well, as they say in merry ol' England, ta-ta, all." Ross walked out of the great mansion.

"Tell me *what?*" Page shouted.

"I have no idea what your uncle was babbling about, Page."

Anne willed herself to calm down. "He'd been drinking. Couldn't you smell the brandy? The fool is going to fall off his horse someday and break his neck."

Page narrowed her eyes. "What is going on, Mother? And don't lie to me. Something is very wrong. I've known it for years. Mother, I am a grown woman. Papa left me a lot of money and holdings. I am a very rich young grown woman. I can do what I damn well please, and I damn well please to marry James Haywood. With or without your blessings. Now that all that is settled, tell me this . . . secret that you and Uncle Ross share."

Anne shook her head. "There is no secret, dear. You're imagining things. . . . All right, Page. All right. Let's don't you and I quarrel anymore. Page, what do you know of this young man's family?"

"Mother! His grandfather is Colonel MacCallister! The famous war hero. The MacCallisters practically settled Colorado all by themselves. They own hundreds of miles of it. They have cattle ranches and sheep ranches and towns and mining and . . . God, who knows what else? James is a little rough around the edges, but he's a gentleman through and through. I simply cannot understand what you have against him."

Anne was thinking fast. She knew only too well how impulsive the young could be. She had to say this right, and do it right the first time. "I have nothing against the young man, Page. Nothing at all. James William is a fine young man. But from what you've told me he comes from a very large family, and you must remember what Doctor Benson told you."

Anne had bribed, and used a bit of blackmail, to force a local doctor—who was quite fond of young Negro girls—to impress upon Page that she must never have children; the labor would kill her.

"I know what Doctor Benson said, and I know what three other doctors in Charlottesville told me. There is nothing wrong with me, Mother. All three have told me I can have as many babies as I like. To repeat what one told me: 'Miss Woodville, you are built for having babies.' "

Anne sat down in the closest chair and grabbed up a fan and started pumping. She felt flushed.

"What's the matter with you, Mother?" Page asked. "Are you ill?"

"I . . . ah . . . no! No. I'm fine. I just felt flushed, that's all. Page . . . ah . . . don't have children, Page. For your own sake, don't. I won't mention it again. But don't have children."

"Why, Mother? Why? Just tell me why I should not have children."

"Because . . . well, this is difficult for me to express. Page, darling, idiocy runs, ah, well, *dark* in our family."

"Idiocy, Mother?"

"Yes. We have some real monsters confined to asylums around the country. Or I should say *had.* They're all dead. But one." Anne's mind was humming now; she had the beat and wasn't about to stop singing the song.

"But, Mother. I am perfectly normal!"

"Your brother isn't." Anne kept piling one lie on top of another.

"My brother?"

"Yes. You have a brother. He's confined to an institution in New York State. He receives the very best of care; you know I would not stint on that. But there is no cure. He's a monster. Page, darling, you must never repeat any of what I just told you. That's what your Uncle Ross was trying to get me to tell you. Oh . . . I'm so ashamed, Page." She put her face in her hands and wept, a great actress playing a role.

Page came over and knelt down beside her mother, taking her hands into her own. "I never suspected, Mother. I swear I didn't. I thought you were just trying to run my life. I apologize for thinking harshly of you."

"Swear to me you won't have children, Page!" Anne lifted her tear-stained face to her daughter. "You've got to swear you won't. It's for your sake and the happiness of you and James William."

"Mother! You mean . . . we have your blessings?"

"Swear it, Page, and I'll give you the finest wedding Virginia has ever seen."

"Oh, I swear it, Mother. On the family Bible, I do swear it!"

That family Bible is full of lies, dear. I know. I put them there. "Then you and James William have my blessings. Page, you must never let on to your uncle that you know. Remember, it's common knowledge that he does have a loose tongue."

"Yes. I know that, Mother. It will be our secret. But . . ." The young woman frowned.

"James?"

"Yes."

"You . . . trust this young man, Page?"

"Yes, Mother. With all my heart."

"Is he strong enough to stand the truth?"

"I think so. Yes. Certainly."

"Then . . ." She sighed, once again thinking fast. "Let me tell him, Page. Let me soften the blow for you young people. I can scatter a few rose petals on the path before I tell him the bitter truth."

"Mother, you are the greatest mother in all the world. Would you do that for me."

"Darling Page, I would do *anything* for you. Just anything at all." Anything at all to keep you from birthing some goddamn nappy-headed pickaninny and ruining everything for me, everything that I schemed and fought for, you spoiled, pampered, hard-headed rotten little bitch!

"Page . . . ?"

"Yes, Mommy?"

"Have you ever given any thought to living in Colorado?"

"Why . . . yes. As a matter of fact, James and I have discussed it. Would you mind terribly?"

"Well, of course I would miss you, dear." About as much as a toothache. "But I think a proper lady must go where her husband wishes. Oh, Page, it would be a grand adventure for you."

"Oh, Mommy! James will be thrilled!"

Not nearly as much as I will. Anne smiled sweetly at her daughter.

31

Kate sat in her chair in the living room of the home in shocked silence for a few moments. Jamie got up and went to the kitchen, stoking up the stove, and putting on fresh water for coffee. Then he stood in the doorway for a moment, looking at his wife.

"Maybe there is some mistake," Kate finally said. "Surely there is more than one family named Woodville in the Richmond area?"

"With a daughter named Page, who has black hair and black eyes and whose mother is named Anne, who lives on a plantation called Ravenswood?"

"You're right, of course," Kate said. "Well! This is somewhat of a problem. Not the fact that he is planning to marry a young lady with some Negro blood in her veins; but does he know about the girl's lineage?"

"Not likely, Kate. It's very doubtful the girl knows."

"So what do we do about it?"

Jamie shrugged his heavy shoulders. "Nothing. What can we do?"

Kate stood up and walked to a window, looking out toward the cemetery, her eyes on the graves of Moses and Liza. The Negro couple had been very nearly middle-aged when Kate and Jamie had first met them, back in the Big Thicket country of East Texas. They had lived a good long life. Liza had died within a few weeks of her husband. Their children, Jed and Sally, still lived and worked in the valley; they were both grandparents.

"Moses would have known what to do," Kate said. "I miss them both."

Jamie came to stand beside his wife, his gaze following his wife's eyes. Titus had died while Jamie was off in the war, but he had been buried Indian fashion, high up in the mountains. His widow, Moon Woman, and their children had gone back to their tribe. Jamie had not seen any of them in years. After Robert's death, his widow had taken their children, all of whom were grown, and vanished without a trace.

"Jed and Sally have no idea what happened to Anne and Roscoe," Jamie said. "The past is dead and, in most cases, buried. All we can do is hope for the best for James William and Page."

"What are the chances of her delivering . . . well, you know?"

"I don't know, Kate. I'd say very slim. But I'm no doctor."

Jamie and Kate fixed their coffee and returned to their chairs on the front porch.

Jamie looked up the street and spotted a cotton-headed little boy running barefoot toward the house. He knew it was one of his grandsons or great-grandsons, but damned if he could remember which son or daughter or grandson or granddaughter the boy belonged to. Kate would know, but he wasn't about to ask her; every time he did she got a big laugh out of it and made some sarcastic comment about his failing memory. Jamie knew his memory was just as good as it was twenty years back; it was just that women seemed to have a knack for remembering birth dates and names and the like.

"Grandpa!" the boy hollered. "Men's a comin'. Two of them. Pa says it's somebody called Preacher."

"Well, I'll be damned!" Jamie said. He had not seen Preacher since before the war.

Preacher looked like death warmed over; but Jamie knew that the man's looks were very deceptive. Preacher was still a very dangerous and very quick man on the shoot or with a knife. Jamie cut his eyes to the young man riding with the famed mountain man. A gun-slick if Jamie had ever seen one. Young, too. Maybe twenty at the most. Wore two guns, one of them butt forward and high up on his left side.

"Howdy, you old reprobate!" Jamie called to Preacher. "Light and sit."

"Howdy, there, Colonel!" Preacher hollered. "Miss Kate. You still puttin' up with this mangy, beat-up ol' coot?"

"I've sort of gotten used to him after forty-five years," Kate replied, as Preacher and the young man swung down from their saddles.

"This here is my pard," Preacher said. "He ain't dry behind the ears yet, but he's a good boy. He'll do to ride the river with. Name's Jensen. I call him Smoke."

"You hungry?" Kate asked.

"Ain't I always. But me and your man got to palaver first. Then we'll eat. Let's us take a walk, Bear Killer. Smoke, you hep Miss Kate."

Falcon rode up, and he and Jensen sized each other up very quickly. Both had the stamp of gunfighter on them. Falcon was a good eight or ten years older than young Jensen. Kate introduced them.

"Howdy," Falcon said.

"Howdy," Jensen said.

"Heard of you," Falcon said.

"Heard of you," Jensen said.

"So far that's the most borin' conversation I ever did hear," Preacher remarked. "Give 'em a year or two and they might say somethin' worth hearin'. Come on, ol' hoss. We got to talk."

On the way to Louie's saloon, Preacher said, "Do you recall a run-in you had with some damned Easterner name of Grover Ellis?"

Jamie thought about that. "Yes. I remember him. Slightly. But it wasn't much of a run-in. I told him to git and he got. Why?"

"Well, he got all right. What he got was kilt over yonder

on the west side of Bearpaw. But he lived long enough to tell one of his boys that it was you who done him in and then lifted his poke."

"That's nonsense, Preacher!"

"Oh, I know that. But Ellis come from West Virginee—feudin' and fussin' and fightin' folks. He's got a whole passel of kin on the way out here to avenge him."

"Damn!" Jamie said. "How much time do I have?"

"Oh, couple of weeks, I reckon. Maybe three. They was provisionin' up at Fort Dodge last week and a pard of mine heared them talkin'. He rode hard to git to my camp with the news. Me and Smoke yonder come over this way to hep out."

"How many men in the group?"

"Not many—twenty-five or thirty, is all. You take five or six. I'll take five or six. Smoke'll take five or six. And Falcon can have the rest. There won't be much to it."

Jamie laughed at that. "Preacher, I don't know whether you've noticed this or not, but, ol' hoss, we're not as young as we used to be."

"I have noticed that I ain't quite as spry as I used to be, Bear Killer. Howsomever, Smoke'll take up the slack for me, and Falcon can take up the slack for you—I got it all figured out. What we'll do is just ambush 'em over near Well's Crick and just blow 'em out of their goddamn saddles. Leave 'em for the buzzards."

Jamie had to chuckle at Preacher's words. In the vernacular of the West, Preacher was a very bad man to fool with. And Jamie had heard of Smoke Jensen. The young man was supposed to be the fastest gun west of the Mississippi River.

They entered Louie's saloon, and Jamie spoke to one of Louie's boys, who was tending to the bar. Louie's wife ran the little eating place that was partitioned off, in case the bar talk got rough, which it seldom did.

"Whiskey for me, boy," Preacher said. "And a beer for the colonel."

Taking chairs at a table, Jamie asked, "Where is Audie and his partner?"

"Lobo? Well, Lobo is probably still holed up in a cave like a damn bear, and Audie done got hisself a whole crate of books. The collected works of Shakespeare, I think they is. He's been readin' to them goddamn heathen Blackfeet all winter. I stayed for about a week, but me and them Blackfeet just don't gee-haw. But they like Audie. They 'bout half skirred of the little bastard; think he's a god of some sort. 'Sides, 'bout a week of him forsooken and harkin' and lo yon maiden in the medder and the like was all I could take. That Shakespeare feller was a strange one, you ask me."

Jamie grinned at the mountain man. Preacher was probably in his late sixties or early seventies, still spry and as full of crap as he ever was. "Where'd you hook up with young Jensen?"

"Kansas. Him and his pa was headin' west. His pa had bad lungs. I kinda took to the lad. Say! I forgot. They was a feller askin' 'bout you last year up north of here in one of them fly-by-night minin' towns. He never did mention his name, but he was a regular gentleman, he was. All of us could tell it. Soft-spoken and all. Said he knowed you durin' the war. He's got him a place up to Goldtown."

"I know where that is. What else did this fellow say?"

"Said he first seen you sitting under a tree by the side of the road readin' a newspaper. Somebody in the place called him Cord, I think."

"Cord could be Cort," Jamie said. "I thought he was dead."

"Well, he ain't. And he's lightnin' fast with them guns of hisn. He's a gambler, and a damn good one, too. I think he's kinda funny—if you know what I mean—but he shore ain't no man to mess with. I think he's a man ridin' a panther, ol' hoss. He's on the prod with a hair-trigger temper and the gun skill to back it all up. He drinks a lot, and when he drinks, he's twicest as dangerous."

"Do me a favor, Preacher?"

"All you got to do is ask."

"You and Jensen stay here and help protect the town against

Ellis' kin, should they come here after me. It's very important that I see this Cord person."

"Consider it done, Bear Killer."

"You think this Cord person is Anne's husband?" Kate asked, as Jamie was putting together a few things.

"Yes. And he needs to know what is happening. Not that he can do anything about it, but as the girl's father, he has a right to know."

"You be careful, Jamie. Discounting Ellis, there are still a lot of people out there who would like to make a reputation by killing you."

Jamie smiled at her. "I'm like an old wolf, honey. What I've lost in spryness I've gained in deviousness. I'll be back."

Jamie saddled up one of Horse's distant offspring and rode out. Lightning was a dusty color, with a jagged white streak running down from the top of his head to near his nose, hence his name. If anything, Lightning was meaner than Horse and a hand or two taller. Lightning had the disposition of an angry puma around anyone other than Jamie; but with Jamie, he was as gentle as a pup.

Lightning started to bow his back when Jamie swung into the saddle. "Don't," Jamie said, and the monster horse settled right down.

"Stay close," Preacher told Smoke. "I'll be circlin' around up in the high country. And stay shut of these fillies," he added with a grin. "I seen 'em swishin' around and battin' their eyes at you."

Falcon and Smoke hit it off about as well as two lone wolves, but each respected the other's prowess with a pistol so they were at least civil with each other.

"Be a weddin' here this summer," Falcon told Smoke. "I'm gettin' hitched. If you're around, you're invited."

"Thank you," Smoke said.

"Think nothin' of it."

With that, Falcon went to one end of the town and Smoke went to the other.

Kate was amused at the antics of the two, but said nothing.

"Like two roosters struttin' around," Preacher said. "They'll be friends 'fore long. But for now, they're just circlin' one another."

Goldtown was a good four days' ride from MacCallister's Valley. Before Jamie entered the boom town, he circled it, stopping often to dismount and look it over through field glasses. On his second day of observation from high up, Jamie spotted Cort Woodville. The man was leaning up against a porch support post in front of a saloon, smoking a cheroot. He was neatly dressed in a pale gray Confederate cavalryman's hat—complete with gold braid—black suit, fancy vest, with white shirt and string tie. He wore two guns, tied down low. Cort had lost all signs of innocence in his face. Even from afar, Jamie could see that the man's expression was hard and unyielding.

Jamie entered the boom town from the rear, stabling his horse at the edge of town. Carrying his rifle, bed roll, and saddlebags, Jamie checked into the town's best hotel (which was quite fancy for the time) and cleaned up, ordering a hot bath and sending his boots down to have them blacked. He carefully shaved and dressed in a dark suit, then went out to eat. It was late afternoon when he pushed open the batwings to the Golden Rooster saloon and walked to the bar.

Many of the men in the place knew who he was and tensed, for it had been a few years since Jamie had strayed from his valley, and they all wondered what was up. Although Jamie was no longer anywhere near a young man, he still carried himself erect, and anyone with a knowing eye could see that he was still powerful and not a man to trifle with. Those big Colts tied down low were a dead giveaway.

But there were those in the place who did not know Jamie Ian MacCallister—men recently arrived from the East, men who still carried grudges spawned from the Civil War—and they took umbrage at the pale gray Confederate cavalryman's hat Jamie had carefully brought with him, packed in a leather case.

Across the room, sitting by himself at a table, his back to a wall and playing solitaire, Cort Woodville smiled when Jamie strolled in. The smile was more than just seeing a trusted old friend, but at the hat Jamie wore. Things could get very interesting very quickly, Cort thought.

"Whiskey," Jamie ordered, then turned to face the crowd, the glass held in his left hand.

Jamie's hair was nearly all gray now, and the lines in his tanned and rugged face had deepened.

"Another goddamn Johnny Reb." A man spat the words out, contempt dripping from his mouth.

"Yeah," another said. "And an old bastard at that. Hey, gramps! You bes' be gettin' on back to your rockin' chair 'fore someone snatches that traitor hat offen your old head and makes you eat it."

Cort smiled and laid the deck of cards aside, both hands dropping beneath the table and loosening the thongs to his six-guns. He had seen when Jamie walked in that his guns were loose in their holsters.

Jamie's eyes were as cold as an icy mountain stream. He looked at the loudmouth and said, "If you must bray like a jackass, go down to the corral and do it."

The man flushed, cursed, and pushed back his chair, standing up. "I don't have to take that kind of talk from any goddamn Johnny Reb."

The bartender, a man from the East and new to the West, whispered, "Mister, that's Jimmy Johns. He's a bad one to mess with. You best back off."

Jamie ignored the bartender and kept his eyes on the loudmouth. "You're still braying like a jackass. I thought I asked you to leave."

Men began quickly getting out of the way, out of the line of fire.

The loudmouth's hands were poised over the butts of his

guns. "You want to make your play, Johnny Reb?" He threw out the challenge.

"That's Jamie Ian MacCallister, Jimmy," a man spoke quietly from the crowd. "Sit down and shut up."

Jimmy Johns' face paled, then flushed as sweat broke out on his forehead. Jamie left the bar and walked toward the man, the glass of whiskey still in his left hand.

"Don't come no closer, MacCallister!" Jimmy hollered. "Don't make me kill you."

Jamie kept walking toward him.

"I got a sack of high grade dust says Jimmy will never clear leather," a miner spoke up.

No one took the bet.

"You're an old man, MacCallister!" Jimmy cried. "I can beat you. I can. Don't make me do it."

Jamie continued closing the distance between them.

"I got friends in here!" Jimmy said, his voice breaking. "I got pards behind you, MacCallister."

"I'll take care of them," Cort said conversationally. "Don't worry about your back, Colonel."

Several men cussed in low tones. If the man called Cord got into this game, the lead was going to fly and no one in the place would be safe.

"Your play, tinhorn," Jamie said, his words dripping with sarcasm. The old recklessness had taken hold of Jamie, and he knew he was crowding the loudmouth. He also knew he was behaving foolishly, but he didn't care. Too many good men on both sides had died in that bloody conflict called the Civil War for any man to sneer at the beliefs of the other side.

"Do it, you bastard!" Jamie said. "Or tuck your tail between your legs and slink on out of here."

The loudmouth's shoulders sagged. "I'm done, Mister MacCallister. I'm leavin'. But I was just funnin' with you." He began backing up, then moving toward the batwings. He backed out onto the rough boardwalk, and the night swallowed him.

"Well, that's over," a man said.

"Not yet," Jamie said.

"What do you mean?" another miner asked.

Cort was smiling.

"Just wait a moment. You'll see."

Several men who had been long in the West added their smiles. They knew what Jamie meant, and why he was still standing facing the batwings, his coat swept back, his guns ready.

Cort shuffled the cards and began laying out a hand of solitaire.

The batwings flew open, and the loudmouth stood there, his hands poised over the butts of his guns. "No goddamn Southern trash talks down to me. Fill your hand, MacCallister!"

"After you," Jamie said calmly.

Jimmy Johns grabbed for his guns, and Jamie shot him twice in the chest. Jamie was not as fast as he once was; but he was still better than most, and more important, he made his first shot count. The challenger stumbled backward and fell to the floor. His bootheels drummed out a death song, and then he was still.

Jamie holstered his .44. "Now it's over," he said, and walked to Cort's table and sat down.

He had not spilled a drop of whiskey from the shot glass.

32

"My dear friend," Cort said. "Please sit down and tell me all about what you've been doing since our magnificent sacrifices for the Southern Cause and our ignoble surrender."

Jamie sat down and smiled at the man. "I'm glad to see you have not lost your wit or the sharp edge to your tongue, Cord."

"Ah, so that disreputable old mountain man did find you."

"Preacher. Yes. We have to talk, Cord."

"You sound serious, Colonel."

"I am. Page and my grandson, James William, are planning to be married. And I know the truth, Cord. All of it."

"You want to explain that, Colonel?"

Jamie did. In full. Starting in the Big Thicket country of Texas and stopping when Roscoe and Anne slipped out of the valley in Colorado.

Cort was silent during the telling. "That must have been quite a shock for both you and Anne when we suddenly appeared at Ravenswood back in '61."

"It took me aback some, I will have to admit. I did some acting of my own."

"Ross told me some of it, but now you have filled in the gaps."

"I'm sorry."

"No need to be. I'm happier now than I have ever been. I have found my place in the scheme of things. But this marriage. Oh, Lord, those two kids."

"That's all I'm thinking of, Cort. Not that Page is a quarter-breed. I don't give a damn about that. MacCallisters have married Mexicans and Indians. My youngest boy, Falcon, is about to marry a Cheyenne princess."

"You are far more broad-minded than I was, Colonel. And I stress *was.*"

"The war matured a lot of men, Cord."

Cort nodded his head and then lapsed into a long silence. The men in the saloon left them alone, moving tables and chairs far away, and even their talk had ceased its boisterousness. "No," Cort finally spoke. "The marriage cannot be allowed, Colonel. Not unless both of them know the truth, and so far as I know, Page does not know."

"My wife, Kate, put it this way: Do we have the right to stand between them and happiness?"

Again, Cort was silent for a time. "No. No, of course not. It is not my intention to do that." Cort lifted his eyes to meet Jamie's, a smile on his lips. "What are we both saying? These kids are a thousand miles away. It probably took a month and a half for the letter to reach you. They might well be married by now."

"Yes. And if that is the case, what do we do, if anything?"

"Ah, Lord, I don't know."

"Page's brother?"

"You do know it all, don't you?"

"Yes."

"I lost track of him just before the war. Then, after I, ah, died, so to speak, I put the Pinkertons on the case and found him. He's a college graduate and working on a newspaper in Boston. I heard he was getting curious about his parents and starting to make inquiries."

"That could bring Anne's world crumbling down around her."

"Yes. Very quickly."

"We need to get the kids out here before that happens, if it happens."

"Your grandson was studying . . . what?"

"He was going to read the law and then settle around Denver. It's a growing town."

"So is MacCallister's Valley," Cort pointed out.

"I thought of that, as well. Will you ever return to Virginia, Cord?"

The man shook his head. "No. I have liquidated all my holdings and severed all ties. There is nothing left for me there." He smiled. "And before you make the offer, no, I will not settle in your valley, Colonel. After you leave this dismal hole in the road called a town, you will probably never see me again. For I intend to fall off the face of the earth and never appear again."

"That's sort of drastic, isn't it?"

"It sounds much more ominous than it really is, Colonel. I have more than ample funds to live out my life quite comfortably. I have this little spot all picked out. Where, is my secret. I left Page quite the wealthy young woman, so she is well taken care of. I left Ben Franklin Washington money. So I think my obligations to my children have been fulfilled."

"It would seem so."

Cort picked up the deck of cards and began shuffling them. "I understand you have a gang of hoodlums pursuing you."

"So I hear."

He dealt hands and was deft at it. Very deft. "You don't appear to be overly worried about it."

"Men have been trying to kill me for over fifty years, Cord. I'm still around."

"Yes, well . . . I assume, then, that we are going to allow our children, my child, your grandchild, to forge their own destinies without parental interference?"

"I suppose so."

"Thank you for the long ride to inform me of the events, Colonel. I guess all we can do is wish them well and hope for the best."

"That's about it." Jamie held out his hand and Cort shook it. "Good luck to you, Cord."

"The best of all things to you, Colonel."

Jamie pushed back his chair and walked out of the saloon. The body of the loudmouth had been dragged off the board-walk and the blood mopped up. Jamie wasn't sure exactly what this long ride had accomplished, but he felt it was some-thing he had to do. He'd provision up come the morning and then ride south and some east. With any kind of luck at all, he'd intercept Grover Ellis' kin and bring another boil to a head. But he'd be doing the squeezing.

The wedding was held on the last Sunday in May at Ravenswood. Ross was in attendance with his two children—naturally, it would not seem right for him to be left out, so Chastity was a flower girl. The couple was going to honey-moon abroad and then settle out west. Anne was deliberately vague about just where that might be. She just wanted the damn wedding over with and the kids gone. The detective agency she used had told her that another detective had been prowling around, asking a lot of questions about Anne and Ravenswood. The detective was home-based in Boston. Anne didn't need a college professor to tell her what that meant. Ben Franklin Washington was on the hunt—and closing fast.

After the party was over, the kids gone and the guests de-parted, Anne sat with Ross on the porch, in the dark, and told him what she had learned. For once, they both were civil with each other.

"Goddamnit, Ross," she finally let her anger loose. "I've provided for the boy and so has his father. He's wealthy in his own right. Why in the hell can't he just leave well enough alone?"

"Why, darlin'," Ross mush-mouthed. "I 'spect the boy wants to see his mammy."

Anne sighed at her brother's dark humor but did not lose her temper—with him. Her anger was directed at her child, a son she had not laid eyes on in more than two decades.

"There is a way," Ross said, all sarcasm gone from his voice.

"I'd like to hear it."

"Kill the detective and the boy."

She cut her dark eyes to her brother. "Are you out of your goddamn mind?"

"It can be easily arranged."

"You're talking about my son!"

"I'm talking about our future and the future of your daughter. If your son is allowed to blow the lid off of our little charade, it's over for the both of us. Oh, we'll still have money. But no position. No standing in the community. We'll be half-breeds and treated as such. You think about that, Anne."

"You know that Cort is still alive. He will know."

"Cort, who goes by the name of Cord Woodson, is a gambler and gunfighter out in the Wild West. He is also an alcoholic who is drinking himself to death. He will eventually die from the bottle or the bullet. But we can take care of him as well. And then no one will know."

Anne got up to pace the porch of the mansion. She whirled to face her brother. "I have never done anything like—"

"Oh, shut up!" Ross flared at her. "Back during our touring days, you poisoned at least three men that I know of for what was in their purse. You stabbed another man to death backstage in St. Louis. Are you forgetting that I helped drag the body out and dump it in the Mississippi River? Don't go all moral and righteous on me now, sister dear. You really don't play the part well at all."

Anne walked to the far side of the porch to stand staring out at the darkness. "I really don't know the boy," she finally said.

"That's my sister of old," Ross said. "Now you're back in character."

"I haven't said yes, yet, Ross."

"But you will. There is no other way. Well, we could have him knocked on the head and shanghaied on board ship down on the coast, but that would only delay the inevitable."

From the darkness she said, "You really are rotten to the core, aren't you, Ross."

He sat quietly for a moment. She could hear his breathing. "You believe in heaven and hell, sister?" he finally spoke.

"No." Her reply was cold. "I think living is hell."

"So if there is no punishment after life, what difference does it make how we conduct ourselves while on this earth?"

Anne came to sit by her brother's side. "Maybe we could talk to Benjamin?"

"Don't be a fool, sister. You think he would take one look at what we have and not want a part of it? My God, Anne! We both fought, scratched, lied, cheated, stole, and murdered to get where we are. I'd kill ten people, fifty people, a hundred people to keep it."

"What changed you so, Ross? You didn't used to feel this way."

"The good life. How many more years do we have, Anne. Ten? Fifteen at the most. I intend to live out my time left in the lap of luxury. And nobody is going to stand in my way. Nobody, Anne. Nobody." There was cold menace in his voice.

"I don't want to know about it when . . . well, it happens."

"You won't."

"Will he be hurt?"

"No. It will be as quick and as painless as possible. I promise you that."

Anne stood up and walked to the door. She opened it and paused there for a moment. "Just do it, Ross. Do it."

"Consider it done, sister."

She walked into the dark mansion and closed the door behind her.

Jamie lingered long in his blankets. When he did decide to get up, he experienced a twinge of pain in his left shoulder. Doctor Prentiss had told him he had a slight case of rheumatism and there was nothing he could do for it.

"Damn!" Jamie said, sitting up and rubbing his shoulder. He did not relish the prospect of growing old. But when the sun came up and warmed his shoulder, the pain was gone, and Jamie did not feel his age. He ate his pan bread and bacon and drank his coffee, enjoying the chatter of squirrels and the singing of birds. This was the year he and Kate would both turn sixty. Jamie just could not believe it. Where had the time gone?

"Sixty years old," he said aloud, pouring another cup of coffee. "Sixty!"

Then he smiled as he thought of Kate. She sure didn't look sixty, although there was a lot of gray among the gold now, and she was troubled with pain in her joints on cold mornings. But her figure was still good enough to put many a younger woman to shame, and the both of them still enjoyed a lively romp in bed.

He laughed aloud at that.

Jamie instinctively looked around him without really being conscious of doing it, checking his surroundings. The horses were grazing and the birds were singing and the squirrels were playing. No danger abounded close by.

Jamie leaned back against his saddle and thought about Cort. The man had changed dramatically. There was a killer coldness about him now. War softened some men, scarcely changed others, and turned a few into hard men. Cort fell among the latter. Jamie felt sorry for the man.

Jamie saw Lightning's head come up, ears pricked, eyes alert. He quickly put out his fire and took up his rifle, moving into cover. From there, Jamie scanned the direction his horse was still intently studying. He could not see or hear anything out of the ordinary, but knew from long years of walking the thin line of danger that something was out there, and Lightning had picked it up.

Then he heard the faint sound of voices. "I tell you I smelt coffee, Cal. I did!"

"Well, I didn't, and my blower's just as good as yourn. What you smelt was your stinkin' feet."

Jamie eased the hammer back on his rifle. The squirrels had

ceased their scampering about and chattering; the birds were silent.

"Look yonder, Cal! That's fresh horse shit. Ain't more'un twelve hours old. Someone's clost."

"Be quiet. We got to have some horses. I'm tarred of walking. My feet is killin' me."

Had their horses stolen in the high country, Jamie thought. Probably taken by Indians who could have just as easily killed them.

Then Jamie tensed as a third voice was added. "Cal, Decker?"

"Right here, Lew."

"Someone was just fryin' bacon. I smelt it. Made my mouth start salavatin'. But the smell was faint. They's a camp 'bout a half mile from us, I figure."

Jamie was about seventy-five feet away. Lightning was as still as a rock, his mean eyes turned wild with rage. The monster horse had picked up the sense of danger from its master, and was ready for a fight.

"Cal, you circle around to the left. Decker, you go to the right. I'm going straight in. Quiet now. Try to shoot them through the head. We don't want bullet holes and a bunch of blood on their clothes. We got to have their clothes."

"Maybe they's some women in the camp," the man called Lew said. "If so, don't shoot them 'til I git a chance to dip my wick."

Nice folks, Jamie thought. Just the kind we need to populate the West. "Come on, boys," he murmured softly. "It's a good day to die!"

33

Fifteen hundred miles away, another scene was being played out, this one just as dangerous and just as life-threatening as the one rapidly approaching a bloody conclusion in the Rockies.

"You were given to a couple down in the slave quarters one night during a violent storm, Mister Washington," the detective told Ben. "The slave woman had just lost a baby a few days before. That woman is now dead. Her name was Georgia Washington. You were given to her by Anne Woodville's personal maid, Selma. Your father, Cort Woodville, is thought to have been killed during the war. But he is alive and living in the West, going by the name of Cord Woodson. He is a gambler, gunfighter, and near-alcoholic. It is my opinion, Mister Washington, that you are in very grave danger."

Ben was clearly startled. "But why? I don't want anything from my mother. I have money of my own. This Cord Woodson saw to that. I'm sure it was he. I don't plan to upset any apple carts."

"I don't believe you will ever convince your birth mother and her brother of that. I'm through, Mister Washington. I don't want anything further to do with this case. Frankly, I'm scared."

"I'll double your fee. I—"

"No. I want out of this. Mister Washington, you are dealing with very dangerous people here. Ruthless. I backtracked this Anne LeBeau. She is suspected of killing several men years ago. But nothing could be proved. Your uncle, Ross, is just as dangerous; perhaps even more so. I fear for your life should you pursue this. Quit it, now."

Ben paid the man off, and the detective walked out of the hotel room and disappeared. Two blocks away he was run down by a frightened and out of control team of horses. The Boston detective's skull was badly crushed, and he died there in the dirty street, lying in a pool of his own blood.

Ben had watched it all from his hotel room, and it scared him. He didn't believe for a second it was an accident. But what to do? He didn't know. Would his mother really try to kill him? Yes, he now believed she would.

Ben was thinking fast, convinced now that his life was in real peril. If he could make it to the railroad station, he could get clear. And that was all he wanted to do. Just get clear and get back to Boston.

He packed swiftly and paid his bill, leaving by the back door. He stepped out into the alley and turned toward the street. Something crashed into the back of his head, and Ben Franklin Washington dropped into a pain-filled darkness.

Jamie waited with the patience of a natural-born hunter. He had played out this game many, many times. For over fifty years, he reminded himself. The only thing about him that moved were his eyes.

Jamie caught movement to his right, then to his left. Cal and Decker were beginning their circle, and they were pretty good in the woods. But with Jamie, pretty good wouldn't cut it.

He knew that by now they had spotted his horses. Jamie allowed himself a small smile. He would just stay quiet and let them enter his camp. It would be amusing to see what happened when one tried to touch Lightning. He waited.

One by one the three men slowly entered the deserted-appearing camp. They stood for a few seconds, puzzled expressions on their faces.

"He's gone huntin'," Lew finally said. He knelt down and shook the coffeepot. Jamie had just made a second pot, so the pot was full. "We'll keep a sharp eye out and have us some coffee while waitin' for him to come back. Cal, you go over yonder and throw a saddle on that horse. Decker, you rummage through them supplies and find that slab of bacon. I know he's got some; I smelt it."

Cal did not notice when Lightning laid his ears back and walled his cold eyes. The animal stood perfectly still as the saddle blanket was laid on his back and smoothed out. Then Cal walked around the horse to fetch the saddle, and that's when Lightning kicked the snot out of him. Jamie winced as Lightning's rear hooves caught the man on the arm and hip and knocked him a good twenty feet. Jamie heard the bones break as the steel-shod hooves impacted. Cal's head banged on a rock and he was out.

"Jesus!" Decker said, running over to him. "Lew! His arm's all busted and looks like his hip may be busted, too. He's in bad shape."

"That's a killer horse," Lew said. "But I'll ride him. I'll beat his head in with a rifle butt and larn him who's boss."

Walk on over there and try to do that, Lew, Jamie thought. This I have to see.

Lew picked up a club from the ground and walked over to Lightning and drew back as if to hit him. Lightning's jaws clamped down on Lew's arm and locked. Lew began screaming as Lightning tried to chew the man's arm off.

"Oh, God, Decker!" Lew screamed. "Get me a-loose from this bastard. He's tearin' my arm up something fierce."

Lightning chose that time to start rearing and kicking with his front feet. Again Jamie winced as the steel-shod hooves came down on Lew's booted feet. Lew was screaming in pain when Lightning finally turned loose of the now bloody and torn arm. Lew fell back onto the ground, one shin badly torn and bleeding and one foot broken.

Jamie rose from the ground, his rifle leveled at Decker. "Just freeze solid, Decker, and I might let you live."

Decker cut his eyes to Jamie and froze to the ground. Lew was moaning around on the ground, bleeding at arm and leg, one foot smashed nearly flat.

"Drop your gun belt where you stand, Decker," Jamie told him.

The gun belt quickly hit the ground.

"Now take Lew's gun out with your left hand, thumb and forefinger only, and toss it to one side. And when that is done, drag him over there." Jamie pointed with the muzzle of the Henry.

Lew screamed in pain as Decker dragged him off to one side.

"Now drag Cal over there beside him," Jamie said, after relieving the unconscious man of his pistol.

That done, Jamie pointed the rifle at Decker. "You can heat up some water now, and see to their wounds. But don't get any cute ideas. I'll gut-shoot you and leave you all for the bears and the pumas."

"Whatever you say, mister," Decker said. "We just wanted some coffee and food."

"You're a liar. You were going to kill me, steal my horses and rape any women you found in camp. I heard you talking."

Jamie poured himself a cup of coffee and backed away from the outlaws. He petted Lightning and calmed him down, then moved to the packhorse and calmed him. Then he sat down on a log and watched Decker work on the wounded men.

"They both need doctors," Decker finally said. "I think Cal's skull is cracked, and Lew is chewed up and stomped on something fierce."

"Goldtown is that way," Jamie said, jerking a thumb.

"Do you mean for us to *walk?*" Decker asked.

"Unless you can fly."

Cal moaned and sat up, rubbing his aching noggin. He blinked a couple of times and stared at Jamie, sitting on the log, a cup of coffee in one hand, the Henry rifle in the other big paw. Jamie held it like it weighed no more than a feather.

"How many of me do you see, Cal?" Jamie asked.

"One," the man said, a surly edge to the words. "And that's one too many."

"He's just got a bump on the head," Jamie said. "Between the two of you, you can manage to get your friend to Goldtown. Take you about two days. Providing you don't run into Indians."

"What about our guns?" Lew gasped the question through his pain.

"They stay with me."

"You're a black-hearted devil, mister," Lew said. "You ain't got no call to treat us like this. We's human beings, not niggers nor Injuns."

Jamie chose not to reply to that. He sat on the log and stared at the men.

"Will you give us some food?" Decker asked.

"I'll give you some jerky and a canteen of water. What happened to your horses and supplies?"

"Stole by Injuns, I reckon."

"Where are you from?"

"West Virginee. We was supposed to hook up with kin of ourn, but we got lost, I reckon. These damn mountains got us all turned around. They some bigger than the ones back to home."

"You should have stayed to home," Jamie told him.

"Cain't do that," Cal spoke. "We swore to avenge our kin. The family honor is at stake."

"So you're manhunters, right?"

"Kin is kin, mister," Lew said. "When a man does a hurt to one Ellis, he hurts us all."

Jamie had noticed that Decker was slowly moving his hand toward his right boot top. Hide-out gun, he thought. "Ellis, hey? I've heard that name. There was a no-count piece of white trash got all up in my face some months ago, demanding this and that and threatening me. I ran him off. His name was Grover Ellis. That your kin?"

"Who you be, mister?" Decker said, his face flushed and his eyes mean with hate.

"Jamie MacCallister." Jamie set his cup of coffee down on the log.

Decker let out a vile oath and grabbed for his boot. Jamie let him get the pistol clear, and then he shot him, the .44 slug taking the man in the center of his chest. Decker stretched out on the ground, dead.

"If you feel lucky, go for the pistol," Jamie told the pair, dropping one hand to his side. "I haven't levered in a fresh round. You might make it."

Cal grabbed for the pistol, and Jamie drew his right-hand Colt and let it bang. Cal was sprawled out on the ground, belly down, one hand reaching for the pistol when Jamie fired. The slug entered the top of his head and exited down near the base of his spine.

"That leaves you," Jamie told Lew.

"You're a cold-hearted, black-souled bastard, Jamie Mac-Callister," the last man said. "But I'll not play no fool's game. You let that damn horse of yourn make a cripple out of me. And you done it deliberate, 'cause you knew what he was gonna do. That makes you snake-shit low. But I'll live. Somehow I'll make it to Goldtown and recover. Then I'll find my kin and we'll come after you, Jamie MacCallister. And if we don't find you, Colonel Layfield and his Revengers will."

Jamie kept his face bland at that. So Aaron Layfield was really coming after him. The man certainly held a grudge for a long time.

"Your funeral," Jamie told him. "Now belly down on the ground, Lew." Jamie walked over to the man and threw the pistol into the timber. "If you raise your head up, I'll kill you."

Jamie quickly packed up and saddled up. He left a canteen of water and some jerky on the ground. In the saddle, he looked down at Lew, who had turned over at Jamie's command and was staring up at him, his face shiny from pain-sweat and his eyes flashing with dark hate. "If you have any sense at all, Lew, you'll give up this hunt."

"I'll see you in hell, MacCallister!"

"Whatever," Jamie said, and rode off.

Jamie paused at the cemetery at the edge of the still-growing town of MacCallister. He sat his saddle for a moment, looking at the headstones, his mind filled with memories. The early settlers were going, faster now as the years piled up behind them. Sam and Sarah Montgomery now lay side by side in the cemetery. Both had lived into their eighties and had died within weeks of each other. But they had left behind them kids and grandkids to proudly carry on their name.

Falcon had seen his father ride up and rode out to meet him. "Any trouble, Pa?"

"None to speak of. How's your ma?"

"Fine. Misses you."

"Any trouble?"

"Not the first sign of it."

"It's coming. And it'll be coming in large groups when it does. Let's go home, boy."

After a long hot bath and a shave, Jamie sat down to eat with Kate.

"Is this Cord the girl's father, Jamie?"

"Yes. And we both agreed there was nothing we could do, or should do, about the marriage—which has probably already taken place. Did you tell Ellen Kathleen about, ah, the, ah . . . well, you know?"

"No. I wanted to talk to you about that."

"Why should we worry her? But on the other hand, if something were to happen, like, ah, with babies . . . oh, hell, Kate, you know what I mean."

"I'm going to have to give that some thought, Jamie. Did you have any trouble on the trail?"

As was his custom, Jamie leveled with her, leaving nothing out.

"Will these men be coming here?"

"I'm certain of it."

She poured them both coffee and put out a fresh-baked berry pie. She cut a small slice for herself and half the pie for Jamie. Age had not diminished his appetite one whit.

"That young Smoke Jensen is a polite young man, but he has the coldest eyes I believe I have ever seen. Falcon says he's the fastest with a pistol and the deadest shot alive, and coming from Falcon, that is a compliment."

"I'd say so. He's a quiet young man, but I'd not want him doggin' my back trail."

Kate looked at her husband to see if he was serious. He was. For Jamie, called Man Who Is Not Afraid, Man Who Plays With Wolves, and Bear Killer . . . for him to say such a thing was practically unheard of.

Kate studied her husband's face. This Smoke Jensen must have really impressed him.

"One thing about being married to you, Jamie Ian Mac-Callister," Kate said. "I have never lacked for excitement in my life."

Jamie looked at her and chuckled. "But it has been a good life, has it not, love?"

"I wouldn't trade it for anything, Jamie. Nothing in this world." She sighed. "I just wish . . ." She fell silent.

"What, Kate. What is it you wish for?"

She shook her head. "Finish your pie, honey. Then we'll talk."

"Tell me now, Kate."

She sighed and said, "It's nothing your gold can buy, Jamie. The Swede is down in bed. Doctor Tom says there is nothing he can do. It was a stroke, Doctor Tom says."

Jamie looked down at his desert plate and pushed it away from him. "I knew Swede was ailing some when I left, but . . . I was only gone ten days, Kate."

She wiped suddenly moist eyes. "He went down very fast, Jamie."

"I'll go see him."

"He won't know you. He doesn't know anybody. Not even Hannah. Jamie, Hannah is ten or twelve years older than us, and Swede is five or six years older than Hannah. That makes him near eighty or better. He's had a good long life. He just . . . ran out of time, honey."

"I've thought about . . . well, what lies beyond this life, from time to time. More so now that I've got more years behind me than what is ahead of me. And, to be honest, the Swede talked to me about . . . when his day came. The Shawnees—indeed most Indians—accept death as a part of life. They don't fear it like the white man. You leave this life, you begin another one. Well, I best go over and talk to Reverend—"

Jamie caught himself and grimaced. Reverend Haywood had passed on three years back. Lydia Haywood had followed him a year later. The new minister, Charles Powell, was a nice enough fellow, but one that Jamie just could not warm to. Many of Jamie's thoughts about the afterlife collided head-on with the new minister's beliefs, for Jamie thought much like an Indian concerning the Great Beyond.

Kate touched her husband's hand. "Hannah and I will see to matters, Jamie. It's late. You get some rest."

Jamie shook his head. "I want to go sit with Swede for a time. I'll be back early, Kate. I . . . ."

He paused as the door was pushed open. Jamie Ian stood there, his hat in his hands. "Pa, Mother. The Swede just died."

Reverend Powell did not understand why Jamie did not attend the funeral of one of his best friends. But he and a few others were the only ones who did not understand why Jamie chose to sit his horse on a ridge high above the valley and look down during the ceremony. Reverend Powell also disapproved when Jamie insisted that some of Swede's tools be buried with him.

"It'll help him get by in the new life," Jamie told the stern young man who always dressed in a black suit and never seemed to smile.

"God will provide all things, Mister MacCallister," the young minister said.

"Even God might need a little help every now and then," Jamie replied. "Besides, Hannah agrees with me, so no more needs to be said about it."

"The man is simply impossible," Charles Powell told his wife, Claudia, after the services. "I do not understand him . . . at all! Sometimes he behaves like a . . . well, like a *heathen!*"

The wife patted her husband's hand. "I know, dear."

"I'll convert Jamie Ian MacCallister someday," Reverend Powell said. "Someday I shall see him Washed in the Blood of Christ. Someday I shall hear him forever renounce the heathen ways of the Indians."

Claudia Powell ducked her head to hide her smile. When hell freezes over, she thought. Then stifled a giggle at her blasphemy.

34

Ben Franklin Washington awakened to a terrible throbbing pain in his head. He lay still for a moment, trying to get his bearings. It didn't take him long to realize that he was in a ditch, or a pond, or lake . . . for he was lying in several inches of water. Slowly, slowly, he raised his head and looked around him. There was not a lamplight in sight. He lay in total darkness. He put out one hand and felt a rise in the earth. He pulled himself toward that rise until he was out of the water. The exertion caused him to lose consciousness for a time. When he came around, the eastern sky was turning pink.

Then panic struck him hard, for his mind seemed a total blank. He did not know his name, did not know where he was, could not recall what had happened to him . . . nothing.

"Calm down," Ben said aloud. "Just calm down and relax. You've suffered some sort of accident, that's all. Your memory will return."

He slept for a time, until the warmth of the sun awakened him. With full consciousness, bits and pieces began returning to him.

"I am a writer, a reporter," he said aloud. "My name is Ben Franklin Washington. I am in Virginia. And somebody tried to kill me."

Then it all came flooding back. His search. The detective. The detective's warning. The detective's death.

Ben pulled himself to a sitting position, only then aware of a pain in his left arm and chest. He looked down. A bullet hole penetrated his coat and shirt, the bullet having nicked the fleshy part of his inner arm and gouged a thin line in the side of his upper chest.

"After I was struck," he said aloud, "they brought me out here and shot me, and left me for dead. That has to be it." He smiled ruefully. Just another dead nigger found alongside the road. Not much would be done about that. But who would do such a vile and evil thing? His mother, Anne LeBeau Woodville, and his uncle, Ross LeBeau, of course.

He patted his pockets. His wallet was gone, of course, and all the change and keys. But Ben was no fool. He looked around him before removing his shoes. He had several hundred dollars in paper money hidden under the inner lining of his shoes. He smoothed that out and then, using a thin rock, pried off one heel and removed several gold coins from the hollowed-out leather. He hammered the heel back on and then did something with his wet and muddy clothing, washing and drying each article carefully. Then he brushed each garment as best he could, bathed his face and hands in the creek water, and dressed.

His head hurt something awful, and he gingerly probed the back of his head. There was a knot about the size of a goose egg there, but he could detect nothing broken. Thank God I have a hard head, he reflected. Then he sat for a time, his thoughts busy.

"Yes. All right. Let them think me dead," he finally said aloud. "I have funds to return to Boston on the train." Providing I can find a train, he thought with a bit of humor. "I'll confer with my editor, and then we'll see about upsetting some apple carts."

Ben rose to his squishy shoes. "I wanted to cause you no trouble, Mother. I just wanted to find out where I really came from. Perhaps see you, tell you I hold no rancor toward you; tell you I understand why you sought to pass for white. And then I would quietly return to Boston and let sleeping dogs lie. You will regret this, Mother. I promise you that."

Ben Franklin Washington started slowly walking down the road. He could see chimney smoke in the distance. He had a terrible headache. He wondered how much it had cost his mother and uncle to have this done.

Two hundred and fifty Yankee dollars.

Lew made it to Goldtown. He said nothing about his dead partners back on the trail. He had rifled their pockets, taken all their money, found the pistol Jamie had tossed into the brush, and fashioned himself a crutch of sorts, then hobbled on, after shoving his dead partners over the side of the ridge. Varmints would soon erase all traces of them. Along the way, Lew treated his badly bitten arm with poultices and said nothing about it when he reached the settlement. As for his broken foot, he told the story that his horse bolted, spooked by a puma, and stepped on his foot. His horse had run off in a panic, and he could not find it. It was a good enough story— it had certainly happened to others—and no one questioned it.

By the time he reached Goldtown, the bones in his foot were beginning to heal, badly, and there was nothing that could be done for it, for there was no doctor in the boom town. Lew would always have a limp, and for the time left him on this earth, when it rained, his foot would ache something fierce.

Lew bought a horse and supplies, and then struck out to find his kin. He had a real score to settle with that damned Jamie Ian MacCallister.

There were still a few Indians left around MacCallister's Valley, and they were all friends with Jamie. They were his eyes and ears, and they did not let him down.

"White men come," the old Ute called Three Horses told Jamie. He pointed toward the east and said, "Four days away."

"How many?" Jamie asked.

Three Horses held up both hands, fingers open. He opened and closed them five times, then shook his head and repeated the same thing twice more.

"A hundred and fifty men," Jamie muttered, although he knew that was only an approximation on the part of Three Horses. It might mean a hundred men, or it might be three hundred men.

Jamie pulled at his shirt and gestured to the east.

Three Horses shook his head. "All same. Blue. But not soldiers like we know. Hat different. Not yellow legs. Red leg."

"Layfield's bunch," Jamie said.

"That first group," Three Horses said. "Second group smaller. Dress all different. Two days behind red legs. I go." He turned his horse's head and rode off.

Jamie stood and watched him leave. Two groups of men, both of them coming after him. Layfield and Ellis' kin, he felt certain. He could not let them strike the town. Too many innocent people would be killed. There were too many kids living here.

With his return from Goldtown, Preacher and Smoke had pulled out. But even had they stayed, the odds would have been too great.

Jamie squatted down and thought the situation over. Falcon and Marie were planning their wedding. Jamie wouldn't want to leave Marie a widow before the couple even got hitched.

Jamie mounted up and rode back down to the village—no, he corrected himself. It was no longer a village: it was a town, with stores and a doctor and a church and everything else that made a community. It had to be preserved, and preserved intact.

This was his fight.

Kate knew from the look on his face when he rode up that something was dreadfully wrong. She sent one of Morgan's children out the back door on the run to fetch his pa.

"What is it, Jamie?" she questioned.

"Pack me a bait of grub, Kate," Jamie told her.

"The men after you . . . they're coming, aren't they, Jamie?"

"Four or five days out. There are too many of them, Kate. Far too many for us to handle here. I've got to slow them down. I've got to thin them out."

"Jamie . . ."

"Listen to me, Kate. If they hit this town full strength none of you will stand a chance. Layfield is a madman. He's insane with hate. He and his men will kill everything in sight. They'll kill children and women alike—they'll spare no one. This is my fight." He put both hands on her slender shoulders. "Honey, there is no law near enough or strong enough to do us any good. The nearest army post is a hundred and fifty miles away. And this is a civilian matter . . . I'm not certain they would get involved. Kate, I'm not asking you to sing my death song. I don't intend to ride off and get killed. I'll be back. But I've got to cut the numbers down. While I'm doing that, this town can get ready to deal with the rest of them. I can't stop them all. But I can damn sure hurt them some. Now go fix my food." Jamie followed Kate's eyes and turned.

Jamie Ian stood in the open doorway, big and solid. Morgan and Falcon and Matthew stood on the porch. "Don't talk nonsense, Pa," Jamie's oldest son said. "You can't face this bunch alone. Me and the boys will get our gear together."

"Stand still, boy!" Jamie's voice was sharp and commanding. "What you'll do is what I tell you to do. This town has got to be preserved. But more important than the town are the people who make it so. The kids, the women, the elderly who can't fight. I can buy you time to prepare for a fight. And I can cut down the odds considerably. Now start layin' in food and ammunition and water. Fill the barrels, for there certainly will be fires to put out. Start fortifyin' the homes and businesses and lay out defensive positions for the men. And don't argue with me about this. I won't stand still for it. Falcon, you go put the pack frame on Luke. He's tough as a mountain goat and doesn't spook. Your ma is goin' to fix me some food. Now don't stand there with your faces hangin' out—move!"

The boys moved. They didn't like it, but they did as their father ordered. Jamie dressed in old and worn but comfortable buckskins. He carefully cleaned and oiled his pistols. Two Colts around his waist, two on the saddle, left and right of the horn, and two more in his saddlebags. A dozen filled cylinders for the Colts. He loaded up two Henry rifles, one on the packhorse, one in his saddle boot.

"You old goat!" Hannah spoke from the barn door. "What you're doing is foolish. You're sixty years old, Jamie Ian MacCallister."

"You don't have to remind me of that, Quiet Woman," Jamie said, using the name the Shawnee had called her. "I feel it on cold and rainy mornings. But when the sun shines, the age disappears like snow in the spring." They both had unknowingly slipped back into the Shawnee tongue.

"I have put together my things. I will ride with you."

"Now it is you who is foolish. You're an old woman. Go home and let your children and grandchildren care for you in your last years."

"Haw! How much you think you know and how little you really know, Man Who Is Not Afraid." She thumped her chest. "I am just as much Shawnee as you. I can still ride and I can still shoot. You cannot stop me. I am nothing without Swede. Nothing. I am like an empty bowl. I will be behind you. I have spoken and that is that." She stepped out of the barn and returned to her own home.

"Perhaps it is the best way," Jamie muttered in Shawnee.

"What did you say, Pa?" Ellen Kathleen asked, stepping into the barn.

Before he could reply, Hannah's singing came to them, a strange and sad chant.

"What is she singing, Pa? I never heard anything like that in my life."

"Her death song, girl."

"Her *death* song? Hannah is in good health. Doctor Tom says she is. What are you talkin' about, Pa?"

"Things of which you do not and would not understand, girl. Go to the house and get my hat. I'll pick it up there."

"Your colonel's hat, Pa?"

"No. The old brown one with the upturned brim."

"The one with the feather in it, Pa?"

"You know which one I'm talkin' about, girl. Now do it."

Jamie fiddled around in the barn, stalling for time. His sons sat on the front porch of the big house with their mother. They listened to Hannah's strange chanting and were all startled when she stepped out into the street wearing an old beaded buckskin dress and carrying a rifle.

"Ma!" Falcon hollered. "You got to see this. Something mighty queer is goin' on."

But Ellen Kathleen had entered the house through the back door and told her mother what Jamie had said. It did not come as any surprise to Kate.

"Leave her be, boys," Kate called from the house. "She's doing what she wants to do and feels she has to do."

"Well, what the hell is she doin'?" Matthew asked in a low tone. "That song she's chantin' is givin' me the boogers."

"That's her death song," Ellen said, stepping out onto the porch, holding her pa's old brown hat.

The townspeople had gathered on both ends of the street, staring at Hannah, listening to the strange chanting.

"What is that heathen sound?" Reverend Powell asked one of Abe Goldman's sons. The merchant had died while Jamie was off in the war.

"I don't know, sir. I never heard nothing like it."

"Where'd she get that dress?" Rachel MacCallister asked. Rachel, one of Goldman's granddaughters, and named after her mother, had married one of Jamie's grandsons. "That's an Indian dress."

Virtually everyone in the valley was related, either by blood or marriage. A genealogist would be reduced to tears long before he figured out who was related to whom and how.

"That is her death song," Tomas Nunez said. "She is riding with Señor MacCallister to meet the enemy."

"But she's an old woman!" Reverend Powell protested. "Besides, what she is doing is unChristian!"

"Charles," his wife said.

"Yes, Claudia?"

"Shut up!"

Charles' mouth clamped closed.

Kate stepped off the porch and went to Hannah. The two women embraced, and Kate returned to stand in front of her house. Hannah's kids and grandkids stood silently on the porch of their mother's house.

When Jamie came out of the barn, riding Lightning and leading the packhorse, Hannah lifted her rifle into the air and chanted, "Iyiyiyiyiyi!"

Jamie spoke to her in Shawnee, and she swung into the saddle with a grace that belied her age. There was a strange smile on the woman's face as she looked toward the graveyard where Swede was resting.

Jamie reached down and lifted Kate off the ground, kissing her soundly. "I'll be back," he said.

"You better," Kate said, as Jamie lowered her to the ground. "If you don't, I'll never forgive you."

Hannah had ridden out to the edge of town. She sat her horse and waited.

"This ain't right, Pa," Jamie Ian protested. "Hannah's got kin and friends here. She can't just ride off to die. She ain't an Indian."

"That's where you're dead wrong, boy," Jamie told his oldest son. "We both have as much Indian in us as we do white." Jamie nodded at his family, plopped his old hat on his head, and rode off.

"I don't reckon I will ever understand Pa," Falcon said.

"Get the town ready for a fight," Kate said, her voice sharp and commanding. "Right now!"

The crowd scattered, and Kate stood for a time alone on the long front porch. She stood there until her man could no longer be seen. Then she walked into the house, into her kitchen, and started rolling out dough for bread. When that was done and the dough laid out to rise, Kate locked the front door and sat down in her chair and had herself a good cry.

35

Jamie rode off toward the east, with Hannah right beside him. The horse she rode was old, like Hannah, and Hannah was comfortable with the animal. Jamie knew why she chose that horse: horse and rider would die together. Jamie would bury them Indian fashion where they fell, with the horse's tail tied to the tall burial platform and the body of the animal under the platform . . . if he was alive to do that.

Hannah was in her seventies, but she could still ride like the wind. She hummed as they rode; other times she wore a faint smile on her lips. Jamie would occasionally glance over at her, and their eyes would meet, a silent understanding passing between them. Rarely did they speak, and when they did, it was always in Shawnee.

Once, Hannah broke the long silence by saying, "It is good, this thing we do."

"Yes. I have felt the years lifting off of me, flying away like eagles."

"I, too."

"Are you weary of this life, Quiet Woman?"

"Yes," she said without hesitation. "I have birthed my children and seen them grow into fine men and women. I have loved my man with all my heart, and I wish to be with him again. Those who do not understand the Indian way would not understand that, would they?"

"Probably not. Most of them anyway. I was raised in the church back in Ohio Territory; I have vague memories of it. But I can't warm to it now. It's too harsh for my liking."

"Do you ever think of the life after this one?"

"I didn't used to. But I do now." He pointed. "We'll camp up ahead. I know a good spot."

The man who now called himself Cord Woodson had won a sizeable pot from some miners and was now sipping whiskey and playing solitaire when a couple of dusty travelers walked into the saloon and bellied up to the long bar. They ordered whiskey with a beer chaser, and after drinking the first mug down to knock the dust from their throats, they took another full mug of beer and the bottle of whiskey over to a table and sat down.

"There's gonna be some big doin's down to that old boom town south of here, boys," one of the riders said. "Some tin soldier name of Aaron Layfield has got him a colonel's commission from the U.S. government to take care of the Indian problem here in Colorado. But before he does that, he gonna clean Jamie MacCallister's clock, so he says."

Cord's eyes turned as cold as the North Sea. He laid down the deck of cards and listened.

"Seems as though Jamie has some old warrants out on him. Personal, I don't think they're worth the paper they're writ on, but until some high-up muckedy muck judge in Washington say they ain't no good, Jamie's got him a fight on his hands. Me and my pard here is fixin' to ride down that way and get us a good seat up in the hills. We both got field glasses, and we intend to see what Jamie does up agin a couple of hundred men."

"A couple of hundred men?" Someone tossed out the question. "Did you say a couple of *hundred* men?"

"That's right. But that ain't all. They's another group of manhunters comin' up behind the *first* bunch. Maybe a day or two behind them. I'm tellin' you, boys. This here is shapin' up to be the grandest fight since Bull Run. An' I ain't about to miss it." He looked at his partner. "Come on, Pete. Drink up and let's get them supplies and get gone. We want to find us a good and safe spot to eyeball this fracas."

The two riders finished off their second beer, grabbed the bottle of whiskey and stood up.

"Wait a minute!" a miner said. "Just hold on. Where did you say this fight was gonna be?"

"Well, I don't rightly know for shore," the second rider holding the bottle of whiskey said. "But the logical place, if you look at a map, would be that no-name town about fifty miles south of here. You know, where the vein played out after about six or seven months."

"Yeah. They had just started callin' that place Bell City. Is that the place?"

"That's the place."

"But why there?" another asked.

The first rider shrugged his shoulders. "I don't know. But that's where everyone I jawed with says it's gonna take place. Don't ask me why."

Several men rushed outside right behind the two riders, scurrying about to get supplies. Cord sat for a moment, idly shuffling the cards. Then he smiled, tossed the deck on the table, and stood up.

"You aren't leavin', are you, Mister Woodson?" one of the bartenders asked. "Don't forget your card game at four o'clock."

"I won't be able to make that game, Clarence," Cord said. "I just remembered I have an appointment." He paused by the batwings, his face a study. "Clarence, should I not return, you can have all my clothing and other personal items."

"Say what?" the bartender asked.

"We're about the same size, so they should fit you well."

"Why . . . thank you kindly, sir. But why would you not return, Mister Woodson?"

"Oh," Cord said with a smile, "call it a hunch. Just say I played out my hand." He laughed. "Yes. That's a good one." Laughing, Cord shoved open the batwings and stepped out onto the boardwalk.

Preacher and Smoke Jensen were just settling down to coffee, stew and pan bread when a voice called out, hailing their camp. "I'm plumb friendly, boys. And that stew do set my mouth to salivatin'. I got some canned peaches that'd go right well with that stew."

"So come on in, providin' peaches is all you got in your hands," Preacher called into the gathering twilight. "I'd shore hate to kill a man by mistake. Why, hell, I'd probably fret about that the rest of the night. Might keep me awake, and I'm a man who enjoys his sleep."

Smoke pointed to Preacher and then to a spot by the fire. "I'm Smoke and that's Preacher. Stew will be ready in a few minutes. Sit."

The man sat—Cautiously, for he knew the reputations of both Preacher and the young gunfighter called Smoke. And they were both quick on the shoot.

"Coffee's ready," Preacher said. "Providin' you got a cup."

"I do have that," the man said. "They call me Tin-Pan. You boys heard the news?"

"What news?" Smoke asked, putting those cold young/old eyes on the stranger.

"You know where Bell City is?"

"I know where ever' rock is in Colorado," Preacher said. "I know ever' spring, ever' crick, ever' tree, and ever' valley. Course I know where that is. What about it?"

"Gonna be a big shoot-out there, so I hear. They's about six or seven hundred men comin' in from the east to kill Jamie Ian MacCallister."

"You don't say?" Preacher filled the man's cup. "Why would they want to be doin' that?"

"Don't rightly know. Way it was told to me, it has somethin' to do with the war. Some sort of a grudge."

"Bell City, hey?" Preacher asked.

"Yep. Folks is comin' in from all over to get them a good seat. But not me. I don't want to be nowheres around when that much lead starts flyin'."

"Bell City isn't that far from here," Smoke said.

"That's right, boy," Preacher replied. "It shore ain't."

"Ain't you a pard of MacCallister?" Tin-Pan asked.

"Been knowin' the man for over forty years. He's a real nice feller, Jamie is."

"When is this fight supposed to take place?" Smoke asked.

" 'Bout four days from now, I heard."

"Ummm," Preacher said. He cut his eyes to Smoke Jensen, and they both smiled.

The old mountain man and scout called Sparks (a distant relative of Captain Sparks from Texas, who had ridden with Jamie's Marauders during the war) sat by his fire in the high-up and mulled over the rumor he had just heard from some miners.

" 'Bout a thousand or so men all comin' together down near Bell City to kill Jamie MacCallister," they had told him.

"A *thousand* men?" Sparks had questioned.

"That's what we heard."

"Yeah," another miner spoke up. "I reckon this is the end for Jamie Ian MacCallister."

"I wouldn't count on that," Sparks replied.

"They's some old woman ridin' with MacCallister," the third man in the party said. "A white woman totin' a rifle, and she's 'pposed to be all dressed up like an Injun." He shook his head and poured another cup of coffee. "The whole thing sounds like a made-up story to me."

Huddled by his tiny fire, Sparks decided he'd pull out at

dawn and just take him a little ride down toward Bell City. There just might be some truth in what the miners said.

"Git your possibles together, you little shrimp," Lobo told Audie. "And leave them goddamn Shakyspear books behind. We got some ridin' to do."

"I am quite comfortable here," the little man said. "Why should I leave such restful and untroubled surroundings to go wandering off with the disreputable likes of you?"

" 'Cause we been wanderin' off together for near 'bouts forty goddamn years, you hard-headed field mouse!"

Audie stared up at the huge old mountain man. "Something is terribly wrong, Lobo. What is it?"

Lobo told him.

Audie stood up, all four feet of him. "*Thousands* of men coming after Jamie?"

"That's what I heared."

"I shall be but a moment, you prehistoric throwback. During the interim, you may saddle my mount for me."

"Is there anything else you'd like for me to do for you, you little turd?"

"Would you consider bathing?"

"I took a bath last month!"

"It was just a thought, a fleeting hope. Forget it. Stay downwind."

An old Nez Perce warrior called Night Stalker heard the rumors about the men coming to kill Jamie MacCallister. Back in '43, he had played a good trick on Preacher and Sparks and Jamie, the story was still told around the camp fires about how he had fooled the men into thinking he was a Sasquatch.*

Night Stalker pointed his horse's head toward the old now-

*Dreams of Eagles—Zebra Books

deserted town of Bell City. A good friend was a friend forever, and Jamie MacCallister was a good friend. The Nez Perce had long called Jamie Brother of the Wolf.

A few miles to the south, an aging Cheyenne war chief called Dark Hand had also heard the news and was traveling toward the old town. Dark Hand was dying and he knew it. His belly was on fire, and there was something growing there that wasn't supposed to be. This would be a fine way to end his days in this life and travel the starry path to his other life. He would die with much glory, and besides, he would be helping an old friend. Dark Hand smiled. Life was good. He just hoped he could get there before the pain in his belly grew intolerable. He patted his horse's neck.

"Carry me there, old friend. We have a better life waiting for us."

Jamie and Hannah topped the rise and reined up, looking down at the deserted town that lay below them in a narrow valley. There was one way in and one way out, the road running right through the town.

"What an interesting place to have a fight," Hannah remarked, looking down at the silent buildings. "A couple of people with rifles at either end of the town could hold off an army, allowing only a few men at a time to enter." She shrugged. "But there is only the two of us."

Jamie smiled. "For now. Come on. We're a couple of days ahead of Layfield and at least three days ahead of those idiots behind him."

Late that afternoon, after Jamie had killed a deer and Hannah was cooking venison steaks, they both heard the sounds of horses walking up the street, the hoofbeats echoing among the deserted buildings.

Jamie looked out what remained of a window and smiled.

"You know the rider?" Hannah asked.

"Yes. Put on another steak."

Cord reined up and loosened the load on the packhorse. He stood for a moment, savoring the smells of cooking meat. He turned to see Jamie lounging in the open doorway.

"Why, Mister Woodson," Jamie said. "What a surprise seeing you here."

"A man never knows where his wanderings will take him, Colonel MacCallister."

"I'll see to your horses, Cord. You come in and make yourself comfortable. Supper will be ready in a few minutes. Let me introduce you to Hannah."

Inside, Cord laid his saddlebags, rifle, and blanket roll on the floor and took off his hat. "Miss Hannah," he said with a slight bow and a smile, neither his eyes nor his expression showing any surprise at the sight of the white woman dressed in a beaded buckskin dress.

"Mister Woodson," Hannah said. "How good of you to join us. I'll have something to eat shortly. The coffee is ready."

Cord took a tin cup from his saddlebags and poured it three-quarters full of strong coffee and then added a touch of whiskey. "For flavor," he said with a grin.

"Seen anybody else on the trail?" Jamie asked.

"Two riders coming in from the northeast. They should be here in about half an hour."

"Good thing I killed that deer," Jamie said. "The place might be filling up with wandering men."

"That's a very good possibility," Cord said with a twinkle in his eyes. "In spite of the vastness of the area and the sparseness of population, news has a way of traveling very quickly."

"Yes. So it does. That packhorse was heavily loaded, Cord."

"Yes. Two small kegs of blasting powder I bought from some miners. You never know when you might want to blow something up." He said it all with a straight face.

"How true," Hannah said, cutting off two more thick steaks.

Jamie went outside to see to Cord's horses.

"Miss Hannah," Cord said. "I know little of Indian ways. Why do you have that single line painted on your forehead?"

"It means I am ready to die," she said.

"I see. Well."

"Are you?" Hannah asked him.

"Quite," Cord replied. "What is it the Indians say? 'It is a good day to die,' right?"

"If the cause is a worthy one."

Cord sat down and began cleaning first his pistols, then his rifle. Then he laid out a dozen boxes of ammunition and began filling cartridge belts.

Jamie returned, carrying a keg of blasting powder under each arm. From the open doorway, keeping well away from the flames in the old stove, he said, "I'll store these away from this building. Tomorrow we'll start constructing some bombs." He looked up the street. "Riders coming."

Preacher and Smoke reined up and swung down from their saddles. Each man led a packhorse. Without greetings, Preacher said, "Let's get this fracas over with, Jamie Mac-Callister. Me and Smoke got business over to La Plaza de los Leones to tend to."

"We'll wrap this up as quickly as possible, I assure you," Jamie said with a smile. "Grub's on inside."

"Good. I shore be hongry around my mouth."

"I'll see to your horses."

"Kind of you, Jamie."

Twenty minutes later, Sparks rode in and swung down from the saddle. "Ain't it surprisin' who you meet on the trail?" he said. "I thought I had this country all to my lonesome."

"I'll cut another steak," Hannah said.

"Best cut several more," Sparks told her. I just spotted Lobo and Audie headin' this way."

"Two more," the voice came from the rear of the building. Those inside turned.

Night Stalker and Dark Hand stood there, both of them painted for war. Their approach had been so silent not even the birds and squirrels had been alarmed.

"Place is gettin' right crowded," Preacher remarked. "I thought you was dead, you ol' horse thief," he said, looking at Night Stalker.

"Not dead yet," the Nez Perce said. He raised one arm and made a circling motion with his hand. "Men gather on the slopes. Have whiskey and barrels of beer. They come to watch, I think. Some women with them."

"We ought to charge admission," Preacher said. "Gimmie another one of them steaks, Quiet Woman. You do have a way with venison."

"How many men are we up agin, Jamie?" Sparks asked.

"Too damn many," Jamie replied, filling his cup with coffee. He heard the voices of Lobo and Audie fussing with each other.

After everyone had eaten, Lobo patted his big belly. "I reckon we bes' be sittin' down and figurin' this here thing out." He had eaten about five pounds of meat.

"Very succinctly put," Audie said.

"Whatever the hell that means," Lobo groused.

36

"An incredible story," Richard Leander, editor of the paper, said, after listening for the tenth time to Ben Franklin Washington's telling of the events in Virginia. He had made him retell the story. This time it was taken down by a Boston police secretary.

Ben had just had the stitches removed from the back of his head, and the grooves in his arm and chest from the bullet meant to kill him were almost healed.

"What an evil woman," the associate editor said. "Let's start legal action against them immediately."

Ben shook his head. "No proof." Ben had also studied for the law. "The detective's death was ruled accidental, and I don't know who hit me, kidnapped me, shot me, and left me for dead. And whatever we write about the incident must be worded very carefully. We don't want to let ourselves open for a libel suit."

Leander tapped a finger on the desk for silence. "I have two men who should be at Goldtown now. They are to interview this Cord Woodson. I dispatched them immediately after Ben's return. One is an attorney and the other a Federal marshal. They are both experienced fighting men and quite capable of taking care of themselves. We'll do nothing about this until I hear from them. When they reach the nearest telegraph lines on their return, they are to wire me."

"Where is that, sir?" he was asked.

"Somewhere in Kansas, I think. But the wires may have been pushed farther west by now. I just don't know. The nation is pushing westward at near breakneck speed."

Leander looked at Ben. "You are aware, Ben, that once exposed, your mother could be ruined?"

Ben shook his head. "Not her. She has money scattered all over the country. So does her brother. We might disgrace her, but we'll never ruin her financially. She's far too smart for that." The young man sighed. "Sir, there are others to be considered, as well. Page Woodville knows nothing of her background. The same goes for Ross's children. I don't have the right to ruin their lives. This is such a sad affair, touching so many people. There must be a way we can handle it discreetly."

"I don't see how that can be done," one of the paper's lawyers said.

"There must be a way," Ben said.

There was, and Anne LeBeau Woodville had already thought of it.

Night Stalker pointed to the crudely drawn map. "Make rock slides here," he said. "Block road. Then men must come in on foot to attack town. When big group is in pass, we use blasting powder to bring down walls of canyon on both sides. Kill plenty, I bet."

"That's mighty good plannin', Night Stalker," Lobo said. "Sounds good to me."

"It's a very good plan," Cord said. "Jamie?"

"Let's get busy."

The two men Leander had sent to Goldtown had arrived, heard the news about the up-coming fight, and were now only a few miles away from Bell City, riding as hard as they dared push their horses.

"Nine men and one woman, at the most, against four or five hundred armed men?" the Federal marshal said. "They won't stand a chance."

"Don't bet on that," the attorney said. "But what we don't want to do is get caught up in this fight. We'll try to see Cord Woodson before the action starts, get his statement, if any, and get the hell out of there."

"I don't want to get trapped in that town," the marshal replied.

The Boston attorney shuddered at the thought.

"You failed," Anne told her brother. "Ben Franklin Washington is still alive."

Ross was stunned. "That's impossible!"

"But true. My detectives say he returned to Boston and has had several meetings with police, attorneys, and Federal people. A big wind is gathering, brother dear. Our house of cards is coming down."

Ross rose to pace the room. "For once I am at a loss for words, Anne."

"I'm not. I began preparing for this the day after I married Cort. How much cash could you get together in, well, say a week?"

Ross smiled. "Quite a tidy sum, sister."

"Enough to live comfortably on for the rest of your life? Be sure now."

"Oh, yes. I've already seen to my children's future. Yes. I'll have quite a sum."

"Get it together. And do it quickly. Return here when you've done it. Then we'll make our move."

After Ross had left, two men stepped out of a room off to one side of Anne's office. "Follow him discreetly," she told the men. "Be here when he returns with the money."

"And then?" one of the men questioned.

"Just be sure you get here a few minutes before he does," Anne said coldly.

"He's in that old deserted town about ten miles from here, Colonel," Layfield's scout reported. "MacCallister and about eight or ten other people. And one of them is an Injun woman."

The scout added that the pass was blocked. Layfield waved that off. "The woman is probably that wife of his. Good work. We'll hit them just after dawn." He turned to the former Union army sergeant and deserter, Carl Miller. "Captain Miller, see that the men are well fed and get a good night's sleep. Tomorrow we finish MacCallister once and for all."

Miller saluted and smiled. "Yes, sir!"

Jamie and Kate's second set of twins, Andrew and Rosanna, now lived in England with their spouses, Liza and Alfred. Andrew and Rosanna were due to return to the States in about a month for the start of a sell-out tour that would begin in New York City, wander around the country, and eventually end in San Francisco. James William Haywood and his bride, Page, were winding up their honeymoon in England and planned to return to the States with the twins and their troupe.

They knew nothing of the events that were rapidly coming to a head thousands of miles away; events that could possibly alter their lives forever.

Jamie and his friends, with the exception of young Jensen, might well have been getting on in years, but what they lacked in youth, they more than made up for in cunning.

Layfield sent fifty men into the pass as spearheaders, picking their way carefully through the mounds of rock. High above them, the fuses to carefully placed packets of explosives were lighted. When the explosives went off, there was nothing the men in the pass could do except look up and wait to die. Every man was lost, buried under tons of rock. When the dust cleared, the pass was forever blocked from the east for anything other than foot travel, and even that was going to be rough. To attack from the west, Layfield and his men would have to travel north for several days, then cut west, then travel south to reach the west end of the pass. It was a long detour, and Layfield had sense enough to realize that Jamie and those with him would be sniping and nipping at their heels the entire way. And he knew only too well how proficient a guerrilla fighter Jamie was. Layfield silently cursed Jamie MacCallister and everyone who was with him. Eight or nine old men and one damned old squaw, or whore—to Layfield's mind, one was synonymous to the other—holding back several hundred men. Well, he silently amended, minus fifty good men who now lay entombed forever under tons of rock.

"We wait and go in after dark," Layfield ordered.

Which was exactly what Jamie and the others hoped he would say.

But Layfield didn't count on the several hundred spectators being there. At night, numerous camp fires dotted both sides of the pass leading to the dark and silent town. And nearly to a person, the spectators were on the side of those in the town. The fires really added little light to the blocked pass far below them, but Layfield worried about them. They were a distraction.

Inside the town, the defenders had no illusions about their situation. They had enough powder for one, maybe two more carefully placed explosions . . . then it would be bullets as Layfield's men made their way through the pass, and blades when they closed. And enough would make it through; the men and Hannah did not kid themselves about that.

At the west end of the pass, with the besieged town in sight, the attorney from Boston asked, "Why don't they just get out? What they're doing is eventually committing suicide."

The Federal marshal replied, "It's a holding action, I suspect. Giving the people back in MacCallister's Valley time to get ready. And also cutting down the numbers those people will have to face when Layfield finally does break through."

"Are those warrants we were told about valid?"

"They're not worth the paper they're written on. But until a judge declares them worthless, there is nothing I can do about this . . . travesty."

"We have to talk to Woodville—if that is Cort Woodville down there going by the name of Woodson."

"It's Woodville," the marshal said. He was thoughtful for a few moments. "I have a plan. See what you think about this . . ."

"Two men carryin' white flags comin' in from the west," Lobo called to Jamie.

One of the men stopped in the center of the street while the second man, his badge pinned to the lapel of his coat, rode up to the edge of the blocked pass.

"Layfield! I'm Red Foster, federal marshal. I need to talk to one of the men in town. Hold your fire until I leave the area. And that is an order. Do you understand me?"

"Red Foster of the Illinois cavalry?" Layfield returned the shout.

"That's right."

"Take as much time as you need, Marshal."

"Thank you," Red muttered, turning his horse. "You pompous, arrogant, over-bearing, loudmouthed jackass!"

The attorney had taken Cord and Jamie off to a separate building and said, "Wait until Marshal Foster gets here. Then we shall explain what this is all about."

Red shook hands with both men, and they sat down on

dusty old chairs while the Boston attorney laid it all out for Jamie and Cord.

When he finished, Red said, "That's the story, Mister Woodville, and we know you are Cort Woodville." He removed a photograph from a leather case and laid it on the table. "This was taken in 1864. Will you deny it is you, sir?"

"No," the plantation owner turned gambler and gunfighter said with a sigh. "I remember when it was taken. Let me warn you of something, gentlemen: Anne LeBeau is a dangerous woman. Much more so than you think. If she has learned that our son is still alive, she will be acting swiftly and with deadly dispatch to rectify that problem. She has always thought Ross to be weak, so it is my belief that once the news of the failure to kill her son reaches her, she will remove Ross first, then take whatever assets he has, and leave Virginia. You will never be able to trace her through her holdings, for she uses many names, through many dummy companies. She will simply change her name, alter her appearance somewhat, and head west, to start all over. Probably in California. And she will leave no one alive behind her to tell the story. Believe that, gentlemen. The woman is as ruthless as a black widow spider."

"So you will verify and sign these papers attesting that the young man named Ben Franklin Washington is your son?"

"I verify nothing and I will sign nothing," Cord said with a smile. "The young man's needs have been seen to, and he is comfortable as far as money is concerned. He will never have to worry about a thing. Now, as ruthless as Anne is, she will not harm Page. I know that. We both have seen that Page will never want for anything. Tell Ben to stop this pursuit after his birth mother. If he continues to dog her, she won't fail again. Tell the young man to accept what he is and drop the matter."

"He will never stop, sir," Red said.

"Then he's a damn fool!" Cord said harshly. "I suspect that Anne let Ross arrange Ben's, ah, accident. That was her first mistake. She won't make that mistake again. The next time, she'll handle it, and Ben will be dead. And all he will have accomplished is to destroy his sister's future. If he continues to pursue that end, and I live through this fight, I'll kill the son of a bitch myself."

"Listen, Mister Woodville," the Boston attorney said, after recovering from his shock at the harsh words.

"No, you listen!" Cord cut him off. "Is Ben so selfish he wants to ruin other lives? What else might he want? To live in a grand mansion and be lord of the manor? He might do that, but he will never be anything other than what he is, and that is a goddamn quarter-breed. I don't care how much money he has; we're not talking about oh-so-proper Boston. We're talking about the South, where passions run high against Negroes. They were slaves four short years ago. You think the stroke of a pen will change the feelings of two hundred plus years? Don't be naive, gentlemen. Tell Ben to accept what he is and drop the matter."

"He'll never do that, Mister Woodville," Red said. "He is one very determined young man."

"If that is the case, gentlemen, what he might well end up as is one very *dead* young man."

"Is that your final word on the matter, sir?" the Boston lawyer said, his words stiff with indignation . . . among other things.

"That's it."

Red cut his eyes to Jamie. "And, you, sir?"

"Why destroy lives when nothing is to be gained by it?" Jamie asked. "If Ben Franklin Washington persists in this, my grandson might well call him out and shoot him. MacCallisters have a tendency to take the shortest route toward a goal. I sympathize with the young man. But in some respects, I have to agree with Cord. Drop the matter. I know Anne. I watched her grow up. That is one dangerous woman. I personally don't think the Negro will ever be fully accepted as an equal by the majority of white people in this country. North, South, East, or West. I can't tell you why that is, but it's what I believe. Maybe in a hundred or so years, but I have my doubts at that.

And neither will the Indian, not in large groups anyway. It's sad, but I think it to be true."

Red stared at Jamie for a moment. "I'm told, Mister Mac-Callister, that there are people of all nationalities living in your twin valleys."

"That's very true. Including two Chinese families. But I handpicked the original settlers—personally. And over the years, I have turned away several hundred or more people who wanted to settle there. Does that answer your question, if it was a question?"

The Boston lawyer sighed. "So what happens now, Mister MacCallister?"

Jamie and Cord exchanged glances, then smiles, and then both burst out laughing.

The Boston lawyer and the Federal marshal looked at one another and shook their heads.

When the two men had stopped their laughing, Red said, "I fail to see anything amusing about this situation, sir. There are approximately two hundred men gathered on the east side of town, with about thirty or forty more coming up behind them, two days away at the most. Yet you seem to find something hysterically funny about it."

"The Indians have a saying, Red," Jamie said. "It's a good day to die."

"Let's return to our reason for being here," the Boston lawyer said. "What about Ben Franklin Washington?"

"If he tangles with Anne," Cord said, "I can assure you she will have him killed with no more emotion than swatting a fly."

The lawyer and the marshal stood up as one. Red asked, "What happens now?"

"The truce is over," Jamie said. "You boys had better get clear. 'Cause all hell is about to break loose."

37

Over the years, Ross had carefully laid out a network of spies around Richmond, and he knew he was being followed an hour after his sister's hired thugs began trailing him. And he knew by the end of that day who they were and who had hired them. It came as no surprise. As a matter of fact, it rather amused him. He knew only too well how evil his sister was. After all, he thought with a secret, silent chuckle, we're cut from the same mold.

Ross went about his business as if he knew nothing of the men shadowing him. He quietly began liquidating what he could and turning that into bank drafts. Just like Anne, Ross had secret accounts in New York City under different names, and just like Anne, he was wealthy in his own right.

But where to go? That was the question. Ross was firmly convinced now that his sister meant to dispose of him. So where would he be safe? Where his sister was the least likely to go to hide and make a new identity for herself. New York City? He shook his head. Doubtful. They'd played there too many times as musicians and actors. The odds were too great they would be recognized. No, New York City was out.

St Louis? No. They were even better known there.

So . . . where?

The more he thought about it, the more attractive the West looked. It was growing, no, booming was a better word.

Over coffee and a sweet roll at one of Richmond's better

restaurants, Ross made up his mind. Denver was a place that was going to grow, and he might as well get in on the ground floor. With his wealth, he could buy, no, *build* a very comfortable home there and live in seclusion and luxury while his wealth grew. Yes. Spread his money around in various banks and invest in the right properties.

There was little chance that he would meet anyone from MacCallister's Valley. After all, it had been almost thirty years since he and Anne had slipped away during the dead of night. Like thieves, the thought came to him, and once more he was amused. Well, that's what they were. Thieves . . . and worse.

He would arrange for any monies due him from his holdings in Virginia—holdings he could not liquidate at this time—to be quietly converted into cash and sent to New York City to one of the banks there. Of course, there were other details to be worked out, but they were minor ones, and could be handled by one of his local attorneys . . . a person that Ross could send to prison for life, therefore one that Ross knew would keep his mouth shut—tightly.

He felt better now that he knew he had things all worked out.

Then he sobered as another thought came to him: now all he had to do was stay alive for a week.

He couldn't arrange to have Anne's hired thugs disposed of; that would tip off Anne that he was on to her plan. So . . . yes, yes, it came to him. He would have a couple of very close friends of his with him at all times. Reasonably prominent people who had a dark side to their lives. Of course, *they* might get killed; but . . . what the hell?

Now he really felt better.

Where to go? Anne thought, sitting in her drawing room. Like Ross, she mentally checked off and eliminated the places where she was well known and simply could not go, and finally settled on San Francisco. But her brother had to be taken care of. She had to see to that. She could leave no loose ends dangling. And she couldn't just disappear . . . she had to let people think she was dead. And she had that worked out, too. It was a fine plan, albeit a chancy one. Everything hinged on getting everybody here at Ravenswood at the same time. But she thought she could arrange all that easily enough.

She told all but one of the servants that beginning Monday, they could have a few weeks off, with pay, of course. She and her personal servant were going to take a little trip. Thelma was just about her size . . . yes. The woman would do nicely. Not that there would be much left to identify.

She let it be known around the city that she was going to take a trip. She placed her better jewelry in a bank box. Page could have that after her . . . she laughed . . . her death.

Then she arranged for painters to come in; while she was gone the place was to be remodeled. She insisted that they bring their materials at once and store them at the mansion. Lots of nice, very flammable materials.

Anne smiled. Everything was working out quite nicely. It was going to be perfect. Anne liked things neatly done.

Layfield's plan to attack during the night turned into a disastrous failure. Jamie and his people heard them coming about ten seconds after they started climbing over the rock-covered pass and were waiting for the men. The leading team of Layfield's Revengers was cut down by rifle fire and forced to withdraw, leaving their dead behind.

"Stupid people," Dark Hand remarked. "This is not much of a fight, hey?"

"I think it's going to get better," Jamie told the Cheyenne.

"Hope so," the Indian replied.

The defenders of the town took turns sleeping and guarding the rest of that night and were all refreshed when dawn split the sky.

Layfield was furious. He had launched two attacks against Jamie. Both of them had failed. Layfield thought about just circling around and riding hard to reach MacCallister's Valley. He had long dreamed of burning down the town, just like MacCallister had done his town. But now the element of surprise had been lost, and the townspeople would be ready for him.

He reluctantly admitted to himself that he had been a fool to stop here and do battle with Jamie. Jamie had wagered on Layfield's vanity and had won.

Layfield knew that to withdraw now would mean a terrible loss of morale among his troops. He had to press on; had to come up with a plan of attack that would bloody those in the town.

Aaron Layfield might have been many things, but he was not a fool. He was well aware that the arrest warrants he carried with him were bogus, and could be recalled at any time. They might already have been voided by a Federal judge.

He looked up at both sides of the narrow pass and grimaced at the sight of all the spectators, cooking breakfast, boiling water for coffee. Many had partied all during the night and were still drunk.

"Disgusting Godless bastards and whores," Layfield said.

The Soiled Doves from Goldtown were working the crowds. The sounds of their grunting and coupling had been heard during the night as the miners bought their fleshy pleasures. That outraged Layfield. He wanted to kill them all. Men and women alike.

Layfield had been going quietly insane for years, and his sickness sometimes nearly overwhelmed him. Ever since the war's end, he had one paramount thought before him: kill Jamie MacCallister.

He had carefully rebuilt his forces, procuring several government grants to do so . . . with the help of a couple of shady politicians in Washington. Now Jamie MacCallister was only a few hundred yards away.

Might as well be on the moon, Layfield thought. The sounds of many horses approaching cut into his thoughts and turned the man around. The most disreputable-looking bunch of men he had ever seen were walking their horses through his army's camp and up to Layfield, standing on the eastern side of the jumble of rocks that blocked the pass.

"I be Clyde Ellis," a man said. "We'uns come to avenge our kin. Git out of the way. We're goin' acrost to settle this score with Jamie MacCallister."

Layfield took off his hat and mock bowed. "Why, of course, Mister Ellis. Be my guest."

One look at the pass and Ellis changed his mind. "That there is a death trap," he said.

"Thank you," Aaron replied coldly.

"But up yonder ain't," the West Virginia man said, pointing to the ridges above the town.

Aaron suppressed a groan. The solution to the problem was so obvious he had overlooked it. What had he been thinking? He felt like a fool for not thinking of it himself.

"We send riflemen up yonder to pick them bastards off one at a time," Ellis said. "I got ol' boys with me that can knock the eye out of a squirrel at three hundred yards."

"Don't even think about doin' that!" the voice came from the ridge, about ten feet off the ground and about thirty feet away.

Layfield and Ellis turned to face a dozen or so miners, all armed with rifles. One of them pointed to the other side. Ellis and Layfield turned. Another dozen or so miners, all armed with rifles, stood or squatted on the other side. Those miners pointed above them and then across the narrow pass. Ellis and Layfield looked all around, and Ellis cussed, low and long. Several hundred men stood from the top of the high pass to almost the bottom, all of them armed.

"There ain't gonna be no back shootin', boys," a burly, bearded miner said. "Y'all got them men down yonder outnumbered ten or fifteen to one or more as it is. You fight 'em on the up and up. You send men up here to back shoot, they ain't gonna be returnin' to you 'ceptin' in one condition, and that's rollin' downhill dead."

"I reckon we understand that," Ellis said.

"You better," the miner said, and then backed off to sit behind a rock.

"Now what?" Layfield grumbled.

"We plan some," Ellis replied.

At Fort Lyon, some one hundred and seventy-five hard miles away, the commanding officer read a dispatch and swore. "That goddamned Layfield again. I thought we were done and through with that lunatic at war's end."

"What's the matter?" his executive officer asked.

"Layfield is supposed to be heading to Bell City with a large force to launch an attack against Jamie MacCallister." He glanced at the date. "Hell, they're already there by now."

"Why would Layfield attack Jamie MacCallister?"

The colonel grinned. "Jamie and his Marauders rode up into Pennsylvania in '65 and burned down his town—remember?"

"Oh. Yes." He shook his head. "Bell City is a hard week's ride from here, sir."

"Yes, I know. Whatever is going to happen will have happened long before we reach there."

"Scout's back, sir!" the sergeant called. "And he's been wounded. He's got an arrow in his side."

"Indians, again," the colonel said, standing up. "Have the men fall out, Captain." He looked toward the northwest. "Luck be with you, Jamie MacCallister."

Those in the old deserted town waited for several days, knowing something was in the works, but not knowing what. They cleaned guns, sharpened knives, ate, stood guard, and rested.

"This is gettin' plumb borin'," Preacher groused. "If all this sittin' around and eatin' keeps up, I'll be fatter than lardass over yonder." He pointed to Lobo.

Lobo gave him a very profane hand gesture, leaned back, and closed his eyes.

Cord was across the street in the second story of a building, watching the blocked pass. Something, he wasn't sure what, caught his eyes. He took his field glasses and went up to the roof of what had once been a saloon and studied the pass. "Well, I'll be damned," he muttered, then climbed back down and walked across the street.

"They're clearing the pass by hand," he told Jamie and those who were not on guard or asleep. "Rock by rock."

"I wondered when they'd get around to that," Sparks said. "It's not going to do them any good. Hell, it'll take weeks to get a path cleared enough to get a horse through. All we have to do is pick them off one at a time as they come out."

Jamie was silent for a moment. "It's a diversion," he finally said.

"A what?" Lobo asked, sitting up.

"A ruse," Audie told him. "A variation on the Trojan Horse ploy."

"Whose hoss?" Lobo asked. "Trojan Ploy? I ain't never heared of him. What a stupid name."

"Go back to sleep, you cretin!"

Lobo looked all around him, his eyes stopping on Cord. "What he just called me, is that good or bad?"

Cord arched an eyebrow and waggled one hand from side to side.

"That's what I figured," Lobo said. "I got to larn to read one of these days so's I can figure out what this sawed-off piece of buzzard bait is callin' me."

"West Virginia is mountainous," Cord spoke from the doorway.

"What?" Sparks said.

"Yes," Jamie agreed.

"So many of those men with Layfield would not be at all reluctant to risk their lives making their way over the peaks that surround us," Audie said.

Night Stalker and Dark Hand grasped what was being said and stood up, rifles in hand. "We stop," Night Stalker said. The Nez Perce and the Cheyenne walked out of the room.

Hannah said, "I thought the miners told . . ." She fell silent and shook her head. "No. They wouldn't interfere if all the men were doing was climbing up to circle around behind us."

"That's right," Jamie said. "But there won't be many of them doing the climbing. The mountain faces are too sheer. Night Stalker and Dark Hand can hold them off. What we've got to do is figure out what those men on the other side of the pass are up to." Jamie frowned, then smiled. He suddenly jumped up and ran to the door, calling for the Indians to come back.

"What the hell . . . ?" Lobo muttered.

"Don't stop the men from getting in behind us," Jamie told the pair.

"What?" Night Stalker said, confusion on his face.

"Make no sense," Dark Hand said.

"Yes, it does. Listen to me. I believe Layfield and Ellis are counting on us to throw everybody toward the rear when those men attack. When we do that, Layfield will launch an attack from the east. He'll be pouring men over those rocks. If enough men get through, we'll be in a box. Trapped."

"Clever," Audie said. "Not terribly original, but clever enough for a man of Layfield's limited intelligence. Ahh! Yes. I see what you're planning. Let Dark Hand and Night Stalker get into position, unseen, and allow those climbers to think they've taken us by surprise. Meanwhile, the remainder of us will have quietly gotten into position close to the east end of the blocked pass. We shall be armed with every gun we have at hand. Night Stalker and Dark Hand will start yelling in panic. Yes. Put Lobo with them. He can roar like a grizzly. The rest of us will lie quietly in wait; perhaps allow the first wave of Layfield's men to actually breech the rocks, and then open up on them."

"That's it," Jamie said.

"Very, very good, Colonel. I'm impressed."

"I'll go with them, too, Jamie," Hannah said. "They'll be expecting to hear a woman screaming."

"That's right. Good."

"Let's get to it," Sparks said. "I'll start making some bombs out of what powder we have left. I'll make them small enough so we can toss them."

"Now it gets interestin'," Preacher said with a smile.

38

Each defender was armed with two Henry rifles and anywhere from two to six pistols. Sparks had rummaged around
and found cans and bottles and had constructed a dozen or so
grenades, filling the homemade bombs with rusty nails and
small jagged rocks; the flying shrapnel would produce
hideous wounds.

During the night Smoke had carefully inched forward to the
blocked pass and planted three heavy charges of explosives,
and that exhausted all the powder the men had brought with
them. Smoke then laid out fuses and backed up to one of the
buildings at the edge of the pass. There, he waited with a box
of matches for the attack to begin.

Audie was on the roof of a building on one side of the street,
Preacher on the roof on the other side. Jamie, Cord, Sparks,
and Smoke were on ground level, waiting.

When Night Stalker, Dark Hand, Hannah, and Lobo had
finished with the men who had climbed down to attack from
the west side of the pass, they were to join the others.

Now all the defenders could do was wait.

In England, Jamie's kids and the honeymooners were
boarding ship for the return to America.

Ben Franklin Washington, along with two attorneys, several reporter friends, and a group of detectives who would act

as bodyguards were leaving Boston on the train for Richmond.

At Ravenswood, Anne was packed and ready to go. A trusted driver was waiting by the carriage in back of the mansion. Anne's personal servant was thrilled—her mistress was actually taking her to New York City. She had been astonished when Anne had given her several of her own beautiful rings to wear on her fingers . . . just a loan, mind you. She was wearing them now at Anne's insistence.

Everything was ready, with just one small hitch: Ross had disappeared without a trace. Anne allowed herself a small smile when her hired thugs reported that to her. So her darling brother had smelled a rat. Well, she might have guessed he would. Ross was anything but stupid.

She watched as the hooligans drank their tea and quietly sank into unconsciousness; death would soon overtake them. Her personal servant was already dead in the kitchen from the poisonous brew.

Anne dragged the body of Thelma to the large living room and carefully placed it across the room from the two soon to be dead men, now sprawled on the floor. She put a small pistol next to the maid's hand; two cylinders had been fired the day before. Pistols were placed close to the men's bodies. Then Anne closed up the house and lit the long, slow-burning fuses that would ignite the flammable materials left by the painters. She carefully locked the back door and got into the carriage.

"We'll stop along the way and have us a picnic lunch," she told the driver. "I just made some perfectly delicious tea for us to drink."

"Sounds good, ma'am." He clucked to the team of horses. Anne did not look back.

Ellis had sent a few more men scaling the cliffs than Jamie had anticipated, but in the end it made no difference. The four defenders at the west end of town were ready for them. Night

Stalker, Dark Hand, and Lobo started yelling and Hannah started screaming, and Layfield sent his troops scrambling over the rocks at the east end . . . straight to their deaths.

Smoke lit the fuses then backed off to join Jamie.

The bombs at the edge of the rock slide exploded and sent pieces of men flying in all directions. Sparks started hurling his homemade grenades, and the rusty nails and bits of glass and rock tore into flesh and dropped men dead or horribly wounded.

When the defenders started firing, it was almost at point-blank range. They didn't have to bother to take aim, for the street was a narrow one and the attackers were running shoulder to shoulder.

It was a very brief fight, lasting only three or four minutes at the most; but it was carnage at both ends of the street for Layfield's and Ellis' men. When the gunsmoke and black powder smoke from the bombs and grenades, and the dust from the explosions finally settled, both ends of the short street were littered with dead and dying.

"Layfield!" Jamie shouted. "Can you hear me?"

"I hear you, MacCallister. You treacherous, traitorous bastard! What do you want?"

"You can send over a small group to collect your wounded, here on the east side. We'll patch up those left alive on the other end of the street."

"Why should I believe the likes of you, MacCallister?"

"Don't be a fool, Layfield. Your wounded are suffering while you're standing over there debating. Come get them. We won't fire on you."

"Your kind heart is going to get you killed one of these days," Smoke said softly. "Especially when dealing with the likes of men like Layfield."

Jamie looked at the young man with the old eyes; eyes that were cold and hard. "You may be right."

Two teams of men, unarmed, came gingerly and cautiously over the mound of rocks in the pass. They stopped just before they reached street level.

"Come on across," Jamie called. "We're not going to fire on you."

Layfield's men gathered up the wounded and left without saying a word of thanks.

"Nice people," Audie remarked. "We should have shot every one of the damned miserable wretches."

"Let's eat!" Preacher called from the rooftop. "All this excitement done made me hongry!"

Layfield was getting desperate while his men were losing the will to fight. They had seen a full third of their comrades slaughtered, and as far as they knew they had not inflicted a single wound on any of the defenders of the town. Layfield had promised them a quick victory and glory. He had promised them wealth and women when they took the town of MacCallister. They had seen none of that which had been promised them.

The spectators that lined the ridges were certainly not helping morale. They hooted and yelled and cussed and cast aspersions upon Layfield's army, calling them all sorts of vile names. And the miners were also giving aid to the enemy, lowering food down to them by ropes.

Clearly, waging the battle against Jamie MacCallister here had been a mistake. Layfield now realized that. But to pull back? That was unthinkable.

Or was it? Perhaps not, he thought, sitting in his tent. No, perhaps that was the way. Not really pulling back, but letting MacCallister think he was retreating. Yes. It might work. He had been studying maps of the area and knew the twin valleys that MacCallister claimed were really not that far away. He could leave a small force behind. . . .

"No," he muttered. That wouldn't work. The damned miners and their filthy whores would tip MacCallister off the instant he started pulling men back.

Layfield got down on his knees and began fervently praying for heavenly guidance. He prayed for God to give him a sign. "Give me a sign, Lord!" Layfield implored the Almighty. "Show me the way!"

What he got was rain. Cold, miserable rain. It started while Layfield was asking God for help in his fight to destroy Jamie MacCallister and continued on through the night. It was still pouring when Layfield awakened the next morning, coming down in cold, gray sheets.

"Shit!" Layfield said, closing his Bible.

Ellis and his men were faring even worse than Layfield. Ellis had lost half his men trying to assault the town from the west side. They had not come prepared for the changeable weather in the Rockies, and they were cold, wet, and miserable.

Lew Ellis' foot was aching something awful. He sat huddled under a tarp and cussed Jamie MacCallister and that damn killer horse that had mangled him. He didn't think he would ever be warm again. These mountains were different from the mountains back home. Lew hated these mountains. They were . . . well, unfriendly, was the best he could come up with. But his hatred for Jamie Ian MacCallister was even stronger. Just thinking about killing that big bastard warmed him somewhat. But he was still cold.

"I didn't think we could pull this off," Sparks said, sitting warm and dry with a cup of coffee in his hand. "But damned if I don't believe we done it."

"The miners say that some of Layfield's men have left him," Smoke added. "But he still has a sizeable force with him."

Night Stalker entered the building through the back door and stood for a moment, warming himself by the fire. "Men will come," he finally said. "Not on horseback, but walking. They have found an old trail through the mountains. They will be here in the morning."

"You're sure of that?" Preacher asked.

"Am sure."

"They used the rain for cover," Lobo said. "It's misty and foggy out there. That's why the miners didn't warn us."

"You can bet they left people behind," Hannah said. "Moving around and tending fires and the like." She started humming. Night Stalker and Dark Hand looked at her but said nothing. They knew what she was humming.

"You get out of here, Smoke," Preacher told his young friend. "You get gone."

"I'll stay," the young gunfighter said.

"He's right, boy," Lobo told him. "You got a whole life ahead of you. Hell, we're old. Clear on out."

"Forget it," Smoke said.

"Your courage and loyalty to a friend is most admirable," Audie said. "But those attributes can sometimes be misplaced. Preacher is right. You should leave. No one will think the less of you for it."

Smoke stood up. "I'll relieve Cord and stand watch while he gets some coffee and warmth. I'm staying." He picked up his rifle and left the room.

"The boy is as hard-headed as you are, Preacher," Jamie said with a smile.

"We ain't lost this fight yet," Preacher replied. "Ain't none of you ever seen that boy up close and in a fight. He's a devil. There ain't a nerve in him."

"He does appear to be right handy with them guns of hisn," Lobo remarked.

"Rattlesnake fast," Preacher said. Then he smiled. "Larned everything he knows from me, of course."

Preacher exited the room swiftly as people began throwing sticks and cups and boots at him.

39

One miner who witnessed the fight later called it one hell of a battle, and the old ghost town of Bell City would forever after be known as Hell City.

The rain stopped during the night and the sky became star-filled. By dawn, Layfield's men were in place, and there was nothing for the defenders of Hell City to do but stand and fight; for Layfield's men now were located at each end of the ghost town, and escape for the defenders was impossible.

"This reminds me of the time I was surrounded by about five hundred Kiowa," Preacher said. "That was back in the late '40's, I reckon it was."

Audie rolled his eyes, knowing Preacher was about to launch into another of his tall tales. Lobo began pulling up clumps of grass and sticking them in his ears while Jamie laughed at the antics of the men.

"They'd ambushed an army supply train, but didn't know there was about a thousand or so rifles scattered out among the wagons and cases and barrels of shot and powder. I couldn't run nowheres, my good hoss had pulled up lame, so I started loadin' up them rifles just as fast as I could. I must have loaded up near 'bouts two/three hundred of them rifles 'fore them painted-up Injuns realized I was there. They'd been busy torturin' them what was left alive. When they seen me, here they come, a-whoopin' and a-hollerin' and a-shriekin' like devils. I commenced to firin' just as fast as I could pick up one rifle and let 'er bang and lay it down and pick up another one. Them Kiowa never seen nothin' like that. They'd charge and I'd bang. I was firin' them rifles like pistols, one in each hand. The smoke was so thick you couldn't see. They was dead Kiowa a-layin' all over the place. It was a sight, let me tell you. We fought near 'bouts all mornin' 'fore them Injuns finally give it up and went ridin' off, carryin' their dead. That was a hell of a fight, let me tell you that, boys—and you, too, Miss Hannah."

Audie stared at him for a moment. "Why, you misbegotten old reprobate, what has that to do with our present situation?"

"Well, I don't rightly know," Preacher replied. "It just reminded me of it, that's all." He walked off to take up his assigned position.

"There was about a hundred of them Kiowa," Sparks said.

"You mean the story is *true?*" Cord asked.

"Yep. Most of it. Preacher must have kilt or wounded forty or fifty Kiowa 'fore they give it up and rode off."

" 'Course it's true," Preacher said, pausing in the street to point toward the rear of the building. Then he walked off.

Audie thought about the stacks and stacks of rifles and belts of ammunition that had been retrieved from the dead and wounded of Layfield's and Ellis' men after their abortive charges. "There was a moral to the story after all," he muttered. "But getting it out of that old buzzard is sometimes as difficult as shaking hands with a grizzly."

The defenders began loading up Henry rifles and Colt pistols and passing them around. "This will give us a little better chance," Cord said, just as he left the room with an armload of rifles and pistols.

"For a fact, we ain't got much of a chance," Sparks said, heading out the door and to his position near the east end of the town.

They looked up as Smoke's pistols barked twice down at the west end of the street.

"The first ones who reached us did not make it very far," Night Stalker called from across the street.

"It's been nice knowin' you folks," Lobo said. "I reckon our string's done run out. But I aim to take a bunch of them bastards with me."

He was carrying a load of weapons that would have staggered a big mule.

"Here they come!" Preacher hollered. "And we didn't kill near 'bouts as many as we first thought neither! They's swarmin' like bees."

Jamie stepped out onto the warped boardwalk, his hands filled with Colts. He emptied the pistols into knots of men rushing into the streets from all sides and watched them fall. He holstered the empties and filled his hands with Colts pulled from behind his belt. The morning was bright, sunny, and rapidly turning bloody in the Colorado Rockies.

Hannah shouted out in Shawnee and used her now-empty rifle as a club, smashing heads until she went down under a mob of blue-shirted men. Jamie did not see his old friend fall, but when her shouting ceased, he knew she was gone. It filled him with a rage he had not experienced in years. He turned toward where he had last heard her shout and emptied Colts that filled his fists into the mob of men. Then he picked up two Henry rifles and began firing them, twirling the rifles like batons to work the levers. A bullet nicked one arm, another bullet slammed into a post and sent slivers of wood into his face, and yet another round burned his right leg. Jamie stood like a rock, loaded rifles leaning against the store front, within arm's reach. He would empty two and grab up two more. The street became thick with gunsmoke and ringing with the pitiful cries of those wounded.

"A thousand dollars for the head of Jamie MacCallister!"

Jamie grabbed up two fully charged pistols and two rifles and ducked back inside the building, running the length of it and exiting out the back door. He turned and came face-to-face with a handful of blue-shirted Revengers. It was too close for rifle work, so he started swinging one rifle like a club. He heard skullbones pop and jaws break under the impact. Dropping the now stock-broken rifle, he grabbed up a Henry from one of the downed men and ran up the alleyway just in time to stand, watching through horror-filled eyes, as Cord stepped out into the street, both hands filled with pistols. Cord had changed clothes. He was now wearing his old Confederate uniform, from his cavalryman's boots to his gray, gold-braided hat.

"Come on, you Yankee bastards!" the former plantation owner shouted. "Meet the gray one more time."

Cord began firing as fast as he could cock and fire. Jamie watched his body soak up lead, but the man stayed on his boots, exacting a fearful toll from the blue-shirted men only a few dozen yards away. He emptied his pistols and sank to his knees in the muddy street, the front of his gray coat soaked with blood. Dropping the empties, Cord pulled out two more pistols from his sash and kept on firing. Cord Woodson died on his knees in the street. But he would not fall over; he remained on his knees, facing the enemy. One more insult to the blue-shirts.

Jamie stepped out of the alleyway and gave the remainder of the men who had killed Cord their final insult: he filled them with lead and watched them fall. Jamie dropped those empty pistols and the empty Henry and jerked out his last two Colts.

Night Stalker screamed out insults from a rooftop and leaped down into a knot of now badly disoriented and frightened men, a knife in one hand and a tomahawk in the other. He began cutting flesh and splitting heads. His body jerked time after time as bullets tore into him, but the Nez Perce warrior would not go down that easily. When he finally fell, he was surrounded by a sea of blue, dead and dying.

Dark Hand, one leg broken by a bullet, and blood streaming down his face from another wound, painfully hauled himself to an upright position, tied himself to a hitchrail, and began screaming insults in Cheyenne. The surviving defenders of the battle of Hell City found him there after the fight;

the Cheyenne warrior had suffered over a dozen gunshot wounds before dying. A pile of blue-shirted bodies lay in a semicircle all around him.

Jamie saw a man cautiously making his way up the street, staying close to the buildings, ducking in and out of doorways, and turned to face the man.

"Step out into the street, you yellow-bellied bastard!" Jamie called over the hammer of gunfire.

"MacCallister?" the man shouted.

"That's right. Who are you?"

"I be Clyde Ellis and I've come to kill you, MacCallister."

The two men were oblivious to the waning sounds of battle around them.

"You can try," Jamie called.

Clyde stepped out from the doorway. "I'll just do that," he said.

"I doubt it," Jamie replied, and shot him twice, one slug taking the man in the chest and the second slug tearing open his throat.

Carl Miller could see that the battle was nearly over, and they had lost. It was incredible. Nine men and one woman had defeated a superior force. It was time for him to haul his butt out of this death trap.

"You going somewhere?" the voice stopped him and turned him around.

Carl faced a young man, no more than nineteen at the most. He grinned. The fool had his pistols in leather. "You damned stupid little pup!" Carl said, and lifted his rifle.

Carl's eyes could not follow the blur of the draw. Gunsmoke bellowed from the pistols and gunfire hammered the morning. The last thing Carl Miller thought before he died was that no man alive could hook and draw that fast.

Smoke Jensen turned and saw that the battle was over. The main street of Hell City was littered with the dead and the dying and the wounded. He looked around for his mentor, Preacher, and a smile creased his lips as his eyes found the old mountain man, walking up the boardwalk toward him.

"By God, now that was a purdee good fight, boy!" Preacher called. "We skunked 'em good, we did."

Preacher's eyes found the hitchrail-tied body of Dark Hand and the bloody body of Night Stalker. "Damn!" he swore.

Audie stood over the battered and bloody and almost unrecognizable body of Hannah and slowly shook his head. "I shall never meet a braver woman," the little man said. Audie had suffered two wounds: one in the side and the other one in his left arm.

Lobo lumbered into the street and picked up his little friend just before Audie hit the ground and carried him off to tend to his wounds.

Sparks had a bullet crease on his noggin and a burn on his leg. Preacher and Smoke and Lobo were unscathed. Jamie stepped out into the street and looked around him. He had four minor wounds, including a slight head wound that dripped blood down onto his face and shirt.

"They're hightailin' out, Jamie MacCallister!" a miner shouted from the slopes of the pass. "Headin' north, they is. 'Bout thirty of 'em, all told."

Jamie waved at the man. "Let's bury our dead," he said.

"That there was a brave man," Preacher said, pointing to the body of Cord, dead on his knees in the muddy street. "He needs some fittin' words on his marker. You got airy?"

"Yes," Jamie said, wiping the blood from his face. "We'll burn into his marker these words: 'His last hand was a good one.' "

Jamie buried Hannah Indian fashion, along with Dark Hand and Night Stalker. He buried Cord, dressed in his full Confederate uniform, on a lonely ridge overlooking a pretty stream and using a hot iron, burned the words HIS LAST HAND WAS A GOOD ONE, into the marker. The miners came down from the slopes and pitched in, helping to bury Layfield's and Ellis' men. They were buried in a mass grave and the spot marked with the date of their death. Then Jamie, Audie, and Sparks tended to their wounds.

The guns, horses, and remaining supplies of those who had come west to kill Jamie were given to the miners.

Preacher and Smoke rode out, followed the next day by Lobo, Audie, and Sparks. The day after that, Jamie pointed his horse's nose toward home. On a hill overlooking the deserted town, Jamie paused to look down at Hell City for a moment, then lifted his eyes to the graves of his friends: Cord, buried on the south side of the town; Night Stalker, Dark Hand, and Hannah, laid to rest on the north side of the pass.

Jamie raised a hand in farewell and then lifted the reins. "Let's go home, Lightning. I think we've both earned a good long rest after this nonsense."

Thirty miles away, to the north, Aaron Layfield and what remained of his army were camped, seeing to their wounds and wallowing in hatred for Jamie. And there was plenty of hate to go around. Aaron had sent a messenger back east to notify the kin of Clyde Ellis of the tragic events that had befallen their relatives. Those who had escaped with the slightly insane colonel of the army of Revengers and part-time lay preacher were the most dedicated and hard-bitten of his men, all veterans of the War Between the States. Aaron had asked those men if they would stay with him, to plan a way to rid the world of Jamie Ian MacCallister. They had all agreed to stay.

"We shall one day be victorious," Aaron declared, after an hour of praying and receiving what he considered to be a sign. "For God is on our side."

The sad thing was, Aaron Layfield really believed that.

Jamie rode into his valley and slowly swung down from the saddle, his kids and grandkids and great-grandkids gathered around him. It was quite a crowd.

Kate pushed her way through the children to stand staring up at her man. "Is it over now, Jamie?" she asked.

"It is as far as I'm concerned. But Aaron Layfield got away with some of his men. I can't speak for him, Kate."

"Tell us where he went, Pa," Falcon said. "We'll ride over and clean out that nest of snakes once and for all."

"Hush," Kate told her youngest. "Let's talk of peace."

"There ain't gonna be no peace until this fool Layfield is in the grave, Ma," Morgan said. "We might as well get it done now."

"Don't sass your mother, boy," Jamie said, and Morgan shut his mouth.

"Hannah?" Kate asked.

"Laid to rest the way she wanted, Kate. She and the Swede are together on the starry path."

"Did she die well?"

"That she did. Audie said he had never met a braver woman."

"Then all the ones who came west with us are gone."

"I suppose so," Jamie said, experiencing a weight of sorrow for a moment as his eyes drifted to the cemetery with its rows of neat headstones, marking the resting places of good friends. He looked at the hundred or so members of the Mac-Callister clan and said, "Let me rest and bathe and eat, then I'll tell you all what happened."

When no one showed any inclination to leave, Kate put her hands on her hips and said, "Move!"

They moved.

40

The westward push from the east was in full swing, with thousands of settlers pulling up stakes and heading for what many believed to be the Promised Land. For some it would prove to be just that, but for many thousands, the lonely trails west would become their final resting place. Every few yards along the Oregon Trail there would be a grave.

Between the end of the War Between the States and 1870, changes, some good and some bad, were coming at breathless speed in America. Dynamite was manufactured in San Francisco. Alaska was bought from Russia. The territory of Wyoming was created. Ulysses S. Grant became the 18th president of the United States. At Promontory Point in Utah, the nation's first transcontinental railroad was completed as the Central Pacific and Union Pacific were linked.

Jamie felt sure that Layfield would strike again, for the man was a fanatic, the most unpredictable of types. But as the summer wore on, Jamie began to relax and enjoy the season. Friends had spotted Layfield and reported the location to him, telling Jamie that Layfield seemed to be waiting for something.

"Supplies, probably," Jamie said. "The army has assured me that Layfield no longer has any government connections." A Federal judge had thrown out those warrants against Jamie.

"Then he'll strike here, you think?" Kate asked her husband.

"I'm sure that's what he plans to do. But I won't give him that chance. I have people watching his movements. When he starts to move, I'll be notified. Then I'll put an end to this nonsense once and for all."

"But this time you'll take the boys and a few of the other men with you," Kate said, and it was not put as a question.

Jamie smiled and patted her on the shoulder. "If you say so, dear."

"I definitely say so."

But Layfield made no moves other than to go into a mining town half a day's ride from his camp for supplies.

As the summer began drawing to a close, Jamie finally put two and two together. Somehow, Layfield had learned that Andrew and Rosanna and their troupe of dancers, singers, musicians and actors were going to play Denver and then come spend a week or so in MacCallister's Valley before heading on to San Francisco. Layfield was waiting until they arrived before striking.

"Now you're endangering my family," Jamie muttered. "Now you've really gone too far."

But this was a bad time to take men away from the fields, for the growing season was short and harvest was critical. Jamie saddled up and rode around his twin valleys—or as much of it as he could in a full day. The valleys were filled with people: farmers and small ranchers. More than six hundred people, at last count, now lived in the twin valleys. They had a government, a sheriff, law and order, schools, churches, and a fine little town.

Jamie sat his horse on a ridge that looked down on both valleys and was filled with pride. He had first seen these valleys nearly thirty-five years back. He recalled digging and letting Swede smell the good rich earth. What was it the Swede had said?

The Swede had smiled and fingered the dirt. "It will grow good crops, Jamie."

Jamie sighed in remembrance. Now the Swede was gone, as was Hannah. Sam and Sarah were gone, Juan and Maria, Moses and Liza and Titus and Reverend Haywood and Lydia. All gone. Dead and buried.

Jamie dismounted to squat on the ground, gazing out over the valleys. "And now I am growing old," Jamie whispered. "And there is more gray than gold in Kate's hair. So what the hell difference does it make if I die protecting and preserving this land?"

Jamie chewed on a blade of grass and fell deep in thought as he looked out over the land.

"Those of us who came first have deep roots here," he murmured. "We will leave behind kids and grandkids and great-grandkids to carry on. I cannot let a madman destroy what we all worked so hard to build."

He would leave Kate a rich woman, richer than even she knew, for Jamie had been digging up and hoarding gold for several decades. He had sacks of gold hidden all over the valley and a deer-hide map in a banker's safe deposit box in Denver with the carefully marked locations of two dozen more veins of the precious yellow metal.

Layfield had to be stopped—and stopped permanently. Once that was done, they could all live in peace for the rest of the time God granted them on this earth.

Jamie stepped into the saddle and rode back. Kate was sitting on the front porch with several of their daughters and a whole mess of blond-headed and blue-eyed grandkids and great-grandkids. It looked like a convention.

"I'm goin' huntin'," he told Kate. "Winter will be here 'fore we know it, and we need to stock up and jerk some meat."

Kate smiled at him. "Are you getting senile, old man? We have herds of cattle and flocks of sheep and hundreds of chickens. Those hard times are years behind us, Jamie. Tell me the real reason you want to ride off."

He returned the smile. Age had not diminished Kate's beauty. It had somewhat dimmed her eyesight, and taken some of the luster from her hair, but she was still a beautiful woman. And her mind was sharp as a razor.

"I just need to get away for a time. I want to ride the High Lonesome 'fore the kids get here."

"Then say so, Jamie Ian MacCallister," she told him. "Don't story to me."

"Yes, ma'am," Jamie said, and the girls all laughed. They loved it when grandma chided grandpa.

"Well," Ross said, after reading the paper. "That is one performance I shall not miss." He poured another cup of tea and tried to recall the last time he'd seen those two MacCallister brats. Ross was now living under the name of Russell Clay.

Andrew and Rosanna and their performers were coming to Denver for a week of shows. Always the actor (ham, might be a better word) Ross could not resist the pull of a musical troupe. He sent a messenger to reserve a box seat at the opera house and settled back to reread the lengthy (and overly flattering, to his mind) article on Andrew MacCallister and his sister, Rosanna.

"Nobody is that good," he finally concluded. He folded the paper and laid it aside. "I'll be the judge as to their talents," he said. "Surely meager, at best."

Then, as always, Ross's thoughts wandered to his sister. He wondered where she had chosen to hide. He would be willing to wager that she was somewhere here in the West. And if he had to take a guess, he would bet it was San Francisco. He made up his mind. He would hire detectives to find her. And then arrange to have her killed.

Anne LeBeau, now known as Andrea Petri, read the article about Andrew and Rosanna coming to San Francisco with great interest. She had quietly followed the twins' careers for years and was anxious to see them perform. She rang for one of her servants and sent him over to the music hall to reserve a box seat for one of the performances.

Anne often wondered where her brother had chosen to hide and what he was doing. He was here in the West, somewhere, she was certain of that. But while the West was vast, the cities were few. She would be willing to bet it was Denver. Anne made up her mind. She would hire detectives to find Ross. And then have him killed.

"Where is Pa goin', Ma?" Morgan asked, moments after Jamie had saddled up Lightning and ridden out.

"To wander the high country for a week or so," Kate replied. "Or so he says."

"Uh-huh," Morgan replied. He went to his home and told his wife he'd be gone for a week or so. Outlaws, he said.

"Right," she said, very drily. "Sure." She had seen Grandpa Jamie ride out.

Jamie Ian walked over to his brother Matthew's home. "Pa just rode out, and he was leading a packhorse. Morgan was right behind him. Something's sure up."

"I'll get saddled," Matt said. "You get together some supplies. And lots of ammo."

Falcon walked over to Little Ben Pardee's house. "You seen Pa or any of my brothers, Ben?"

"I seen Matt and Jamie Ian ride out a few minutes ago, leading a packhorse. What's up?"

"I think Pa's gone off to fight that goddamn Layfield."

"Damnit!" Little Ben swore. "I'll saddle up."

"I'll get the supplies."

Half a dozen of Jamie's grandsons, now grown men with families of their own, gathered at their grandmother's house. "Where's Grandpa off to, Grandma?"

"You . . . stay . . . here," Kate said, carefully enunciating each word, steel in her voice. "And I'll brook no backtalk from any of you. Understood?"

Perfectly. When Grandma put her little foot down, it went down firmly.

Jamie topped a ridge and swung down from the saddle, letting his horses blow and then water and graze for a time. He looked behind him and swore. He knew by the way the rider sat his horse that it was Morgan about a mile back. That dust a couple of miles behind Morgan was surely more of his sons coming up.

"Might as well wait until they catch up," Jamie said. "I taught them all and I won't be able to shake them."

Jamie built a small fire and put on water for coffee.

Morgan rode up and stepped out of the saddle. He walked over to the fire and squatted down. "Going for a little ride, huh, Pa?"

"That was my plan. Alone, too."

"Ma suggested I sorta tag along with you. Man of your advanced age, you know?"

"She said that, did she?"

"In so many words."

"I just bet she did. You ought not lie to your pa, boy."

"Me? Tell a lie to you? Not me, Pa. That's Jamie Ian and Matt comin' up behind me."

"Wonderful."

"And them two behind them is surely Falcon and Little Ben."

"That's just dandy."

"I think it's kinda nice for a father and his sons to get together for a huntin' trip ever' now and then."

"Sure it is. No tellin' what kind of game we might bag this trip out. You make up your mind to give up scoutin' for the army permanently, boy?"

"I thought I might. Me being married and all. I bought that piece of land the Simmons give up."

"That's real nice, boy. Your ma will be pleased."

" 'Sides, somebody's got to hang around to look after you. In your advanced age."

Jamie sighed. After a couple of seconds he ducked his head to hide his smile and dumped the coffee in the boiling water, then added a bit of cold water to settle the grounds.

"You goin' to kill this nut Layfield, Pa?"

"I'm going to first try to talk to him, boy. If he'll let me. I want to tell him the war is over and done with. And to leave me and mine be."

"And if he don't care to listen? And I'll bet you five horses to one he won't."

"He better listen," Jamie said. "I think I'm being right charitable toward him. He and his men killed Hannah, Night Stalker, and Dark Hand. Wounded me and Audie. Speaking just for me, I'm willing to let it pass. But if he don't want to do that, then we can let the killin' begin."

Morgan stared at his father for a few seconds. He'd heard that tone in his pa's voice only a few times and knew what it meant. His pa was killing mad inside, but very controlled on the outside.

While Jamie leaned back and chewed on a piece of jerky, which he always carried in his saddlebags, Morgan studied his pa out of the corner of his eye, being careful to not stare directly at the man.

He knew that his pa was considered an old-timer. He also knew that his pa was about sixty years old. But old-timer and close to sixty years old or not, Morgan sure as hell wouldn't want his pa to haul off and hit him, for Jamie was still bull-strong and, for a man his age, could move damn quick.

"What are you thinkin', boy?" Jamie asked.

"A lot of things, Pa. Why does this Layfield hate you so? Why you, particular?"

Jamie shook his head, just as the sounds of approaching

horses became clear. "I don't know, son. But he sure singled me out . . ." Jamie smiled. "Years before I burned down his damn town."

Morgan laughed. "Burnin' down a town might tend to piss some people off, Pa."

"It was war, son. But . . . with Layfield, it's something deeper than that. I think the man is crazy. I just happened to come along at the right time when he was looking for something, or someone, to hate."

Jamie Ian and Matthew rode up and dismounted. "We thought we'd just tag along with you, Pa," Jamie's oldest said, smiling.

Matthew got a cup from his saddlebags and moved to the fire, pouring a cup. "Yeah, Pa. You might get lost in the woods or something."

Jamie pointed to the two riders rapidly closing the distance. "Who is that behind you?"

Jamie Ian squinted. "I don't rightly know, Pa."

"Try Falcon and Ben Pardee. See how that fits your mouth."

"Well, now. It just might be them."

"Uh-huh."

"Pa?" Matthew said.

"What?"

"How come you hittin' Layfield and his bunch now, after all this time?"

"Andrew and Rosanna."

The boys were silent for a moment, mentally digesting that. Jamie Ian nodded his head. "I see. Layfield's been waiting 'til we all gather in the valley. He wants to be sure he gets all the MacCallisters."

"That's my thinkin' on it, boy. And James William and his new bride will be there, too. Even though Layfield's only got about thirty or so men, he could do a lot of damage. 'Cause I don't think the man cares whether he lives or dies, just as long as he gets me. That's why I wanted to go this alone."

"Pa," Jamie Ian said softly. "Just as long as there are two MacCallisters or kin alive, the other ain't never goin' to be alone."

Falcon and Ben Pardee rode into the camp. Jamie said, "Light and sit, boys. Let's plan this out . . ." He grinned. "Since this is gonna be a family affair."

41

"Miss Kate," a man who farmed a section of land at the far end of the valley addressed her. "Meanin' no disrespect, but we just can't let your man and your sons carry the whole burden of fightin' this crazy man, Layfield. Jamie Ian MacCallister and you and them few who come with you to this spot, why, y'all pioneered this land. You carved a garden spot out of the wilderness. Y'all made it easy for the rest of us. I been elected spokesman to tell you this, ma'am. Now, this is what we plan on doin' . . ."

Rosanna and Andrew and troupe had arrived in the boom town of Denver and were staying at the finest hotel in the city. They were all anxious to get the shows over with and head for MacCallister's Valley. It had been years since they'd seen their parents. They had lots to talk about and new babies to see and lots of mama's good homecooked meals to eat. Kate had written them both, and Ellen Kathleen had written James. Everybody was looking forward to a big eatin' on the grounds and to some fine entertainment from world renowned professionals.

And Jamie and sons and Little Ben Pardee—among others that Jamie was not yet aware of—aimed to see that everybody got their wishes . . . everybody, that is, except for Colonel Aaron Layfield.

* * *

"There's a whole passel of folks paralleling us, Pa," Morgan said, after being gone all of one morning. "But I couldn't get close enough to see just who they might be. They're stayin' to the flats as much as possible."

"How many folks?"

" 'Bout fifty, I think."

Jamie thought about that. "The army?"

"No. And I'm sure of that. And I'm also sure they're not outlaws, either."

"How can you be sure of that?"

"I went into one of their camp sites. It was all cleaned and tidied up. Stone fire rings was careful laid and the fires careful put out. They even dug latrines, Pa. And filled them in when they was done."

"You're right. That was no outlaw camp."

"What do we do, Pa?"

"Nothing. Layfield's camp is a day and a half away, and I want this issue settled once and for all. I don't know what those other men are doing out here, but they're staying a distance away and leaving us alone. We'll do the same for them. Let's go."

"Jamie MacCallister and a few others are coming, Colonel," Layfield was informed.

"Good, good!" Aaron Layfield beamed, rubbing his hands together. "Have the men get into position."

"They're coming under a white flag, sir."

Layfield thought about that, his smile fading. "Very well. I shall honor a white flag of truce. Let them enter the camp."

Layfield carefully dressed in his best uniform and laid out his plumed hat. He pulled on his freshly blacked boots and buckled on his sword. He brushed his hair and combed his beard and stepped out of his tent. He walked to the edge of the camp and waited for Jamie Ian MacCallister.

At last! Layfield thought. I've got him at last. And he is coming to me.

Jamie and sons and Ben Pardee rode to the edge of the camp, Jamie in the lead. He stopped about fifty feet from Layfield.

"Don't he look nice, now?" Little Ben muttered.

"Elegant," Morgan returned the whisper.

"Colonel Layfield," Jamie said.

"Colonel MacCallister," Layfield returned the military title.

"I've come to talk peace," Jamie said. "The war is over."

"Not our war, sir. Not until one of us is dead and in the grave will it be over."

"Why?" Jamie asked. "Why does it have to be that way?"

"Because we are enemies."

"Colonel, the war is over and done with. Your side won. Lee surrendered. I have no reason to fight you and you have no reason to fight me."

"Are you forgetting that you destroyed my town, Colonel MacCallister?"

"Are you forgetting that you destroyed several *dozen* towns in the South, Colonel Layfield?"

"That was different," Layfield said quickly. "Oh, my, yes, sir. Much different."

Jamie blinked at that. He stared at the man. "Different, sir? How? Why?"

Layfield smiled, then laughed; a sound without humor. "You were the enemy, sir. That's why. And because you were the enemy, you are the enemy. That's in the Bible."

Jamie doubted that most sincerely; but he was no Bible scholar and let it pass. He also felt that attempting to argue the Bible with a man like Layfield would only add fuel to the fire. He just did not know what tact to take.

"That was quite a fight you put up in that old town, Colonel," Layfield said. "Yes, indeed. Quite a fight. But there was something missing there."

"Oh? What?"

"The Rebel flag, of course."

Jamie sighed. "Sir, the war is *over*. It's been over almost five years. Hostilities have ceased."

"Not for me, sir. Never for me or for those who follow me. You burned my town."

Jamie sighed. This was getting nowhere. "Would you like for me to apologize, sir?"

Layfield slowly shook his head. "Don't be ridiculous, sir! That was war. One never apologizes for acts committed during war."

The man is truly crazy, Jamie thought. His cinch strap is too tight. Where the hell do I go from here?

"I think we have said all there is to say to each other, Colonel MacCallister. You should withdraw now and prepare for battle."

"Gird my loins?" Jamie asked drily.

"Quite, sir."

"Nuttier than a pe-can pie," Falcon muttered. "Man needs to be put in an insane asylum."

"What's that?" Layfield shouted, his face turning crimson. "What did you say, sir?"

"I said you're nuts," Falcon told the man. "You're holdin' the reins too tight."

"You can't speak to me in such a manner!"

"I just did," Falcon said. "You . . . nitwit!"

"Prepare for battle, sir!" Layfield shouted, waving his arms. Spittle oozed from one corner of his mouth. He jumped up and down and began shouting orders to his men.

"Thanks a lot, brother," Morgan said, twisting in the saddle to look at Falcon. "Your mouth has done it again."

"My God!" Ben Pardee said, looking at the ridges all around the little valley.

"Cease and desist, Layfield!" came the shout from above the two groups of men.

Jamie looked up. Troops of the U.S. Army cavalry lined one side. He cut his eyes to the other side, where about fifty men from his valley stood, all armed with rifles.

"You are under arrest, Colonel Layfield!" the shout came

from the side of the cavalrymen. "I am Major Paul Silver, United States Army. Order your men to lay down their weapons and do so immediately."

"Never!" Layfield shouted, pulling his sword. "I have God on my side. I shall never surrender. Death to all traitors!"

"Get ready to leave the saddle," Jamie said. "Get behind those rocks yonder and keep your heads down. It's about to get real wild here."

"Fire, men!" Layfield shouted. "Fire!"

"Now!" Jamie yelled, and threw himself from the saddle.

Layfield's men opened up, and the canyon thundered with gunfire as the men lining both sides returned fire.

It was a slaughter. But a carnage that Layfield miraculously survived. When the firing stopped, Layfield was still standing, turning around and around, waving his sword and shouting orders. But his orders fell on dead ears.

Jamie stood up and walked to the man, grabbing his arm and taking the sword from him. Morgan tied the man's hands behind him and sat him on the ground.

"I am a colonel!" Layfield shouted. "I cannot be treated in such a manner."

"Hush up," Morgan told him. "You're going to have a nice long rest, Layfield. You need it."

"Strike this infidel dead, Lord!" Layfield screamed. "Fling a lightning bolt from the heavens with Your mighty hand and destroy this heathen!" He tried to bite Morgan, and Morgan jerked his hand back just in time.

"This guy is nuttier than a tree full of squirrels, Colonel," Ben Pardee said, just as the men from the valley and the cavalrymen rode up.

"Colonel MacCallister," the officer in charge said, dismounting. "I am Major Silver." He offered his hand and Jamie took it. "We tried to get here in time to arrest these men peacefully. But we were delayed."

"You got here just in time, Major." He looked at the men from his valley. "What can I say, men?"

"You don't have to say anything, Mister MacCallister," Minister Powell said. "We were only too glad to help."

"I'll have President Lincoln court-martial you for high treason against the United States government and hang you all!" Layfield shouted.

"Somebody needs to tell him that Lincoln is dead," Jamie Ian remarked.

"More importantly," Major Silver said, "somebody needs to tell him that the war is over and the nation is healing."

"Charge!" Layfield screamed. "Slay the infidels. Kill the slavers. Blow, bugler, blow!"

"The bastard is crazy!" a sergeant said, after jumping to one side to avoid being bitten on the leg by Layfield.

Layfield had toppled over to one side and was thrashing about on the rocky ground, kicking his legs. He began singing about John Brown's body.

Jamie looked at Layfield. "What will you do with him, Major Silver?"

"I'm sure he'll be confined to a lunatic asylum. If he doesn't have a heart attack before we get him there. Excuse me for a moment, sir. Sergeant Bowren! Get the surgeon up here and dose this man with laudanum. Keep him quieted down for his own safety."

"Yes, sir."

Reverend Powell touched Jamie on the arm. "Let's go home, sir. We have much to do before the performers arrive."

Jamie smiled at the smaller man. The reverend was carrying a rifle, and Jamie had no doubt but that he had used it. "Let's do that, Charles." He leaned down and whispered, "But I still think the Indian way makes more sense."

The reverend looked stunned for a moment; then he threw back his head and roared with laughter. "I'll convert you yet, Jamie Ian MacCallister! You just wait and see."

42

As Ross LeBeau, now going under the name of Russell Clay, sat in his expensive box seat and watched the performers on the stage, he was filled with a strange sort of sadness. It was like nothing he had ever experienced before.

He remembered Andrew and Rosanna MacCallister with a smile. He would have recognized them anywhere. And, he was forced to admit, they were superb performers; much more talented than he expected them to be.

He thought of his own children: Garrison and Chastity, the boy and the girl he would never see again. That, he realized with a start, was the reason for his sudden sadness. Paternal instincts rearing up quite unexpectedly. He missed the boy and the girl. That was the simple truth Ross was forced to admit. They were a part of him that could not be denied.

He had detectives working to find his sister's whereabouts; but that was going to take some time. Months, probably. A bitter smile creased his lips as he reflected on the past. A house of cards, Anne had called their lives. Well, Ross thought with a sigh, that was a very apt description. A house of cards.

Roscoe Jefferson, who had changed his name to Ross LeBeau, and who now lived under the name of Russell Clay, sat alone in his box at the theater and silently wept as the performers on the stage below went into their grand finale to the sounds of thunderous applause from the packed house.

Hundreds of miles to the west, Andrea Petri sat in her grand home, surrounded by expensive and lovely possessions, and was alone with her thoughts. Her ruminations, however, were not nearly so gentle as her brother's. She did love her daughter Page, in her own strange way, and for a time, she had felt some affection for Ben Franklin Washington. But no more. That quarter-breed had very nearly ruined things for her; and Anne was not the type of person to forget and forgive.

Now she had learned that Ben Franklin Washington was continuing his snooping around Richmond. "You're a fool," the woman who now called herself Andrea Petri muttered. "And unless you back off, it's going to cost you most dearly— your life, you idiot. I missed once, I shall not miss the next time."

The authorities had ruled that Anne Woodville had died in the tragic fire that had consumed Ravenswood Plantation. It was plain for all to see that two men tried to rob Mrs. Woodville and she, although mortally wounded, had managed to shoot them both. During the struggle, lamps had been overturned and the great house set on fire.

Ben Franklin Washington didn't believe a word of it. It was just too pat. First his Uncle Ross mysteriously disappeared, then his birth mother died in a fire. Nonsense!

He tried to speak to some of the Negroes who worked the land. But they rebuked him coldly.

"You want me to talk bad about the lady who done give me this parcel of land I'm workin' clear and free and taxes paid," one man told him. "You must be some sort of fool, boy! I don't even know what you is, much less who you is. But you shore actin' like some goddamn ignorant swamp nigger! Why you want to stir up trouble and woe agin the memory of that grand lady? I knowed Georgia Washington. Her last boy-child died when he was just a young'un. Right out yonder in them swamps." He waved a hand. "Drowned in the black water. Now you come 'round here tellin' folks that you be he? Damn, boy, you a fool! You bes' carry your breed ass back north. 'Cause you shore ain't gonna git no one 'round here to put no badmouth on Mrs. Woodville. Now git on out of here. I got work to do."

Ben Franklin Washington returned to Boston, but he was more determined than ever to learn the truth. One way or the other, by hook or crook, he would start digging up bones, so to speak, and uncover the truth.

And he no longer gave a damn whose apple cart got upset.

Jamie rode back with the men from his valley. For the first time in years he was at peace with himself and the world, and it was a very strange feeling. So far as he knew, he had not a single enemy left in the world—at least not that he could think of.

He had some good years left him, a few more anyway, and now he and Kate could grow old together, side by side and peacefully.

As he rode, with the company of good and loyal friends all around him, Jamie again thought that he had everything any man could ever hope for. He and Kate had their health, nine kids who were all as fertile as any bottom land in the country, more grandkids and great-grandkids than he could count—much less call their names—and ample time to sit back and take it easy and enjoy life.

Lord knows, Jamie thought, Kate has sure earned some quiet times with her man staying close to hearth and home. He'd been gone months at a time scouting for the government, then almost four years off in the war. Tell the truth, he was looking forward to some quiet times with Kate.

Falcon had put off his marriage to Marie until the trouble was all over and his brother and sister came to the valley. Now that was set for next month.

Jamie smiled, thinking that it was about time they got married, for Falcon had already fathered two kids out of Marie, twins, a boy and a girl. An event that Falcon had wisely kept from his mother for almost a year. Indians had told Jamie, but he had kept his silence, knowing that Kate would fly off the handle when she learned of it. Which she did, just a few weeks back, and she let her feelings be known to Falcon in no uncertain terms.

"But, Ma," Falcon had protested. "Me and Marie was married in the Cheyenne way!"

Kate had stamped her little foot, said, "Shit!" and grabbed her son's ear and damn near twisted it off. Falcon had done so much hollerin' half the town turned out to see if someone hadn't got themselves all tangled up with a mountain lion.

"You go get the pulpit-pounder, Ma!" Falcon yelled. "Me and Marie will stand up and be married in front of God and everybody. Just please turn a-loose of my damn ear!"

Kate did, then promptly grabbed the other ear. "Don't you swear in front of me, boy!"

"Lord have mercy!" Falcon hollered, towering over his mother.

Jamie had beat it off the front porch when Falcon had told his mother about the twins. He'd already ridden to the village to see them, and knew at first glance they were Falcon's kids all right. Both had dark hair, fair skin, and very pale blue eyes.

"Boy," his dad had told Falcon, "I don't know how you're gonna break this news to your ma, but when you do, you leave me out of it."

"I was kinda hopin' you'd sorta, ah . . ."

"You want *me* to tell her?"

"Ah . . . yeah, Pa. As a matter of fact, I do."

"Hell, no!"

As they rode along toward home, Jamie cut his eyes to Falcon. "How's your ear, boy?"

"My what, Pa?" Then he flushed, remembering. "Aw, Pa," he said with a grin. "It's all right. To be no bigger than a minute, Ma sure has some strength, don't she?"

Jamie laughed and rode on ahead. Falcon was a good boy,

but he could be as wild as the wind. Marie though, both he and Kate hoped, would settle him down. Falcon would be the last of their kids to marry. The last eagle to really leave the nest. Jamie recalled a conversation he and Kate had 'bout a month back.

Jamie had pointed to a couple of blond-headed, blue-eyed youngsters walking past their home, a boy and a girl. "Now those have to be MacCallisters, Kate, but damned if I know who they belong to."

Kate had laughed. "They're Pat and Joleen's kids, Jamie. Number forty and forty-one."

"Forty and forty-one what?"

"Grandchildren, Jamie. Our grandchildren."

"Jesus Christ!" Jamie muttered. "Don't those kids of ours ever get out of bed?"

Kate started naming names until Jamie's head began aching. He finally got out of his chair and went for a walk. He'd never heard so damn many names in all his life. Walking didn't help much: seemed like every other person in town, grown-up and kid alike, had blond hair and blue eyes. And nearly half the kids called him grandpa.

When he had finished his walk and finally returned to the porch and sat down in his chair, Kate had said, "Look at it this way, Jamie: there will be someone to take care of us in our old age."

"Yeah," Jamie replied drily. "Providing we can remember their names."

43

Falcon stayed around long enough to greet Rosanna and Andrew and all the troupe, and James and his new bride, then took off for the hills to fetch Marie and his kids. Andrew's wife and Rosanna's husband both arched an eyebrow and looked a little cock-eyed at that news—both being European and raised in very wealthy and proper homes—but said nothing. This was, after all, they thought, the Wild West of America where people did things differently. Much differently.

Falcon was back the next day, with Marie and the twins, and everybody in the twin valleys *oohh*ed and *aahh*ed and carried on over the black-haired, pale-eyed twin brother and sister. The members of the troupe had never met a real life Indian princess before, and Marie played her role to the hilt, even though she spoke perfect English and nearly flawless French.

Marie and the twins were to stay with Jamie and Kate, until after the wedding ceremony, while Falcon would stay at his own house he had just built.

"Ain't that kind of like lockin' the barn door after the horse has already been stole, Pa?" Falcon asked sourly.

"Shut up, boy," his dad told him. "Just keep in mind what your ma did to your ear."

"Both of 'em!" Falcon said with a quick grin.

"And get shut of those guns, boy. Are you planning on being married wearing two guns?"

"Got to stay ready for trouble, Pa."

"Good Lord, boy! There will be the entire population of a Cheyenne village up in the hills around the valleys. You think anyone is going to attack the town with them around?"

"That is something to consider, ain't it, Pa?"

Marie's immediate family, including aunts and uncles and cousins, were in attendance, in full regalia. The Cheyenne warriors were some of the most magnificent of all the plains Indians, and they were most impressive. They made some of the Europeans very nervous, but the foreigners soon were at ease when they realized the Cheyenne were old friends of Jamie's. The Cheyenne also had a high sense of humor, and after a time pointed out to the Europeans that they were dressed for a ceremony, not war. Soon Indian and white kids were running about, playing games, and the men were chatting while the women exchanged gifts and gabbed about this and that.

Almost too quickly, the wedding was over, the bride and groom disappearing into their house. The troupe members looked around, and the Cheyenne were gone without a trace.

Jamie and Kate were keeping the twins until the honeymoon was over. Everybody had gone home, and Reverend Powell was quite pleased that Marie and Falcon had been officially married in the eyes of God (even more pleased that Jamie had actually set foot in his church). The troupe members were staying in various homes, and Jamie and Kate were alone on their front porch with the twins playing and cooing and gurgling in their crib.

Jamie looked at the twins. "Is that number forty-two and forty-three?"

"Yes."

Jamie shook his head in disbelief.

Kate laughed at the expression on his face. "We've certainly come a long way, haven't we, Jamie?"

Jamie took a sip of his coffee. "Two scared kids running west. Your pa disowning you and me with a murder warrant on my head. My God, Kate, that was forty-five years ago. That's just damned hard for me to believe."

"Seems like yesterday, Jamie. Jamie? Do you feel old?"

"Not really. I like to go to bed a bit earlier than I used to. Linger longer under the blankets come the morning. I enjoy sunsets and the risin' up more than I did when I was younger. But old? No."

"Jamie Ian and Ellen Kathleen are both forty-four years old. Our youngest is thirty-one."

"Woman, how in the hell can you keep all those dates and names in your head? It boggles my mind just thinkin' about it."

Kate laughed, and her grandson chose that time to spit up all over himself. Kate rose to clean him up. She plopped the girl in Jamie's lap and took the boy into the house. The child promptly snuggled up in her grandfather's arms and went to sleep.

"My little breed," Jamie whispered. "You've got a hell of a background, girl. Scotch, French, German, Cheyenne, and God only knows what else. I won't live to see you finally pick a man and settle down. But you're gonna be a heartbreaker; I can tell that right off. And a wildcat; you got that blood in you. You're going to see things happen in your lifetime that your grandma and me couldn't even dream of. This old world is changin' fast. And you're gonna be a part of it. I envy you that . . ."

Jamie's eyes caught a flash of sunlight off of metal high up in the hills. It came and went in a bright sudden wink, but it was there. He studied the hills for a time, but the flash did not come again. He grunted and sighed. "Travelers, I guess. Place is sure fillin' up, girl. When your grandma and me came out here, there wasn't nobody but us and your folks and the like. Now there's wagons rumbling through near 'bouts every day, seems like. Civilization is upon us. I reckon that's good. Couldn't have stopped it if I'd wanted to."

The day was warm, and Jamie fell asleep on the front porch, holding the child in his arms. Kate stepped out a few minutes later, saw the sleeping pair, and gently took the girl without waking her husband, then went into the house, placing her on a pallet on the floor, beside her now cleaned-up and sleeping brother. Kate stepped back outside just as Jamie was opening his eyes and looking all around him.

"I took her," Kate said. "She's asleep on a pallet with her brother." She shaded her eyes and looked up the road. "Riders coming."

That was nothing new. The ever-growing town in the twin valleys had opened up, and riders and freight wagons came and went constantly. MacCallister now had a stage that ran twice a week and mail service. The town also had a fair-sized hotel and a bank. The town of MacCallister was growing and prospering; even more so since gold and silver had been found all around the twin valleys.

"Enough for everybody," Jamie had said with a smile, with only Kate knowing what that smile meant.

There were five riders, and they wore long dusters, a garb that was growing ever popular among travelers. There was nothing about the riders to arouse suspicion, so Jamie paid them no mind. He stood up, stretched, and went around the house to the well to draw a bucket of cold water. He sloughed his head with the cold water and that woke him up.

Then he suddenly recalled that five other riders had ridden in the day before and taken rooms at the hotel. And they, too, had been wearing dusters.

"Odd," Jamie said. But then he recalled that Louie Huske, who owned the new hotel, had said the men were polite and well behaved, did not drink too much, and caused no trouble. And they were also trailing pack animals heavily laden with mining equipment. "Well, that explains that," Jamie said, and forgot about the men.

He started doing some repairs around the house that he'd been putting off all summer. Jamie lost himself in the work and did not notice the five other men who rode slowly into town, or those who followed about half an hour later. The last bunch did not ride into town, but camped about two miles outside the settlement, in a thick stand of timber along a creek. The land on either side had not been used for farming that year because of flooding and was a perfect place for a small group of men to hide out.

Jamie woke up suddenly in the middle of the night, remembering that the next day was the day of the month the stage line always sent an extra stage, one in the morning and one in the afternoon, to bring in cash and to carry out gold from the new mines. But he drifted back off to sleep, wondering why he should be thinking about that. The stages were always heavily guarded, and he'd heard that this line was under contract to Wells Fargo, or some big outfit, and nobody in their right mind messed around with companies like that. Their detectives would spend a lifetime hunting men down.

When he awakened the next morning, Jamie had forgotten all about the riders.

Jamie ate his usual breakfast of several eggs, about a half pound of bacon, a bowl of oatmeal, and half a dozen biscuits smeared with butter and honey. Falcon, Jr., picked out the bits of dried apples and then poured his bowl of oatmeal over his head, his hi-chair and the floor, and then grinned at everybody while Katie promptly followed suit.

"Wouldn't you just love to have them to raise, Jamie?" Kate asked.

"I don't think so, honey. I really don't."

Megan came over just after breakfast and took the twins back to her house for the day, Jamie carrying Falcon, Jr., for her. After dropping the twins off, Jamie walked into town and stopped in at the hotel for a cup of coffee with Doctor Tom Prentiss and Louie Huske. Out of long habit, Jamie had tucked a pistol behind his wide leather belt.

Tom opened his watch and checked the time. "About time for the stage to arrive," he said.

"Whose horses are those at the hitchrail, Louie?" Jamie asked. "I don't recognize the brand."

"Beats me, Colonel. They was tied there when I opened up this morning. But they haven't been there long. No droppin's around them."

"I seen Matthew ridin' out 'fore dawn," a man spoke from the table next to theirs. "I waved at him, and he said there had been some trouble up to one of the minin' camps. Said he ought to be back around noon."

Jamie nodded his head. There was always some sort of minor trouble at one of the raw camps, but it seldom amounted to much. Matthew ran a tight county and would brook no serious trouble, and everybody knew it. Matthew would run a man out before the troublemaker could blink.

"You're quiet this morning, Jamie," Doctor Tom observed. "You feel all right?"

"Fit as a fiddle, Tom. I just have an odd sort of feeling, that's all. Not physical, mental."

"Kate all right?"

"Ornery as ever," Jamie replied, and that got a laugh from everyone within earshot.

The man who ran the bank, Paul Carrington, strolled in and joined the men at the table, ordering breakfast. Jamie noticed that the man looked worried and asked about it.

"Hell of a double shipment coming in today, Jamie," Paul spoke in low tones. "More than twice the usual amount of cash and we've changed schedules. We're shipping out on the return run." Paul cut up his breakfast steak and sopped a buttered biscuit through his eggs.

"You have plenty of guards, don't you?" Louie asked.

"I sure as hell hope so," Paul replied. "I'm sitting on a fortune of gold at the bank. It's got me jumpy. Matthew rode out to one end of the county this morning to check on trouble, and the two deputies rode out to the other end. That leaves us with no lawmen."

"There is more to it than that, Paul," Jamie said. "Come on. What's the matter?"

"The Nelson gang. Miles Nelson escaped from the territorial prison and was spotted heading this way. His old gang ran anywhere from twenty to fifty men. And no bigger band of cutthroats exists anywhere."

The Nelson gang had formed up and started their dirty work while Jamie was away in the war and had grown bigger and stronger during the years. They were perhaps the most brutal and cold-blooded gang west of the Mississippi. Miles was a college-educated man who planned his raids brilliantly and was almost always successful in carrying them out. The Nelson gang was notorious in that they seldom left any witnesses alive. To a man, they were vicious killers and rapists.

"Surely they wouldn't attack a Wells Fargo stage or bank," Tom said.

"They'd attack anything," Louie said. "Way I heard it, Miles Nelson is connected to some big money back east. Has political connections, too. He and some of his men are blood related to a group of powerful men back east name of Newby and Saxon."

Jamie stared hard for a moment at his old sergeant major. "What did you say, Louie?"

Louie repeated it.

"Something, Jamie?" Doctor Tom asked.

"Maybe. The Saxons and the Newbys are old enemies of mine and Kate's. A blood feud that goes back more than forty years. You armed, Louie?"

"I ain't carryin' one on me. Hell, Jamie, you're about the only person in town who packs a gun . . . other than Falcon and Matthew and his deputies. There is never any trouble here. This is the safest spot in all of Colorado."

"It might not be today. Get a pistol. All of you."

"Jamie," Doctor Tom said. "No one in their right mind would attack this town. Would they?"

"Miles Nelson might. And he might be doing it for more than one reason."

"Damn!" the banker said, and pushed away from the table, forgetting his breakfast.

"Here comes the stage!" a citizen shouted from out in the street. "No. They's two of them this day."

Jamie rose and walked to the windows of the dining room. He watched as eight men got off the two stages, all of them wearing dusters and all of them carrying rifles. "Goddamnit!" Jamie cursed. "Dusters. Dusters. I should have put it together. I must be gettin' old."

"That's odd," Louie said, walking to the windows and looking out. "Must be nigh onto thirty men done come into town . . . all wearin' those fancy dusters."

"The Nelson gang wears dusters!" the banker said. "That's the Nelson gang out there!" He pushed open the batwings and stepped out, frantically looking up and down the street.

Women were beginning to appear on the boardwalks, ready to do the day's shopping. The school bell was ringing. School would commence in fifteen minutes. Boys and girls were all over the place, all of them slowly walking toward the schoolhouse.

"Oh, God," Jamie said. "This could turn into a slaughter." Then it came to him: Miles Nelson had *planned* it this way. Townspeople would be reluctant to shoot for fear of hitting women and kids.

Jamie turned, walked across the room, and jerked the pistol from the waistband of a very startled traveling drummer who had just sat down to eat.

"Say now!" the man blurted.

"Shut up," Jamie told him. "And get down. All hell is about to break open here."

The drummer left his chair and stretched out on the floor. He was relatively new to the West and had heard all sorts of terrible tales about shoot-outs and renegades and outlaws and savage Indians. "I didn't want to come out here in the first damn place!" he said.

Paul Carrington was hurrying across the street when one of the duster-wearing men coldly pulled out a pistol and shot the driver of the stage out of the box. The outlaw leaped onto the stage and grabbed up the reins. Paul turned and took a bullet right between his eyes.

"Here we go!" Jamie shouted, and pushed open the batwings, a pistol in each big hand.

44

Jamie shot the outlaw out of the driver's box, and the team panicked, running up the street, wild-eyed and frightened.

"It worked, boys!" someone shouted. "There's MacCallister. Kill him!"

Set-up! the words flashed through Jamie's mind. This whole thing was a set-up to get me. Or at least a part of it was. He ducked back into the hotel dining room just as the lead really started flying.

"They's outlaws comin' from both ends of the street!" a man yelled. No sooner had the words left his mouth than a bullet doubled him over and left him dying in the dust.

Kate! Jamie thought. The outlaws would have learned where we live. Oh, Jesus, Kate! He ran out the back door and headed for his house, ducking behind houses and into alleys. A duster-clad man, both hands filled with pistols, stepped out in front of him. "Gottcha, MacCallister!" he said.

Jamie shot him in the face and kept on running.

Another duster-wearing man came galloping up the street in front of Jamie's house, firing at the frightened and running women and kids in his path. Jamie shot him out of the saddle just as Kate stepped out of their home, a Henry rifle in her hands. Amid all the other shots, Jamie heard the round that brought Kate down. She slumped bonelessly to the porch.

"Kate!" Jamie screamed, and ran across the street just as a heavy explosion shook the earth. Someone had blown the

safe at the bank, but Jamie's thoughts were not of money or of gold. He jumped up onto the porch just as his sons and sons-in-law threw up a circle around the house and drove off any of the Nelson gang who might have had the stupidity to remain within range of the MacCallister boys' deadly fire.

Jamie knelt down beside Kate. He was weeping almost uncontrollably, the tears falling onto Kate's dress, thick and sticky with blood where the heavy slug had passed clear through her slender body, between her breasts.

"Jamie," Kate said, her eyes clear and bright. But her lips were pink with bloody froth; more so each time she breathed. Jamie knew then the slug had cut a lung. "I'll be waiting for you on the Starry Path."

"Kate . . ."

"Don't say anything, Jamie. I know. I can't feel anything from the waist down. The bullet nicked my spine." She coughed up blood. "I'm not in pain, love. I'm at peace." She cut her blue eyes. "Baby Karen. I see her."

Doctor Tom Prentiss was running up the street, ducking and dodging the flying lead from the outlaw guns, making his way to the MacCallister home, carrying his black bag. He leaped the white-painted picket fence that Jamie had just repaired, ran into the yard and jumped up onto the porch.

The fire from the MacCallister guns had driven the Nelson gang far away from that end of the street. No one among the outlaws wanted to face those angry guns.

Jamie leaned down and kissed Kate's bloody lips.

"Jamie," Kate whispered. "Don't fret. We'll be together again."

Tom Prentiss had taken one look at Kate and stepped back, leaving the man and wife alone on the porch, knowing there was nothing he could do. He looked at the MacCallister boys and shook his head.

"You be good, darling," Kate whispered, her voice fading as the life ebbed away from her. "And take care of yourself. I'll be waiting."

"Oh, God, Kate!" Jamie cried out, his anguish-filled voice ripping into every person within hearing distance. "Kate, Kate!" Jamie put his arms around her and held her close.

But Kate said no more.

She died quietly in Jamie's arms.

45

Jamie held Kate for a long time. No one tried to interfere. Long after the gunfire had ceased and the outlaws had galloped out of town, Jamie gently lowered Kate to the porch floor and stood up. His crying was done. He was dry-eyed. He felt a coldness take him. He looked at Ellen Kathleen. "Take care of your ma," he said. He cut his eyes to Jamie Ian. "Help your sister, son." Jamie stepped into the house and buckled on his twin Colts. He reached up to the peg-board and took down his scalping knife and walked back out to the porch.

"What are you going to do, Jamie?" Reverend Powell asked in a breathless tone. He had run all the way from the church.

"Find out where the gang went," Jamie said.

"How?" the reverend asked. He shivered at the cold light in Jamie's eyes.

"You ever seen a man skinned alive, Reverend?"

"Good Lord, no!"

"Then you better plug up your ears," Jamie told him. He stepped off the porch and started walking toward town.

"He doesn't mean that," Reverend Powell said.

Falcon spat on the ground. "You wanna bet?" He pushed past the man and went to his mother's side.

Jamie dragged one slightly wounded outlaw off the street and into a blacksmith's shop and closed the big double doors.

Those outside heard the outlaw curse, and then say, "You go to hell, MacCallister. I ain't tellin' you nothin'!"

Then the screaming began.

A few minutes later, Jamie stepped out of the smithy's and walked back to his house. There was a bloody scalp hanging from his belt.

"I'll fetch the dress that she bought in San Francisco," Megan said, her cheeks still wet from tears.

"No," Jamie told her. "Your ma always said she wasn't cut out to be silk and lace. She said she wanted to be buried in gingham. Pick out a simple dress." He looked at his children and the crowd of other kin that had gathered. "They's plenty of tragedy to go around in this town today. Some of you go give solace and aid to others. Jamie Ian, you get a couple of picks and shovels and meet me up yonder where Grandpa is buried. That's where your ma and me planned to be planted. Go on, now."

"Pa?" Falcon said. "Did that outlaw tell you anything?"

"He told me plenty."

"We gonna ride?"

"Not we, boy. Just me. And don't give me no sass about it."

"Yes, sir. I mean, no, sir. I won't."

Jamie looked at his family, still standing in the yard, on the porch and in the street . . . they made up about one-fifth of the town's population. "There is nothing that can be done for Kate. But there are plenty of others in this town who are badly hurt and there are lots of scared kids. Go help. Make yourself useful. That's what Kate would have done."

Jamie turned and walked toward the barn. A few minutes later he rode out, toward the high ridge where his grandfather was buried.

Kate was buried late that afternoon, just as the sun was beginning to sink in the west and the shadows were long. Reverend Powell kept it short, as Jamie had requested. After the service, Jamie told everybody to go on back home. He was going to stay by the grave for a time.

Jamie built a small fire and put on water for coffee. He had fixed him a poke of food from the house before leaving to dig the grave.

"I'll have a proper headstone up 'fore I take off, Kate. I promise you that. Then I'm goin' to find those that both plotted and carried out this terrible thing. I know that don't come as no surprise to you. Kate, some of the kids will be up here most every day after I pull out, puttin' flowers and such on your grave. Then it'll taper off to once a week and then once a month and then once a year. But that's the way it is, Kate. They got to live their own lives. I'm goin' to make you a promise, Kate. And I'll do my damndest to keep it. I will be laid to rest beside you. The kids will know that 'fore I pull out, and some of them will come get me no matter where I fall or where I'm planted."

Jamie sighed and took a drink of the hot, black, strong coffee. "Kate, we had just over forty-five years together, and to my mind, they were good ones. I loved you the first moment I put eyes on you, and I love you now. There has never been another woman for me. And there never will be. I think you've always known that, but I just wanted to remind you one more time.

"Kate, I'm not ridin' off to get myself killed. You know me better than that. But it ain't gonna be right without you here, honey. I'm feelin' . . . well, sorta lost right now. I guess you know that, listenin' to me ramblin' on like an idiot. But there are things I have to say, and I got to say them now."

He drained his coffee cup and leaned back against the mound of earth that covered Kate. He took comfort in being just that close to her, and he was silent for a long time, drawing strength from her nearness.

"Well, old woman," he finally spoke. "I thought I had a great deal to say, but I reckon I've said it all. They was said silently, and I truly believe you heard them. I'll sleep now, beside you for the last time on this earth, and then tomorrow I'll see to your stone and then I'll be gone.

"Good night, Kate. Sleep in peace. I love you, Kate."

Jamie chiseled these words into a huge stone. KATE MAC-CALLISTER. B. 1810 D. 1869 BELOVED WIFE OF JAMIE IAN MACCALLISTER B. 1810 D.

He left that blank.

Jamie packed up his tools, saddled up, and rode down to the town. Matthew was sitting on the front porch of the house. Someone had cleaned up Kate's blood; or tried to. Jamie could still see a spot where Kate had lain.

"I got to talk to you, Pa," Matthew called.

"So talk, boy. I'm goin' to put on some water for a bath and a shave. You can talk while I'm doin' that."

"Pa, we got laws in this country now."

"Is that a fact?"

"Damnit, Pa, don't make light of that. This territory is soon gonna be a state." That was a few more years away, coming in 1876 as the 38th state. "But we got to show the folks back east that we're civilized enough for that to happen."

Jamie built a fire in the stove and placed a huge pot of water on to boil. Matthew winced as his dad lifted the huge heavy pot with no more effort than pluckin' a petunia from the ground. His pa was still one hell of a man. Jamie turned from the stove, and his eyes were cold with controlled fury. "Your ma lies yonder on that ridge, boy. Cold in her grave. And you're goin' to talk to me about laws? Don't waste your breath, boy, and my time."

"Pa, every sheriff in the territory has been notified about what happened yesterday. It'll be coast to coast in a few weeks. Maybe less time than that. The Nelson gang will be found, Pa. I guarantee it."

"I guarantee you they will be found, too, boy. By me."

"Pa, you're sixty years old. You're not a kid. You're a

grown man with lots of sense. Pa, I'll stop you from doin' this if I have to. I'll—"

Jamie knocked him from the kitchen, through the living room, out onto the porch, and sent him tumbling to the front yard, unconscious.

Falcon, Morgan, Jamie Ian, and Andrew sat on the porch and watched Matthew hit the ground.

"Sounded like Pa hit him with the flat side of an axe, don't it?" Falcon said.

"Pa slapped me open-handed one time," Jamie Ian recollected. "I was, oh, 'bout sixteen, I reckon. I bowed up to him. Once. My head rung for two days and I couldn't hear out of my left side for a week. I never bowed up to Pa again after that."

"Pa's killed men with his fists," Morgan said.

"You reckon we ought to throw some water on our brother?" Andrew asked.

"Naw," Falcon said. "He was up all night. He needs the rest."

Matthew was up, staggering around and holding his head and moaning and cussing, when Jamie had finished bathing and shaving. "What the hell did Pa hit me with, a singletree?" he finally managed to croak.

"Naw. His fist. You're just lucky you got a hard head," Morgan told him.

Matthew stuck a finger in his mouth, felt around, and said, "I got me some loose teeth."

"They'll tighten up," Falcon said. "Just eat soup for a few days."

Jamie's tall bulk filled the doorway. "Don't you ever bow up to me again, boy," he told Matthew. "You understand me?"

"Yes, sir."

Jamie ducked his head to hide a small smile; then the smile faded as Kate's face drifted before his eyes, smiling at him. He was silent for a time.

"Boys, listen to me. Of course I feel sorrow. Deeper than

I can describe. Your ma and me was together for forty-five years. We fell in love as children and we're still in love. And we'll be in love forever more when we meet on the Starry Path on the way to Man Above's home. True love lasts forever, boys. It don't ever die. Not even the grave stops it. And that's all I got to say about it.

"Now, you boys say your goodbyes to the family for me. You know I'm not much for long farewells and I don't want to see no tears. I've seen enough to last me for a time. Matt, you go pack my blankets and other possibles. Jamie Ian, put together some food for me; you help him, Andrew. Morgan, go help Falcon; he's about half-scared of that big buckskin."

He ought to be, Morgan thought. That big son of a bitch is mean as a cornered puma. "Yes, sir."

The boys left to do as their father had asked.

Jamie sat alone on the porch until the boys had saddled up and packed up the horses and led them around. Jamie watched as more funerals were carried out among the townspeople, for the outlaw raid had left a dozen dead and several dozen more wounded. He could hear the faint crying of the families as the dead were buried.

"Plenty of grief to go around," Jamie muttered. "Gonna be grief in some outlaw camps 'fore I'm through, too. There'll soon be blood on the moon."

"You say something, Pa?" Andrew asked.

"Just talkin' to myself, boy."

Jamie shook hands with his sons and stepped into the saddle. He did not look back as he rode off, right down the main street of the town that he and Kate and few other adventurous pioneers had settled, so many years back.

Little Ben Pardee, Doctor Tom Prentiss, and Louie Huske stood on the boardwalk in front of the hotel and saluted as Jamie rode by. He returned the salute and kept on riding, putting the town behind him.

Jamie rode up to Kate's final resting place, dismounted, took off his hat, and stood by her grave. The kids had been up on the ridge, for the mound was covered in flowers. There were signs that Indians had visited the grave, for their tokens of tribute and sorrow were there, too.

"Well, old woman," Jamie said. "This is goodbye for a time. I reckon I just got this to say: Your love will be a constant with me, as my love for you will be. I'll see you on the Starry Path, Kate."

Jamie mounted up and sat for a time looking down at Mac-Callister's Valley. "All that down yonder would have never happened had it not been for you, Kate. That's your real monument down there. Folks livin' and lovin' and workin' and fussin' and makin' up and then goin' on about their business of buildin' a future for their kids and grandkids and the like."

Jamie smiled. "Yes, ma'am. I reckon that's what it's all about."

Jamie lifted the reins and rode toward the north.

High above him, soaring on the currents, an eagle screamed.

Don't miss William W. Johnstone's

SCREAM OF EAGLES

a March, 1996 Kensington hardcover

For a sample chapter of this exciting continuation of the
MacCallister family story. . . just turn the page

Prologue

Jamie Ian MacCallister and his wife Kate were both fifteen years old when they were married in the river town of New Madrid, Missouri. They remained married and faithful and true to one another for forty-five years. By the time Kate died in Jamie's arms after an outlaw raid on the Colorado town they helped found, Jamie and Kate had produced a houseful of kids and dozens of grandchildren and great-grandchildren.

Jamie had already lived longer than many men of that time, but somebody forgot to tell Jamie about that. For a man his age, he was still bull strong and wang-leather tough. His hair was gray, but his heart was young. He used eyeglasses to read fine print, but he sure didn't need glasses to shoot.

The loss of Kate hit Jamie harder than anything ever had over the long and tumultuous years. For several weeks after her violent and untimely death, Jamie could not clearly focus on anything except her dying and the lonely grave overlooking MacCallister's Valley. He holed up deep in the mountains and let his grief take control for a time.

Jamie relived over and over each and every memory shared with Kate. The good and the bad. The laughter and the tears. The pain and the pleasure.

The pleasure far outweighed the pain.

After a couple of weeks, Jamie began to realize that Kate would not want him doing this. All the grieving in the world would not bring her back from the grave. She was at peace now, having climbed the Starry Path to be greeted by Man Above. She would wait there for him.

Jamie looked up at the high cloudless blue of the sky. He sighed and then smiled. "You know what I have to do, Kate. I couldn't live with myself if I didn't do it. Of course," he said drily, "I might not live much longer doing it. But I reckon that would be all right, too. 'Cause then I'd be with you."

Jamie buckled on his pistols. Twin .44s, model 60 conversion. He wiped the dust off his rifle, a Winchester model 68. He tidied up his camp, packed the frame on the packhorse, and saddled up his big, mean-eyed buckskin. One of his grandchildren—he couldn't remember which one, much less the child's name, Kate had always kept track of those things—had named the huge animal Buck.

It was turning colder now, with winter not far off. During the weeks that Jamie had spent wrapped in his grief, those responsible for the attack on MacCallister's Valley, and the death of Kate, the Miles Nelson gang, would have scattered like dust in the wind. Any trail would be as cold as the stars.

"I got a few good years left in me," Jamie muttered. Buck swung his big head around to look at him. "And I'll use them finding you all. My son Matthew talks of book law and justice. That's his way. I'll have justice my way."

He swung easily into the saddle, the movements like a man twenty years younger.

"I'll find you all," Jamie repeated. "And I'll kill you."

Overhead, soaring on the winds, an eagle screamed.

1

Jamie topped the crest and looked down at the town nestled deep in the Rockies. Another mining town. A number of buildings with boarded-up windows told him that already the gold or the silver was playing out and the miners were moving on. What made him certain the town was dying was that among the empty buildings were several saloons.

"Let's go find you boys a warm stall and some hay to munch on," Jamie spoke to his horses. "You both deserve a good rest. It's cold this day."

About twenty degrees above zero, with the ground covered with snow. Jamie wasn't sure, but he thought he had passed the new year in a cave, sitting out a blizzard. "That would make it 1870," he muttered, his breath steaming the air. "Kate's been gone almost six months now." And, he thought, the trail I've been trying to find is as cold as the weather.

Almost six months, Kate lying cold in her grave.

No, he corrected his thoughts as he walked his horses onto the wide street, deep-rutted from the wheels of many heavily laden wagons. That is only the shell that contained the flesh and blood of my Kate. Her soul is with Man Above.

Waiting for me.

Jamie stabled his horses at the livery and told the man to brush and curry the packhorse. "Don't touch Buck," he warned. "He bites and kicks."

"I wouldn't touch that big ugly son of a bitch for fifty dollars," the young man said. He jumped back just in time to avoid the flashing teeth of Buck, who was doing his best to take a chunk out of the livery man's arm.

"Don't hurt his feelings," Jamie cautioned him with a small smile. The smiles were coming more often now, but they were still rare. "He's very sensitive."

The young man rolled his eyes and began forking hay into the stall, muttering about horses in general and Buck in particular.

Jamie took his rifle and saddlebags and walked up the boardwalk to the only hotel that was still open in the dying town. He checked in and stowed his gear. The desk clerk froze as still as death when he reversed the book and read the name.

Jamie Ian MacCallister.

The legend himself. In person. In his hotel. My God!

The clerk took in Jamie's size. Big as a mountain. His hair was almost all gray, but the big man moved like a huge puma. The clerk sensed danger shrouding Jamie like clouds on the high peaks.

"I'll have a haircut and a bath," Jamie said. "Where's the barber shop?"

"Just across the street, sir. To your left as you leave the hotel. May I say that it is an honor to have you here, sir. I . . ."

But Jamie was already out the door. The clerk called for one of his swampers and told the rummy to spread the news. Man Who Is Not Afraid was in town.

Jamie soaped and scrubbed and did it again with buckets of hot water. Then he had the barber cut his long hair short. After Jamie had left, the barber carefully swept up the graying hair. There were people who would pay a lot of money for a few strands of the hair of the man many Indians still called Man Who Plays With Wolves. Still others called the living legend Bear Killer.

Others called him one big mean son of a bitch, but never to his face.

Dusk was settling over the mountains as Jamie went into the hotel bar and ordered a whiskey. "From the good bottle," he told the barkeep. He would linger over the amber liquid, savoring the hard flavor, and then have dinner. The menu on the chalkboard was beef and potatoes.

The men who had lined the bar shifted to one side, giving Jamie the entire left side of the long mahogany. Everyone in the West knew the story of the Miles Nelson attack on Mac-Callister's Valley, the death of Kate, and that Jamie was on the prod.

After ordering his whiskey, Jamie spoke to no one in the bar, and no one spoke directly to him. A man wearing a star on his coat entered the room, looked at Jamie for a short time, then left. He did not leave because of fear, only because he knew MacCallister's reputation and knew Jamie would not deliberately provoke an argument with any innocent citizen.

But the marshal also knew there were a couple of ol' boys in town who thought themselves to be tough, and when they heard that MacCallister was in town, they would brace him in hopes of gaining a reputation. The marshal didn't want to be around when that happened. He knew that while the two so-called "bad men" were strutting around, talking about what they'd do to MacCallister, Jamie would just shoot them and be done with it.

And when the smoke had cleared, MacCallister would go eat supper.

The marshal went home to eat his own supper, and to hell with those two clowns who thought they were tough. In about fifteen minutes, or less, they wouldn't be tough—they'd just be dead. And in two days, forgotten.

Jamie had just lifted the glass to his lips when the front door banged open and cold air swept through the barroom. Jamie did not turn his head to see who it was. He had positioned himself so he could watch the front door by using the long mirror behind the bar.

Jamie sighed as he watched the two young men. Trouble, he thought. Local toughs wanting to make a reputation. Go away, boys. Go away.

The pair swaggered toward the bar. Both of them were wearing two guns, low and tied down.

Damn! Jamie thought.

The young men bellied up to the bar, and one called for whiskey in too loud a tone.

The barkeep slid a bottle down to them. He was being very careful to stay clear of the line of fire. The knot of men at the opposite end of the bar left to take tables. No one wanted to get shot.

"Howdy there, old-timer. The name's Pullen," one of the young men said. "Jim Pullen. You heared of me, I reckon."

"Can't say as I have," Jamie said, after taking a small sip of whiskey. Jamie was not really a drinking man, but he did enjoy one or two drinks occasionally.

"Oh, yeah? You don't get around much, do you? Well, I reckon a man of your advanced age pretty much has to stay close to hearth and home."

Jamie smiled. There wasn't much of the West he hadn't seen at one time or the other.

"My pard, here, is Black Jack Perkins. I *know* you've heared of him."

"Can't say as I have, boy."

"Well, he killed a man in Black Hawk, he did."*

"I'm sorry to hear that," Jamie said, after taking another sip of whiskey. "Terrible thing, having to kill a man."

"Huh! Well, I killed my share of men, too. I ain't lost no sleep over it."

Jamie said nothing. He placed his shot glass on the polished bar and waited. He had left his heavy winter coat up in his room and wore a waist-length leather jacket over a dark shirt. Dark trousers and boots. Out of long habit, he had slipped the leather thongs off the hammers of his twin Colts before entering the barroom. He waited.

"You're Jamie MacCallister, ain't you?" Black Jack asked, stepping away from the bar and facing Jamie.

*The town also went by the name of Doe for several years.

"That's right."

"I been hearin' 'bout you all my life. I'm sick of it. I don't think you done half of what people say you done. I think most of it was piff and padoodle. Now what do you think about that?"

Jamie was growing very weary of the pair of would-be toughs. But he didn't want to kill either of them. He turned to face the young man and smiled. He lifted one hand and waggled a finger at Black Jack. "Come here, boy."

Black Jack strutted up to Jamie, a curious expression on his face.

Jamie hit him with a left that produced a sound much like a watermelon struck with the flat side of a shovel. Jerking one of the young man's guns from leather, and holding the nearly unconscious Black Jack up between himself and Pullen, Jamie closed the few feet and laid the barrel of the gun against Pullen's head. Jim Pullen hit the floor, his lights turned out.

Jamie popped Black Jack again, and Black Jack joined his buddy on the floor for a nap. He took their pistols and walked out back to the privy, dropping the six-shooters down the twin holes. They disappeared forever with a splash.

Back in the bar, the men seated at the tables winced at the power in those big arms as Jamie reached down with both hands and grabbed the sleeping young men by the backs of their shirt collars and dragged them outside, depositing them both in the street.

Returning to the warmth of the bar, Jamie signaled the barkeep for another drink and then turned to the crowd. "Am I going to have any more trouble here tonight?"

The men slowly and solemnly shook their heads.

"Fine," Jamie said, then took his drink into the restaurant and sat down and ordered dinner. Outside, a citizen helped one of the marshal's deputies drag the unconscious young men across the street. The deputy tossed them into a jail cell and slammed and locked the door.

"Damn fools," the citizen said.

"They're lucky MacCallister didn't kill them," the deputy said. "He may be gettin' on in years, but that is still one war hoss, and no man to brace."

"Reckon how long he'll stay in town?" the citizen questioned.

"As long as he damn well pleases," the deputy replied.

"It's from Pa!" Matthew shouted with a wide grin, waving the envelope the stage driver had handed him. Matthew looked up at the driver. "Where'd you get this, Luke?"

"Another driver give it to me. It's been passed around some, Matt. I figure it's taken near'bout two months to get here."

Matthew sat down on the porch of the Goldman Mercantile Store and carefully opened the envelope. Abe and Rebecca Goldman were long dead, the store now operated by their youngest son, Tobias.

The entire town, more than five hundred people, soon gathered around, waiting in silence as Matthew read the letter.

"Pa's well," Matthew finally said. Matthew was one of triplets—Matthew, Morgan, and Megan—born in 1832. "Pa was in Central City when he wrote this. He's picked up the trail of some of the Nelson gang and was leavin' out for Wyoming next mornin'."

"What's the date?" Matt's youngest sister, Joleen, asked.

"There ain't any. Hush up and listen."

"Don't tell me to shush, you ox!"

"Shut up, the both of you!" Jamie Ian told his brother and sister. "Read," he told Matt.

"There ain't much more."

"Isn't," Joleen corrected.

Matt sighed and returned to the letter. "Pa says to tend to Ma's grave site and plant some flowers around about. He says if he comes back here and finds the site all grown up with weeds, somebody's butt is gonna be in trouble." He looked up into the faces of his brothers and sisters, in-laws and nieces and nephews and what have you. "That's it."

"I wonder where Pa is now?" Megan said.

"Atlantic City," Jamie read the faded wooden sign, "Welcomes You."

Jamie had bypassed South Pass City, giving it a wide berth and riding on toward Atlantic City. He had heard that several of the men he was seeking were loafing around that mining town, gambling and whoring and making trouble.

Jamie was about to put an end to all that.

The government had recently started building a fort near Atlantic City. It would be named Fort Stambaugh, after a first lieutenant who had been killed by Indians near Miner's Delight. It would be abandoned in eight years.

After the raid on MacCallister's Valley, the Miles Nelson gang had broken up and scattered. The Pinkertons and Wells Fargo detectives, many sheriffs and town marshals all over the West, as well as federal marshals and the U.S. Army, were after them. With the gold and money taken from the bank and the stagecoach, the gang members could live well for a couple of years. By then, the heat would be off them and they could regroup . . . or so they thought.

But they hadn't taken into consideration one Jamie Ian MacCallister dogging their trail, riding with hard revenge burning in his trail-wise eyes.

When the gang had struck MacCallister's Valley, the Nelson gang was the largest in all the West. Actually there were five gangs, each with about fifteen men, robbing and raping and looting and burning from Kansas to California. Miles had pulled them all together for the raid that killed Jamie's wife. Twenty of the gang had been killed, wounded, or captured during the raid in the valley. That left about fifty-five outlaws still on the loose. Fifty-five of the meanest, sorriest, most worthless dredges of humanity ever assembled.

It had taken Jamie about six months to do it, but he had put together a list of men who were part of the Miles Nelson gang. To do so, he had visited with every sheriff and marshal in every town he passed through, looking at dodgers and talking with men in lock-up. A rustler might steal your cattle, but when it came to raping and killing women, shooting little kids down in the street, that was going too far. And most of the men in jail talked to Jamie.

Jamie had a list of fifty-one names, and if it took him the rest of his life, he was going to visit each name. After the visit, he would draw a line through that man's name.

These men had robbed him of the most precious thing in his life.

Kate.

And if it cost him his own life checking off those names, well, so be it. Without Kate he was nothing.

Just . . . nothing at all.

THE EAGLES SERIES BY
WILLIAM W. JOHNSTONE

__Eyes of Eagles
0-7860-1364-8

$5.99US/$7.99CAN

__Dreams of Eagles
0-7860-6086-6

$5.99US/$7.99CAN

__Talons of Eagles
0-7860-0249-2

$5.99US/$6.99CAN

__Scream of Eagles
0-7860-0447-9

$5.99US/$7.50CAN

__Rage of Eagles
0-7860-0507-6

$5.99US/$7.99CAN

__Song of Eagles
0-7860-1012-6

$5.99US/$7.99CAN

__Cry of Eagles
0-7860-1024-X

$5.99US/$7.99CAN

__Blood of Eagles
0-7860-1106-8

$5.99US/$7.99CAN

Available Wherever Books Are Sold!

Visit our website at **www.kensingtonbooks.com**

THE MOUNTAIN MAN SERIES BY
WILLIAM W. JOHNSTONE

__The Last Mountain Man	0-8217-6856-5	$5.99US/$7.99CAN
__Return of the Mountain Man	0-7860-1296-X	$5.99US/$7.99CAN
__Trail of the Mountain Man	0-7860-1297-8	$5.99US/$7.99CAN
__Revenge of the Mountain Man	0-7860-1133-1	$5.99US/$7.99CAN
__Law of the Mountain Man	0-7860-1301-X	$5.99US/$7.99CAN
__Journey of the Mountain Man	0-7860-1302-8	$5.99US/$7.99CAN
__War of the Mountain Man	0-7860-1303-6	$5.99US/$7.99CAN
__Code of the Mountain Man	0-7860-1304-4	$5.99US/$7.99CAN
__Pursuit of the Mountain Man	0-7860-1305-2	$5.99US/$7.99CAN
__Courage of the Mountain Man	0-7860-1306-0	$5.99US/$7.99CAN
__Blood of the Mountain Man	0-7860-1307-9	$5.99US/$7.99CAN
__Fury of the Mountain Man	0-7860-1308-7	$5.99US/$7.99CAN
__Rage of the Mountain Man	0-7860-1555-1	$5.99US/$7.99CAN
__Cunning of the Mountain Man	0-7860-1512-8	$5.99US/$7.99CAN
__Power of the Mountain Man	0-7860-1530-6	$5.99US/$7.99CAN
__Spirit of the Mountain Man	0-7860-1450-4	$5.99US/$7.99CAN
__Ordeal of the Mountain Man	0-7860-1533-0	$5.99US/$7.99CAN
__Triumph of the Mountain Man	0-7860-1532-2	$5.99US/$7.99CAN
__Vengeance of the Mountain Man	0-7860-1529-2	$5.99US/$7.99CAN
__Honor of the Mountain Man	0-8217-5820-9	$5.99US/$7.99CAN
__Battle of the Mountain Man	0-8217-5925-6	$5.99US/$7.99CAN
__Pride of the Mountain Man	0-8217-6057-2	$4.99US/$6.50CAN
__Creed of the Mountain Man	0-7860-1531-4	$5.99US/$7.99CAN
__Guns of the Mountain Man	0-8217-6407-1	$5.99US/$7.99CAN
__Heart of the Mountain Man	0-8217-6618-X	$5.99US/$7.99CAN
__Justice of the Mountain Man	0-7860-1298-6	$5.99US/$7.99CAN
__Valor of the Mountain Man	0-7860-1299-4	$5.99US/$7.99CAN
__Warpath of the Mountain Man	0-7860-1330-3	$5.99US/$7.99CAN
__Trek of the Mountain Man	0-7860-1331-1	$5.99US/$7.99CAN

Available Wherever Books Are Sold!

Visit our website at **www.kensingtonbooks.com**

THE FIRST MOUNTAIN MAN SERIES BY
WILLIAM W. JOHNSTONE

__**The First Mountain Man**
0-8217-5510-2   **$4.99**US/**$6.50**CAN

__**Blood on the Divide**
0-8217-5511-0   **$4.99**US/**$6.50**CAN

__**Absaroka Ambush**
0-8217-5538-2   **$4.99**US/**$6.50**CAN

__**Forty Guns West**
0-7860-1534-9   **$5.99**US/**$7.99**CAN

__**Cheyenne Challenge**
0-8217-5607-9   **$4.99**US/**$6.50**CAN

__**Preacher and the Mountain Caesar**
0-8217-6585-X   **$5.99**US/**$7.99**CAN

__**Blackfoot Messiah**
0-8217-6611-2   **$5.99**US/**$7.99**CAN

__**Preacher**
0-7860-1441-5   **$5.99**US/**$7.99**CAN

__**Preacher's Peace**
0-7860-1442-3   **$5.99**US/**$7.99**CAN

Available Wherever Books Are Sold!

Visit our website at **www.kensingtonbooks.com**

THE LAST GUNFIGHTER SERIES BY
WILLIAM W. JOHNSTONE

__The Drifter
0-8217-6476-4   **$4.99**US/**$6.99**CAN

__Reprisal
0-7860-1295-1   **$5.99**US/**$7.99**CAN

__Ghost Valley
0-7860-1324-9   **$5.99**US/**$7.99**CAN

__The Forbidden
0-7860-1325-7   **$5.99**US/**$7.99**CAN

__Showdown
0-7860-1326-5   **$5.99**US/**$7.99**CAN

__Imposter
0-7860-1443-1   **$5.99**US/**$7.99**CAN

__Rescue
0-7860-1444-X   **$5.99**US/**$7.99**CAN

__The Burning
0-7860-1445-8   **$5.99**US/**$7.99**CAN

Available Wherever Books Are Sold!

Visit our website at **www.kensingtonbooks.com**